THIRST

Also by Giles Foden:

Freight Dogs
Turbulence
Zanzibar
Ladysmith
The Last King of Scotland

THIRST

A novel of the hydrosphere

Giles Foden

W&N
WEIDENFELD & NICOLSON

First published in Great Britain in 2024 by Weidenfeld & Nicolson,
an imprint of The Orion Publishing Group Ltd
Carmelite House, 50 Victoria Embankment
London EC4Y 0DZ

An Hachette UK Company

The authorised representative in the EEA is Hachette Ireland, 8 Castlecourt Centre,
Castleknock Road, Castleknock, Dublin 15, D15 YF6A, Ireland

1 3 5 7 9 10 8 6 4 2

Copyright © Giles Foden 2024

The moral right of Giles Foden to be identified as
the author of this work has been asserted in accordance
with the Copyright, Designs and Patents Act of 1988.

All rights reserved. No part of this publication may be
reproduced, stored in a retrieval system, or transmitted
in any form or by any means, electronic, mechanical,
photocopying, recording, or otherwise, without the
prior permission of both the copyright owner and the
above publisher of this book.

All the characters in this book are fictitious, and any resemblance
to actual persons, living or dead, is purely coincidental.

A CIP catalogue record for this book is
available from the British Library.

ISBN (Hardback) 978 0 2978 6822 4
ISBN (Export Trade Paperback) 978 0 2978 6929 0
ISBN (Ebook) 978 0 2978 6823 1

Typeset by Input Data Services Ltd, Bridgwater, Somerset

Printed in Great Britain by Clays Ltd, Elcograf S.p.A.

MIX
Paper | Supporting
responsible forestry
FSC® C104740

www.weidenfeldandnicolson.co.uk
www.orionbooks.co.uk

For David Barton, who also did servitude piking bales,
and Billy Keane, who served where stories begin

'But it's no use now,' thought poor Alice, 'to pretend to be two people! Why, there's hardly enough of me left to make one respectable person!'

> Lewis Carroll, *Alice's Adventures in Wonderland*

1

Starting the engine

June 2014

Above the town, the sky had suddenly let the sunshine in. Birds were sounding and – further away – a couple of the region's dark-maned, almost extinct lions were roaring. All in the sequence that humans describe as dawn. Who knows what lions might have called it as the sun began to warm their backs? One would need to *think lion*.

In more or less the same moment, Captain Xin's vehicle pulled up outside Catherine Brosnan's bungalow in Dekmantel. Its tyres made a slight swish of sand.

Catherine had been there nearly three months. Waiting mostly for Xin to act. Previous meetings with him had only added to an instinct that her purpose there was being endlessly deferred. All the while, the clock on her research project had been ticking down – like everything on the planet seemed to be ticking down. For it was again one of those years full of canary-in-coalmine warnings about climate change. It was in her nature to pay attention to such moments – but there had been so many. And now (but that latch-opening of now was always closing), it would take so many moments of self-sacrifice for anything useful to happen.

The time waiting for Xin's help had seemed so long. She'd spent too much of it painting her toenails, tooling about on social media or looking at stupid apps. A satellite-driven community service gave an internet signal to the main part of the town, but as soon as one went even slightly into the desert it began to lag, then stopped abruptly.

Frustration had furred her mood all this while, clogging like particles of moss in one of the old lead pipes which – long before her birth thirty-five years previously – had first brought water direct from the spring in the Well Field to her old family house in Ireland. Sometimes, here in the Namibian desert, she had wept for that childhood home in dampest Kerry.

Home, where a little Virgin Mary shrine still sat on its sconce on the rough white-plaster wall, dripping fitful electric light from a plastic candle. Home, where wild geese called from the mouth of the night. Home, where tiny red arachnids crawled over her rubber boots when she helped her brother save the hay in summer.

Bloodsuckers was the odd family word for these tiny spiders, because crushing them left a large reddish spot. Clover mites scientifically, *Bryobia praetiosa* – odd enough in themselves, in that they were entirely female, their eggs not needing any male input. Not now so often seen, because of the changes in climate.

But her own purpose, now and in Namibia? Here, in this dusty little town, Dekmantel? To find a vast reserve of groundwater. An aquifer, as scientists like her called it.

What aquifers are, how they work, what they look like – why they're important and worth a lot of risk to find: all not much understood by non-scientists. Except maybe by those people who, living not in cities (as most now did), depended on boreholes for their water. So Catherine had constantly found when asked what she did, usually by unwelcome blokes in bars.

Precious things, aquifers, waiting in the darkness, mostly unseen, sopping up water, holding water, letting it seep out . . . layers of subterranean rock, sand or gravel that can draw up water but also allow it to flow, acting as a containment for the future.

Discovered in the present, an aquifer might assuage thirst, making a massive difference in a bone-dry place like Namibia, where human or any relationship with water was extremely fragile and dangerously contingent.

Trying to ease that relationship was exactly why she was here in Dekmantel, waiting for the Chinese captain – the one who'd at last arrived, along with dawn, noisy birds and distant lions whose roaring was already becoming a thing of the past, just as humanity might.

Xin's vehicle had been followed by a military truck, chugging out fumes. Until they halted, the cylinders of both vehicles moved to the repetitive tempo beloved by both Henry Ford and Li Shufu, China's latter-day model of the American automobile tycoon.

Had she not been eating a bowl of cereal in the kitchen of the bungalow, Catherine would have seen the military truck fishtailing over rugged dunes. As if it were empty. In the back of it all the same: six of Xin's marines, along with some tents, water, other provisions.

She would have seen Xin's own transport too: a lighter-duty, off-road utility item. Its original design depended on serial inheritances from previous eras: Russian off-roaders, American Jeeps and British Land Rovers.

Known as a Beijing jeep, anyway.

The captain knocked on the door. Catherine started up, at once embarrassed by the flaking paint on the bungalow porch (even though it was just a rental) and the fragments of Nature's Source Muesli Crunch lodging between her molars.

She dodged her head outside, said she'd be just a minute. After a quick brushing of teeth, wanding of lashes and panicked dabbing of concealer on an inconvenient spot on her forehead, she duly emerged in Lycra leggings, trainers and a fresh white T-shirt to meet Xin under the sun-blistered porch.

By now Xin seemed impatient, if she interpreted correctly the slightly raised eyebrows and cocked head that greeted her. For it had been the longest minute, the delay mostly relating to disguise of the spot. Laughable, really, that last night she'd been looking at an app that showed a carousel of celebrity female faces, offering Botox or fillers that could make her look like them, if she could ever afford it.

Well, that was the promise, but now here she was, presenting her authentic self; stood in the doorway of the bungalow, looking at the unadulterated face of a Chinese naval officer – handsome enough, if slightly hawkish.

He said, 'Hello, Catherine.' She said, 'Hello, Xin.'

Not one drop of this perfunctory exchange got anywhere near the well of mutual understanding, if not intimacy, that she'd inferred from their previous meetings. *Maybe I've made a mistake about that . . .* so she added, more formally: 'Sorry to have kept you waiting, Captain Xin.'

He gave an odd, nervous smile. 'Really no need to call me Captain.'

'OK.'

An awkward pause followed, during which they hovered about each other under the porch. It was almost as if he were as anxious as she, although he really didn't seem the anxious type.

Catherine herself carried in her heart a heap of anxiety, on her back a small rucksack containing maps and a few necessaries, and across one shoulder a plait of jet-black hair. The same plait that sportive young men at university had occasionally tugged, in the name of banter. Why she started learning the martial art of Muay Thai: to tip those lads on their backs – put them in order, knock some heads.

Never actually took them on it, though, that intercranial journey.

Now, locking the bungalow door behind her, she felt – despite the self-supposed censure of Xin's gaze – excited at the prospect of this trip with him. Some high-voltage crackling at last, after all this time in furlough. Her encounters with Namibian and American as well as Chinese authorities had so far harvested little response, neutral at best, negative at worst.

The aquifer she was seeking lay across the border of two zones of corporate control – ones so roughly under the national aegis as to be provinces of foreign powers, ones whose deployment of technology exceeded by far the resources of the state. Yet despite the advances of technology, where the aquifer *exactly* was remained frustratingly unclear. The models that predicted it on screen had not yet produced it in reality.

Still conscious of her tardiness and appearance – face a tad pale, apart from the spot – Catherine walked alongside Xin to his jeep, feeling uncertain.

Head down, looking at the sand, not wanting him to see her forehead, she noted boots daintier than might be expected on the feet of a military man. High-laced but thin-textured, they were almost like the monkey boots those chancers who tried to get the shift off her back in Kerry would wear on Friday nights. The country lads were at least more polite than the university guys.

There was one country boy, Ger Sweeney, with whom she'd had some fun times, but it fizzled out when he stopped being an apprentice and began building up his own business. Kerry Heating Solutions, as she remembered, *here for all your oil-fired boiler install and servicing needs.*

'Just the thing to cause a tipping point in the climate system,' she'd told him on their final meeting, over pints of Guinness at John B's in Listowel.

'What's a tipping point?' Ger had said, which remark pushed that already on–off relationship over a critical threshold.

Something fired now inside Catherine as she neared Xin's jeep, but she was not fully sure it was sexual attraction. Maybe just the blowback of all those lost opportunities for pleasure that she had dutifully denied herself. In pursuit of what . . . academic attainment? So much keyboard action.

Grabbing the handle of the passenger door, she wondered if she should, when younger, have grabbed faster whatever it was she needed, copying some other type than that of the nerdy academic her stern teacher Mary-Ag had implicitly thrown before her.

All past conjecture, now that she was on the Skeleton Coast. A place where vast dunes and occasionally rusting ship-hulks dominate vision. A place where the cold Benguela Current lifts dense fogs as the Atlantic hits desert heat. A place where humans scratch a living in towns that hanker on. Such as Dekmantel, so named because every morning a cloak of sand settled on the green tin roofs of its houses.

All past conjecture, now that she was thirty-five and single – a pale Irishwoman getting into the jeep of Captain Handsome.

Thirty-five! Not a great age in the history of the planet, but old enough to sense that she might not ever have a baby – even if she was wary enough of the banal way in which this topic was treated in magazine articles and in all sorts of other advice, education and public engagement.

Almost a bombardment, really. One that seemed to have pursued her all the way from her Leaving Cert science teacher's classes in Kerry (that same Mary-Ag) to an undergrad course at Trinity College Dublin – then an MSc and PhD beyond, at the same institution. And now this academic research project that had landed her in Namibia.

Putting his walkie-talkie on the dashboard, Xin pulled back his cuff and looked at a watch. Quite old, with a seagull image in the middle of its dial and a strap as green as broccoli. The walkie-talkie made a wailing noise.

She had just not yet found the right father, she'd kept telling herself – someone kind. Or at least fucking chivalrous. Her own da had been neither, dying some years before, at the same time as her mother.

'Ready to roll?' Xin asked, more by way of instruction than question. Next he picked up his walkie-talkie, said something in Chinese to the marines in the truck behind.

No reply.

Catherine looked at his thighs, gapped either side of the steering wheel. He was wearing the same light-brown uniform as that first night they'd met in the old Portuguese fort, Dekmantel's only slightly upscale hotel. That was nearly two months ago. She'd been on her research trip just a few weeks then, and still believed she could prove something.

Her academic plans had been turned upside down since she first met Xin. They'd had a couple more meetings afterwards. But he'd kept refusing her permission to go into the Chinese corporate mining zone. Officials of the American mining company, the Scursail Corporation, had also said no: she'd had a particularly unpleasant encounter with Scursail's head of security, a South African called Glen Cole. Namibian government officials in Windhoek, the capital, had been more courteous but equally unhelpful.

Beside her now in the jeep, Xin sighed – spoke again in Chinese into his radio, more barkily now. Then said to her: 'My apologies. Those guys behind are not the brightest.'

'No problem,' she said. 'I've waited long enough.'

He gave her a look, and she immediately regretted having vented.

With time on the research trip dribbling away (the whole thing was only a year; after which the chances of her post being extended got even slimmer), she'd found herself immured here in Dekmantel, unable until now to evaluate on the ground the hypothesis she was being funded to test.

Once more, Xin pressed the button on his walkie-talkie and said something and, on getting no reply (why didn't he just get out and go remonstrate with them in person?), turned his head to the window opposite her and looked out over the mist-haze as it dissipated over the outskirts of Dekmantel . . . mist-haze mixed with kitchen smoke from bungalows like Catherine's, plus a number of concrete blockhouses and a few thatched huts.

Dekmantel. A one-horse town of emblematic type, the kind of place where someone might make a dope western if they could handle the hassle of the heat. It sat on the edge of a vast desert. Somewhere crossed by the lines drawn in blood by impious adventurers, who in bygone times of empire had hunted down prey, and not just animals. Hunted down other people's tax money, other people's land, other people. No pains, no sacrifices were spared in eliminating those others of the past, who were chased from one waterhole to the next. Then were hanged or shot. Or died from drinking poisoned water.

Nowadays, the many travel writers for glossy magazines who visited the region struggled as to how to treat this issue of genocide. Or so Catherine had intuited in her reading in preparation for coming here.

'What's wrong with these people?' muttered Xin – almost on the instant finally getting a reply on the walkie-talkie from the marines in the truck.

And then, turning to her: 'I'm sorry about this, Catherine.

The dumb fellows behind us lost the key to their truck. I was on the point of saying bye-bye to the stupid eggs, but they finally found it!'

She didn't reply, not much liking the way he was talking – just looked at his thighs again. They seemed, like the rest of his body in that moment, to flex with his own frustration at the continued delay. Behind them the engine of the truck yawped at last.

Lions, too, she'd read (in the slightly more enlightened travel articles), the whole shower of invaders also liked to shoot lions, brutishly exterminating them. And now both the descendants of the hunted lions and the descendants of the hunted humans were still searching tenaciously, amid a chaos of sand and rock, for freshwater springs. Which was why the Irish Research Council had allocated her grant, though less for lion reasons than human ones.

One of that latter species, Captain Xin, now fiddling with the key of his own vehicle, gave what sounded like a curse in Chinese, before mumbling – half to her, half to himself – the words: 'Steering lock; now it's my fault.'

Finally (finally!) he started the engine. As he did so, she found herself recalling their first meeting. That, too, had ignited something.

2

A twist of sand

She had guessed it was him right away, even in the gloom of the bar of the old Portuguese fort in Dekmantel. Now called the Hotel Bom Jesus, its name illuminated a flashing neon sign outside. The bar was somewhat erroneously dubbed a 'cocktail lounge', wrong because its habitués drank beer, neat spirits or soft drinks. Sodas, as they were locally known. A cocktail lounge only insofar as there were many prostitutes there, seeking military clients. The Bom Jesus sat exactly on the dividing line between the two zones of corporate control, so far as mining and in fact much else was concerned. Many Chinese soldiers and also many paramilitaries (the American mine used South African mercenaries for security) were in the bar that first night Catherine met Xin, which had made it a bit scary for her to enter.

Among these other military, Chinese and South African, demarcated by table choice, Xin was distinguished by pure presence and by sitting alone. He was smoking a cigarette and drinking a glass of whisky, his broad forehead and closely cropped hair bent over a book.

Fierce concentration. A few years older than her maybe (ashes in that black hair), but still . . .

He closed the book – it seemed to be about fishing, at least it had a picture of what looked like a trout on the cover, and some Chinese writing. It surprised her that he might be a fisherman, if her intuition was correct.

She sat down next to him, made her introduction, said her piece. No need: infuriatingly, he'd known at once what she wanted from him – a pass into the Chinese mining zone of the Namib. It was the same thing that everyone wanted from him, he told her almost straight away.

Adding, though not unkindly: 'There's no point in my granting it. You're bound to fail. It does not matter how tough you are. All fail in the Namib.'

Namib meant 'wide place' or 'a place where there is nothing' in Khoekhoegowab, one of the main local languages. A place that despite being mostly sand was, remarkably, created by water, running from ephemeral river sources far inland. Grinding away rock, carving gorges, depositing the sand that made it, most likely, the oldest desert on earth. It stretched for more than 2,000 kilometres along the coasts of Angola, Namibia itself and South Africa – coasts along which Atlantic currents and winds constantly swept tonnes of sand back into the foreshore and beyond . . .

And now, as the jeep pressed further into all that sand, followed by the diesel-chugging truck, Xin wore sunglasses. Wrapped round his neck was a white silk scarf. In combination with a khaki jacket, this attire made him look much more raffish than he had in the bar, that first time and the other times they'd met, him stonewalling her permit request but also suggesting they meet again, until finally coming round, as it now seemed.

Had he put on this outfit for her?

Xin brusquely requested the co-ordinates she had estimated for the aquifer. They corresponded with a place called Serra dos Leões, near the border with Angola, in the Kunene region. But she had told him all that before. Scrabbling in her rucksack, she found a plastic folder and passed it over. It was already extremely hot in the cab. Embarrassing that he might feel sweat from her own palms on the cover.

She knew that their chances of finding the fabled water source were slim. Watching Xin enter the co-ordinates into his phone, holding the steering wheel between those khaki-clad knees, Catherine was reminded of a dusty allusion that one of her colleagues in Global Water Studies back at Trinity, Professor O'Connor, used to like making: *The map is not the territory.*

In other words: despite the probabilities of the scientific models seeming secure, at least when one sat in front of a screen, everything she had previously thought about the aquifer and its location could be wrong. O'Connor like to apply the same dictum to his own discipline of earth science, reminding young students that he was old enough to remember when it was confidently predicted that the planet was getting colder, not hotter, as it now indubitably seemed. He used this, she remembered, as a way of emphasising the importance of the long view, in which individual human perspective was of almost negligible significance.

Their small convoy passed alongside a dried riverbed. Maybe, Catherine speculated, it was a tributary of one of the larger rivers that fed or fed off the very aquifer for which she was searching. A place that she suspected existed not just from scientific data but also from fugitive references in the anthropological literature. These mentioned, vaguely enough, sacred underground water sources that tribal elders kept secret, some of the journals showing cave paintings of animals and humans supping at springs.

So hot in the cab . . . Luckily, Xin soon opened the windows, apologising that the air conditioning was not very effective.

Piles of dry brushwood snapped under the jeep's tyres as they traversed something that was not quite a road, not quite plain sand either. There was no breeze today. Even the stir of air produced by the passage of the vehicle was stifling. The plastic covering on the aerial of Xin's walkie-talkie seemed to be melting.

They passed some thorn trees on a bank of dry grass, at which goats were nibbling. The billy raised its head to stare at them. Catherine wondered what it thought, and in the same moment what the man driving her was thinking. She was becoming increasingly aware how little she knew Xin, or Hai (that was his given name, he'd told her once), despite the evenings they had spent together in the bar of the hotel . . .

Evenings when she'd told him about her life in Ireland, how her brother Tony hovered as busy and irksome as a midge over the family farm.

And your parents? Xin had asked, only out of politeness she'd thought, and then she'd explained how they'd both been killed in a car accident on the way into Limerick to get a replacement dressing gown for the same Tony, who then had to take over the farm when still a young man.

Evenings when Xin himself had described his own youth in Qingdao. A coastal city in eastern China, he'd explained, in the province of Shandong. His grandmother had been a senior political figure there, he'd said, adding how he, as a result of the privileges her position brought, became something of a wastrel: a drunk, a gambler, a driver of fast cars. All freely admitted. 'I stupidly wanted to be a pop star,' he'd told her – with a sideways, down-lit grin that showed his teeth, slightly pointed – but he couldn't sing. This period of his life ended when his grandmother fell into political disgrace. He'd then joined the Chinese Navy, in which 'my aunt, Yu Ping' was one of the few female figures of high rank.

Evenings when there'd been, she thought, a flicker of erotic interest between them. But around Xin she was aware of red flags, back then in the Bom Jesus and now in the jeep as he altered the revs of the engine to get a balance between maintaining momentum and spinning the tyres on millions of grains of sand.

They came to a spit of land where dry grass had caught fire, then been choked off by sand. It had left a small area of cinders, in some parts still smouldering, giving off black whisps. Further away, previous tendrils of smoke were diffusing slowly, making stepping stones in the sky.

Soon the riverbed petered out. They entered the desolation of the dunes proper – dunes that she knew moved across the landscape at a rate of about fifty centimetres a year, pushed by winds – the two vehicles climbing up and falling down them like insects.

Every grain of sand in the massive piles they were driving across stored up heat and radioactivity. The physics and chemistry of these grains talked to each other like batteries in series, increasing exponentially the total dune system's ability to store energy. And all this was happening as that whole community of grains moved on, centimetre by centimetre, year by year, century by century, across the landscape, ignoring human borders.

Professor O'Connor once light-heartedly proposed in a lecture that these grains had almost human-type bonds, before immediately referencing communication between ants. It really was as if temperamentally he didn't make a distinction between different parts of a whole-earth system – all this in a lecture when his doltish students weren't getting the whole at all, though Catherine thought she had.

After about two hours, mounting yet another vast dune, one shaped like a star with radiating arms, the truck behind got stuck. Xin picked up his radio and spoke into it again.

They waited outside the jeep as the marines dug out the truck, cigarettes jutting from their mouths as they angled in spades and strutted metal boards, rolled wire netting up the incline. It took over an hour.

'Drift sand,' said Xin, as they got back in the jeep. 'That's the worst.'

Catherine accustomed herself to the throb of the engine as they resumed their wriggle up the dune. The bumping of the jeep as it met successive elevations of sand awoke something within her, the same feeling she'd had when she'd met him in the bar of the Hotel Bom Jesus.

At the crest of one dune, Catherine was struck by the apparent absence of wildlife and plants. None of the country's famous dark-maned desert lions or scavenging jackals here. No desert elephants or desert rhinos and certainly not the near-mythical golden mole. Nor even one of those plants that had developed survival abilities to fit the ephemeral nature of water in a desert. She'd been hoping to spot one called a quiver tree – effectively a large sponge (to hold onto water when it arrives), but with small cactus-like leaves to minimise its loss of water between brief periods of abundance. Only a few lonely birds, making slow circles in the blue high above, and flies, coming occasionally into the vehicle and wavering about till they escaped. She thought of clouds of blackfly in the Well Field back home in Kerry, buzzing species of meadow flower, of moorhen peeping from their sedge, and the whole arrangement of roots that lay under the sodden soil.

Pausing, Xin took off his sunglasses and put binoculars to his eyes. There were no tracks, only vacancy. She could see that well enough unaided.

'You do realise', he said, 'that it's very unlikely we will find any sign of water.'

'Everyone keeps telling me that. But I have to try.' She looked across the empty sweeps of sand. 'I was surprised that you agreed, Xin.'

He was silent for a moment. 'Did you not want me to come?'

'I didn't say that. Just thought you would keep saying no.'

He shifted uneasily in the driver's seat. 'There's a big difference between preferring not to get involved and doing what you actually want. I could lose my job granting this pass, escorting you now.'

'I understand that very well,' she said, looking at the sulphurous sand ahead, unclear about what he was saying to her, or communicating. Not perhaps the same thing.

The great space appeared to lay itself out as a willing scapegoat under the sun. Behind, the gear changes of the truck came loud – individually distinguishable, like someone arguing with themselves.

Heading north, they crept on for most of a day, not stopping for lunch, instead eating from a large packet of hard, bland biscuits as they drove and drinking water from the holy chalice of Xin's canteen, which tasted of iron and fire, and its own rubber seal.

The heat from the sun burned her thighs through her canvas trousers. The heat from the jeep engine burned the soles of her trainers. Colloquially, back home: her runners. She wanted to take them off, and the little socks underneath, put her feet on the dashboard, but was embarrassed about what Xin might think of her painted toenails. It would be an impertinence, surely, to do the thing she wanted.

The wind outside began to rise. Because of the open windows, sand blew into her face, scratching her eyelids. Now she wanted him to close the windows again, but knew that would make it too hot.

'We'd better stop,' Xin said as they crested another belt of dunes. 'This wind is getting very strong. Better to get down low if a storm comes.'

They descended the next dune at a sharp angle, the chassis of the jeep seeming to flex as it skidded from side to side. The sand streamed next to them in little rivulets.

'Perhaps we should turn back,' said Catherine, after about twenty minutes more of this up-down torment.

'It was you who wanted to come.' He gestured over the sand, which was now suddenly featureless, level as linen all around them. 'I hope you're not disappointed in what you find.'

'I was expecting . . .'. Her voice trailed off; she had hoped it would all have been easier than this.

Overwhelmed and vulnerable was what she now felt: not even knowing now what she'd thought she had expected. Something better than failure, anyhow, which is what this expedition now seemed like. Something better than a sense that people like her, so-called experts, should have their expertise so immediately called into question by the local landscape. It struck her that were she not with him, she would be so lost; and he wasn't even local himself, Xin.

Looking again at the sand, which seemed to shift in the haze, Catherine realised that she was wrong about the landscape being featureless. Where, not very long ago, there was desert that had appeared completely smooth, now there were bars, ribs, definitive patterns evolving. Peaking and troughing along their run, they looked like enormous skeletal remains of antediluvian creatures.

Yet because of the rising wind there was also a sense of incipient movement, a feeling that the vast skeletons were on the point of waking up from millennia of sleep. It was really hard for her to judge how large they were, these moving carpets of ribbed sand. People liked to use the analogy of football pitches, but they outstripped that measure completely.

Even as Catherine (ever the scientist) was mentally abstracting the nature of such comparisons, forward particles of sand within these wind-driven waves were striking at the streamlined edges of the jeep, plucking at its painted surfaces as if they were obstacles to be deflected.

In the distance, a stripe of inky cloud was scratching towards them. Blown sand again flitted through the open windows, once more pricked Catherine's eyelids, causing her to close them but get caught on the counter-attack every time she reopened them.

'Come,' said Xin, 'we should eat before the storm.' He picked up the walkie-talkie and gave an order in Chinese.

Shortly afterwards they halted. Producing a petrol stove from the truck, the marines cooked up, remarkably quickly, a meal of black tea and polished rice and slices of processed meat. The meat tin was mostly covered with Chinese characters, but there was another, overprinted label that read HENAN PORK in English. Henan's a province, Xin told her. Both the meat and the rice were white as milk and had practically no taste. The slices of tasteless pork were extremely regular in shape; she imagined the machine that cut them, in faraway Henan, which he told her adjoined his own home province of Shandong.

'You OK?' he said.

'I hate the feeling of sand in my mouth,' she said. 'And on my face.'

Yet squatting down next to Xin – watching him scoop up food, a slight movement for a body she reckoned capable of leaps, aggressions, feats of strength – Catherine was now content. Apart from the sound of their utensils and the odd comment from the marines, eating their own meal a little distant, there was a couple-like quiet between them.

Once they had finished the meal, Xin ordered that tents be erected in the lee of the vehicles. The marines did this no less speedily than they had prepared the food. Soon there were three white tents up: one large square one for the marines and two small triangular ones for Catherine and Xin. All these were guyed with weights, pegs being useless in sand.

'You should take shelter now,' Xin said with a tight smile. 'Try to sleep. We will aim to reach the site tomorrow.' Then he added: 'The supposed site.'

'Goodnight.'

She went inside her tent, the fabric of which was flapping in the wind. As darkness fell the storm took hold of the camp more firmly, dense flurries of sand wrenching the canvas. She lay still, looking at the moonlight through the moving, semi-transparent envelope of the tent.

The canvas seemed to eddy as the sand disclosed light differently with each blow. It altered second by second, now fat, like a bright-white cow on the material, now thin, a starveling creature, now something else, and something else again, each kinetic image caught in a wrinkle of time or twist of sand.

3

Her own desire

A few hours passed, during which Catherine intermittently woke. During the periods of wakefulness she thought about the past few months and the ways in which she'd struggled with the idea that the Chinese and Americans (through their South African overseers) had so much power in this land. Mainly because it had uranium, in global reserves of which Namibia presently ranked third, after Kazakhstan and Australia – a desired commodity if you were building nuclear power stations or nuclear weapons.

In Namibia, these mining companies were operating in a sovereign territory. Yet it had often seemed to Catherine that the Ministry of Mines, with which she'd had some dealings, was itself undermined by these foreign interests. The corporate activities of those interests were focused only on profit, with little concern for the national interest.

Lately, Russians, too, had been in the local resource-extraction game. They had also been mining uranium, she knew. But that crowd of gangsters had recently suffered a setback and been expelled. One of those moments when the ministry fought righteously back against foreigners, squeezing harder those who hoped to extract nuclear juice out of communal earth.

To the planet, Catherine thought wildly as she lay in her tent, its fabric all the while still penetrated by the dispassionate if jerky gaze of moonlight, the centuries which all these corporations had spent mining must seem just a blink of an eye. She had long persuaded herself that her own research subject – water and its sources and deployments – was of different value to uranium and those other metals and gems, the mining of which had more or less disembodied this part of southern Africa since the days of Rhodes. She had allowed herself a broad moral latitude on that subject. But sometimes she doubted the ethical superiority that she had perhaps too easily assumed. Water, after all, was a resource like any other.

Her thoughts turned again to Xin – there in the other tent, just a few metres over – and wondered why he'd finally agreed to help her by permitting an escorted trip into the Chinese mining area. He hadn't been obliged to do so. All these mining areas, after all, were policed as strictly as the former *Sperrgebiet* (German: 'Forbidden Zone'), a diamond-rich expanse of sand that lay more southerly on the Skeleton Coast, access to which by unauthorised persons had been strictly prohibited during the previous century.

To an extent she was hoping the reason was that he liked her, but that hope came with complicated attachments, as if hope itself were a slight against her professionally, even if it was emotionally welcome.

This whole show in Namibia stank – but she couldn't let that turn her away now. She was on a job, and if she were to keep her post the job had to be completed to schedule. Especially now that the university was, yet again, in a period of strategic review.

She tried to sleep, losing consciousness all too slowly as grains of sand pit-pattered on the canvas . . .

After some time she was awake again, lying there with a sore throat and dry eyes that now saw nothing. The patterns on the canvas of the tent had gone to black, light having been swallowed up in the depths of the storm.

She sat up with a start – feeling hugely, terrifyingly alone.

Visibility was low, but, opening her tent and looking out, she could just see the figure of Xin in his. He was crouched, illuminated by a lamp. It was by now well past midnight; why was he still awake? Not even lying down.

Surprising herself, she ran over in bare feet and unzipped his tent. He was wearing black socks, she noticed, but apart from having removed his jacket and boots was clothed exactly as before.

'Can I sleep here?' she asked him, knowing why she asked but not wanting to admit it to herself.

He looked at her, again with an expression she couldn't read. Bewilderment, possibly. 'If you're sure.'

She was expecting him to say something more, but he didn't; so she came inside the tent – pressed down internally on the doubt dissuading her from owning her own desire, from being the person she thought she could be.

They moved awkwardly around one another in the tiny space, revolving on the groundsheet until she was able to find a small space and sat down. He shuffled off a foam mat and passed it to her before rolling into his sleeping bag.

'Are you frightened?' he said after a few seconds, asking her the question that she'd thought he might pose before. 'Is that why you came?'

'I'll be all right,' she said, trying to pass him back the foam mat, the ends of which were curling up.

'Please do take it,' he replied. 'The sand gets very cold at night.'

There was very little else in the tent: a small khaki valise with zipped compartments; some extra uniform; a canteen of water. A head torch, hanging from a hook in the middle of the tent. The only other light came from the purplish display of his walkie-talkie. Still switched on, it emitted a soft hiss of static.

He was watching her look around the tent, she realised. She returned his gaze.

'Do you mind if I turn off the light?' he asked. 'We might need the battery.'

'OK,' Catherine said. The light went off. Then: 'Look, the moon has come back!' She felt a bit stupid saying this, as it was obvious. At the same time there was an impatience, secret and guilty, that something else was meant to happen and had not started.

Sand had again begun striking the tent. It made a dry, rolling noise. Turning, she saw the silhouette of his face and experienced a strong desire for him to kiss her. It seemed as if Xin also wanted that, from the way he angled his head. Perhaps their evenings together at the hotel – the conversations that surprised them both, the apparent ease that had grown between them – had always been heading towards this. Perhaps, also, the vastness of the desert night was just too much for both of them.

'How would you feel', Xin suddenly asked, shifting closer, 'if I kissed you now?'

She cleared her throat, dry from so much sand running down it during the day, and said: 'I don't usually permit strange men to kiss me.' Then she smiled in the secret darkness, thanking the genie that had so quickly granted her wish, and moved herself closer to him.

After a little time, he turned on his side and slipped an arm over her. It felt good to be held again at last.

'Catherine Brosnan,' Xin later declared in the most unromantic manner, 'wait for a prophylactic.'

He reached out an arm, scrabbled around for the valise in the pearly darkness, unzipped it. Producing a silver-foil packet, he ripped it with his teeth and handed her the contents.

Having rolled it on, she drew him to her, guiding him in with her hand, then gripping him by the hips. He lasted a long enough time, waiting for her to come first.

They lay there for a while afterwards, breathing together as one, his slightly scratchy chin against her neck, her hands now in the small of his back. Outside, the storm was moving on, setting up its big top in another place.

Shortly afterwards a mechanical tone burst out of his walkie-talkie. He moved off her, picked up the radio; listened; pressed the talk button; said something forceful in Chinese. Another voice replied, no less urgent-sounding.

Taking off the condom, he quickly donned his uniform and went outside, continuing to speak to his interlocutor.

4

The morning after

Catherine woke in a fit of breathlessness. The heat of Xin's tent was a prison. No sign of him. Her belly and thighs were crusty; she wished there was water in which to wash. Panicked, she dressed, before emerging into sunlight so bright it made her want to clap her hands over her eyes.

The marines were packing their big tent into the truck. She looked about for Xin in the ocean of sand, finally spotting him on a small incline. In uniform, present and correct now, he was inspecting the montage of dunes through binoculars.

Getting nearer, she wanted to hold him again. He let the binoculars drop on their cord and turned to her as she approached.

'Good morning,' he said, unsmiling, as if last night had not even been real. He seemed preoccupied.

'What are you looking at?' Behind them she heard the clank of tins as the marines began making coffee.

'The configuration of the dunes has shifted because of the storm,' he said, not even glancing at her. 'I was looking at something beyond, in line with those trees. Here.' He offered her the binoculars.

'Do you think we've found it?' she asked.

Xin shook his head. Catherine lifted the binoculars to sore eyes. She saw three small palm trees a couple of kilometres off. Some 200 metres nearer, half buried in one of the dunes, was a military vehicle.

'A Land Rover!'

'Don't think so. Maybe something like my troops' transport. We'll take a look anyhow.'

He went back, got a rifle and a canteen of water from one of the marines, and started walking with Catherine towards the vehicle. They progressed in silence.

As they approached, it became clear that it was indeed not a Land Rover, nor a Beijing jeep, but a small military truck. It was smaller than that of his marines, and much older.

'How did it get here?' Catherine asked.

'Driven, of course. Very long time ago.'

'I can see that.' Was he making her feel stupid on purpose?

A single red star, faded now, was painted on the bonnet. Russian. This insignia, and the truck's green paint, had flaked and faded after long years under the sun. The canvas flaps on its sides had hardened to the consistency of tree bark. Its wheels and lower body were sunk in deep.

It was impossible to open either of the doors. Xin didn't even try, instead grabbing the rim of the cab roof, hauling himself up one of the inclines of yellow sand into which the vehicle was buried so his eyes were level with the driver's seat.

'There's someone there,' Xin said.

'Surely not.'

'Human remains. A body.'

She pulled herself up, joining Xin at the not-quite-closed window. The glass was pitted.

Inside were indeed the remains of a man, his desiccated body and army uniform embalmed by the sun and blown granules of sand, which half filled the cab; he was lying on the double seat with his booted feet up, crossed, and his back against the door opposite.

His capped skull, too, was packed with sand. It flowed from his wide eyes and his too-large nostrils and his open throat down onto his lap. The heat and glare made the horror of his face – the grinning jaw, and the big cap with its own red star, still red despite the passage of time – too much for Catherine to comprehend.

She felt at once disgusted, a little afraid, but also scientifically curious – having never seen a body except when identifying those of her parents, which were so mangled it was an imprecise exercise. Didn't want to remember.

Xin pushed down the window glass with considerable effort. 'A Russian soldier from long ago, when they too tried to control this place,' he announced.

The strangest thing was the way the skeletal hands of the body were holding, with something that looked almost like casualness – half open, on his lap – a little notebook.

Xin reached in and took hold of the book. Sand fell out of its shrivelled black-leather covers and its yellow, almost-brown pages as he opened it. He flicked through it, shaking his head in bemusement as he looked at the roughly written scrawl inside.

'Cyrillic script.' He handed it to Catherine but she demurred, thinking of her parents in the morgue and not wanting to touch leather covers that had been between dead hands.

Chuckling a little at her reaction, Xin put the book in the pocket of his khaki jacket. He did this swiftly, as if whatever account was within its covers could be concealed with a snap of the skeleton's bony fingers. Then he said: 'Like I have told you, all will fail. Look, we need to get back.'

'But what about the co-ordinates? We've not got to the aquifer.'

Xin looked at her for a moment, then back at the body of the Russian. This time his eyes were dull. 'Can you not hear what he is saying?' he said flatly.

'What do you mean?' A sense of doom came, as if he was already retreating from her.

'This body is telling you the same thing I did at the hotel. We were foolish to come. Besides, the radio call I got last night said I had to return to base urgently; it was my naval superior – something serious.'

All the same, as Catherine absorbed this information he reached into the cab and removed the dead soldier's big hat, flicking it to get rid of the sand inside. Then he turned and they began walking back to the camp, which the marines had mostly already packed up – Xin carrying the dead man's sandy, red-starred headgear without looking back, or at Catherine.

Later, back in Xin's jeep, with the dead soldier's Soviet hat between them – it really was absurdly large – they sat in near-silence. The atmosphere between them could not have been more different from last night.

As they drove back along the dunes towards Dekmantel, roughly following their own tyre tracks from the way there, Catherine again thought of their initial meeting in the bar in the hotel, when she'd asked for the permit, and Xin had first told her she would fail.

'Why?' she had asked him.

'The same reason the Portuguese who built this fort in the sixteenth century failed. And the other foreign powers, like the Russians who fought here covertly in the 1980s. And you British, who were the biggest failures of all, firing on the natives with cannons from ships two hundred years before.'

'I'm Irish,' she'd told him – playfully, she hoped – as they'd stood on the parapet outside the bar, watching the sun track down over the desert landscape beyond. The truth was that she felt no great connection to her nation, but abroad her sense of being Irish was amplified. Especially when someone accused her of being British. *On the contrary* . . . Within that resistance, too, folded within its Irishness, was a sense of always wanting instead to bring her own self into focus.

'My apologies,' Xin had said with a smile. 'Anyway, from a Chinese point of view, the British are irrelevant now. All that backward focus on empire has worn them out! There are new empires of which they seem oblivious.'

'What do you mean?'

'The Americans running the other side of the mining territory here. Us too, in our own sector.'

'I'm just trying to find an aquifer that will help people survive, ideally Namibian people.'

'Do you not think your aquifer would have been found before, given that the Portuguese, British and South Africans, the

Russians and now the Americans and also my own people have been looking for it for so long?'

'I guess – but that does not, in itself, mean the aquifer isn't there. And it seems from the stories that some Namibian tribes might actually have found it. Or found it sometime in the past.'

'You just want to believe that to confirm your science. Science is only another kind of story, after all.'

'It could be important if we found it – it could improve people's lives. Why are you always so negative?'

'I'm not. It's just, well . . . the same as it always was. This whole business. I could never say so to my superiors back in Beijing, but wherever invasions happen, local populations eventually take back control. Become dominant themselves. Rightly. So there is not much point in us outsiders being here at all. And long after humans, when evolution has its way in the future, who knows? New forms of domination – I'd put my money on spiders surviving us all!'

'What?'

Xin had chuckled, seeming distant (back then she had experienced the same annoyance she felt now in the jeep), looking into her eyes over the rim of his whisky glass. 'No . . . how's it said in English? . . . I'm pulling your legs.'

'Leg,' and she had laughed, despite it all. 'But about that permit?'

He'd shaken his head at the time. 'I'm sorry.'

Now, with his hands on the steering wheel, the hands that had touched her last night, he didn't seem sorry at all – more like he was ignoring her.

It was late in the afternoon when they pulled up in front of her bungalow in Dekmantel. Often during the journey, leaning her head on her hand, her elbow on the sill of Xin's jeep, Catherine had begun to feel very sleepy. The excursion into the desert had taken the better part of two days. It seemed somehow longer, this abortive attempt to find an aquifer that remained, despite all her efforts, half fable.

At Dekmantel, even the setting sun seemed different. No

romantic vibes arose, as Xin ratcheted back the handbrake. The passion she'd sensed, and thought he'd sensed too, now seemed like a convulsive fit.

Passing her the Soviet hat, Xin said, 'Here, a souvenir.'

He leaned across and pecked her on the cheek. But he did not look at her, not properly. By the time she had shut the door of the jeep and turned back in hope, he was already moving away.

Feeling melancholy as Xin drove off, Catherine looked up and saw a curl of fog in the sky. Smoking downwards, its tongue began licking the roof of the bungalow.

5

The years after

2014–2039

After a bitter further couple of weeks in Namibia, Catherine returned to Ireland. Within another six weeks of her return, following a visit to the university medical clinic, unwelcome news came.

News that Catherine put down to Xin having ripped the condom packet with his teeth, or the condom being past its sell-by date, or maybe degraded by the harsh climate. Or something.

After more time, still bitter but longer, she lost her academic job in Dublin, on the basis of brutal research-power metrics. The aquifer project in Namibia was deemed a dismal failure by the university authorities.

She went back home to live with her brother Tony.

The Brosnan family occupied a deceptively imposing Edwardian-era farmhouse, on the front field of which Tony raised calves, just one part of a broad dairy-related enterprise. Deceptive because there was never, had never been, much money in the family. The farm lay in a townland of north Kerry, near where the lordly River Shannon bounds that county and neighbouring Clare. Here, Tony maintained a thirty-strong herd of Friesian milkers on boggy ground. And a single bull, nicknamed Big Business.

A tall, taciturn individual, never coupled never mind married (perhaps on account of his hairy face and grumpy manner), Tony soon began treating Catherine like a servant. He expected her to do the shopping, compile the farm accounts, and now and then help with the cows. These tasks lessened a little after she finally shared the fact of her pregnancy.

Tony remained remarkably incurious about his sister's experiences in Africa. Beyond the most cursory enquiry, it was as if he didn't care how she had ended up back home and expecting. He did note to himself, in his costive and querulous and almost entirely self-absorbed manner, that as well as an embryo Catherine had brought back from the desert a strange item of headgear.

That absurdly large cap with metal grommets and airholes and an internal leather headband. With a Soviet red star above the brim and a plastic chin-strap, from which it now hung from the hook on the door of his sister's bedroom, next to a tatty woollen dressing gown nominally hers since she was a teenager.

She had never worn that dressing gown, getting another one, silky and floral, from Shein online. It had arrived from China in what seemed like minutes, delivered long before she'd met Xin and the baby that had developed inside her, even if the effect of that now seemed just as sudden as the arrival of the parcel.

The tatty dressing gown was too big for her anyway, and horribly scratchy, being handed down years ago when it was discovered that Tony had a wool allergy. Probably they should have got rid of that garment, the journey to get a replacement in Limerick having been the occasion of the death of their parents.

But old houses like the Brosnans' were full of such clutter: bizarre, dilapidated articles hanging on hooks or hiding in the backs of wardrobes, which despite present disuse nonetheless ported back to a whole forest of significant events. Tony never got a new dressing gown, wandering about in cotton pyjamas, his half-harboured belly and sinuous chest hair sometimes giving Catherine a fright when they crossed paths in the corridor.

He reacted violently to the sun as well as to wool, often having to slather on calamine lotion. Drink, on the other hand, turned his skin canary-yellow. His cheeks would often look that colour after a long night at Mullarkey's Lounge down in the village. Such expeditions he possibly allowed himself too often, sometimes insisting Catherine join him. He liked to play darts there, and a board game called Shut-the-Box. In summer after these sessions, when the effects of sun and porter combined, he could look as red and yellow as his favourite vintage tractor, a David Brown Implematic from the mid-twentieth century.

He seemed much more interested in repainting that tractor than in his niece when she was born, her bold cry announcing herself at the hospital in Tralee, as if saying: *I'm taking my place in this world.* It was a feminist act, calling her Catherine, too, or so her mother had thought. But Cat she became by name, which perhaps defeated whatever point was being made by that doubling.

That said, jumping back a generation or three, the Brosnan family was in fact rife with Catherines. Perhaps during this process of naming and renaming daughters there had, despite the turning tide of time, always been an expectation that eventually one single Catherine would – like a beachcomber on the shore of genetic history – turn up some form of resistance to the prevailing current of men laying down how things should be.

The tattlers of the townland were more inquisitive about Cat's arrival than Tony, but they'd long been that way. The very oldest among these biddies remembered earlier periods during which young women of the region had often turned up with unexplained babies. At least one (Shona Gossip, as she was locally known) had once been in that position herself, though the tourists who dropped into the provisions/souvenir shop she ran wouldn't have known it.

Because the Brosnan farm was once a famine burial ground, it too was on the local tourist trail. It even featured on the 'Discover Kerry' website. Coming in coaches, these tourists brought in good fees, but Tony hated them, as giving out the history of the place used up a lot of oxygen. His audience loved the part about the skeleton an ancestor found when replacing the back-kitchen tiles. Tony was always glad when the coaches departed, depositing the visitors at other places on the 'Wild Atlantic Way', as the tourist website had it.

The same Atlantic that crashes on the Skeleton Coast so far away in Namibia – somewhere Catherine often thought about as baby Cat became a girl, and then a young woman. During this period Catherine, resenting the way motherhood had subsumed her other identities, often dreamed of the aquifer for which she'd searched. Its luring rhythm lapped on even as she slept, percolating in the spaces of her mind.

Sometimes the effects of these dreams were so powerful that she couldn't get out of bed the next day – becoming, in Tony's unkind phrase, 'increasingly slug-like'.

At the end of the front field where the calves were raised stood twin gateposts, their crumbling stone half-covered with moss. Between these posts – in further years, as she grew up – Cat would wait for the school bus to Ballylongford, stared at by passing motorists.

In the classroom, Cat was occasionally teased for her slightly Asian features. But not mercilessly, perhaps only because they were not very evident and plenty of Irish girls had straight black hair. Cat's teacher at least – that same Mary-Agatha Mulvihill of Ballylongford who'd also taught her mother, and by Cat's time was very ancient of days – paid no heed at all to her looks. In fact, despite a reputation as being rather fierce and retrograde, she took Cat under her wing, being the *fons et origo* (Miss Mulvihill in her Listowel nursing home later liked to use that very term, explaining it strictly to bewildered Polish health visitors under a duty of palliative care, as Latin for 'source and origin') of Cat's rapid academic rise. A rise that eventually brought Cat to Trinity College Dublin to do the very same degree in Global Water Studies as her mother, and then an MSc in the subject.

It wasn't just the familial template that drew Cat in this direction. More and more, scientific models were suggesting that hydrology – the distribution and movement of water both on and below the earth's surface, and the impact of human activity on water availability to humans and other forms of life – was a key factor in how climate change could be confronted.

Throughout Cat's further education, another inspirational figure exerted a powerful sway on her. One Professor O'Connor, now very elderly, influenced her just as he had her mother, emphasising again in lectures that 'the map is not the territory'.

Cat would more or less map out similar in temperament to her mam as the years passed: kind-natured but intense, a bit jumpy also . . . anxious overall, and maybe a little anachronistic in how they both fronted up to an ever-changing, increasingly tech-driven world. But they lived in a remote place where tech made some difference, though not an enormous one.

Partly because humans resisted it. Although his cows were milked by machine – a robotic process involving the attachment of milking equipment, the cleaning of teats, primary suction, the massaging of the back of the udder to relieve any held-back milk, followed by secondary milking – Uncle Tony still mucked out by hand. Scraped twice daily with a long-handled shovel, dextrously landing cowpats in a barrow. He'd resisted the lure of automatic yard-scrapers, of 'moo monitors' that measured when cows were in heat, or the market in gene mutations creating hornless calves that would eliminate the need for painful de-horning. The smell of burnt horn used always to turn young Cat's stomach.

The farm, backward enough as it remained, was primarily a place where a black-and-white river of cows – streaming from field to parlour, parlour to field – bulked large in her imagination. The contrasting colours of Uncle Tony's herd played as powerfully on her peculiar sensibility as did the sound of the differential gears of her uncle's tractor.

Those gears turned hardest in the place that the family referred to as the Well Field, which was a wet meadow. The ground there gurgled greenly – subject to unseen, mostly unexamined subterranean passages of water as they traced their secret text beneath the surface, on occasion veering so wildly as to cause Uncle Tony's tractor to get stuck. That was a topic he'd return to with vehement curses when they were all round the kitchen table for meals, a table holding festering liquid under oilcloth nailed down long before any of them had been born. The liquid was most likely tea: every meal in that house was served with tea.

Loose tea, spooned into a dimpled steel pot. Cat missed that at Trinity, where it was only teabags of course.

★

University life, in Cat's experience, was dominated by an over-emphasis on beer on the one hand and culture chat on the other: opinions on books and films and podcasts and the latest storm on the socials. Plus a lot of people looking down at other people (so-called poets, especially, looked down on her), together with a broad sense of somehow always failing, always being in default or abeyance or another negative space.

Partly (at least Cat observed it like that), the disdain was because she was a scientist, even though she was maybe as well read as any humanities student, such as probably didn't know what stochastic meant, or annulus, or that a Darcy was a unit of intrinsic permeability. In a student pub quiz once, asked what a Darcy measured, she was the only person to get it right, one joker putting down 'manhood of male lead in Jane Austen novels'.

Few of these literary stuck-ups had heard of William Rowan Hamilton, Trinity's most famous mathematician. Also a great fan and friend of Wordsworth, to whom he even sent a few poems of his own. Cat was sure Wordsworth told him to stick to the 'hard sums' and he came up with imaginative ways of extending the spatial dimension of complex numbers . . . ways that contributed to modern mechanics, computer graphics, crystallography – all things she had used in her own research.

As well as snobbery, now and then a sort of cringing, performative 'anti-racism' was directed at her as a half-Chinese person by other students, and sometimes staff too. This mortified her, amplifying a sense of states in conflict within her. To city folk, meanwhile, who picked up on her Kerry accent, she remained just a *culchie* – an apparently unsophisticated person, come from the country to the metropolis.

At the same time, paradoxically enough, she was also a figure of distant exotic interest to male students. Many of the young men in her orbit were so terrified of a wrong step that they struggled to speak clearly, much less do anything so brazen as ask her directly for a date.

So one way or another she was alienated at university. This added to a wider feeling of being separate from the city itself. She especially hated the orgy of shopping in Dublin. Dundrum disgusted her and Henry Street was ghastly: all those people grappling for the same objects of commerce. On Black Friday, when door rushes happened, it was as if it might come to mob violence, the Fanta-faced mothers with gold-chained handbags almost trampling their own children as they rushed towards their one desire.

Together the city and the university made her feel miserable, sometimes almost suicidal. Once, having been with mates to see a vintage Studio Ghibli film called *My Neighbor Totoro*, which concerned a mother recovering from a long-term illness, she almost did it – running in the direction of a bridge on the quays and thinking of throwing herself off it.

Baulked when it came to it. She was lucky to have those friends, who used her phone location to come and find her. They were a disparate bunch, very into retro culture (Miyazaki films were a big deal, along with a host of forgotten indie bands with names like Obi, Mexican Pets and Flying Saucer Attack). It was odd, the retro thing, as otherwise all this group were very future-focused, some of them almost petrified in a mode of apocalyptic thought, others driven to activism and ethical change, one or two falling prey to fringe conspiracies.

Many of this friendship group had tattoos and piercings and colourful clothing. Others, like Cat herself, wore only black and white and would never in a million years countenance cutlery on their faces. It was a subculture really: a reaction to the wider world becoming ever more mainstream and right-wing. AI had made all this worse, in Cat's opinion, causing so many people to think on tramlines as the technology regurgitated received orders.

As well as getting support from friends, Cat sought out counselling, student services, all that. Going back to Kerry helped a bit, escaping Dublin digs so dingy they offended any civilised notion of cleanliness and proper hygiene. Mould was a big factor.

When these trips back home got too boring, she found relief by dashing out along the Kerry lanes on one of the big black bicycles that were in the farm sheds, encrusted by cobwebs and bits of straw; Uncle Tony had happily helped her get one of these heavy vehicles roadworthy, informing her that he and his siblings had used them in their own youth. On these excursions Cat often got soaked through, but almost enjoyed the electric danger of the summer storms that so often struck the county.

In the same season, she would help her uncle save the hay, taking odd pleasure in watching the bloodsuckers crawl on her runners as she piked up bales in the barn. Servitude that beefed up her biceps.

A stray ginger cat hung about in that barn for some years, staring at her, blinking at her, blinking at her more when she blinked back, as if messages were really passing between them. It mostly ate the mice in the barn, but now and then she gave it the odd scrag end of meat, or a rind of bacon left over from dinner. Which she often had to cook, her mother by now sometimes spending all day in bed and rarely leaving the farm. But the place's agricultural cycles went on nonetheless, just as they had more or less done for centuries.

The path from the farmhouse to the fields led to a blistered steel gate secured with a frayed piece of green baling twine. Another gate – a cast-iron kissing gate, a remnant of the Edwardian origins of the farm – also led on to these marshy pastures, or once did. Never nowadays being in use, it was choked by brambles.

Wearing a rubberised green mackintosh and tub-like wellingtons, Uncle Tony would halloo the cows through the steel gate and down into the disinfected parlour every morning and evening – moor them there in stalls. Maybe cast an eye on the way at that old kissing gate, possibly thinking of one of the well-formed widows Cat sometimes saw him chatting to through the half-curtained windows of Mullarkey's as they downed their rosé spritzers. But he'd never set his cap at any of them.

As her own path to adulthood developed, Cat would naturally ask her mother about her father, more and more as she got older. Looking furtively to check Tony was not present, Catherine would reluctantly draw a finger across the world map on the kitchen wall. The oilcloth-covered table in that room sported an old Powers Whiskey jug (intended to add water to alcohol but now used mainly for milk). It was a bit of a throwback, that jug, the kind of thing you'd only see in the house of an oldish rural bachelor like Uncle Tony.

On the map, Catherine would trace the outline of the Skeleton Coast. She would, if pressed, tell Cat about her evenings with Xin on the parapet of that fort-hotel, where Chinese soldiers coincided with South African mercenaries; and she and Xin, leaning side by side, looked out over the landscape, where coloured flashes from the neon sign of the Bom Jesus competed with spectral moonlight on side-slips of sand.

She would also, with deep sighs, tell her daughter about their trip to the deeper desert, and the dunes that shifted like strange animals. Once or twice, too, she told the girl how, much later in this history, China brought the aircraft carrier *Zheng He* to Walvis Bay and decanted troops into the interior, trying to claim the uranium-rich areas in totality, causing a diplomatic incident; and also how she'd discovered that Captain Xin had been sent back to China for his part in all this – she wasn't sure why.

And then, according to the *Irish Times*, how American-employed South African paramilitaries had taken over some of the area where she'd thought the aquifer was; and how they, too, had failed to find it; also how there'd been a brief stand-off with Chinese troops, an incident about which *The Times*'s 'Eye on Nature' columnist (champ of the hour, who happened to be on safari there) gave a dramatic report.

RTÉ swiftly followed up with a 'country in the news' profile, one watched by Catherine and her brother. All these Namibian incidents were characterised by Tony as 'Suppose it's between the Reds and the Yanks?' Adding when the TV showed a half-naked Himba tribesman, 'with your man gettin screwed over as usual?' Correct; which is not to say Tony had carried his investigation into the depths of geopolitics very far.

And when on later occasions Cat herself asked the much more important questions, such as 'What did my father look like?' Catherine, giving even deeper sighs, would describe the khaki uniform and the black hair and broad forehead that her daughter had inherited.

But Catherine did not tell Cat that she could no longer, to her own distress, remember Xin's face exactly enough; and that when she imagined him at night, while she was lying in the slated farmhouse, his head angled towards her in other moonlight, it was no longer his face that she saw but the skull of the Russian soldier whose hat was on the bedroom door; and that as he smiled at her, whether she was awake or in dreams, from the dark portals of his eye sockets flowed two thin streams of sand.

6

The tub of despond

July 2039

One summer evening, Cat was lying in the bath of the farmhouse in north Kerry. The bathroom was ill-lit: one yellowish, round ceiling fixture with a green wire, circa whenever, and a few weak spotlights, more recently inserted and haphazardly placed.

Back for the hay yet again, but all had changed in her life; the turn of spring to summer had become in her mind an uncouth, almost hideous thing, just as the turn of university terms had. By now (aged twenty-four), she had a PhD and a post-doc research project, but even though it paid court to the protection of early-career researchers, the university was treating her pretty badly. Everywhere she turned there seemed to be a man saying no.

Professor O'Connor had been kind (maybe feeling guilty about what had happened to her mother), but although distinguished he had little power in the department now he was so old, cutting a pitiful figure as he struggled with online presentation software. Now and then, outside the university, she saw him shuffling about in SuperValu, buying a pie for his tea.

Cat was looking at the wiry hairs of a brush that she sometimes used to clean the bath she was in, Uncle Tony never doing so. It was jammed behind the taps, next to a degraded bar of soap that might be rejected if there were any other option. She reached for it as if it were a lifebuoy – foamed first one armpit, then the other.

Outside it was getting darker. Uncle Tony was probably in one of his sheds elsewhere on the farm, cursing the paucity of an arc lamp as he polished that favourite tractor of his, the yellow-and-red David Brown Implematic.

Cat used the stub of soap to rub her nose, hoping to cleanse stopped pores. Her chin she avoided, as this particular brand of soap caused the skin to dry out. She tried to toss the soap bar back near the taps. It missed and slipped underwater. She held her nose and lowered her face beneath the surface, opening her eyes, so the yellow lamp with the green wire on the ceiling went all wiggly.

Work away, she silently said to the lamp as if it were some insect eating a strand of weed.

She came up from under the bathwater, blinking her eyelids, shaking liquid from her ears like a dog, wondered what she was hearing. Was that Big Business calling?

Keeping Cat awake, the bull often roared on summer nights. The cause of his roaring was the smell of cows on heat. Drifting from the apertures of the cowshed's computer-controlled ventilation system, these aromas danced from furrow to furrow – reaching the bull where he stamped in his field, before dissipating westwards to the Shannon and the sea.

Cat found the disappeared soap – leaned forward, water streaming from her shoulders, put the pitiful bar in its proper place, next to the brush behind the faucets. But it soon fell into the water again.

Lying back in the bath, she cocked a second ear. Was that really the bull she'd heard? Nope – this evening Big Business was quiet, having emptied his balls enough. What she'd heard was a roaring in her own head, throbbing like timpani between her temples, there in the tub of despond.

The only real noise in the bathroom was the sequential dripping of two taps. On each drop Cat focused her eyes as well as her ears, thinking of blood and her miserable mother – present yet to her memory, but left . . . six years now, was it? She dipped back under the water again, said hello once more to the hazy ceiling, said hello once more to the yellow lamp with the green wire, which from underwater now seemed like a cartoon character.

Came back up again, bubbles sliding down her cheeks as smoothly as the characters in the cartoon series of which she was thinking popped between different realms. Maybe that could one day be a thing, now that everyone was talking about quantum computers, here in Ireland and elsewhere, too, everyone everywhere talking about quantum all at once together, connecting like the talking feet in Irish dancing.

She'd been made to do all that – grudgingly go off to evening dance classes in some hall, waiting for another bus between the mossed gate pillars at the front of the farm. Memories of rinkas and slip jigs, once embedded in her very limbs, had now faded.

She raised her hips, flicked her own moss where it floated in the water, but decided she couldn't be arsed. Soaped her toes instead, putting fingers between them – in that process lost the soap again.

What had happened with Mam had affected her sexual appetite, sometimes making her want more, sometimes having quite the opposite effect, causing her to turn away even from men who were both hot and kind.

Stupid, as the hot/kind combo didn't come along so often. Not so stupid as to always say no, but those lovers she had taken had turned out to be the wrong choices. When would she allow it to start, the real man adventure, or any other kind of adventure?

What had happened was that soon after Cat turned eighteen and went to the same seat of sweaty learning as her mother, Mam had upped and offed again to Africa, to Namibia, that same country where Cat was conceived.

Fuckload of sames. God preserve me from sames.

She listened to the squirrels scratching across the roof and thought she should probably exfoliate, so reached for the loofah and began scraping her shins.

Mam had left during her first year at university. So far as Cat had gathered, in a poor enough harvest of information, Mam had heard from Captain Xin that he had returned to Namibia, inviting her to do the same. Her mother had sent Cat an incoherent text message, which had arrived during one of Professor O'Connor's lectures, half explaining all this.

Actually, not really explaining at all. Only reeling out a laborious itinerary, which excluded anything emotional, involving departure from Farranfore, the local airport, flying to Dublin and then Amsterdam, a layover in Luanda, then arrival in Windhoek: from where, Mam had added, she was to get a smaller plane to Walvis Bay.

A long journey, and one with a long psychic history. Like a *Rinnce Fada*, Cat speculated as she soaked in the tub – thinking again of the dances she'd once been made to learn as an extracurricular activity. Part of Irish heritage and culture, romantically supposed. Was there also some romantic mania parcelled up with Mam's sudden decision, something that had dammed off the more rational part of her?

At any rate, when she'd flitted her mother had taken with her the Russian hat that used to hang on the back of her bedroom door, perhaps hoping it would doff its way to the location of the lost lover.

The lost lover! Cat used to scoff inwardly when her mother had occasionally talked of Xin in that way. Now, submerging her face in the bathwater again, she hoped that the reason her mother had gone was more a matter of being led by her mind rather than her heart, but that was a hard measure for anyone to tread.

She rose from under the water with a gasp to hear from far off the clank of a bucket as Uncle Tony went about the closing-time business of the farm. Sluicing out, most likely.

Cat tried to find the long-lost soap. It was by now turning the bathwater into the Milky Way. Couldn't locate it. She looked balefully at the emerald-green or maybe urine-yellow encrustations on the taps, whose successive drips seemed to tell her own tale as the bathwater cooled around her.

A tale of trying to find a mother who often seemed absent and had now pissed off. It wasn't the end of the world, not everything had fallen to pieces. She knew that Mam had struggled with motherhood, but still – did she have to run off so quickly?

Perhaps all of our stories are the same thing, she thought, trying to remain objective. We must simply grow up and climb out of pain, having been thrown into this well of the world like dogs without bones. These are the facts – and all our complaints as we get older, by which time we are quite tired and out of breath, are nothing more than a puppy's bark, sounding faintly in the distance.

I miss you so much – but it was so mean, Mam, leaving me like that. *Didn't you hear me calling?*

The bathwater was getting even colder. Just as the whole idea of Mam being 'in love' with Xin, even if her mother had sometimes talked like this, always seemed colder than Mam implied. So far as Cat understood her – always a difficulty with parents – her mother hadn't appeared like someone likely to cast herself away, hoping to board the raft of romance.

Adjusting her position in the bath, she reflected that there had been plenty of good times as well as dark ones. Her mother had never totally withdrawn affection, and there had been many times when Cat had been happy to model herself on her. Like those nights at Mullarkey's when, with Cat in tow, her mother and Uncle Tony had sung 'Whiskey in the Jar', accompanied by the blind auld fella on his accordion. Afterwards endless happy hours, as it had seemed to Cat, of the board game Shut-the-Box. But now the box of affection was well and truly shut, even though the tune came back insistently from time to time. An earworm, like.

Still, those moments had put a fair bit of light into Cat's childhood, giving her a sense that her mother might have been a woman who'd been pushed off course by 'that trip to Africa', as Uncle Tony liked to put it, but was gradually righting the ship. Perhaps there was even the bold notion that she was being properly mothered after all. But Mam had gone off, and after a man; and how could that ever be forgiven?

She leaned forward to pull out the plug, turned on the hot tap for a refill, then leaned back, trying to feel the pleasure of the creeping heat despite the way her mind was going. When the bath was near-full again she jammed a heel in the plughole, lay there for a few more seconds before hauling herself forward and replacing the stopper.

But she could not stop the past. She often hated herself for having done nothing much to find her mother in the six years since she'd left, but her view was that it was for the mother to come back, not for the daughter to go and find her. Yet it all hurt so much, hence the days – no more than two, usually – when any sense of being able to cope with the everyday slid out of her grasp and she took to her bed, as her mother had. She'd survived, but all the time the feeling of an absent mother wore away at her.

The milk of the dissolving soap had by this stage caused a flecky scum to form on the surface of the bathwater. Cat was reflecting on how it sort of made a temporary alphabet, like the old Ogham symbols carved on local standing stones, when there was a knock at the door:

It was Uncle Tony, saying there was a call for her. 'Foreign fella,' he informed her through the wood. 'Says they're an admiral.' As if that were a perfectly normal thing to say to anyone, never mind someone in the bath.

By the time Cat got downstairs – dark hair turbanned in a raggedy old towel, body wrapped in the confused flowers of her Shein dressing gown – she found her uncle listening to a news item on the radio. It concerned the Minister for Local Communities. A member of a flat-capped Kerry dynasty of political gombeens (as Uncle Tony called them) now reaping the benefits of a violent shift to the right in the country. In part this had happened because the refugees who used to go to Britain now went to Ireland, something which had provoked an uneasy union between forces linked only in their hatred of immigrants, wokeism, globalism and the rest.

She went into the good room to take the call, glancing at wooden cases of never-used porcelain. Once, when younger, she'd taken out some of the cups and saucers, plates and jugs, got a little sense of them being handled by all those prior Catherines.

Next to the crockery was another, smaller wooden cabinet showing the dual-heritage medals of a distant ancestor. Timothy Brosnan. He'd been a Republican doctor, once treating Michael

Collins himself – before, sickening of the violence of the Civil War, he'd fled the country. Hiding in the Royal Navy, of all places, doing sterling service in the Second World War as a ship's surgeon, winning British medals that now sat alongside his IRA ones. Sometimes Uncle Tony had told stories about him.

Cold drops running down her neck from under the towel, Cat picked up the VoIP line and said hello. The voice at the other end revealed the identity and also the rank of the speaker, if not much else. Except maybe signalling, through its raspiness, that the speaker was a heavy smoker.

'Hello, my name is Admiral Yu Ping of the People's Navy of China. I'm calling you from Namibia, where my country has a base. Am I speaking to Catherine Brosnan, daughter of Catherine Brosnan and Captain Xin Hai?'

Cat assented to this description, while insisting, 'But I'm Cat now, Cat Brosnan,' even though she was not so clear about that sometimes, the warring states within her seeming to erode the possibility of any definite identity. Right now, caught in confusion, she deemed herself as dissolved as the soap in the bath she'd just got out of.

Then the Admiral said: 'I understand from my sources that you are following the same path as your mother, in the study of water?'

'That's right, I have a PhD in that field,' Cat confirmed, talking into the mouthpiece with astonishment.

'Well,' said the Admiral, blithely enough, 'I knew your father, Captain Xin – in fact, he's my sister's son. Something has come up about the work he was doing here in Namibia – well, work they were *both* doing. Do you understand?'

'Sort of,' said Cat, wanting answers more than questions, a need that was almost like panic, emotional supplement of the simple question of her own that followed: 'Is my mother now with him?'

'I believe so. Well, I hope so. But after some years living together in a house in a town called Dekmantel, they both disappeared, my dear, having gone in search of the same aquifer she was looking for when she was first here. The issue now is, I need someone to help me unlock the details of their disappearance. Having investigated you and your own studies, and because it concerns the location of the aquifer your own parents were seeking, I have the sense that you'd be the best person to help me.'

'Disappearance? What's happened to them?' She did not much like that word 'investigated'.

There was a pause and then the Admiral said: 'I don't exactly know. Look, the best thing is that we meet in Walvis Bay – it's a port city in Namibia. Walvis is where I'm currently situated. I'll send you a plane ticket and explain once you arrive.'

'I can't come until mid-December,' Cat said, feeling of herself that this was a strange, oblique way to react, now that news of her mother had finally come. 'I've obligations at my university,' she tried to explain.

'Very good,' said the Admiral. 'We all must do our duty, but in fact that's exactly why I am contacting you. I am afraid I have to insist that you come as soon as possible if we are to find your parents.'

Cat remained silent at first, feeling angry that she was meant to act, very suddenly, on behalf of two people who had abandoned her. 'I have a life here in Ireland,' she eventually said – fairly mutedly, because it was not much of a life.

Another pause came: static on the line.

'You are right,' the Admiral eventually replied. 'But you are also Chinese, and there are things here in Africa that I need you to do – to find your parents, as I say, but also in the service of your second nation. I will arrange transport and send you money. Your destination is Walvis Bay via Windhoek; details to follow by email.'

'OK,' Cat found herself saying, her thoughts immediately veering away from this executive matter to that of whether or not a Chinese admiral would really consider a half-Irish person to be Chinese. It was almost warming to think so, and perhaps that feeling had an effect on her eventual decision.

But how does this person even have my email? she wondered next as the phone went down.

She went back upstairs and sat on the bed in her Shein gown, feeling uncertain. Had she agreed? And what exactly had she agreed to?

Suddenly, everything struck her as extremely complicated. Partly, an academic career was at stake – not quite sure what it really amounts to now, she was thinking: something that's going to have to be interrupted, whatever it is. There was also, having suddenly been given this weird opportunity, a strong compulsion to find her mother and (as a way of getting a footing for that unresolved career?) another need to take on the challenge of finding the aquifer. The two in this moment gave the impression of being impossibly entwined.

Unwrapping the towel-turban on her head, she underwent a tug of war between those two joint-seeming options and a third, which was simply to stay at home. What course made sense? So far she'd always thought of herself as a sensible young woman. Despite all the wobbles her mother had caused her, and the antagonisms of identity that she often felt in her bones, and that one moment of suicidal ideation (as her therapist had termed it) on the bridge, she had at least mostly been practical.

And so, getting dressed, she regretfully decided to reject the Admiral's offer after all – regretfully because it seemed exactly the call to some other form of life for which she'd been waiting.

But on hearing an account of all this, when Cat finally got down to the kitchen, Uncle Tony banged his hand on the table, making the Powers jug shudder. The rich white milk trembled inside it.

'You've got to go,' he said, as red round the neck as a Cork shirt, because he was wearing his favourite Ireland's Eye jumper (it was much colder within the house than it was outside), even though he well knew he was allergic to wool. 'You need to find my sister. Might be our only chance to know, Cat. She was a pain in the arse, but I miss her. And family is family.' And then he said something really unexpected, which made her realise he had more self-knowledge than people ever gave him credit for. 'Look what's happened to me, sticking on this farm all these years! I'll give you whatever cash I can manage.'

It was this short, unprecedented speech – from a relative who she'd never thought loved anyone very much, but there was now certain evidence he did love his sister – that set Cat on her way. The light in Uncle Tony's eyes, as he was urging her to go, reminded her that he hadn't always been the grumpy git he so often seemed nowadays. Light in his eyes like when he'd taught her to ride a bike on high-hedged lanes. Light in his eyes like when he'd won a smallish prize on the lotto and bought himself a smartwatch. Never worn, but still.

Having said his piece, Uncle Tony shouldered his way through the back door and went off to Mullarkey's. To watch a Gaelic football match between Cork and Kerry, one that would end in defeat for their own county, which had been dominant in the GAA for so many years, and in this crucial match almost pulled it back at the last minute but unaccountably failed.

As he told her over rashers the next morning: 'We should have been more humble.' It was true, Kerry always went into these matches with an expectation of victory. Entitlement, even.

They ate the bacon in silence. Left too long on the range, it had become dry and pithy. The eggs, hard and bubbly underneath, weren't much better.

All through the day that followed, as the cycles of the farm continued like the brook that fed the spring in the Well Field – pursuing their courses with a decisiveness that she felt was lacking in herself – Cat kept thinking: should I go or not?

What was *should* anyway? 'Should' had not mattered much to her mother, who 'should' have stayed or 'should' have at least made one phone call in six fucking long years. A better 'should' seemed to lie more in the zone of work than that of family dynamics – a 'should' that might boost her post-doc with this trip and find in Namibia achievements that would make it impossible for all the departmental male high-ups to keep saying no to her.

7

The Admiral

It was early morning in Namibia when Cat left the Protea hotel one of the Admiral's staff had booked for her. Even though drifts of Atlantic fog were curling through the port of Walvis Bay, the weather was hot. So hot it was melting already the resolve with which she'd arrived, which was to treat all this more as a matter of scientific research than a personal quest.

Having passed along city streets and been admitted at the main gate of her destination, she was now crossing a gigantic compound, its walls topped with razor wire. She was on her way towards the stepped entrance of the Central Secretariat (West African Sector) of the People's Liberation Army Navy of China. As established by permission of the Namibian government.

On her way – and very apprehensive, not far off being downright scared. But here she was at last: in the exact spot at the appointed time, less than a fortnight after the Admiral's call.

Her journey, following more or less the same itinerary as her mother's, had been long. At the first layover, in Dublin, tension was palpable in the transit lounge, where TV news was continually playing – showing scenes of burning buses and smashed shop windows. Masked men, like ghosts from Ireland's past, had been rioting in response to the rape of a young woman. The perpetrator was said to be an immigrant, but this had not been confirmed.

Hoping it would all settle down by the time she got back, Cat continued crossing the dusty square of the base. Sweat was pooling under her armpits, running down her ribs as she tried to remember details of this other city she was now in, having looked into its history on her phone during hours waiting at airports.

Previously, long before it had come under Chinese control, Walvis Bay had offered its inestimable status as an Atlantic naval base to other powers: Germany, Britain and later South Africa. In its South African incarnation, long ago in the 1980s and early 1990s, the base had played a role in the Namibian War of Independence and the Angolan Civil War, supporting operations of the apartheid government in those two closely intertwined conflicts.

What I am doing here? It was a question she kept trying to answer from the point of view of her work, pushing away the matter of missing parents, which appeared just too big to confront. Or too fugitive – like chasing ghosts? She remained amazed at the absurdity of her position.

The idea of an aquifer was important, both for her as a scientist and for the survival of local people and, clearly enough, important to the Chinese (and the Americans) too – because water was needed for the extraction of uranium in an energy-challenged world that was increasingly relying on atomic power.

If the aquifer existed, the question of who would own it was crucial, an issue driven by economics and power . . . thoughts of this type kept trying to march on in her head before being swept away again by the personal. Did she really want to find two parents who had abandoned her? Or had she come just for an adventure?

An adventure would be so much easier. As she walked – it was a very big compound – her eye was caught by the sight of a piebald crow settling on one of the razor wires. It kept shifting from foot to foot and she wondered how it did so without cutting its claws.

She finally reached the big wooden doors of the Secretariat. A guard in naval uniform with a cigarette stuck to his lower lip was sitting on a stool on the top step. After a longish phone call, Cat was finally admitted to the interior of the building.

Guided by another sailor, she entered the main complex,

passing through a series of rooms until they reached one with a massive desk, with a notice on the door in Chinese characters and then underneath in English, ADMIRAL YU PING. The sailor opened the door for her into a room that smelled strongly of tobacco.

Behind the desk, swallowed up in an almost throne-like chair, sat a thin person dressed in a white uniform tied with brass buttons and cinched at the neck. Above the neck a distinguished face topped by grey frizz stared at her. To Cat's great shock, this individual was female – counteracting presumptions both she and Uncle Tony had made in Kerry on receiving the phone call from Admiral Yu.

For this was the Admiral, her face as wrinkled as parchment. Cat stared back. The woman in front of her looked like someone in a painting, an effect accentuated by a wall-mounted lamp that shone on her forehead.

For a second or two there was silence, in which the two of them considered each other. Cat intuited that the sombre, somewhat severe face framed by the back of the huge chair was one that might transmit a kinder expression, perhaps even a smile. But it wasn't happening yet.

There was a large cut-glass ashtray in front of the Admiral, full of butts. Nearby, on a smaller desk to the side, sat a computer and printer. The screensaver of the former showed the star, anchor, sextant and waves of the emblem of the People's Liberation Army Navy.

The woman in the big chair finally stood up and said: 'Thank you for so swiftly answering my summons. Have a seat.'

Cat nodded, and then, sitting back down herself, the Admiral at last smiled, saying: 'The child of my nephew! I hope you have not had too difficult a journey.'

'No, it was fine,' Cat replied, wondering wildly if this information made her – surely she must be? – Yu's grand-niece. Then she asked, bluntly enough: 'You have some news about my parents?'

The old Admiral gave another smile, sadder this time, before declaring: 'In time, my dear; first we must go into some previous history. You are aware of the Angolan Civil War of 1975 to 2002? In the earlier parts of which many Cubans and a smaller number of Soviet forces aided the Angolans against incursions by the South African Army from here in Namibia?'

'To an extent,' Cat replied. She'd studied the Cold War in Africa as part of her Leaving Cert, but didn't remember much.

'It was closely mixed with the South African Border War, which brought this country its independence. It's well known that South African forces operated here and in Angola itself. What a lot of people don't know is that Soviet troops were also stationed here at that time, secretly in the desert, along with Cubans.'

The wars to which Admiral Yu referred were among those largely forgotten conflicts in which African liberation struggles, the monstrosity of apartheid, and obtuse angles of the broader Cold War, all got mixed up in extraordinary ways.

Cat vaguely recalled her history teacher saying something about how the name 'Border War' emphasised the conflicting ideologies of opposing forces, being used by the apartheid state to imply protection of borders rather than invasion of foreign territory.

The Admiral, with some panache, lit a cigarette. 'Well, when my nephew, your father, Captain Xin, was helping your mother for her search for an aquifer in 2014, they came across an abandoned vehicle which contained a body. Also, a little notebook written in Russian script – a diary of sorts. Do you know anything of this?'

'A little. There was a hat, a Russian military hat, that my mother took with her when she bolted.'

'Bolted?'

'Left me with my uncle.'

'Yes, well, all that is probably to be regretted. And I'm sorry to say, my dear, that some of it was probably my fault.'

'What do you mean?'

'I will explain. After your mother and my nephew were . . . together, Captain Xin went back to China and took that notebook with him.'

'And?'

'Many other things occurred later, nothing directly concerning the case in hand, matters instead to do with a changing picture of threat in this part of the Atlantic and the need to increase the operational capabilities of our navy here.'

Cat had no idea what she was talking about. For her, the Atlantic meant the rip tide on Banna Strand; candyfloss and seaweed at Ballybunion; surfers at Inch, slick as seals in their black wetsuits. Plus occasional news reports on RTÉ about the decline of the Irish fishing fleet.

'By then my family had run into some political trouble,' Admiral Yu continued. 'Your father went back to China while you were growing up, becoming – how's it said, *persona non grata?*'

'Yes,' Cat said after a pause.

'Well, after some years, our family's political fortunes recovered. That's why I'm back here, running this base, developing our increased aircraft-carrier programme on the African coast, hoping to achieve true blue-water capability.'

'What does "blue-water" mean? And what's all this got to do with my mother – and with Xin?'

'I'm sorry. Blue-water is naval shorthand for conducting flight operations from an aircraft carrier outside the range of an airfield. A high-risk endeavour, one which means aircraft carriers need a base. Like this one we are in. As for your parents, I will come back to them, I promise.'

Shifting in the big chair, Admiral Yu produced from a pocket a handkerchief – no less white than her uniform – and proceeded to cough noisily into it. Cat caught a glimpse of brown phlegm – must be the smoking – then Yu continued.

'The notebook your parents found when your mother was first here, back in 2014? It was a diary kept by a Russian soldier fighting with the Cubans. It disappeared for a few years before we had it translated.'

'What happened to it?'

'Well, we had difficulties as a family, as I say . . . I mean in politics in China. It sometimes happens there; it happened to my mother too.'

'*Your* mother?' said Cat in some wonderment. She thought what was being inferred was that figures and families in high-up Chinese echelons fell in and out of favour, but she wasn't ready for the jump back in generations.

'Yes, your father's grandmother.' Straight came the answer, though it did not resolve Cat's bewilderment.

'So both I and your father had to clear out of Beijing for a while, go back to Qingdao. The diary of that Russian got left in the attic of our house in Beijing, in the bottom of a box of your father's fishing tackle.'

'My father was a fisherman?' For some reason this knowledge dumbfounded Cat.

'Yes, his favourite hobby – is this not what you imagined?' The Admiral gave an oddly girlish laugh, then continued. 'We both were suspended from our positions for a while. Then, as also happens in my country, we both got rehabilitated. But this caused a delay in translating that diary, which is why the exact location of the aquifer hasn't so far been determined. It's hard enough to locate them even with data right in front of you, and this is so different.'

Cat felt exasperated, unable to spool forward from this account to where she was now. 'I must make it clear, Admiral Yu, that I'm only here to find my mother.' As she said these words, she wasn't quite sure they were true, feeling in bad faith about how, as she came into this place, she'd begun prioritising the scientific quest over finding her parents. And now already it all felt different.

The truth was, from a scientific perspective there really was something fascinating about the idea of a large aquifer existing in a place so dry. A place where an aquifer could be of such critical importance, given how life here, and not just human life, was so dependent on water. If she got to the site first, it would be the beginning of a professional goldrush, even if the aquifer was still not a verified fact. And the whole mystery of the diary her parents had found and what it pointed to – well, that was intriguing too, albeit in a way that seemed light years from verified fact.

The Admiral paused, briefly rubbing fingertips across her forehead, its wrinkles accentuated by the rays of the wall-hung lamp. 'The point is, the Russian soldier's notebook mentions a large aquifer. The same aquifer that your parents were searching for, whose existence your mother had assumed from her research. And when they came back here six years ago your parents began living together, quite happily I believe, in a house in the town of Dekmantel. Did you know anything of this?'

'She did not contact me at all.' These few words did not do justice to what Cat was experiencing. In no way approached the profound feelings she had about her mother, which were basically that the narratives ought to have been switched. All this period, the thirst she'd had for her mother to get in touch should instead have been her mother's for contact with her daughter.

'I'm sorry,' said the Admiral. 'Did you not think of contacting her?'

A burst of anger came. 'You think that was easy? I was just a student. Look – I just want to know now, basically: why am I here?'

'Well, first I must say I am sorry for your pain. I can see it on your face. It can't have been easy being half-Chinese.'

'What do you mean?'

'Being half-Chinese in Ireland. And from what I've learned, well, your mother had her own challenges too. Xin showed me some of her emails, and I am also a mother, so believe me, I'm not ignoring those challenges in any way.'

'Some of her emails?'

'Yes, she and Xin were in touch sometimes while you were growing up, though not in so easy a manner, I should say.'

Cat was shocked. All the time she'd supposed her mother might have been pining for Xin (at the same time as sometimes speaking of him in anger), messages had been travelling between them? Hot-and-cold messages, she guessed, from what the Admiral said, but she needed to know. For possibly as long as eighteen years, her mother had been in intermittent touch with her father but had not bothered to contact her own daughter in the subsequent six!

'What do you mean, not so easy?' Cat asked, her own anger now bubbling furiously.

'Dear girl, they were apart and from two very different cultures ... persons who kept a warmth in their relationship, sharing many things of which you are the most important, but also facing real practical difficulties. One of those was that my nephew had, as a naval officer, for reasons of security, to be very careful about his contacts with foreign nationals.'

'OK,' Cat said sullenly, wanting to say *bollix* or some such but not daring to do so.

'As to your earlier question, after this time living in the bungalow in Dekmantel, they began searching for the aquifer again. This was part of Xin's job, in fact, securing water supplies for our mine here, but they restarted the search on their own.'

'And what happened?'

'About a year ago, they sent me, direct from Xin's phone, some physical data about the location of the aquifer but then nothing. Ever since then I have been looking for them. You should know, Cat – I have dispatched other people after them, with no success ... before taking this big step of asking you. Because you are family, and because you understand the science, as well as reasons of command; I need to know where the aquifer is for my job as well as to find your parents. And find them soon. Not just for family reasons but also political ones: the paramilitary outfit that ruthlessly protects the interests of American mining companies here has the muscle to rival us in the race to secure rights over a significant new water source in the region. It always causes diplomatic trouble when we send in more troops; that has happened before.'

'What did the people you sent find?' Cat asked. 'I mean recently.' She was trying to remain practical, despite what her feelings were telling her. For she was experiencing a weird, half-subconscious sense of being in communication with her mother ...

'Nothing much, well, little signs only. The difficulty is that the aquifer location noted in the Russian's diary that your parents found has turned out to be within the American zone of control, near a place marked on maps as Serra dos Leões. It's right by the border with Angola, in Kunene, quite near the town of Opuwo.'

'Serra means mountain range, right?'

'Yes – it's a Portuguese word, referring to how jagged mountains look from a distance like the teeth of a saw. But oddly, there don't appear to be any mountains there. Leões means lions, of course.'

'Why can't you send your own people there again? Why do you need me?'

The Admiral gave a deep sigh, her chest wheezing a little. 'It has already proved very difficult for anyone associated with the Chinese military to go in there.'

'Why?'

'Because the American mining company, Scursail, has secured the concession in that area. They have already built a new headquarters in Kunene. And are beginning to police the whole area, albeit at this stage only with drones. Which is where you come in.'

'What do you mean?'

'I'd like you to go into the interior and check out the location of this aquifer.'

'Why would I? You've brought me all this way to go blundering around in the desert on my own?'

'Dear girl – believe me, I'm not trying to make you do something you don't want to. The reality is, this is your best chance of finding your parents. And mine. It's just not possible for me to send Chinese troops after the Namibians I sent – people on our payroll but under the radar, as it were.'

'So I'm to be just another like that?' She didn't mean for her voice to sound as rude as it did.

'Look,' said the Admiral, 'your parents went off looking for that aquifer and nobody has seen or heard from them since, apart from the couple of messages I got from Xin, showing the results of physical tests for water they'd conducted.'

'What exactly are you asking of me?'

'I'll be direct. That you go and find them: keeping your head down, pretending – if I can ask it, and I feel uncomfortable doing so – when you meet any South African guards of the American mines in those parts that you're just a scientist, neglecting to disclose a Chinese connection.'

Cat trembled with anger (*just* a scientist?), but all she let show was mild irritation. 'You want me to be a spy?'

The Admiral almost laughed, but soon corrected herself. 'No, it's really not that at all.' She coughed again, magicking the hanky out of her pocket in the same way as before. Cat wondered if she was ill. 'My apologies. No, I want to find my nephew, just as you want to find your father, I presume, and your mother. So please be assured that my first motivation is emotional, just as I am assured yours is.'

'I don't know—'

Now it was the Admiral's turn to interrupt Cat. 'Let's focus on a practical matter, that of finding out what happened to your parents in the desert.'

Yu got to her feet, went to the computer on the desk, dislodging the navy-insignia screensaver with the slightest nudge of the mouse. After she had pressed some buttons, the printer started spewing out pages.

'I was intrigued by what I read in the Russian diary,' the Admiral commented, taking one sheet after another from the printer tray. 'As I've said, it looks like the aquifer we need to find is in the Angola–Namibia border region. Serra dos Leões is a name on some of the oldest Portuguese maps, going back to the seventeenth century. I went to the trouble of getting some satellite scans done. And we got a hit, a patch of subterranean blue. It is a little unclear because I am told by experts that some of the area concerned is under a large rocky structure made of a mineral resistant to satellite imaging. I gave this same data to your parents before they disappeared.'

The Admiral seemed oblivious to the emotional effect these remarks might be having on Cat, who was again thinking, why am I here? Do I even want to find my parents at all? And how am I going to manage out there in the desert?

She handed Cat the printed sheets, each displaying penetrative satellite mapping of the arid area of Serra dos Leões, uncovering the hidden groundwater resources at scale.

As she held the pages in her fingers, it was as if they could bring her at once to the space they represented. But as soon as she laid them down on the desk in topographical order, flattened out, their power seemed to ebb. She remembered again Professor O'Connor's wisdom about the map not being the territory.

She studied the maps closely. As well as nearby towns such as Otjirova, Ruacana and Opuwo – the town the Admiral had mentioned – they showed the aerial extent of rock bodies, their assumed potential for water (given as blue patches), along with various overlaid hydrodynamic features, such as the direction of groundwater flow. There were also numerical side panels on the still-wet pages, suggesting the size of pore throats in the grains of sand and gravel packed around host rocks.

Cat knew from her own academic study that this local detail – the sorting of these grains, their size and angularity, specifically the degree to which they can rotate – were all key factors in the viability of aquifers, which must have limited porosity for containment but be sufficiently permeable to allow rain to fill them up. This was presumably the kind of thing her mother, with Captain Xin's assistance, had been looking at in what the Admiral referred to as 'physical tests'.

Cat asked, wanting confirmation: 'These local details, did my mother source them?'

'Yes, I told you: she and my nephew sent me some info before they disappeared, which is what you see there on the side. But then they just went dark, although I got further info from my own studies. And then, as I said, I sent a lot of people after them. From what my own experts say, and what the Russian soldier says in the diary, the aquifer seems to be roundabout here.' She pointed at a place on the map next to which the words SERRA DOS LEÕES were printed.

'That's the top end of the Damara Sequence,' Cat said.

'What's that you say?' the Admiral asked.

'It's the basic geology of northern Namibia.'

This was true. Anyone who'd done world geology would know it. They'd also know that these maps with blue patches were still just models, only representations of reality, not reality itself, just as Professor O'Connor had warned. Entities not to be trusted.

Admiral Yu said: 'I hope that having read this diary, you'll become convinced that the course of action I am suggesting is a good one – the best way to find what has happened to your parents.'

She went behind the big desk, opened a drawer and produced a perfect-bound booklet.

'So, Cat, this is what the Russian soldier wrote – translated first into Chinese and then English. There may be some mistakes in that process, but I hope it will persuade you. The truth, my dear, is that I just don't know whether the maps are right, or where your parents ended up; it's a very big desert out there.'

With this she gathered up the map pages spread on the desk and put them inside the booklet.

Cat turned her face, still unsure. Was this really about finding her parents or was there something hidden, some mechanism by which she was being covertly controlled?

'Please,' the Admiral said forcefully, as if she herself suspected Cat's suspicion; and then added with a softer inflection, while holding out a liver-spotted hand: 'At least read the booklet, look at the maps. I want to find my nephew as much as you want to find your father, your mother, and that's as much your responsibility as mine. I have ordered you a taxi and put more money into your account. And also got cash for any further transport and subsistence while you are here. Do think about what I've said, Cat; it's about people we love – both of us . . .'

Cat's self-resolve wavered. Admiral Yu must then have seen something in the perplexity on her face, for she simply shoved the sheaf of documents into Cat's hand. And then picked up a phone, making a call in Chinese.

'All right, I'll look at it,' Cat heard herself saying, even though she had no idea how to meet this charge of responsibility. 'But I am not promising anything. Or accepting your plan in any way.'

She tucked the documents under her arm and said her goodbye to the Admiral, convincing herself that she had not been compromised; and then the same sailor who'd brought her in materialised to escort her to a taxi waiting to return her to the hotel.

Cat read about half the pages of the diary in her room there, her head propped on pillows both too fat with foam but oddly too thin at the same time. As the double-translated voice of the Russian journal began to imprint itself on her mind, the challenge of what she was attempting struck her like the summer lightning that bounced around her bicycle as she sped down Kerry lanes.

8

The Russian diary (I)

1 March 1989 – Serra dos Leões

Now we hear this war will soon be over. Most of the Cubans left a few days ago – off to Angola to get shipped back to Havana. We've all been together since the fighting in Cuito, so it will be strange, not having those beardy fuckers around. The camp is very empty, except for when the Angolan allies bring us supplies.

All that's left on this lump of rock now is just the three of us: me, Alexi Yazikov and Vadim Luzhin, among the last Soviet operatives in the country, possibly. And hidden under the rock, what our superiors call a supergun, a massive piece of artillery. The Pion.

Not much of a party. Alexi is a member of a gang back home, basically a criminal (covered in tattoos), and I can tolerate him so far. Luzhin I actively hate – looks more anteater than the KGB man he is. But a nose big enough to put into other people's business, that's for sure.

We've mostly been sitting on our backsides, smoking, playing guitar, telling bad jokes – trying to avoid an argument, although Luzhin doesn't play that game well.

I'm still trying to read my poetry volumes and do some proper writing of my own – but filling up the pages of a diary isn't literature. Hard to get much real work done when it's so damned hot.

No more decent meals to look forward to now the Cubans have gone – the only thing we really miss about them is their cooking. Somehow they managed to make some good stuff from what's in our stores – sacks and sacks of pasta and tins of chopped onions, but also some tinned tuna and beef. It was clever, what they managed to turn out, asking the Angolans to bring particular herbs (as well as the herb we smoke!).

But we won't starve. Enough pasta here to feed a regiment. And we're growing our own garlic, which does surprisingly well in sand.

I shouldn't complain. This place is a lot more mellow than Afghanistan – many of our comrades were killed in the Maravar Pass there – and the Angolans brought us a bag of fresh grass last time they climbed up here; so we've been working our way through that for a few days. Really helps us stop going crazy.

4 March 1989 – Serra dos Leões

So, more days pass inside our big red rock. Smoking weed, playing guitar, pleasuring ourselves: these are the only things that keep me and Alexi from going crazy in this land of scorpions and black-maned lions.

It's hard to stick with the plan of our mission. We're meant to be guarding this secret artillery emplacement but there doesn't seem much point now the conflict is with Western forces and their South African allies is about done. Back home, it looks like things are falling to pieces. The radio guy in Cuito says that Gorbachev has been making noise about the country changing – 'loosening' I think he said. What the hell does that mean?

Vadim continues to shout orders at us nonetheless. This morning he got us greasing the Pion for the second time in a week. What's the point? It was a lot of work, craning the thing in here, but looks like we've now lost our chance – someone else will have to blow the Boers a new arsehole. Vadim should shout instead at the two lions who have started to circle our base late in the evening – sometimes the bloody things watch us like television.

Gives me a bad feeling, how clever those lions are. Raking out beehives with their claws or picking up melons to suck on. So clever I sometimes imagine them explaining ideology like Vadim does.

Yesterday's lesson was the Failure of Romantic Individualism. Today's was False Consciousness of Holism in the Capitalist System.

6 March 1989 – Serra dos Leões

Vadim went off to Cuito yesterday to see his superior officer, to plead our case for transfer – I hope not just his alone, the fucker. He has taken with him my books of French poetry to check they are legitimate. It amuses me to think of the KGB puzzling over my Mallarmé, my Valéry.

While he was away, me and Alexi had a few vodkas. I read him the first bit of a satirical poem I'm working on, and Alexi started strumming along on his guitar. Like good Soviets we turned it into a military anthem. Alexi enjoyed the bit about a pride of lions raising a new nation. Maybe the desert heard the call – by sundown, four lions were sat outside the fence.

They probably hate the smell of our little camp on the rock, as it stinks of booze, sweat and marijuana.

Vadim came back late just now, was very quiet. He said his application to be transferred out of Africa had been turned down. Before bed I heard him weeping in the latrines, the pussy. He did bring back my poetry books, though, to give him credit.

8 March 1989 – Serra dos Leões

After yet more pointless housekeeping of the gun, I tried to contact command a few times but there was no reply. We needed some music after listening to the dead air between here and Cuito. We spent most of the afternoon sat round the radio, tuning it to non-military frequencies.

One track took me straight back to my Zhanna, the two of us lying together in Voronezh with my little red transistor. I was enjoying drifting back there, to her smile, to her skin; until Alexi ruined it by mouthing off about wanting to get home to 'put his cock in the till' – searching for rich women.

That guy! His attitude to women is all wrong. Better to be 'extraordinary gentle', like my sage Mayakovsky advised. *Not a man but – a cloud in trousers.* That was always how I approached my Zhanna. Once, I remember, she was hanging up washing – on a line strung from apple tree to apple tree. I so wanted to grab her bum, her hips, but didn't – instead taking a pegged white sheet and letting it fall on her bare shoulders.

Well done me, but now we're in such a different place.

– by example, when we were eating dinner just now, Alexi held up his arm with one of the tattoos on it, a small blue one of a corkscrew entwined with a snake. He keeps asking me to join his gang when we go home. I reminded him that I'm a writer, not a gangster.

& he: 'What are you doing here then?'

& I: 'You know I had no choice, any more than you.'

& Vadim: 'Choice is a bourgeois abstraction.'

& Alexi: 'The Party, the army, the whole system, is just as much a gang as the Shtopor. (That is the name of Alexi's gang.)

& me: 'There is nothing so sad as tattoos on an ageing body. You should think about that, Alexi. When you are older that thing on your arm will make you look ridiculous.'

& Alexi: 'Fuck you. And fuck your poetry too.'

& Vadim: 'People with tattoos are troublemakers, and so are poets.'

And with that we go into the hut, listen awhile to the radio, lie down on our mats . . .

Unable to sleep, I get up again as Voice of Russia drones on, write more of this journal in the soupy, insect-thick light of the lamp, going through its lines, one turning after the next as my pen reaches the edge of the page. At each margin, the absence of my lover strikes my consciousness, patent as the thump of the generator.

Do you hear me, Zhanna? Do you feel the natation of my words, sliding over your skin? I want to send you signals, hoping you too have your ear to the radio.

Listen hard, my love, we've eased into the audible zone now, passing tone squelch and middle C. Like Superman, we're surfing the *grandes ondes* together now, taking ardent flight in wavy circles through the whirling vortices of the air, dodging what streams, what rocks, what darts in beams out of Hilversum, Droitwich and Krasny Bor.

From Krasny to here in the desert, Serra dos Leões, Voice of Russia announces itself, with the interval signal 'My Country's Vast' playing on chimes, followed by the chatter of the DJ, which my well-tried wrist is rushing to transcribe:

Something like – *And at this very point I'd like to say hello to all our listeners in the United States of America. Keep it tuned, don't let video kill the radio star . . . hello there, now here's a letter from Laurie Deightner in Newcastle, Pennsylvania, USA.* 'I've recently started listening to Voice of Russia. I enjoy it very much. I am a student at Slippery Rock University. I have travelled in the Soviet Union and one thing I liked was the music there. I would like to hear more contemporary and rock music from Russian artists. I especially like Time Machine, Autograph and Aquarium. Young people everywhere like this type of music. If young people in my country hear the music of your young people, we shall see that we are not so different after all.' *Well, Laurie, that's what Voice of Russia's all about. Thanks for writing and remembering that music makes friends. Here's Aquarium and Dreams of Something Bigger.*

Pretty idea, kid – but best keep a Pion supergun under the rocks, just in case? Strange to think of our massive artillery piece, sat down there on its platform, all fused and ready to blow its hat off – just waiting, waiting. Probably be waiting a long time now, as it seems the West has won.

11 March 1989 – Serra dos Leões

I'm getting worried. We haven't been able to establish contact with Cuito for two days now, and I'm beginning to wonder whether command has shipped out. Did they think of us: well there's only three of them up there, so why bother with a rescue? And who's going to miss guys who officially never were here? It makes me think the whole system is going down.

We've got tins of beef and fish and sacks of pasta (so much pasta) to last a while and we have our little pump tapping the aquifer. Apparently it's massive, that water supply, so we're not going to run out. But we're going to have to get out of here at some point.

In the meantime, I have been experimenting with *makaroni po-flotsky*, which is a navy dish made of pasta, onions and braised beef . . .

9

Decision time

August 2039

Lying on the bed in her hotel room in Walvis, Cat put the printed pages aside, leaving the second half unread. She was tired, and it was hard to process everything the diary's writer had said. Had said fifty years ago! It was disconcerting that the Admiral considered it still worth investigating after all this time; but as Professor O'Connor used to say in his lectures, pointing at similar deposits to those she'd viewed on the maps, 'There's treasure in them there hills!'

She tried to sleep but found it difficult, all too aware that she was very far from home and that what she was now attempting was so huge. Why did she feel any compulsion to continue with the mission that the Admiral had suggested? Especially since she had such mixed feelings about her mother, and the father she did not know?

She got up, went to the window and drew back the dreary brown hotel curtains – but the view over Walvis to the ocean was blotted with mist. Closed them again, feeling unease about how she used to do exactly this when younger back in Kerry, looking out of a window that gave on to the front field and wondering where her life was going.

Back in bed, trying to arrange the bendy hotel pillows, she thought again about the reference in the Russian diary to an aquifer. It seemed like evidence of the water source her mother had first come here to find.

Maybe enough to go on with – more anyway than she found in the half-disdained memory of her mother, embarrassing as that was to admit to herself. At the same time she wondered, as she lay there trying to escape her own head: has Mam died out there in the desert?

The resolution to do some actual, real scientific research at last pulled that doomy thought from her head. Strange how bad thoughts needed to be extracted like that, as if they were physical. Sometimes when she was younger and a bad thought came, she used to shake her head from side to side, hard, as if the unwelcome thought were a worm that needed to fall out of one of her ears.

The next day, Cat went back early in the morning to see the Admiral within the forbidding confines of the naval Secretariat. On the way, despite an earlier resolution in favour of work, science, rationality (whatever it was), the streaming, fog-draped windowpanes of office buildings caused memories of her mother to prick in her eyes, maybe because they brought back those of that same figure's own mascara-streaked weeping. Cat felt almost nauseous, far from home – in this place where half of her was mirroring her mother, the other half trying to fulfil her own destiny but didn't seem able to.

All this now appeared to be mixed up with facing Admiral Yu again, as if that woman were not someone seeking her services as an expert hydrologist but someone who might be another link in chains that she was trying to break.

But slowly, with every pace, she galvanised her thoughts, realising that not trying to find the aquifer could in the future seem a greater wrong than turning tail. Because the water that might be in the aquifer; Namibians needed it, yes?

She tried to slow down her brain as she entered the razor-wired perimeter of the base, one of the guards giving her quite the quizzing.

Admiral Yu herself was extremely solicitous once Cat finally found her way back to the room with the high-backed chair and the ashtray filled with butts. 'So I hope you trust me, having looked at the diary your parents found?'

'Yes, though I haven't read the whole thing yet.'

'You mean you will go?'

'Yes.' Yes, even though shadows passed over her as she said so, even though something dropped in her soul as she spoke.

Quickly enough, the Admiral outlined details of her trip from Walvis to Dekmantel, the town from which her mother had disappeared.

'There's a safe house there we use,' the Admiral explained. 'Dekmantel in part intersects with the American zone, so we have to be careful.' She was coughing into the handkerchief a lot more than yesterday. 'The house is disguised under the name of a water charity called Clear Course. I came up with that English name myself. Not such a big thing, the Americans have their own houses the same way. Xin was there before. There's a caretaker we pay there, a young woman called Nadine. Little too young for the job, but seems capable.'

As the Admiral spoke, Cat experienced a whole cocktail of emotions – excited, nervous and suspicious all at once, and hardly able to absorb the information that was being given, wondering if she also was too young for the job.

'When your mother came back here six years ago, Nadine's mother was housekeeping for both her and Xin. A refugee from Angola. But sadly she died recently, so we passed the job on to her daughter.'

The idea of something being passed on to a daughter immediately struck a chord in Cat, but there were more practical matters to consider. 'How am I meant to get there? And live money-wise when I do?'

'Don't worry about any of that. I will give you money. Some of it for the girl at the house, which is on the road that goes into the gravel pan. It has the odd name of Spit Street. Number 15. Your flight from here to Dekmantel will be paid in advance. And this is the contact number you need for transport.'

She scribbled down some details on a notepad and handed them to Cat, saying: 'The contact is a pilot called Sean Morrow. He's one of those adventurous whites who hang around these parts – kind of foreign locals, always acting like they are the last man standing in a forest of eunuchs.' She flashed Cat an unexpected smile, making her think the Admiral was a more sassy figure than she'd so far appeared. Then Yu added: 'I will organise your flight to leave in the morning. At Walvis Bay Airport; look for the booth of Desert Air.'

It had seemed like the meeting was over, but then the Admiral went on: 'So, you should be aware that all this time the Americans have been trying to find the aquifer, just as we have. I think it is wise that you go to Dekmantel under a different name, in case the South African mercenaries who work for the American mine try to mess with you. There is no need for a passport, Cat; it's an internal flight. But do be aware that your ticket is booked under the name Mary McLaverty – people will assume she's an Irish national like you. Is that OK?'

It did not feel OK. 'Why is it necessary?'

'You need to trust me. The security people who look after the American mine are dangerous.'

'What do you mean?'

'There is a possibility they might otherwise know who you are, i.e. Xin's daughter.'

'It makes me feel I shouldn't go.'

'Please just trust me on this; is that OK?'

Cat supposed it was, but it still seemed dodgy. On the other hand, having come so far, what option did she have but to trust the Admiral – who was, after all, her father's aunt? Who now passed her a zip-locked plastic packet containing the flight details. Also a bundle of cash, held together with a blue rubber band.

'Oh, and one more thing.'

'Yes?' Holding the packet and the band-wrapped notes, Cat was thinking of containment, and not just in its hydrological sense. More of how much in life, including one's own self-possession, came down to what could be kept separate or together; but today's problems weren't like that; risk of one type or another seemed always to intrude.

'Be careful: there are some anti-government rebels active in the area where you are headed. But this is really the best, if not the only, way of finding your mother.'

'OK,' Cat said, though she was still far from feeling so. Yu's remarks just seemed to confirm her anxiety.

'You don't need to worry when you are in here,' the Admiral said, waving an arm around. 'We have this place swept for bugs daily. But outside, in the desert, you do need to be careful about who's watching, who's listening. Every human being sticks out there.'

'OK,' said Cat again, hoping she could turn into the person who might just be able to do this, even if she'd made so many emotional turns in the past few days that she didn't know whether she was coming or going. Might as well be a flea running up and down the contortions of a corkscrew!

'Take this too,' the Admiral said, giving her a business card with a logo on it: the name CLEAR COURSE integrated with a water-drop design. And a name: that of the figure of strategic illusion, Mary McLaverty, plus a PO Box address in Windhoek.

'The number on that address is only an answering service, but any message you leave there will get to me. Do not use it unless in a real emergency, as there's always the chance that those South Africans who work for the American mine could be tapping it. One of my men will lead you out. Remember: this is about finding your parents.'

As she said goodbye, Cat put the card and the zip-locked packet into her rucksack and followed a sailor who then appeared. As she walked behind him through the halls of the Secretariat, her resolve strengthened on the two counts about which she had felt doubt: whether the Admiral was somehow hoodwinking her, and whether what she was being asked to do would really help her find her mother and that aquifer. As her steps sounded on the concrete floor of the building, the future seemed slightly more certain, slightly more possible . . .

That night she read the other half of the printout of the Russian's diary. Swishing through the pages, she was oddly aware of the presence of paper between her fingers; although she knew that it was not the paper that had been found in that sand-buried scene, it felt strangely displaced. The document had already been through two instances of translation, from Russian to Chinese, and then Chinese to English. Her own understanding of what she read seemed like a further translation.

10

The Russian diary (II)

1 May 1989

Cuito has been in touch – finally! They are not as sorry as us that they've had transmitter trouble. Half of March and the whole of April they left us in the shit, here in our iron-roofed hut.

So it looks like the war really is ending but we've been told to stay up here in case hostilities start again. The word is that Namibia will have independence within a year or so – and before it does, both us and the South Africans will be thrown out.

But nobody trusts nobody, and the high-ups in the Kremlin are saying that we need to stay here nonetheless – ready with the big gun in case peace talks fall through. An officer on the radio tells us in confidence that Gorbachev and Yeltsin and the KGB are going at it like the clappers. So, for the foreseeable up in Camp Lion's Arsehole, it's going to be a lot more doing fuck all, apart from checking that the South Africans haven't turned up to cut our throats. Or the bloody lions haven't found a way in. There were seven of the monsters outside the gate the other night.

And Vadim is still trying to keep us busy. Any day soon, we'll be polishing our own shit. Which at least would give us a break from greasing our dicks. We seem to do that more than wash these days. And not much else – we eat, drink, shit, wank in a small orbit.

★

It's getting quite hard now, the waiting. Life feels very distant. It's not easy, living in this little cabin, just the three of us. Alexi still chats on but Vadim barely talks now. Turns out I hate the guy even more when he shuts his mouth – his silence is full of poison.

15 May 1989

It is time to write this down now, as so much has happened. In case me and Alexi don't get out of this fucking place too. I still can't really get it out of my head . . . but Vadim is dead.

Writing it, to the moment – well, not really, I'm very late in coming back to the turn of my pages – feels terrible. I didn't like the man but that's no way to go for anyone.

– three nights ago, Vadim went to check the gates, as we always do each night. He seemed to be at it a long time, so I shouted to ask whether everything was OK. As he heard me he turned round and sprinted back up into camp; went crazy, pointing his Tokarev pistol at us, shouting at us about duty – about how disgusting we look and how we haven't kept the place ready properly. After about a minute of this, he suddenly let the gun fall and stood there, just staring – it was like someone switched the fucker off.

Fearing that next time he went crazy he might shoot us, as he had often threatened to do, Alexi and I jumped on him and tied him to a chair outside the cabin; he didn't even struggle, which was strange – he's a big man and could have made it hard for us.

We called Cuito later, then Moscow itself, which was against regulations, but we just got dead air. I went out to adjust the radio aerial, and on the way back I poured some water down Vadim's throat and threw a blanket over him. We had decided to leave him outside for the night while we worked out what to do.

For a few hours after that, me and Alexi listened to the radio, trying to stay calm by working out some of the English on Voice of America.

In the silence when we turned the radio off, I think I heard

Vadim crying outside. But Alexi and I had begun to talk – and drink. We agreed that the Cubans and most of our own people (except us dead souls) had probably left southern Africa by now. Not a great time to be sat in secret on top of a rock. We got through a lot of vodka; I lost count of the glasses we poured. We were both too drunk – and too freaked out – to check on Vadim by the time we lay down on our mats.

In the night I heard some weird noises, a thump against the wall of the cabin, then a single cry – high and desperate, like a baby – but all mixed with the tangled washing of my dreams; I was dead drunk, gone, and so was Alexi. We just turned over and went back to sleep.

It shames me now to say so – how we slumped like the sots we are (important to recognise one's own nature!) in our little camp of wood and corrugated iron, perched above a massive gun that itself sits in a cave above possibly the largest aquifer in Africa, one topped by an enormous lump of rock in a flat expanse, about the geology of which we have a couple of thousand goddamn questions.

And all this time not giving a fig about our fellow human, hateful as he was.

I went out for a piss early the next morning as the light was coming up and . . . no Vadim. Gone. And only two legs of the plastic chair we'd tied him to were there – raggedly snapped off and covered in drying blood. There was a lot more blood on the aquifer roof, a great bloom of it, with another broad red smear leading towards the fence. And more blood spattered on the cabin and some piles of equipment. The sight of it made my stomach drop.

The gate. We had forgotten to check it. It was wide open, maybe had been all night – God knows why, did Vadim unlock it during his crazy moment before?

Shaking, not wanting to accept what the bloody ground was shouting at me, I went inside the cabin to get Alexi – and my gun.

Me and Alexi travelled quickly from cabin to fence. We were

very scared – bristling creatures ourselves, bristling a rifle each, swinging them anxiously backwards and forwards through 180 degrees. When we reached the gate I locked it, and as I did so a big female lion pranced into view, up onto boulders just outside the fence. It turned its head towards us, and we saw that the fur round its mouth was soaked with blood. This sight sickened me. Without really thinking, I picked up my gun and shot the creature. At that range, the AK split it open.

The lions have been coming every night since they killed Vadim. There are over ten of them, now, we think? They sit outside the fence like dogs near a door. Waiting. I've mostly been lying down even during the daytime – but I find it hard to relax for a second when I know they're out there, their cold yellow eyes blinking. Alexi's the same. And we haven't touched the vodka since the night Vadim died.

I have brushed the blood off the hut and our other equipment, best I could, and thrown the chair legs off the cliff of the monolith. What will we tell HQ, if they ever bother to contact us, and what will they tell his mother?

20 May 1989

Last night I dreamt of being suddenly jerked sideways, consumed in wild jaws, vanished. I am getting scared of going to sleep.

Alexi is spending a lot of time servicing the supergun; he says he wants to make sure everything is lubricated, in case. It's lions, not the South African Army, we need to worry about now, but if it keeps the guy happy. . . He says the Pion will stay ready to fire for a thousand years.

We still haven't been able to make radio contact with Cuito. Not sure if it's the transmitter again or if they've left without us. Either way, looks like there's no rescue coming. We're going to have to get out of here by ourselves.

The dead lion has started to stink. Hard to eat with the smell about, but neither of us dares go beyond the fence to drag the body further from camp. We don't talk about what happened. I keep hearing that weird baby's cry inside my head. Why didn't one of us check on Vadim?

Since I shot the lion, we haven't seen or heard others in the daytime – only at night, their eyes burning like boughs in a bonfire – prissily arranged, they seem to me, maybe in expectation of our prompt execution. It's almost as if the spirit of Vadim has entered them along with most of his body parts. A big group of them come now, and we keep our rifles handy. They don't seem put off by the body of their friend – but when did you ever see a lion's eyes look sentimental?

I've been pondering why they are here. It must be to get water from the aquifer, possibly accessing it through a cave system at the base of the monolith? Maybe coming back here, at certain times of year, when possibilities of water elsewhere have dried up, has been bred into them over generations?

Has this installation of ours blocked hundreds, possibly thousands of years of lion traffic? And that's why they keep coming back. That or poor Vadim has given them a taste for human meat and me and Alexi are next on the menu.

We don't have the spirit to go outside the gate – rifle or no rifle. Not yet.

But we must. I fear that if we don't leave soon, our minds will begin to weaken. Alexi has begun to sleep next to the Pion. We don't talk much now. I feel more and more afraid.

24 May 1989

Over the last few days, we've been outside the fence a few times. We are getting braver. The fear of staying is getting greater than the fear of leaving. We have decided to leave tomorrow, using the hottest part of the day to get back down to the truck in relative safety – we hope the heat will keep the lions away, ceasing their vigilance even as we hope it will seize our sinews and fire them into action.

We spent the afternoon taking stores of food and barrels

of water down the side of the mountain, where our truck is hidden; one carrying, one following, swivelling, with a gun for protection. When we check it, the truck still starts, thank God.

Before we leave we are going to make one last broadcast on the radio, in the hope that if Moscow is listening they can send a plane to pick us up. Can't see it happening, though.

Alexi says he wants to spend one last night with the gun. I hope he doesn't do anything stupid tomorrow. Whatever happens, I am going to be driving towards that wide desert horizon, leaving this rock full of lions' teeth. Alexi can do whatever he wants – but I myself will not falter.

11

Ice-cold Mary

Lying in bed in the hotel in Walvis, Cat once again put aside the printouts of the Russian's diary. Her lip twisted in disgust, imagining how Vadim must have died. Such a terrible end! Although far quicker than what must have been an agonisingly slow, thirsty exit for the Russian who wrote the diary, stranded in the desert, the one whose body her mother and Xin had found in the truck. And what had happened to Alexi, she wondered. Maybe he never made it to the truck? Did the two of them argue? Did Alexi strike out into the desert on his own, or stay behind and suffer the same fate as Vadim?

Having turned out the light, Cat was unable to settle, needing to shove and punch the annoying hotel pillows, hoping as much to get them into sleeping shape as to feel more certain about what she was doing here and who she really was.

Didn't you hear me calling? That again.

After Mam left, she'd often got a weird sense of hearing an interior voice: not her own exactly, and not her mother's either, more a strange blend of both. Back in real life, when her mother was on the farm, it was like she was always being jumped out of her own hide when Mam shouted for her like that, asking her to do this or that. Afterwards the calling seemed unreal, of course, at least if one thought about it in a conventional way; but what happens in our heads is also real. 'Human feelings and thoughts, our very own, ladies and gentlemen – they, too, have their place among the layers upon layers of the whole-earth system, which operate like the membranes of an onion, delicately separate but also connected.'

So Professor O'Connor had once said in a lecture – making Cat think, as she'd sat on a hard bench, of intimately folded bodies, connected thighs; because why among all these guys beside me in the lecture hall is there not one who seems right for me?

Desire of that type now seemed as distant a memory as the Narnia stories she'd read as child, only a few lines remembered from books once held to heart. *Please, you're so beautiful, you may eat me if you like.* Or: *That's why Aslan kept on my left. He was between me and the edge all the time.*

But why's Mam calling in my head now, here in a hotel in Walvis Bay? Thought it had stopped.

Feeling as cold as a cliff, she got up and tried to turn off the air conditioning in the hotel room, but the remote control was too complicated, showing so incomprehensible an array of erratic numbers and jumpy letters, other symbols too, on its pale-grey screen that it might as well have been a device for summoning down aliens.

Got back into bed, cuddled the duvet round her.

The frequency of that unreal voice of her mother's had diminished a lot in recent years, as anger about her departure had settled into melancholy, and after melancholy something like acceptance. A process aided, perhaps, by medication, but that produced other problems, including weight gain, which she'd done her best to counter in gym classes.

Yet it was after she had started taking the antidepressants that what she thought of as the core of herself, the academic formed by the example of Mary-Ag as much as by that of her mother, started to change, becoming someone more free, sometimes almost whimsical but definitely stronger. Increasingly during this period – the time between Mam leaving and her getting the precious post-doc – her focus had turned outwards, towards travel and enhancing her own independence.

She had become more robust, she reckoned, able to exercise a form of denial against her mother that made her more effective in getting on with life; despite a secret lack of confidence, she had enough resilience, enough reserves of power, to go forward on her own.

This, anyway, was the view she took of herself as she again shook the mam voice from her head and tried to sleep, attempting to keep thoughts from burrowing into her head like baby moles, furless but indefatigable, their spiky paws gouging at her self-possession. Once she'd looked moles up on Google, trying to figure out why there were none in Ireland. Something to do with rising sea levels in the Ice Age.

The air conditioning was almost unbearable now, the room so cold she felt as if she were being embalmed by the machine's chilly vents. Remembered then as the next thought came (next!) that baby moles are driven from their home territory by their mother at five weeks old.

It was not so very tragic and heaven hadn't fallen, but couldn't Mam just have stayed and found a way to be relatively happy? Rather than being so selfish and, occasionally, cruel. Once, when Cat was twelve, her mother had told her, while making Bolognese in the farmhouse kitchen, that she thought giving birth had robbed her of being the person she could have been, had stopped her having adventures. Who would say that to their own child?

She turned over, trying to forget.

And yet there had been times when Cat reckoned that her mother loved her very much; she had not been consistently neglectful, certainly not always withholding affection.

Which made her having checked out even worse. The emotional switching on and off before was bad enough – unsettling, like trying to stand steady in the current at Banna – but to go, Mam, after seeming to get yourself right? That was like the ultimate betrayal.

She turned over again. Thirst, was that the problem? Got a glass of water from the bathroom, threw it back, refilled, refilled again, and a next time too . . . finally threw herself back on the bed, which was by now so cold it might evidence the Snowball Earth theory Professor O'Connor had sometimes mumbled about in increasingly incoherent lectures.

Soon she was turning over yet again. Punching yet again the fat-thin foam pillows. Imagining her mother doing the same when she first arrived in Namibia (had she, too, stayed in Walvis?), before she went off into the deep desert in search of something more, something like adventure.

She knew, Cat Brosnan, that she herself was having such adventures herself now, supposedly independent at last; but why was this adventure somehow reproducing the same toxic sense of unease that thoughts about her mother's exit always induced in her?

Sleep, when it finally came in the small hours, at first soothed her mental pains, lulling her with its charity. But later became a hydraulic dream. Oh, water, water – so much water in all its doubles, currents, flows and circulations – that it refused its official designation of H_2O and became right there and then her most immediate reality.

She needed, of course, to pee.

In the morning, while doing so – it took a long time and was alarmingly loud – her back hurt strangely, right near the kidneys, as if she had a UTI. But it was so long since she'd had sex that hardly seemed likely. As the dreams half returned, she fancifully wondered (still sitting on the throne) if the excess of water in them had somehow leached out the synovial fluid in her spine. But that was even more unlikely than the previous hypothesis. Maybe something fishy in all that tapwater she'd drunk?

After a shower she got dressed, ate a quick breakfast and checked out of the hotel, catching a taxi to the airport. It entered a long snake of traffic from Walvis Bay, some industrial, some military.

Eventually, she presented herself and her rucksack at the Desert Air booth, feeling a little nervous given that this flight would be her debut as Mary McLaverty. Soon a pilot, about her own age, in shades and a short-sleeved white shirt appeared, and she was pleased she remembered to introduce herself as 'Mary – from Clear Course'.

Nodding at that, then announcing himself as Sean Morrow, without any of the other usual formalities he escorted her onto the airfield. His hair was almost horribly blond – yellowy, like custard – but this was mitigated by a likeable enough face and quite extraordinary blue eyes.

It was exciting, and a little scary, to get into a small plane with just six seats, empty apart from his in the front and hers next to him.

And so they took off, the vibrations of the plane's little wheels as it trundled down the runway translated into the cockpit, trembling the wings of the plane like the arms of gardeners who've just trimmed a hedge. She remembered doing that once, on Uncle Tony's instruction – by the end being hardly able to wind up the cord and put the trimmer back in the shed, her hands were shaking so much.

Once they'd risen, there was something about the desert that soon unfolded beneath them that appeared to cancel time: take-off itself, and now all the looking down, made her feel unsteady, humbled by an immensity of rumpled rock, sand dunes, gravel plains and flat-topped mountains.

Now and then they passed over little circular settlements, herds of cattle, occasional sheep farms, but mostly it looked like there was no life there, only geology.

The salient element of the journey was Morrow slowly turning his blue eyes towards her as they banked over one of the mountains, the cockpit lights flashing, and him saying: 'Hope you said some proper farewells, Mary, 'cos it's hard to come back from the desert. It sucks people up. Last time I flew a Clear Course employee to Dekmantel, two people disappeared!'

Fright – no other word for it, as she immediately started to suspect that there were gaps in what the Admiral had told her about her parents.

They were hooked up with mics and headphones. Jets of air were coming into the cabin, drying the sweat on Cat's face; it was an odd sensation, as if the future was being blown into being.

'Who were they?' she asked finally.

'One was a guy who's lived here for years. Or lived in the desert at any rate. A kind of DIY zoologist who researched lions – Max Cloete.'

'Oh yes?'

'Kind of a Robinson Crusoe *ou* who lived rough in the desert,' Morrow continued. 'Sleeping in his truck. Wore gold-rimmed specs – sort of an intellectual, artistic type; never wore shoes. He'd tracked the same group of lions for years and knew much more about them than any other scientist.'

'So what happened?' Cat asked.

'He came into Walvis to get some new radio tracking equipment and seemed in a real hurry to get back. Something about a water source—'

'What?' Her ears pricked up at this, squashed as they were by big ancient headphones.

'*Ja*, a water source. What do they call it, aquifer? Loads of people come here looking for those and never find them.'

'OK,' Cat said, feeling dread.

'Well, Max was worried about some aquifer or underground lake or something, place where his lions got water, being threatened.'

'By what?'

'All the mining companies round here are always looking for water, and so are the big agricultural outfits, as well as all the ordinary Namibian farmers.'

'OK.'

'Anyway, Max was pretty amazing with those lions; had enormous speakers on the side of his truck, played courtship roars on MP3 files to lure them away from danger. The word later was – he went into the desert and hasn't been seen for over a year. Her neither.'

'Her?'

'The other person I flew – this was on another day. Don't think her and Max knew each other then, but they definitely met.'

Cat was confused. 'Who're you talking about?'

'Employee of Clear Course, a water charity – Catherine Brosnan – which I'm guessing must have Chinese funding.'

Wanting to scream into the little foam microphone on the stalk in front of her mouth, Cat tried to play it cool, as if she was the ice-cold Mary she was meant to be. 'Did you know

Catherine?' she asked in as neutral a tone as she could manage, though it seemed fake even to her.

'No.' He gave a little laugh. 'Just another passenger. Don't know whether she and Max were really a couple or not either, though they did seem so once. Mostly she was with a Chinese Army guy.'

Cat was shocked that her mother might have had other lovers, if what he said was true. 'What happened to her?' she asked, still trying to keep her voice as level as the plane, even if it was rattling a lot and what she'd just heard was vomit-inducing.

'Interesting enough story, and I only saw the next part of it a month or so later.'

'Saw what?'

'Well, I was doing a drop-off at one of the safari lodges in the desert – usually we stay the night. So Max drives into the camp in his truck, says we're gonna have a party, and uses his big speakers to boom music across the *vlei*. There was a bonfire and everyone got pretty drunk, myself included. This Catherine must have been staying at the lodge, because next thing I know she's dancing with Max. I remember seeing her throw her arms round him . . . kissed him, *ja*?'

Amid that endless rattle, as the air whooshed past and the plane rushed above a landscape that now seemed like an abstract painting, Cat opened her mouth; but no words came out.

'Then the Chinese guy turns up. You could tell he was jealous, angry . . . And no doubt why – she was a real looker. That woman would be a cosy berth for Max or any man, but maybe a little crazy, that's what it looked like that night.'

She didn't quite know what he meant but experienced anger, embarrassment and weird pride all at the same time.

'Mind you, Max was crazy too. Next morning, he's gone, and she's looking moody enough when the Chinese guy rocks up next to her again.'

'And then?' Uncomfortable, interrogating him like this. But she knew she had to do so, to allay the deeper discomfort she was experiencing. Luckily, he seemed oblivious. He reached out and touched some button on the instrument panel.

'Then she also disappeared, the Chinese guy too – and next various folk are sending out messages everywhere, asking what's happened to them. Including your Admiral, who was paying the tab then too. No one ever worked it out. What're you going to Dekmantel for, anyhow?'

Cat wondered what to say, in part intrigued – wanting to know more about her father and other men her mother might have been involved with, which now seemed actually possible.

'Eh?' Morrow said.

Cat realised belatedly he'd been asking her something and she hadn't been listening.

'I asked why you're headed to Dekmantel?'

Not sure what to say, she hit him with science. 'To conduct a water-resource survey. So communities can better parcel out their water.'

Morrow laughed, turning his blue eyes on her. 'Where you're going, lady, they usually do that with a gun. And it's just gonna get worse, because let me tell you, this place is about to blow up. Lots of folk very unhappy about how the miners are sucking up all that H_2O. So unhappy they're ready to take direct action.'

'Who're you referring to?'

'Rebels. Militias is what they call themselves, but rebels is what they are, because this is a perfectly democratic country. Ha!'

Cat thought he was probably manning up, trying to scare her; would Yu really have let her come here if war was about to break out?

'You heard about this trouble?' Morrow asked.

Cat remembered what the Admiral had said, warning her to be careful. 'A little. Is it serious?'

'Lot more than the Caprivi conflict, which was the last time anything like this happened here. About forty years ago – before I was born.'

'What do the rebels want?'

'That's unclear. And there are different groups of rebels here, anyhow. But water's in there somewhere, in what they want. The biggest group is led by a woman called Ma Shango. Nigerian, it's said, and hard to understand – she talks funny. I met her once.'

'What's a Nigerian doing in Namibia?'

'There're a few here, heck more in Joburg. I had to land near her camp once – lots of irregular troops, with Toyota pickups. She herself had a quad bike. Quite a sight, seeing that big lady get off it, rock up to me in her camouflage gear, asking what the fuck I was doing. Told her I desperately needed fuel, and to be fair she sorted it once I paid up. Sent off one of her men to get aviation fuel. I spent a few hours with her next to a *braai*, drinking distilled spirit. Never will forget it; that lady has shaved off most of her hair, leaving a topknot like the leaves of a pineapple.'

'But they must want something?'

'Who?'

'Her troops?'

Morrow shrugged. 'They want to get rid of the miners, get that cash . . . but it's more like – what the fuck else to do? There's an epidemic of joblessness in this country. And it's also filling up fast with people from neighbouring places that have gone to shit. Anyway, you should be careful as there's quite a few of those *skelms* round Dekmantel.'

'What's *skelms* mean?'

'Ah, kind of rogues, scoundrels sort of. There are two other mobs besides Ma Shango's, one called the Skeleton Crew, the other the Ruga-Ruga. The first lead by Sol Spinnekop, who has a spider tattoo, the other by a fellow called Zowa the Brave. A weightlifter, wears a bowler hat.'

It made her anxious, hearing all this, partly believing it, partly wondering if Morrow was talking bull. 'Do I need to be worried?'

'Well, those bands don't really get involved in Dekmantel town, as that's protected by the mining company forces: Chinese soldiers at their place, Karunga, and South African mercenaries at Scursail. Don't worry, you'll be safe.'

'How often do you go there?'

'Not so much, since tourism to the safari parks dropped off. No water equals no animals equals no tourists. To tell the truth, I've started dabbling in the water business myself to make ends meet. My brother and I have got our own little desalination plant in Walvis Bay – there's these amazing new filters; made of graphene. We get them from China and use them to distribute our own bottled water. You have to be an entrepreneur to survive in a place like this. Me and Dickie – my bru – we reckon this graphene's the juice.'

She'd heard of this wonder material. Carbon atoms tightly bound in a honeycomb lattice, graphene had many applications, mainly electronic; but it was also a very good filter for liquids, water included. Some of the maths that her famous Trinity predecessor Hamilton had invented, the poetic mathematician that poets hadn't heard of, was involved in its uses.

'Shame the whole country can't get access to graphene,' Cat commented as Sean leaned across her and made some adjustment on the winking panel in front of her.

'You can't really use it on a mass scale, not yet anyhows. Too costly, too early in the innovation curve. Which means we'll either make a mint – or get nailed.'

Cat was puzzled. 'So you do that and a bit of flying?'

'My family have always done some commerce hand in hand with whatever else, ever since they first came to these parts from Ireland, after the famine. It goes a long ways back. Where're you from, Mary?'

'I'm Irish too,' she said distractedly, watching his lean brown arms operate the controls. It seemed far too strange a synchronicity that the pilot who'd flown her mother was now flying her, and had Irish heritage.

'You don't look it! Despite your name. Not that I do, either; a lot of Dutch in my family now, thus all this . . .' He lifted a hand from the controls and filliped a lick of yellow hair from his forehead.

For a few seconds she put it off through superstitious aversion, but then had to say: 'Tell me more about Catherine Brosnan.'

He gave her a sudden look, the earphones angled strangely on his face. 'Brosnan, yes, that was her surname . . . She split, that's about it. Very pale skin. So you must have met her yourself, from the way you're talking?'

She realised that he might have rumbled her. 'No,' she

replied. 'Just heard her name through work. What do you think happened to her?'

'No idea. Look, a lot of people come out here and get *bosbefok*.'

'What's that mean?'

'Crazy from the bush. It started in the wars that happened here in the eighties, kind of like PTSD, but it's not just soldiers who got it. And then all the other shit that's happened since – well, mainly the effect of the uranium mines.'

Cat nodded. She'd read up on the mines, as they had the biggest effect on water supply in the region, alongside cattle farming.

'Basically, since the wars and economic problems after, it's just piled it on and on, generation by generation. More for the poor folks here than my type, but still . . . Now everyone's pretty much *bosbefok*.'

The two of them stayed silent for a while. Looking at the landscape below, Cat watched earth formations roll by beneath: wedges, skirls, dimples of red rock and yellow sand dunes rucking in endless waves, along with dead-straight lines of man-made tracks and roads – some meeting with the classic X of treasure maps, the cross's vast scale made small by the height of the plane, whose shadow also showed, far below but slightly behind, like something moving at the same pace but in a different time.

'Where do they go to, those roads?'

'Small towns, villages. People live here but most of them are fucked over by mining companies, which are a very different thing than in my great-grandfather's day.'

'That's why there are rebels?'

'Not just that. Here, if you're poor, and believe me even if you're not, there are just so many reasons to be angry.'

'I thought you said Namibia was democratic.'

'It is, and a much better place to be than many of its neighbours, but—'

Cat felt, oddly enough, the same frustration she'd sometimes experienced when schooling undergraduates. 'But what?'

His reply was, 'Babe, it's really complicated . . .'

Babe! She bit back a retort.

They didn't talk much more until they came over Dekmantel, Morrow making a speculative turn over shacks that sagged with plastic sacking, bucketing blown sand over tall mounds of rubbish, some of which were burning; over expanses of white gravel that seemed to have no purpose.

He landed the plane on an airstrip – really just a patch of scrub near the edge of town. It was overlooked by low, scrubby hills festooned with the towers of giant water pumps.

Here they were at last in Dekmantel, a little town in northern Namibia, so far as she knew the last place where her mother's location had been definitively pinpointed, among so many other matters (not only spatial) that remained uncertain.

When Cat got out the pilot handed her a six-pack of one-litre mineral water bottles, brand-named Elim.

'Gift from me,' he said. 'That's our product, mine and Dickie's. You'll need it here.'

Before he turned away, Morrow suddenly reached up and, with the flat of his right hand, touched the side of her face. 'Take care.'

The gesture was gentle but she flinched, moved her cheek away from his hand.

'OK?' he said, having registered her reaction.

She nodded, unsure of herself, wondering if what he'd told her about being safe was true. But mainly offended that he had touched her.

'Hey, and if you need anything, my office number is on the label of those bottles.'

'I've got your mobile number already,' she said. 'The Admiral gave it to me. And I texted you, didn't I?'

'Of course. And yes, you did text me. But this is another number. Call me either way if you need me and I'll be there. Any time, any place, anywhere. "Sean Morrow, be there tomorrow!"'

'What?'

'It's a joke I like to make.'

'Right-oh,' she said, thinking that this was an exceedingly futile conversation.

She carried the pack of water as she walked away from the

aircraft, feeling its plastic wrap slowly rip from its own weight, idly wondering what sort of man Morrow really was.

Then she turned and watched him take off, Sean Morrow with the custard hair. The buffets of the plane's propellers beat on her face, raising a little storm of sand.

12

Dekmantel

Only when Sean Morrow was a dot in the sky did Cat take in the barren actuality of the place in which he'd deposited her. All cacti and sand and rubbish and shacks, together with a clutch of houses with green tin roofs and, standing out starkly, a brown-coloured fort. It had castellated battlements and a neon sign, which blinked even in bright sunlight: HOTEL BOM JESUS, HOTEL BOM JESUS, HOTEL BOM JESUS.

This was, Cat suddenly realised, the place Mam had talked to her about when she was young, where her mother and Xin first met. The pulsations of the sign seemed to touch her from the past – as if separate steps of time, and maybe models of identity too, were being brought closer together.

Vague thoughts I must avoid . . . and anyway the time-trance she'd suddenly found herself in as Morrow's plane flew off was cancelled by time's great opposite: space. Dekmantel was surrounded by massive dune tops that loured over the town like the backs of whales.

Cat was also aware, once the plane had taken off, of a grinding sound. It filled the air as if the whole place were inside a loudspeaker. There was also a pungent odour, similar to that of the muck heap on the farm back home.

Near the airstrip, a toothless old man in a grimy wool hat was sitting outside a shack. He seemed to be doing nothing more than moving pebbles from one hand to another. When she got nearer, she saw that he had a large, trembly bleb in the middle of his forehead. A blister of some type, vibrating inside with serous fluid, she reckoned, but as weathered on the outside as a dried apricot.

The blister was startling enough to prompt other questions in her mind as she stared at it, questions like: what do these people do for healthcare?

'Do you know how I can get to Spit Street?' she finally asked, knowing it was probably a useless enough question to put.

The old man shook his head, muttering something in a language that she did not understand.

'Clear Course?' she said next. 'A bungalow where a white woman once lived?'

His eyebrows lifted, and next he indicated a road behind him. Then – standing up, moving with a hobbled gait – he approached a patch of sand clear of pebbles where he drew a simple map, making a mark with one of his feet and throwing down some of the pebbles that had been in his hands.

'Spit Street,' the man eventually intoned, as if all this while he had been searching for words that she herself had just uttered.

It didn't seem, at least from the map the man had drawn, like so long a walk, but boy was it depressing. Dekmantel was a such a shabby, sunstruck place, enough so to make other miserable examples of linear development – like those thrown up in north Kerry in her own lifetime – as resplendent as Ballsbridge or one of the other fancier districts of Dublin.

The piles of trash she'd seen from the air appeared monstrous close up. Smouldering mini-volcanoes in which greasy peelings of melons and discs of cattle dung, empty tins and pieces of plastic had stiffened into a hard crust. Amid this mess, brown and white dogs were snouting about, ribs showing through their fur. She spotted a couple of large rats too, one momentarily sitting up on its hindquarters like a rabbit.

From the windows of grim little dwellings the odd suspicious face looked out at her. All along the street were piles of plastic water bottles. Most were other brands, but one or two were the Elim type Sean Morrow had given her.

Lugging her own pack of the same bottles, she passed a few shops with ads on the walls: FANTA ORANGE . . . IS FUN; HUNGRY

LION BIG BOSS DOUBLE BURGER MEAL; TAFEL LAGER — SHARE YOUR PRIDE. Other signs, hand-painted, simply showed people buying groceries, or doing other things such as having their hair done or making phone calls.

After the shops and bars, she passed a clinic. DEKMANTEL MEDICARE: its logo was half like a heart-trace monitor, half like the peaks of sand dunes. Clever design. Next to the clinic was a bakery, then a wall topped for security with broken bottles embedded in cement – and then the blue sign of a betting shop: this made the promise 'youplaywepay', as if that sequence was guaranteed, as joined-together as the words on the sign itself.

A group of youths was gathered there watching horse racing on a screen, the commentator speaking in English but with a strong South African accent. The gabble of the commentary fought in her ears with the grinding noise she'd heard earlier. She suddenly realised that it must be coming from the mines, whose machinery could now be seen in some places, poking over the dune tops like the antennae of giant insects. The pungent odour must come from the mines too, she thought as it stung her nostrils again: yellowcake, or Urania – a step in the processing of uranium ore.

There were two mines in Dekmantel, she'd learned from her conversations with the Admiral and the pilot, as well as from research she'd done before coming here. The one called the Scursail Deep was owned by an American company, but based in Toronto, and run by South African overseers. The other was a similar mine, run by a Chinese company, for which the Chinese military provided security under licence from the Namibian government. Its name was Karunga.

The line of control between the two concession-holders ran down the middle of the town – bisecting exactly the Hotel Bom Jesus. That must be why the two contingents sometimes met there, Cat thought as she walked on, recalling one of the stories her mother had told her as a child.

The pack of water Morrow had given her now seemed even heavier than before. She wanted to drop it, leave it there, but was aware that would be unwise. A teenage boy in a green T-shirt with Chinese characters on it and sporting a Karunga Mining Company baseball cap of the same colour passed by on the other side of the street, smiling into his mobile. On her side of the street a much older man in white overalls emblazoned with the legend Scursail Deep almost bumped into her, his hard hat pulled down low over his nose.

As she continued, other labourers passed, walking on this side of the street or the other, all in company gear. Did the workers of the two concessions live in different organised communities? That might explain why they were walking in opposite directions.

Either way, the whole town appeared subjected to an intersection of foreign financial interests, sucking out material resources at an ever-increasing rate: not just uranium but also water, if what Sean Morrow had said was right.

Where was it, this Spit Street? It was now 4.30 in the afternoon, and it was clear from the increasing passage of people either side of her that there was a night shift as well as a day shift.

After a few wrong turns, she finally turned into Spit Street. It rose on an incline, giving her a view of one of the mines and its operations on a dune. Not so very far away . . .

Diverting from her destination, trying to ignore the weight of the water-pack in her hand, Cat went closer to the mine, wanting to see what one of these places was like – these places that had, as Sean Morrow put it, turned so many people here *bosbefok*.

This diversion involved crossing over a plain of white gravel. As she walked – soon regretting the decision, because the plastic strap of the pack of bottles was now cutting into her palm ever more deeply – her heels crunched salt deposits and other areas of dried, off-white mud. The whole glistening surface of the gravel pan was pocked with thorn trees and stunted acacias.

Some earthmovers and trucks – mostly yellow, one or two a lurid orange – were moving on the crest of the dune beyond; then some tiny human figures appeared, walking in a double line. The machines were very big, even at a distance, dwarfing the figures of the workers going to and fro. It seemed like their heads and faces were wrapped in cloth.

It was a long way to the dune, much too far!

Her body suddenly told her almost in panic that she had to get back, find the Clear Course bungalow.

The late-afternoon sun by now was very hot, and there was a sense of constriction in her throat – almost as if the climate itself were choking it. The noise of the machines was rumbling so deeply that she could sense it through the soles of her feet, which were hurting from the heat. Her rucksack, though it contained only a laptop, clothes and toiletries – together with the pages of the Russian's diary and the map printouts the Admiral had given her – suddenly seemed as heavy as the water-pack.

Day's already full as a tick, as Uncle Tony liked to say. Odd how fragments of his voice, too, though not half so insistently as her mother's, came back to her at unexpected times.

And now really was the time to turn back, but she'd got herself a bit lost.

Looking at Google Maps on her phone as she walked, she came off the gravel pan, went along a ribbon of track no less gravelly, meeting en route a herd of fat-tailed sheep – hard to tell one from the other as they divided before her, then contracted behind her on the pebble track, which eventually became tarmac road. It wound up through some narrowly sequestered, near enough suburban streets before swinging over a bridge above what might once have been a small railway leading from the mines to an abandoned industrial unit but was now thick with thorn trees, finally reaching Spit Street, confusingly surrounded by gravel.

But it was the right street and there at last, a little way further along, was a dilapidated sign announcing CLEAR COURSE. The sign sat on a wooden post at the entrance to a modest bungalow with a perimeter fence, an outhouse within a scrappy garden, a green tin roof and metal-framed louvre windows. All around the dwelling she could see the gravel pan again; had she just completed an enormous circle? She realised slowly that Spit Street was so called because it projected into the pan like a spit of coastal land.

On the sun-blasted, wind-splintered sign was the same water-drop logo imprinted on the business card the Admiral had given to her. Or, as the card itself announced, had given to 'Mary

McLaverty', as whom she approached the flaking porch of the bungalow and knocked. Almost immediately, a thin-hipped teenager in a purple nylon dress appeared – not from the bungalow itself but from the outhouse nearby. She was thin but pretty, with the kind of eyelashes many women in easier climates might envy.

13

Actions and reactions

The girl let her in at once, seeming to assume without question that Cat was the new mistress of the house. Presumably the Admiral had sent prior word. She told Cat her name was Nadine, confirming what the Admiral had told her. Cat introduced herself as Mary. Surreal, to announce oneself as one's double. Nadine began showing Cat around the bungalow, ringlets of coiled hair bouncing on her bony shoulders. The bedroom was clean, thank God, the bed made up with crisp white sheets and a coverlet, even though it creaked when she sat on it to take off her runners, her feet feeling hot from all the walking.

'How long will you stay here, *dona*?' the girl asked later.

They were standing in the kitchen by now, and Cat was enjoying the cool of its tiles on her bare feet. Apart from an oven and a kettle, and an aerosol of insect repellent that stood like a little obelisk on one of the scarred worktops, it was fairly bare. There was also a round steel trash can, the big kind that might normally be outside.

'What do you mean, "*dona*"?'

Nadine explained that it was a Portuguese word, a courtesy title used to address ladies in Angola, adding, 'Some of my people are from there; after Kwanyama, Portuguese was my next language. English came later.'

'I see,' Cat said, even if what she really meant was more 'I hear.'

'You stay long?' Nadine repeated in a slightly pleading way, which made Cat think she needed companionship. 'If so we will need to get more water. Sometimes, when too many people are washing or cooking, it does not come from the mains.'

'OK, but I'm not sure how long I'll be here,' Cat replied as they entered the kitchen. 'Maybe two or three weeks?' Then, unable to resist her own curiosity, asked: 'Has anyone like me stayed in this house before?'

'*Dona* Brosnan!' Nadine replied brightly. 'You sound like her.'

'I do?'

'Yes, funny speaking!' Nadine gave the sweetest smile. 'She was here with her Chinese husband for a number of years. My mother looked after them, but then she died and I was given the job of caretaking this place. *Dona* Brosnan was very kind to me.'

Husband? Had her mother and Xin got married here? If so, it was like a further betrayal. At the same time, it gave her a feeling of warmth that Nadine had obviously liked her mother, and that made her warm to her. Even if the idea that her mother had been kind to the girl also caused a perverse twinge of jealousy.

But all Cat said was, 'What happened?'

'One day – it was not long after my mother died, so I was in a bad state – they just packed their jeep and went into the desert.'

'Why did they go?'

As Cat put this question her foot hit a tin bowl on the kitchen floor, making it rattle and spin. Must be for a cat.

Nadine shrugged, tossing the coils at the back of her neck. 'I don't know. Many of my people go into the desert for one reason or another. Whites, not so much.' She gave Cat a challenging look. 'To me, she was very good, the other *dona*.'

It was like an injunction to contend with. Was Mam good? It sometimes hadn't felt so. Either way, could I be?

'How old are you?' Cat asked, pressing down again that sense of a type she must imitate.

'Sixteen.'

Nadine was *so* thin, her face especially, in which disconcertingly plump cheeks protruded like little apples. When she smiled they stood out even further, the skin creasing round them and her long eyelashes batting as beautifully as those of a calf – something Cat had once said to a gathering of fellow students in a bar and been laughed at for raucously. But it was true, they just didn't know about farms, no more than she really knew about Nadine.

'How did your mother die?' Cat asked, probing further.

'Illness.'

What horrors, what pain, did that vague term contain? Was it something to do with the mines? There were studies that showed respiratory disease was a consequence of living near or working where uranium was processed.

But it felt rude to pry any further, so instead she said: 'You want to stay here, cook for me?'

Again Nadine shrugged. 'That's my job, from the Chinese.'

'OK.' She wondered how much Nadine really knew of the whole set-up; likely much more than she did.

'Give me money. I need to buy food.'

Cat happily gave her some of the Admiral's cash, asking her to buy some coffee and beer, and more bottled water.

'No beer here. Only at Hotel Bom Jesus. And water very costly.'

She gave her some more money.

Once Nadine had left, Cat turned on a tap. Instead of water it coughed out into the steel sink pipe-shaped gouts, liquorice worms of gritty black mud. The issue of water supply that Nadine had mentioned was worse than she'd implied. Was it really, as the pilot said, something to do with the mines? Sometimes people blamed things unfairly on corporations, but in this case it seemed like it might be true.

Opened a cupboard. Some battered pots and pans, and chipped willow-pattern crockery. A bag of dry cat food.

As if on cue, the cat appeared. A small orange tabby with a flat back and peculiar long ears. It kept mewing and trying to rub itself on her shins, which gave her the creeps, making her think of fleas jumping from one species to another.

Cat explored the house further, wondering if there might be any clues here as to why her mother had disappeared.

There was a small electric fan in the main room, unplugged. A tattered basket chair sported a blue cushion, on which a pair of binoculars sat; surely Mam would have taken those if she went into the desert? The dining-room chairs and table were made from rough-carved red wood that seemed a little damp, as if it were still oozing sap. There were some hydrogeological maps lying on the table. Why hadn't she taken those too? Maybe they weren't Mam's, maybe she was making assumptions? Assumptions being always the parents of fuck-ups.

But who else could they belong to, these maps, if not Mam? If the timings both Admiral Yu and Nadine had given her were correct, her mother had left this place about a year ago. It seemed a long time for maps to be lying on a table, but there was no dust on them. Did Nadine clean them, shake off the sand that was everywhere else?

The map that would have shown the border region and Serra dos Leões was missing, and maybe that itself was significant; lucky, then, that Cat had brought the ones that the Admiral had given her . . . but did the absence of that particular map mean that her mother and Xin had really gone to the Serra? Probably, from what the Admiral had said – but Cat had learned to distrust probabilities. She got her own maps out of her bag and sat down at the table to think about these conundrums.

Long ago, as her own, more detailed maps showed, there was once a river running south from Serra dos Leões on the Angolan border, down towards Dekmantel and the two mines. A river clearly now dry, or underground, most likely half choked with sand. A bracketed legend near the dotted line of the old river gave up a name. *Former Alfaib River*, it said. An understanding of this, geologically speaking, made the Admiral's suspicion that the aquifer was at Serra dos Leões more likely; and Serra dos Leões was also mentioned, after all, in the Russian soldier's diary.

It was so hard to stop herself building inaccurate pictures in her head of the water that might lie beneath all that sand and rock in that zone of what seemed like mere nothingness, an apparent Out There beyond civilisation. But she knew well enough that ideas of nothing, ideas of a naked desert, were just bullshit of the type Big Business squeezed out daily. There were animals and people and plants amid the supposed nothing, and every sort of systemic and ecological activity, organic and inorganic, each one being worthy of attention down to its merest atom.

Water, finding water, was a crucial part of that imagined total structure, maybe more now in a period of climate emergency as at any other time; but the past could not be discounted, no more than the future. She passed questioning fingertips over the surfaces of the maps. All this involved so much more than the human need to have H_2O on tap, the requirement of one person to have a drink and a decent wash paling before the necessity for water on a larger scale. Here supply was different, everything depending the non-equilibrium nature of water, on ephemeral rains as well as ephemeral rivers, flowing intermittently over both time and space; but also on the occasional fog, that benison wished for by humans, animals and plants alike.

Feeling hungry, which was probably significant, she experienced a rush of anger at Admiral Yu. Why was that representative of the Chinese government sending her into something so dangerous, to find a water source that remained ill-defined – sending her here, into the Out There, with only a basic understanding of the hydrogeological map of southern Africa? Surely there were local or Chinese experts who knew more? Why had she sent a young European graduate with (it was her own admission) zero local or logistical smarts?

So far Cat had only been out of Ireland twice: both times to the Canary Islands, where she'd got almost as red as Uncle Tony and couldn't sleep for the creaking of cicadas. How, she wanted to ask Admiral Yu right now, was she meant to cope with all this, having got to Dekmantel, with so much more still to achieve in finding her mother and the aquifer?

Those two separate things had developed an umbilical-like connection in her mind – as if they really were linked but at the same time were not, just as the tracery of underground riverine systems on the maps in front of her seemed linked to reality but always had to be doubted.

The cat stole by, brushing its fur against her trouser leg as questions continued to race to and fro in her mind. Why would the Admiral trust her with such a challenging role – and then support her so badly: only a base in Dekmantel, some money and an emergency phone number?

Overall, it didn't really make sense. Cat looked again at the maps on the table, again felt a bite of hunger in her stomach; she began to reckon with some certainty that the only reason for her having been chosen in this crazy way was that the Admiral had somehow let family sentiment win over a pragmatic assessment of the facts.

Did the Admiral believe it was her destiny to find out what had happened to her parents? Destiny was a thing in China, wasn't it, as in so many other places too? The belief that in the course and culmination of human life there existed some objective certainty beyond human control.

At the same time, even if that maybe were true – by definition, destiny could never be tested until after the fact – there was something chilling there, something much more basic: the idea that to the Admiral she was just a usefully non-affiliated, 'in-the-family' person who could be relied upon not to sell out the location of the aquifer to a rival power.

She leaned forward over the table, pressing her fingertips into the maps, as if doing so might cause them to offer up answers.

After an hour or so, Nadine returned with two large square bottles of water and very welcome provisions: a parcel of chicken pieces and sweet potatoes. These she began cooking up into a sort of rough curry, chopping up onions and garlic, using Mazola to fry the meat.

'What do you do for water here if you these bottles are so costly and the mains goes off?' Cat asked, watching Nadine cook, feeling oddly like a parent observing a student child in their digs, as her own mother had once briefly done.

'There's a pump in the middle of that big stretch of gravel outside,' Nadine replied, stirring the pan. 'Just one pump, hardly working, and hundreds of people. The mines take all the rest. We manage, but it's always a struggle, something at the back of your mind.'

'Surely if they house all these people, and need them to work, the employers would make sure there was enough water?' But Cat knew as she spoke, from what had happened when she'd turned the kitchen tap and got nothing but muddy squidge, that this wasn't the case.

That in itself maybe confirmed that the search for the aquifer, which her parents and, it seemed, so many others had undertaken, had some real value: that what she'd embarked upon could be of real significance in this parched country.

Nadine turned to look at Cat, her little apple cheeks gleaming in the light. 'Yes, you would think that the directors of the mines at least did that. The Priest says they don't do so in order to control us. Those companies suck the place dry without investing in us; they focus on feeding the mines, not the people.'

'Who's the Priest?'

'The pastor of my church. Jackson Kwambi. Also leader of – a group of people. There are a lot of us; we have a flag with a red cross. He sometimes says in sermons – he has a very strong voice when he preaches – that there should be more pumps. Or at least that the one out there should work better.'

She scattered a handful of spices over the sizzling chicken.

'The pump doesn't function?' Cat was frankly amazed that international corporations let things stand this way, if she understood Nadine properly. But the young woman's reactions were hard to judge.

'You have to hit it to make it work. The pump's tap sucks up from an old *vlei*.'

'What's a *vlei*?' Cat asked, sure she was pronouncing it wrongly.

'Shallow lake linked to underground water and rainfall when it comes. This one, he's dead on top. Only gravel remains there, but the pump connects it to water that flows much deeper down. But the Priest says one day the lake will be reborn and fill.'

'What does that actually mean?' The hot spices had caused an irritating vapour over the stove; Cat watched Nadine almost lift a hand to her eyes to rub them, then catch herself, maybe knowing the onions and garlic on her fingers would make her eyes worse.

'Well, he's a preacher, like I say,' the young woman continued, blinking her long lashes. 'So I can't explain everything he says.'

'What's he like?'

'Well, he wears a black cassock with a lion skin on top when he gives sermons. Until recently he was also a foreman at Scursail, the American mine. He resigned a few months past.'

'Why?'

'Nobody knows, though people say he did not get on with the head of security there. Maybe he left to concentrate on his vocation.'

'Meaning what?' Sometimes Cat regretted the tone of a scientific investigator that came into her voice.

Nadine looked at her as if she was stupid. 'His religion!'

'OK,' Cat said, suddenly realising that belief here was still a very powerful thing, as it had ceased to be back home.

'But I don't know exactly why he left,' Nadine continued, stirring the pan with a wooden spoon. 'The main thing he speaks of strongly is the drying up of water. Anyway, he was the best controller of the labour force when he was at the mine, stopping resistance. Now, many of the Scursail labourers come when he preaches. Also people from the Chinese mine.'

'That's Karunga, right?' Cat asked, remembering something the Admiral had said, and the Karunga T-shirt with Chinese characters that she'd seen while wandering about the town.

'Yes. Both mining uranium ore and turning it into yellowcake. Which is what you're smelling here, all the time. It's what I think killed my mother. Emphysema.'

So she was right. 'I'm so sorry. We should both try not to stay here long.'

'I have no choice,' Nadine said, and Cat could have sworn she saw tears prick the young woman's eyes, whether from the spices or emotion. The moment passed quickly as she continued: 'There are very few jobs in this country for young people. I'm so lucky to have the money from the Chinese. When my mother died, they could easily have got in someone older. But Captain Xin insisted and put me in touch with a lady he called his aunt, also sometimes called an admiral, and after he left with *Dona Brosnan* that same admiral or aunt rang me and got my bank details and said she trusted me to keep looking after the house.'

Feeling confused by all this information (did she trust the Admiral herself?) and quite unable to say anything useful in reply, Cat changed the subject. 'Does the Priest have an actual church, a building?'

'No, he preaches by the pump now. Once he was a seminarian at the Catholic church in town. He was instructed by the old priest there, Father O'Rourke, a Jesuit who taught him, he always says, how to think. But Kwambi was too revolutionary for the Catholics and they made him leave when O'Rourke died and a new priest from Ecuador arrived.' Lifting one of the plastic bottles, she poured a little water into the curry.

Reckoning she was making Nadine uncomfortable by asking so many questions and also by watching her cook, Cat went out on to the veranda.

Sitting on the step there, she again felt uneasy that the Admiral had not only sent her here to do something for which she believed herself to be professionally ill-equipped, but had also, even if accidentally, introduced this other human factor in Nadine.

The view of Dekmantel showed itself again: a sprawling, sand-choked settlement with a horizon of dunes, many dunes, some nearly a quarter of a mile high. Smells of dust and woodsmoke mixed with clatters coming through from the kitchen as Nadine finished her dish.

Far off, Cat heard dogs barking, the kind that comes from dogs kept in kennels.

She watched a very large scoop loader, its paintwork bright orange, speed across the white gravel plain. It must have been thirty tonnes at least, the monstrous machine swerving to avoid pits and berms, those same marks of lost water on the skin of the earth that she had viewed from Sean Morrow's plane. Apart from this activity, the place seemed almost empty.

Within the compound, in front of the bungalow, there was a little coffin-like storehouse made of corrugated iron. Cat went over to it, her feet ploughing through the burning sand, and pushed open the door, which was just a sheet of iron mounted on a wooden frame.

Inside it was dark, very stuffy and hot. There was a small metal bed and items of clothing hanging from nails. A board game on a little table. Was this really where Nadine lived? It made Cat want to help her somehow. And at the same time guilty of invading someone's privacy.

'Do you want to eat with me?' Cat asked, back in the kitchen of the bungalow a little later as Nadine served up, putting down the plate of curried chicken with a deft touch, almost a flourish.

She shook her head. 'I go to my house.'

'Take a plate, then.'

Nadine served herself in silence, then carried the plate to the door. She paused, looking at Cat gloomily over the steaming food. '*Dona* should lock the door. Many types of bad men outside, in Dekmantel. Sometimes I think it would be better, Miss, if all we women could go where men can never mess with us. Flee there, somewhere apart.'

'OK,' said Cat, as if this was just nothing. But she reckoned she should have said more, showed she was in solidarity.

'Also, *dona*, we need to be very sparing with water. There was a town meeting last night. Everyone's very worried about the water, and some are saying we should all join with the militias.'

There it was again: the violence of a species. First Yu had warned her of it, then Morrow, and now Nadine. As she thought about all this, Cat did feel something lying behind the already vaguely disquieting atmosphere of Dekmantel and its surrounding dunes, even though Morrow had told her not to worry.

After she had eaten, Cat tried to do a little work on her computer in the living room of the bungalow. She was hoping to piece together what she so far knew about the location of the aquifer – but really it was just twiddling on her laptop: all to no greater purpose, it seemed, than the striking of the represented letters on the keyboard.

Cat kept trying to work, but darkness was coming. She exited Windows and went over to the real window. It was obscured by a thin curtain showing a semi-abstract design. She drew it aside. On the louvres behind, dark little gluey fixtures, moving a little, were picking out negative space on the dusty slatted glass:

half-dead flies, dreaming themselves fully alive in a dingy orange haze, behind which drifting mist felt its way over the gravel pan and the dunes beyond.

After locking the door as Nadine had urged, she went to the bedroom, undressed, got into sleeping gear – the grey jogging bottoms and soft T-shirt that she had used as pyjamas for longer than she cared to remember. The wooden bed squeaked every time she turned. With slight horror, she found herself thinking of what it must have sounded like if her parents had made love in it.

Ducked away from that thought.

Eventually glided off, though, on her own haze of hopes and memories, which crumbled in her mind as it went through its own gears and dreams began. Dreams that crunched up yellowcake, its falling powder coinciding with elements of a comic she'd once read in which the Sandman sprinkled magical sand onto people's eyes. Dreams that macerated Nadine's teeth and lips as she said, over and over again, 'I have no choice.' Dreams that marched like spiders into her nostrils, pulling cobwebs behind them with industrial vigour.

But nobody wants to hear about other people's dreams – even those triggered by a real, actual smell, seeping in on the mist through the metal-framed louvre windows of a bungalow in a remote part of the world's driest desert.

14

Traffics and discoveries

Cat was woken by the sound of tramping feet, her eyes feeling gritty, nostrils too. There was no sign of Nadine. She went through to the living room and pulled aside the curtain in front of the window. It was just before dawn. The stars had gone, and the moon was paling over the grey dunes, blurring itself out. There was still a little of the drifting mist or fog of last night, but further off the desert horizon was beginning to pink up. Nearer, the dark outlines of the two mines towered over the town. She became aware that a stream of labourers was the source of the tramping noise.

Vague, troubling memories came back, all that usual mix-up of dreams . . . was it something about cake? Or one of those little yellow plastic ducks that some bunch of dopes once released in their hundreds on the Shannon? . . . and amid it all a sense of pity for Nadine, with whom she was beginning to feel a bond.

Humans are really part of the same web of feeling, she was so sure of that, even when they seemed obtusely otherwise, or when people were saying vociferously (my God, all that viciousness on social media!) that they were just themselves and everyone else should stay in their lanes.

Not so. It was important to communicate.

Outside the window, labourers of the morning shift from the mines were making their own lanes across the gravel pan, mostly in the distance, but some were passing right by the bungalow, on Spit Street itself: helmet-cradling, overall-wearing figures who seemed like tired robots in the stinking, foggy air.

She went to the bathroom, washed her face. Also wetted a

tissue and got out from her nostrils the sandy snot that had taken up residence overnight.

Should also be getting out of the house and looking for transport today. And sorting out the science. As she brushed her teeth, the links of a hydrological hypothesis started to form a chain in her head. Difficult because Namibia's hydrology was especially mysterious, given how its rivers are ephemeral, don't always reach the Atlantic, seeping into seas of sand instead.

Centuries ago, the Alfaib must have flowed freely to the Atlantic all year round, coming south, then curving east; but now its path was blocked by dunes, and only a small portion of the river got through on occasion, filtering along subterranean corridors. Somewhere the mass of water that once fed that river lay waiting. That place might be the location of the Admiral's aquifer. What if the same thought had occurred to Mam? It struck Cat that her thinking itself was taking on an almost riverine mode. But where, she wondered, was that kind of internal babble going to get her? Professor O'Connor would not have brooked mental divagations of this sort: despite the importance he attached to the involvement of human thought and feeling in the earth system, layers of an onion and all that, he stressed equally the need for vigilance about allowing things to become too complicated, as that got in the way of the practical solutions that were so urgently needed.

She went back to the bedroom and got dressed, once again feeling a sudden change of heart. Finding Mam, that was the crucial thing, wasn't it? That emotional challenge trumped whatever agendas others might have, however much the scientific issues around the aquifer's location, which seemed like they were defeating her, continued to offer a challenge of its own.

In the kitchen she made coffee. Instant was the only choice – a pot of Nescafé as dry as the sand outside. Carried on thinking. Being right about the proposition scientifically was one thing; physically getting to the source of the old river, now underground – that was quite another.

She didn't have a vehicle, anyway. Again she considered herself stupid to have come here at all. Her desire to find her mother aside, as no one could fault her for that, it was as if she had allowed herself to fall under the proverbial self-deception that the grass is greener. And here, after all, there was very little grass.

Mug in hand, she went outside to sit on the veranda steps, watching the walking labourers who were tailing off as they disappeared into the gantry structures of the mines. She began to form firmer plans to hire a car. Probably wouldn't be easy.

As the sun rose higher behind the mines, their machinery sounded loudly again across the former *vlei*. She turned her head and looked towards the endless waves of the true desert, which was warming now, its dun curves growing yellow. Was it really a good idea, setting out into that? Her understanding of the maps might be completely wrong. Was it that in this place, her mental models of hydrology (Mam's too, maybe) would always be shook up, displaced, based as they were on the wet, green, equilibrium meteorology of Ireland – equilibrium meaning that it rained on so many days? So much in human history, Professor O'Connor used to say, the patterns of our minds mirror those of the places from which we've come. Adding that this is most important when one travels from an abundance paradigm to a scarcity paradigm.

Wrong was how she identified, as she drained her coffee: wrong and scared, wrong and regretful, wrong and anxious. Homesick too.

The futility of finding a car-hire place, or even a taxi, was confirmed later that day as Cat wandered along Dekmantel's paltry main street, whose stores were full of dusty bars of soap, battered tins of tomato paste and old-fashioned radio cassette players in torn blue-and-white boxes. Also quite a few places selling portable desalination units – for which dog-eared posters, almost childlike in their design, were propped up in the shop windows.

Everybody she asked about more ordinary transport responded with just 'No,' 'Not possible,' or other negatives.

The impossibility of arranging travel continued to preoccupy her as, between the end of the afternoon and the start of the evening, she began making her way back to the bungalow – along a red laterite road, weighed down by a new purchase of bottled water. At the end of a hot day, it seemed a very tall order both to discover what had happened to her mother and find out the truth about an aquifer that might or might not have fed the enfeebled Alfaib River. Or indeed been fed by its albeit ephemeral flow.

As she knelt down to stretch a handle out of the plastic covering of the water-pack, just beyond the DEKMANTEL MEDICARE sign a little group of blue-uniformed schoolchildren passed her. They had loaves of bread in their hands – sweet-smelling loaves, clearly just collected from the baker. Some were tearing off pieces and shoving them in their mouths. They seemed so happy it made her feel guilty about feeling low, when really she had relatively little to complain about, didn't she?

After she had been walking for another ten minutes or so, a big red 4x4 stopped next to her. The window wound down to reveal a fleshy white face and lips with the blueish tint of one who might suffer heart trouble.

'Howzit?' the lips mouthed, wolfishly.

'OK.'

'What's a sugarplum vision like you doing in a shithole like this?' He had a strong South African accent, this corpulent man. 'What's your name?'

'Mary McLaverty,' she said curtly. 'I work for Clear Course.' She was pleased with herself for having remembered both the false name and false place of work.

'Clear Course?' The man gave a long whistle. 'That outfit. Shouldn't you have a fleet of jeeps and little guys from China following you in them?'

'What?' She struggled to contain her irritation, but knew at once that the cover the Admiral had given her might be blown. 'And you are?'

'Glen Cole. Head of security at the Scursail Deep.' He poked his thumb in the direction of one of the two uranium mines on the edge of town. 'Seriously, what're you doing here, walking alone? It's not safe.'

'Seems fine to me. I was trying to find a car to rent.'

'Good luck with that. Why'd you need it?'

On the basis that being in plain sight was sometimes the best subterfuge, she thought she might as well come out with it, see what sparked. 'I'm looking for someone,' she said. 'Catherine Brosnan.'

'That Irishwoman who was here a while back?' Cole rummaged in the glove compartment, pulled out a pack of cigarettes and lit one, then got clumsily out of the car, moving as slowly as a slug. His feet and shins were encased in cowboy boots, tanned and pointy-toed. 'She went into the desert with that crazy fucker Xin.'

Even though she didn't know her father, it hurt to hear him referred to like that. 'Why do you say "crazy"?' she asked, even though it seemed crazy to feel hurt about a father she'd never met.

'That batshit was always stirring up trouble between the two mines. Almost caused a war!'

By now this man, Cole, was sitting on the bonnet of his vehicle, smoking his cigarette, feet up on the bumper. Besides the cowboy boots he was wearing jeans and a blue-and-orange striped shirt. And far too much cheap aftershave. Also he had a pistol in the holster on his belt. She hadn't expected that.

'What do you think happened to them?' (She almost added 'my parents'.)

'They're dead, lady. You go into that desert, don't come back, means you're dead, finish *en klaar*.'

She felt a sting at the possibility that her mother might indeed be dead, a likelihood that she tried not to engage with, calming her voice. 'I need to know. And that means I do need to get a vehicle somehow: could you help with that?'

'Very difficult, these days,' Cole said, giving her a lazy smile. 'I guess you're staying at the Clear Course bungalow?'

Cat didn't reply. During the silence, Cole flicked his ash into the sand – appraised her body like he was aiming at a target. Still saying nothing, he got back in his vehicle in the same ungainly manner he'd got out of it. Even from here she could smell his cologne, so strong it overpowered the stink of the factories processing uranium ore.

He spoke to her through the open window, his blue lips seeming to snarl. 'Lady, do you think I am stupid? I know, and I'm pretty damn sure that you know I know, that Clear Course is a Chinese front. And that you're here, like Catherine Brosnan was, to look for that aquifer. You look a bit Chinese yourself!'

She took a step back. How does he know my business? It made her feel even more wrong and regretful and homesick than she had done before.

Mainly, scared.

Cole's broad face, his eyes full of lascivious twinkles, was framed in awfulness by the window of the car as his voice talked ruthlessly on. '*Ja*, don't look so surprised. It's not news that there might be an aquifer out there. All the data says so.'

Was it true, what he was saying? Did other people have the maps Mam had?

'Just no one knows quite where the *fokker* is. Near enough knows, but not quite. But the word is, some Admiral in Walvis is hot to trot on it. Female Admiral! *Sjoe, dis wonderlike nuus.* Why don't you jump in and tell me all about it?'

Shocked, she took another step back. 'I need to get home.'

He dangled out a puffy forearm, drumming fingers on the metal of the door. 'Well, it's at least a click to where you are staying . . . But I didn't mean to there, I meant my place. I'll cook you supper. Who knows? Maybe, if you play nice, I'll be able to magic you up a vehicle.'

His implication was more than clear. 'I really don't think so,' she said.

'You sure?'

'Yes! You can go.' Creeped out.

'Sure you don't want that lift?'

'No, thank you.'

'Suit yourself,' he muttered, 'but my best advice, babe, is that you get out of here. Nothing good ever comes of associating with the Chinese in Africa. Look what happened to your Irish Catherine.'

Was he threatening her? 'What do you mean?'

'Hung out with a Chinese, disappeared in the desert. Basically, that's what happens to anyone who resists my employers. Come back to my place and I'll explain it properly.'

His eyes were now roving all over her. She summoned up the

courage to say: 'You know what, just fuck off, will you?'

'Oh, so you have a cracking personality.' His voice mounted in pitch, raising almost to merriment. Looking at her with what seemed like deliberated malice, he started the engine, then shouted out of the window: 'Or a crack and a personality!'

He then drove off, leaving in his wake clouds of dust and her own disgust.

She began walking again, feeling extremely anxious. Horrible. The heavy water-pack cut into her fingers, reminding her of the day she arrived. The road to the bungalow passed between the *vlei* and the dunes, and this part of the pan was covered with thousands of little white pebbles, round and smooth as glass beads.

Suddenly the air went cold. The sun was going down, very quickly. She mended her pace, but the sand and pebbles made it hard to walk.

On the other side of the road, high up on one of the dunes, she thought she caught sight of an antelope, one with a harlequin pattern of black and white patches. But she wasn't certain. Apart from its horns (she was sure she saw those), the beast's outline was cryptic, half lost in the fading light. Nearer by, bats wove to and fro above the raked orange hues of the dunes.

Back at the bungalow Nadine was waiting, sitting forlornly under the lamp on the veranda.

'What the fuck's wrong with this place?' Cat said as she clumped up the steps, throwing down her burdensome purchase. 'It's like a weird zombie town, and some arsehole of a man was just very rude to me.'

Nadine seemed shocked that Cat had sworn. 'What do you mean, *dona*?'

'I need a car, Nadine.'

'Who was rude to you?'

'I can't talk about that now. Why can't I hire a car?'

'None much of those, at least not here. But there are some taxis, where do you want to go?'

'First off, to Serra dos Leões.'

Now Nadine looked even more shocked. 'That's one of the

sacred sites of my Kwanyama people, a place associated with water but also animals. You know *leões* means lions?'

'Yes,' Cat said, thinking of the stories of secret seeps, secret springs, often linked to lions, that she'd read about in anthropological journal articles about the area. Many of these mentioned both humans and lions returning to special places where water was known to be, often over quite long periods. There were enough of these mythic whispers for them to have some scientific credence. And the harder science concurred with the whispers.

'Our queen still wears a lion skin on ceremonial occasions, but basically this is only symbolic now.'

'What's the connection with lions?'

'I don't really know – all that got lost when a border was made between Angola and Namibia. Maybe something to do with lions having long ago led my people to places where there was water? And lions having a first claim on it that had to be recognised.'

'Do you believe it?'

'What?'

'The link with lions.'

Nadine shrugged.

'How can I get to Serra dos Leões?' asked Cat, a little impatiently.

'I will try to help,' Nadine replied, 'but it's very far and the journey hard.'

'Do you know a man called Glen Cole? He was the one who was rude to me. Well, more than that really.'

'I'm sorry. Yes, I have heard of him. The Priest's old boss at Scursail, head of security there. People say he is a bad man.' During this exchange her face had become jumpy with panic. 'Does *dona* want supper?'

'Yes, whatever you can do. Thanks a million.'

As Nadine cooked, gnats danced round the lamp in the living room, which made a faint hissing sound, as if it were a paraffin one rather than electric. It struck Cat that Nadine was her only ally in this place.

Encountering that unpleasant man, Glen Cole, had really upset her. The discovery that he already knew the Chinese connection to Clear Course suddenly made the whole Mary McLaverty disguise seem a waste of time.

After eating, feeling fearful, she hauled herself off to bed, getting into that familiar sleeping gear, which almost made her hope she could be back in Kerry, listening as Uncle Tony clattered about downstairs. But the only sound here was the insistent clanking of mine machinery and the fainter sound of barking dogs.

It was as if a whole day had passed uselessly – that all her trafficking to and fro, intended to provoke action, had simply got in the way of any practicable discoveries, apart perhaps from what Nadine had said about Serra dos Leões being connected to water.

Feeling stuck, Cat wondered as she tried to fall asleep if this was what Mam had endured when she spent whole days curled up in bed, unable to move; or if she did, only to sip some beef tea brought upstairs by Uncle Tony. Her pale face at these times had showed listless monotony and she reacted almost mechanically in the negative when it was suggested she would do better to get herself up, take a walk, feel the sun on her face.

All this had enraged Uncle Tony. While sometimes he acted as if he really did believe her mother was sick, he said he could see no reason for it (as he often said he could see no reason for the challenges to Cat's mental health, which were reported to him by the university). Sometimes he made reference to past family members who, he argued, had had many more reasons to have been miserable but had survived, pushing on through.

Now she wished that Uncle Tony was here to advise her, even if he were to say again, as indeed he'd once said (alongside other hurtful things), that her ma did not resemble the mother she'd hoped to be. Which Cat had taken to mean that Mam had an ideal model of being a mother, which she did not live up to in her own mind. But maybe it was more about what he himself thought, which he often summed up as: 'Just have to be yourself in the end, that's only common sense.'

It was so hard, untangling the contours of all these feelings – her own, her mother's, Uncle Tony's . . .

The map is not the territory. But you do resemble her, he'd added at the time – 'almost the spitting image, though your hair is blacker'.

Yet sometimes, even when drunk, after her mother had left, Uncle Tony had spoken to Cat in ways that suggested her part-Chinese ancestry represented something like a bad ghost to him; but she knew he was really just struggling to come to terms with whatever had happened to his sister. Anyway, the Brosnan lineage had plenty of bad ghosts of its own; for example, those said to live in the stream that came from the Well Field and fed the water supply of the farmhouse, actually running under it. These ghosts – or maybe fairies was a better word – had (as a matter of folklore, not just in the family but also the wider townland) been seen as the cause of past family traumas and, it was implicitly proposed, could provoke future ones.

Cat didn't believe a word of it, putting it all down to the fact that the place had been a famine burial ground. But she suspected Uncle Tony did set some store by the apocalyptic text of water, not least because water affected so much of his day-to-day life as a farmer. The most common cause of foot rot in cows, he liked to tell her, was when cattle quickly went from wet conditions to dry ones, which caused cracking of the hoof and skin, allowing necrotic bacteria to enter.

Caught in a yellow half-circle of fog above Dekmantel, the moon was shining in through the bedroom curtain; she wondered what he'd think of this place, that uncle who always took great notice of the moon, as its movements affected cattle almost as much as rainfall and drainage. Sometimes he'd deliberately leave a cow that was late in calving out in a field overnight, exposure to the moon often doing the trick.

It didn't do anything useful in getting her to sleep, there in the little Namibian town, which now seemed as bad a place to doze off as that freezing hotel in Walvis. After about half an hour of turning about, and untrussing herself from knotted sheets, she got up, pulled a light jumper over her T-shirt and went outside. Now the moon was almost completely encircled by fog, but it continued to shine all the same, both penetrating and reflecting off the fog, which as she looked up seemed to Cat like a piece of semi-transparent paper held next to a desk lamp.

She went over to the outhouse. It was weakly lit inside. Knocking lightly but hearing no answer, she gingerly pushed open the thin tin door – to see, sitting at rickety table, the plate of her half-eaten meal pushed aside, Nadine bent over a board game.

'I'm sorry, *dona*,' she said, looking up from the black and white pieces in front of her. 'I thought it was the wind at the door.'

'No problem; just thought I'd come over and say hi. Couldn't sleep.'

'Me neither.' The eyes above Nadine's little apple cheeks suddenly seemed so filled with tiredness and anxiety that Cat felt a rush of pity. 'What're you up to?'

'Playing draughts against myself . . . I used to play with my mother.'

Cat sat down on the chair opposite. 'Well, what about us playing?'

Nadine's face brightened. 'OK!'

'Not sure whether I remember how,' Cat said, then Nadine laughed and replied: 'I teach you, even if I batter you.'

'What's that?'

'Beat you the best. Want some tea?'

'Yes, please.'

Nadine went to a little gas-fuelled stove and boiled a kettle, eventually bringing back to Cat a mug of red, earthy-flavoured tea that tasted right then like the best drink ever.

They settled down to play. In the course of the game – in fact, several games – leaning on the table with one of her bony elbows, Nadine told Cat some stories that made her laugh.

But she destroyed her at draughts all the same, giving her the broadest smile at the end. There was something about this young woman – girl, really – that made Cat want to hug her.

Afterwards, going back to the main house, Cat locked its door, as Nadine had the previous night suggested, thinking it didn't seem that secure anyway. But she pulled off her jumper, got into the rickety bed and slept at last.

15

The pump

She entered Cat's room without knocking.

'Nadine! Is it really getting up time?'

'Yes, *dona*. And there's big trouble in the town – the pump has run dry. The *vlei* has finally stopped supply, there's been a riot.'

Cat knelt up in the shonky bed. 'What do you mean?'

'The pump has stopped and I am afraid,' Nadine explained again. 'Scursail people, South African people – gone, fled. I went to the pump, trying to get water. The Priest was starting one of his sermons, speaking louder than I ever heard him before. I asked some schoolfriends and they said that earlier in the morning the Scursail men released dogs on the rioting miners, tried to club them with nightsticks, then, not daring to shoot, ran away, Cole at their head. Miners was going to chop them hard, so angry there was no water. Now Cole and the others have rushed to Walvis in their jeeps, people say.'

'What?'

'*Dona*, I must tell you, it's like revolution what's happening out there. At Karunga, Chinese troops are shooting, but over the heads of the crowd. Many new people in the town too. Militias coming in from the deep desert, with vehicles and guns. Town people looking for water barrels in the mine sheds. I tried myself at the pump but there was none. We need to take steps as the water in our bottles will not last forever.'

With that she went back through to the kitchen.

'Christ.' Cat got off the bed and quickly began to dress,

pulling on fresh pants, bra, canvas trousers, a T-shirt, short socks and a pair of Puma runners.

She went into the living room, pulled aside the curtain. In the midst of the *vlei* was a tall, thin figure in a black cassock with what looked like a lion skin thrown over his shoulder. He seemed to be marshalling a band of khaki-clad young men and women, all within a circle of pickups and other vehicles. Many of the youths were wearing caps and carried white flags with a red cross.

'That's the Priest,' said Nadine, coming to stand beside her at the window. They both looked at the rake-like figure waving and pointing, trying to get his people in line. 'And those in caps are his choir.'

'Why are they dressed like soldiers?'

'I don't know, they've always been that way. The Priest is a very serious person. I think he was maybe, when he first gave that order, thinking of the Salvation Army.'

'And what's with the crusader flags?'

'Crusader?'

'The red cross.'

Nadine tutted, her bony shoulders moving geometrically under the fabric of the hoodie. 'I told you before, *dona*. It's the symbol of his new church, which took over when the Catholics made him leave the mission.'

The choir began to sing a hymn that Cat half recognised from her own childhood. It carried across the sand, prompting a memory that wouldn't quite come.

Between the choir and the mines, Cat saw a further collection of vehicles gathering. She could hear their engines racing as they manoeuvred.

'More militia,' announced Nadine, still stood beside her.

'Yes, of course. I understand.' But what Cat meant was – I see. She was far from understanding, seeing in any deeper way, really only feeling increasingly powerful waves of fear. Which displayed oddly. Not in freaking out, or pacing about, or packing her bags, but in a simple question: 'What are we going to do, Nadine?'

'I don't know.' And then, almost comically, but perhaps because she too was afraid: 'I need toilet.'

Nadine went outside to the loo by the outhouse.

The curtain flapped listlessly as a fragment of the hymn sung by the Priest's choir came through, faster than Cat remembered it, and with more of a martial rhythm:

> *What great events on small depend*
> *Then learned the glory of his name,*
> *The Well of Life, the Sinner's friend!*

In the distance came the sound of more motor engines. Cat wished she knew what to do. Should get a move on – act. But move how, act how? The only logical course was a retreat, a dignified withdrawal back to Ireland. This whole thing was a misadventure.

The cat jumped up onto the outside sill, stared at her through the glass.

She went back to the kitchen, checked the number of water bottles. She took a cautious sip from one and then ate a dry bowl of cereal, cornflakes sticking like paste to the roof of her mouth. As she ate, she heard a scratching noise back at the window in the living room.

She returned. The cat there again, and then a second later not.

Must have jumped down.

Quiet as a cat herself, Nadine came back and said: 'I will try the pump again. Sometimes you just have to hit it harder.'

Cat wanted to say, *Wait, let's think; why bother if it's not working? It could be dangerous.* Words of that nature . . . but the girl was already headed out across the salt pan, carrying a tin bucket that reminded Cat of the ones that Uncle Tony used on the farm.

She's impetuous, Cat thought, like I have been in coming here. And if she's afraid, I should be too.

She looked at the pile of plastic bottles overflowing from the kitchen bin. All that waste, she thought, wondering if it could ever happen here: the total ban on plastic bottles that had been enforced in Europe and the US. Spotting one of the Elim bottles, she went over and peeled off the label with the address and phone number of Sean's company. Might be useful.

Going into the bedroom, she grabbed her phone from her rucksack and waited for it to turn on. It took ages, and there weren't any messages. There was no point in messaging Uncle Tony, who almost never turned on his phone. Almost on a whim, she tapped in Sean Morrow's mobile number, hoping he might be able to come and get her. No answer. Then tried the other number; the one on the label. No answer from that either. So much for 'Be there tomorrow, any time, any place, anywhere,' or whatever the hell the pilot's catchphrase was.

She wondered if she should call the number on the card the Admiral had given her, but this wasn't quite an emergency yet, was it? She was frightened enough for it to feel like one, but something stopped her digging out the card – maybe embarrassment at failing so fast.

She sat on the bed, trembling a little, unsure why she was really so afraid. Because Nadine had said she herself was? But that young woman had shown gumption, going back out onto the *vlei* – why could she not summon the same courage and initiative?

16

Choices and abandonments

Arriving at the pump in the middle of the dried-out lake – the pump that had caused all the trouble but was now, as triggers so often are once they've had their moment, being more or less ignored – Nadine pushed through the crowd. Like so many others before her had done earlier that day, she put her bucket beneath the outlet.

Cranked the handle.

Again, it didn't work. Using the large wrench that hung from a length of blue cord, she hit the rusty upright, again employing the strategy that everyone in Dekmantel knew was needed when the pump played up.

No luck.

Across the dead *vlei*, the sound of her hitting the pump rang out, skipping over the distance between Nadine there in the gravel pan and Cat in the bungalow. Hearing it, Cat went onto the veranda, tried to see more clearly what was happening, wondering whether she should follow Nadine, whom she could just spot in the distance, her arm moving to and fro . . .

His choir dismissed, their music replaced by the cautionary clarion of the wrench, the Priest was also watching Nadine. He had by now retreated some way off, to the VW Kombi camper van in which he now lived, since resigning from his job at the mine.

With his deep-set eyes, which sat behind black plastic-framed spectacles, the Priest thoughtfully studied the slender girl at the pump through the windscreen of his vehicle. Every morning, ever since he could remember, young people like this one – Nadine was in his congregation, so he knew her face – had trooped across the gravel flat to haul water back to their homes.

Once the Priest himself had been one of those young people. Long ago, there was a time of peace, a time of enough water. The noise of the wrench reminded him of a bell, a sound from when Father O'Rourke's mission was still running and he was a schoolboy here in Dekmantel, behaving himself amid the rustle of soutanes, the strop of stitched leather hung on a nail, the beds tucked in neatly.

Leaving no shadows, the sun glared off the white gravel. A faint breeze was blowing over, providing leisurely uplift for a falcon that turned high above the young woman as she whacked the pump – but it was not refreshing. Already the air was too dry for even the whole Atlantic to wet it.

Vacated by its South African overseers, the Scursail mine was being looted by the members of various militias. Small figures were crawling over the site's blackened steels like diligent ants. The sheds, standing alongside gouged craters surrounded by mounds of rock and sand, had mostly been emptied even by the time the Priest's choirboys had finished their hymn.

There had been stacks of plastic sacks there, containing yellow-cake waiting to be transported, and a fleet of large vehicles. The sacks were gone now, and most of the vehicles had been driven away. But one or two earthmovers remained, and the Priest had sent some of his boys over to see if they were in any way serviceable, or if fuel could be drained from them.

The Priest was well known in the region. The most important foundation of his fame was his oratory. Schooled in the arts of discourse by Father O'Rourke, he knew how to move an audience to action with words. So far, the fluency of his speechifying had been seen to good effect only in the tumultuous meetings in which the leaders of the rival militias met to air grievances.

These meetings were often a prelude to sporadic fighting out in the sands beyond Dekmantel, but the Priest's charismatic rhetoric had been noticed by other significant figures in the penumbra of the town, including Ma Shango, Zowa the Brave and Sol Spinnekop. They had seen how even their own followers listened to his tall, bony figure. So they respected him, but also suspected that his choir of khaki-clad boys was just another militia in the making.

Now, as the Priest observed Nadine from the driver's seat of his Kombi and heard the sound of her hitting the pump, the thought of action entered his mind as if it were a new idea; but in fact it'd had many parent thoughts in the past, thoughts that had been lying in the sediment of his consciousness for some time.

This, in any case, as he watched Nadine, was how destiny came to the Priest that day in Dekmantel, the day he finally determined to become a new Napoleon, one who would turn his habitation of religion into one of violence, even if it was violence with a righteous aim.

The aim involved countering a coming drought, as signified in the failure of the pump, by direct action against those who had caused it: the agents of foreign capital, as represented by the American and Chinese mines, and those in government who enabled them.

The Priest had kept his ambitions closely hidden from the world. He had previously considered the onset of drought from all angles. With methods of analysis learned from Father O'Rourke, he had split details as finely different as the hairs of the magnificent lion pelt lying on the passenger seat next to him. He had seen, as if prophetically, the immediate reaction to a total failure of water supply in Dekmantel, and then perhaps something of what would come after. He knew that the end of the water here, if indeed that was what was happening, spelt a very big shift in the power balance, in particular in terms of what foreign interests would or would not do in the future.

A fly settled on one of the lenses of his spectacles. He watched it move its wings. We Africans will no longer be able to endure in our homelands, he reflected, resisting the temptation to bat at the fly. We need a leader if we are to survive.

The fly lifted into flight. His hand rose, fast, and he grasped the insect in his palm.

With the killing of the fly there came to him a sudden

awareness that this was a chance that only came along once in a lifetime: an opportunity to be a catalyst among the oppressed.

And so, freeing himself from the torments of all the precautions he'd previously observed, the Priest abandoned himself to destiny.

He reached into the glove compartment of the Kombi and produced from it an old-fashioned revolver. He put the gun on the lion skin draped over the passenger seat, then started the engine, which ignited with a rattle and a puff of blue smoke. He honked the horn once or twice and drove nearer to the pump and Nadine, who paused her bashing away at it.

He sounded the horn again, in long blasts this time, as if summoning those gathered about in different groups across the *vlei*, with its pump in the middle like the statue of an idol.

His own khaki-clad choir, carrying their white flags with the red cross, filtered among the swelling crowd. Most were little more than teenagers, former orphans who had flocked to the Priest when he offered them safety and the opportunity to learn how to better themselves. To identify with his faction, they often hung rough-hewn wooden crosses round their necks.

More people were now swarming across the salt pan, running after the Priest's vehicle as its tyres kicked up a white haze of carbonate dust and pebbles.

The Priest stopped and left the Kombi. Putting the pistol in his belt and throwing the lion skin over his shoulders, he continued on foot towards the pump, following a furrow in the dried mud. Ahead of him, pulling up the sleeves of her hoodie as if she really meant business this time, Nadine had resumed her assault on the pump.

As he walked, the Priest was trying to remember the girl's name . . .

In the same moment, Cat herself began walking across the gravel pan, having finally gathered up the courage to act. There were so many people here now, all moving about like pieces of straw in a stream, crowding one on the other.

All seemed again to be listening to the anguished clatter of the wrench on the pipe as Nadine continued hitting the metal upright, making it once more the centre of attention. It struck Cat as she approached that there was a lot of pent-up anger in Nadine, for she had been striking the pump for quite a long time. Perhaps others also sensed that anger, as more and more eyes in the crowd were fixing on Nadine's thin brown arm, lifting and hitting.

As Cat was swallowed up more deeply among those others, still feeling frightened but also oddly exhilarated, her tread and that of the crowd around her was causing the white gravel of the *vlei* to flick up with each successive movement, as if hit by a deluge of rain. Was this the adventure she'd for so long hoped to have; was she making a choice at last, or was it yet another eventuality happening to her, something encountered in the stream of life?

She didn't know, but she carried on towards Nadine, knowing at least, as her heels trowelled up more pebbles, that she had to look after that girl, thinking of how Uncle Tony had (after his fashion) looked after her when her mother left.

The Priest – she saw as she walked – was also heading towards Nadine, the shadow of his tall figure shortening on the sand as the sun rose towards its zenith.

17

Errors and imitations

Reaching Nadine before Cat, the Priest stayed the girl's hand, and the clanking stopped. The number of people on the lakebed was by now so large as to suggest everyone in Dekmantel and its environs had turned out. The Priest's choir, spread throughout the crowd, were shouting his name, or rather his title. 'Priest! Priest!' they cried, raising their hands in the air.

The crowd was meanwhile still being swelled by fighters from the different militia crews, mainly those who'd earlier been roaring around the pan in pickup trucks – now returned from the mines, with cargo beds full of plunder – but also others, who were arriving on horses and camels rather than in vehicles.

Members of all these crews were assembling on that patchwork of gravel outside Dekmantel: a patchwork equivalent to their varied political sentiments and personal motivations. Some were just in it for themselves. Others, like the Priest, genuinely hoped to defeat the tyranny of corporations, and the related tyranny of being subject to the proxy conflict of foreign powers bent on milking the resources of the country, battening on its throat like dogs. But there were plenty on the pan who were foreigners themselves, being immigrants beaten from their homelands by other crises prior to the broad water emergency that seemed to be happening. If one could ever put general human rights apart, it could be argued that these outsiders had no dog in this fight. But the same sun was rising over all.

★

The militia arriving across the lakebed on camels and horses was called the Skeleton Crew. A mixture of Cape Malay and Afrikaners, its members were hard-looking, yellow-skinned men, some with brass earrings or amulets round their necks or felt sombreros on their heads. These horsemen and cameleers were part of a larger network of semi-nomadic commandos that operated up and down the Skeleton Coast, and also in desert parts of South Africa. Some of the Skeleton Crew were Muslims; all revelled in their mixed heritage, seeming to find a fierce freedom in it.

The leader of this band was one Sol Spinnekop: the ink of the spider's web tattooed on his face that gave him his name was as black as his close-cropped hair. He rode a white stallion and, like a number of his followers, carried a sword as well as an automatic weapon.

On getting down from his horse, Spinnekop greeted the Priest with a solemn *Salaam*, pressing his palms together. The two men respected each other and had so far managed to avoid conflict between their groups. But nothing could be ruled out in the Damara badlands, this crucible of change where a geopolitical sequence was unfolding – more or less a battle between China and north America.

Unfolding as Cat continued across the sun-throttled *vlei*, time seeming to slow down as she ploughed through the gravel. Homesick again, even though all there was to be homesick for was a few acres of marshy fields, thirty-odd milkers, one bull and a grumpy unmarried uncle, who often seemed more concerned about the slates on the farmhouse roof than her state of mind.

Why was she feeling homesick anyway? What was happening to her was so new, so intense, she shouldn't be having those thoughts. *But I am having them*, she retorted to herself, as the gravel flicked against her calves, stinging like unhived bees.

The leader of another militia was female. She'd just arrived on a quad bike with a Strela surface-to-air missile launcher strapped to its roll bars. Bulky in camouflage jacket and trousers, wearing a machete at her waist, the leader of this group was Ma Shango.

She nodded warily at the Priest on arrival. Her big face was scarred, as if it had only ever recorded violence and pain.

Shango's soldiers brandished their weapons as they came in her wake, regarding the Priest with suspicious eyes as they approached. Like the Priest's own group, this outfit was mostly in military uniform – but in their case a heavily variegated camouflage rather than simple khaki. Shango's men were known as the Mai-Mai. Many of them came from Congo, but her group also contained others from elsewhere in the Great Lakes region.

The gravel Cat was passing over was now as white as milk. Back on the farm – drawing from cows which for medical reasons could not be milked by Uncle Tony's machines – she used to feel, as her hands moved in rhythm and the liquid spat into the tin pail, that mental impressions were passing to and fro between her head and the flank of the cow where it rested.

But now she detected no conversation with nature save a sense that she had to get to Nadine as soon as she could. Something very strange was happening here, as the sun pelleted its beams at her forehead and the pebbles beamed their pellets at her calves.

The third militia looked different again. Rather than wearing military clothing, they were mostly wrapped, toga-like, in tattered red-and-black tartan blankets. Over their motley clothes some of these had rigged fragmentary armour fashioned from pieces of flattened lead, cow-hide pads and lengths of steel chain. One or two had AK-47s and there was also a bazooka in the mix, but most of this group had old-fashioned 'daneguns' – homemade, single-shot wooden hunting rifles bound with wire. Those who did not have guns had spears, bows and arrows or weapons, sharpened to points or studded with nails.

This group, mainly Zulus and Zimbabweans, together with a number of Malawians, was known as the Ruga-Ruga. Their leader was Zowa the Brave, a huge, muscular man who wore a large black bowler hat pinned with car badges: Dodge, Ferrari, BMW and Alfa Romeo. He carried a pair of sawn-off shotguns holstered in a maroon-leather backpack, the straps of which, filled with cartridges, acted as a bandolier. Easy enough to insert those cartridges into the chambers of the shotguns.

Hot wind was now blasting across the *vlei* and Cat's feet made a scratching noise as she ran across the milky gravel. The sun continued to rise.

Finally reaching the pump, she approached what was happening there – the great babble of what was happening there – like the stranger she was, people noticing her, some even grabbing at her clothes as she came through.

Cat watched as the black-robed Priest placed a hand on Nadine's head. Then, removing his hand, he took the wrench from Nadine's own and, soliciting a knife from one of his lieutenants, cut the blue cord with which it was tied to the pump.

Holding the wrench in the air, the Priest began speaking in English with a rich and powerful voice: 'This girl! She has found out what we all knew was coming, that we will have to seek water amid the hearth-fires of our foes. And who are our foes?'

Expectation rippled through the assembly to whom he was now speaking. Fearful, Cat was trying to make herself inconspicuous by hiding behind one of the big earthmovers parked nearby but failing because a lot of people had already noticed her – looking at her hatefully, she thought.

'They are those who came to the desert and filled it with machines.' He gestured at the jungle of derricks on the other side of the *vlei*. 'It is the South Africans and Americans and Chinese and the others to whom our masters in Windhoek have sold us. Once more, my brothers and sisters, we must take up arms to fight for freedom, as our forefathers did in the wars of liberation.'

Another tide of fear washed over her, as she sensed the potential for aggression against her in the crowd because of the colour of her skin. The thought shamed her, but there it was. She watched the Priest circle the wrench in the air.

'You have seen this wrench. You have all, like this girl, hit the pump with it, knowing that sometime this day would come. Well, now it *has* come, and I say to you all that we must – *move!* I say that we should go across the desert to Kunene where Scursail has built a new headquarters.'

Cat remembered that Admiral Yu had spoken of this; and Kunene was near where all the evidence pointed to the aquifer being, and possibly her mother too. Was this an opportunity?

At the moment, as the Priest continued speaking, it didn't seem so. 'Yes, we shall go across the great sand sea into that stronghold of one of our foreign controllers, go there and take back from them what they have stolen from us. Those foreigners came to rule us before and took our lands openly. Now they take our lands in secret. We close our eyes too long . . . and when we wake up, hey, our lands belong to them!'

A roar of assent passed through the crowd, that mixed group of townspeople, militias and hard-hatted miners.

'The technique of these foreigners, it is to take away the riches beneath the earth and pollute the ground itself. They besmirch the earth in which we once grew crops. The earth on which we once danced, in the old way, in the bosom of our tribes.'

A brief silence followed, during which it was as if everyone seemed to consider this fabled time of communal calm.

Still holding the wrench, the Priest again laid a hand on Nadine's head. Cat thought she saw in the girl's eyes the same fear she herself was feeling. Too many people with guns . . .

'We had full bellies in those days, we had plenty of water. Now they have taken our oil for their vehicles. They have taken our copper to use in the wires for their computers. They have taken our lead for their batteries. They have taken our coltan for their cellphones. They have taken our gold for their jewels. They have taken our nickel for their magnets. They have taken our uranium for their nuclear weapons and power stations. Almost any mineral or metal you can name, they have stolen it from us.'

The Priest's voice rose further. 'But that is nothing as to what has now happened. Now, because of what they have done here, they have also taken our water! All this has such a long history, my friends. Only because we occasionally fight back do these greedy people from beyond the sea send their own armies or hired soldiers to control us.'

He wagged a wand-like finger in the air. 'We sent the first foreigners away in the end because we were stronger, but then they came back in altered form. Our job, our job now is to sweep Africa clean of all these malefactors. Americans, Chinese, even those whose faces, as black as my own, cover a false allegiance in the manner of a mask.'

The Priest paused, allowing the audience to absorb the effects of his speech, and again circled the wrench in the air above his own tall frame and Nadine's quivering body. Watching it with mesmerised eyes, the crowd seemed gripped by a strange collective passion. It was almost as if they were an orchestra that the Priest was conducting, with the wrench as his baton.

Again fear struck. Cat's eyes flickered from the swaying rows of faces in front of her up to the wrench – worrying that she was a supposed emblem of foreign power, about to get attacked.

'Yes, my friends,' came the voice of the Priest, again seductive and commanding, 'on you I now call to come with me to Kunene. We shall gather more people with us on the way and be a strength to the poor. We shall leave here as pilgrims but arrive there as warriors. Above all, we shall slake our thirst!'

This last statement produced a strong cry from the crowd, encouraging the Priest's verbosity.

'Yes, and once we take Kunene we shall go to other places where our livelihood is being stolen. Yes, we will make the whole of southern Africa better. Only in this way shall we be released from bondage. I now call upon the other militias to join me. Brothers, sisters, let us spring from our fetters together!'

Another great cry went up. Beginning with the Priest's cross-wearing boys, the cheers soon spread to the troops of the other militias who had arrived. One by one, their leaders – Spinnekop and Ma Shango, Zowa the Brave too – came closer to the Priest. They did not acknowledge his superiority nor offer him fealty, but there was a recognition that the ground had shifted, that some, if not all, power had been carried over to him. They would now have to work together, that much was clear.

As they came up to him, the Priest gave each militia leader

the wrench to hold for a moment, as if to symbolise the new bond between them. To cheers and whistles from their different followers, Sol Spinnekop of the Skeleton Crew, Ma Shango of the Mai-Mai and Zowa the Brave of the Ruga-Ruga each held the wrench in turn before returning it to the Priest, who then resumed his speech in much the same vein.

The mixture of his spiel made Cat uneasy as she skulked behind the earthmover. For all his talk of collective action, it seemed to her as if he was mostly speaking to his own inner addressee, gaining conviction (for his speech had certainly increased in volume) whenever the crowd responded.

Yet more cheers and whoops were still coming from that wider audience, who did not at all appear to share her doubts. The Priest called on one of his choirboys, João, a young Angolan with a barrel chest and muscled, oblong thighs, to hoist Nadine up.

Watching, Cat experienced a by now familiar sense of uselessness, as if she should intervene but couldn't. An intimation of personal futility, diving deep inside her: it wasn't like she was the US State Department or something, not getting involved because to do so might make things worse in a foreign place, or upset domestic voters if involvement happened. If she was going to step forward, now was the time.

Nadine fluttered in the boy's arms like a captured bird. Rooted to the spot, still unable to move as she watched, Cat was again conscious of awful inertia. Passive in itself, this feeling wasn't passive in how it was affecting her: more like it was mocking her, playing with her, toying with her, even laying hands on her, if that made any sense when speaking of feelings, thoughts, all those ripples of consciousness that creep up on us – waiting like the Well Field fox used to wait by the pond there, before striking at moorhens, causing almost comic hysteria. But that was all in her head; what was happening to Nadine was truly physical.

Once Nadine was up on João's shoulders, the Priest cried out again: 'Friends, water has aroused this girl's heart. Let her be our mascot. And if you shall have me also, I will be your general and lead you, but only as one of you, all walking together behind this wrench.'

Swiftly raising his long, cassocked arm, the Priest flung that implement above the delirious crowd. Spinning upwards, it glinted in the intense sunlight – hung in the air, as if about to deviate into errancy.

In the next few seconds there shot through Cat's mind a rapid succession of thoughts: first, that she cared about was what happening to Nadine; second, that whatever else was going on, all this was really about water, something she knew a lot about; and third (the biggest realisation of all), that this might be a moment in which she could actually achieve what she came here for, turning events to her advantage. If the aquifer and Mam were near Kunene, it made sense for the Priest to at least hear her voice . . .

Heaving in breath, suppressing fear, she came out from behind the earthmover, walked forward as if all worries had been settled, plans had been laid, and the turn she'd intended was about to take place.

The wrench fell back into the Priest's hand like a drum major's baton. 'Yes, the true leader is this girl.'

He pointed the wrench at Nadine, who was looking very scared, grimacing up there on João's shoulders. 'She shall be the icon of the hundreds of thousands of young people who will swell our ranks. For it is on their behalf that we will march on Walvis and the other seats of false government. And do you know what? We shall win. And *why?*'

An inconclusive murmur passed through the crowd that now jostled around Cat. She desperately needed to do this, make that turn, but didn't know how.

'I will tell you,' continued the Priest as Nadine started to struggle, but João was holding her shins.

'We shall win because we've been told there's been progress but most of us have not seen its fruits. And we shall win because many of the governments of Africa are in terminal decline. Some hardly exist at all, their leaders spending more time stealing gold and securing monopolies than they do governing. So focused are they on selling our birthright to foreigners that they will not have the strength to resist this girl, whom we will take as our symbol.'

There was a pause and suddenly, bursting forward from the people about her, Cat shouted: 'Wait! You can't just take her.'

It did not feel to her like her own voice, but she had finally spoken.

18

Transformations

As soon as Cat had spoken, movement stirred in the ranks around her. Hands gripped her, pushing her forward. The crowd cleared and here she was, in front of the Priest, still by the pump, still with the wrench in his hand. Next to him stood João the Angolan, Nadine on his shoulders. Nearby were two of the other militia leaders, Spinnekop with his spider-web face and Zowa with his crossed guns and bowler hat.

The Priest's eye fell upon Cat. 'As a foreign person you are brave to speak up in this company. But you should go back to your own country, not interfere in our business. Trouble is coming in this land, and it's not well to be a stranger in such times.'

Odd voices in the crowd spoke up, quite a few in fact, shouting that they too were strangers, but the Priest, puffed up with his own prestige, ignored them completely.

With an effort of will Cat spoke again, aware of all the faces watching her, some filled with what she read as menace. 'You're right to try to help your people, Priest. But this is not the way to do it. If you go to Kunene, you'll be attacked by Cole's men.'

'What makes you think that?' asked the Priest with a derisive laugh. 'You think you know more than we do?'

'It's a matter of firepower. You must know how strong the Scursail people are – that man of theirs, Glen Cole, he said to me himself that anyone who resists that company ends up dead in the desert.'

'The same Cole who this morning ran like a rock rabbit from

Dekmantel to Kunene. As I say, on this as other matters, I think I know better than you do.'

'Maybe so, but isn't it better if the people here are transferred somewhere where there is better access to water? There are strong indications of an aquifer in Kunene, Russian soldiers were once . . .'

She knew it was morally dubious to pursue her own agenda of getting to Kunene, finding Mam and the aquifer, but –

The Priest cut across her words: 'We've heard such stories before. They're always false, these promises. Another white woman who was here in this town before you, some years ago, she used to say such things too.'

Rocked by hearing an unexpected mention of her mother, Cat had to consciously regather her strength. She pointed at Nadine, still up on João's shoulders, still looking very uncomfortable: 'And that girl, she's my assistant. I need her for my work.' Not quite true, but the best she could do.

'You are indeed a brave woman,' the Priest observed again, as Cat got jostled, 'but I cannot allow that.' He gave a deep cough, as if after this stream of speech the fluency of his voice had finally given out. 'She's now a symbol of all we must fight for in the hard days ahead. Besides, I believe that as a stranger your work here is not necessary.'

'She's not a symbol,' Cat said, her own voice becoming a little frantic and rising in pitch. 'And you can't just kidnap her!'

'No,' said the Priest, 'but then we're not. She's a member of my congregation, I believe. Come down, young lady.'

João helped Nadine climb down from his shoulders. 'So which', the Priest asked her, 'would you rather do – come with us and fight Scursail, or stay here with the foreign woman?'

The crowd laughed as if once more a single identity, those dispersed voices who'd previously protested their difference subsumed again in the stubborn unity of the whole.

Eyes cast down, Nadine only mumbled at first, and to Cat it seemed as if she didn't want to be held in common in the same way, shattered by the hammer of the Priest's rhetoric as the others had been.

'What's that?' asked the Priest. 'Speak up.'

Nadine looked at Cat with pleading eyes, then turned to the Priest. 'Go with you.'

'Nadine, no!' cried Cat. 'Don't do this, please.' She had raised her voice, trying to address the whole crowd, sure from what she knew of Glen Cole that what the Priest was planning was going to end in disaster. She was thinking, too, of the miles and miles of empty desert she'd flown over, and how hard it must be to survive in it; and at the same time – why isn't anyone else speaking against this crazy plan?

But she spoke again all the same: 'Look, this is pure madness. You'll be killed if you attack that mining company. I've a better idea, which is that I help you find water. It's shortage of that which has caused all this.'

A shiver of discontent eddied through the assembly. There came the sound of a shot. For a moment panic ensued, a milling of limbs and voices, before silence fell again. The Priest was standing with the pistol in his hand, a wisp of smoke rising from its barrel.

'Enough,' said the Priest, suddenly looking a little anxious, as the other militia leaders watched him. 'It's settled. We will gather supplies and move out today, heading for Kunene.'

'Nadine!' Cat called out again in a strangled voice.

Coming close to her, Nadine shook her head. 'I am sorry, *dona*, but it's just that he's right. We can't stay here any more. The water is gone from this town.' She touched Cat's wrist as if in assurance, seeming in that moment like someone much older than sixteen; it was almost as if she were the person looking after Cat right then, rather than the other way round.

Cat looked at her face, not sure if Nadine was including her in that 'We can't stay here'; then looked at the Priest, assessing them both in turn, trying to remain rational, calm her voice, keep true to why she'd come here and what she thought was right. She was silent for a moment, then spoke. 'Yes, she is correct, from here the water's gone. But not from everywhere, not at all. If you are going to move, let me help you. I know where there's water.'

Even as she spoke, Cat knew that what she was saying was not fully factual. Despite a few data points, as Professor O'Connor might have put it, the aquifer's location remained a mystery. Something that couldn't yet be pinpointed by existing geological knowledge.

Amid these thoughts a big woman with a topknot and camouflage jacket materialised. Cat slowly realised it was the famous Ma Shango of whom the pilot had spoken. This figure – ambling towards them, as baggy-kneed as a cartoon bear, but still forbidding in aspect – was followed by a couple of her soldiers.

Nodding her heavy head, she pointed at Cat: 'If she sabi am where water, why not give her show us it already? Let her go speak, anyhow.'

It took a few seconds for Cat to process this, to properly comprehend the sort of patois or pidgin in which Ma Shango was speaking, and then to remember from what Sean Morrow had said that she was different from most of the people around here, being of Nigerian heritage.

One of Ma Shango's men touched Cat's chest with a rifle, making her start backwards as she was still trying to work out what the woman had just said.

'Leave her,' instructed the Priest. And then to Cat herself, in a manner that riled her: 'You may speak.'

'My name is Mary McLaverty.' Recovering from being touched by the gun, Cat was pleased that she had at least managed to hold on to the fiction of her false identity. 'I work for a charity called Clear Course. I'm a scientist.'

Her words brought a jeer of mistrust from someone, as if they, too, knew she had no more alibis to spare, but she carried on: 'Along with other scientists, I've been collating aquifer data as part of an initiative to wrest back control of clean water on this continent for the people of Africa. We have been working to avert the very water shortages you and others are suffering.' Even as she spoke, Cat recognised that what she was saying had more than enough of the cant of white saviours about it.

But she pressed on in spite of her self-doubt: 'Science can help you and your people, Priest. Water and its sourcing – its flow and rationing – dominates everything here, but science can help find an answer to where great supplies of it could be lying.'

Again, even as she spoke, summoning all she had learned about these situations – about how when the expert confronts the people affected in the field, all is governed by power dynamics, hierarchies of knowledge and the entangled history of haves and have-nots – she knew she was failing. Presumably they were jeering again because of that?

Yes, they were, louder and louder.

'This is all very kind-minded, but we've heard it before,' said the Priest. 'You think we don't know all this shit you're talking? What exactly is it that you propose?'

'That I really *do* help you,' Cat said, a sudden strength of purpose surprising her, despite the jeers. 'That I actively help you find the location of the water, and that you reconsider your decision to attack the mine headquarters in Kunene, avoiding bloodshed.'

'What's in it for you, and why should it concern us?'

It was the ultimate question – even if thinking about it individually did not really help solve problems like water shortage or climate change and other complex global challenges with the same profile: because discussing those didn't just involve stating one's own belief system in terms of those of other people, which she thought was what the Priest was asking, it also involved doing the same in terms of the whole-earth system of which Professor O'Connor had so often spoken.

Too hard a task, but Cat wanted to meet it honestly. All one could do in the end was detach one's own little life experience – the very tiniest sliver of O'Connor's onion – and hope it resonated with others. But she didn't know what to say.

What came out in the end, too late, and spoken to a fairly impatient audience, was full of risk: 'My mother was here before, and went looking for the same aquifer I'm looking for now, a source of water in Kunene.' Have I given the game away, she worried, in hinting at her real identity?

It did not seem so, the Priest just shrugging in response, as if he reckoned it extraordinary that she could offer a different future to the one he envisaged. 'Lady,' he told her, 'you forget that water, too, must sometimes run red.'

Oh, fuck off with the lady, won't ye? But the anger that had replaced uncertainty was also too late.

'We go where we go, only because we must go,' the Priest forged on. 'What you think, as a foreigner, is irrelevant, even if your scientific knowledge might be helpful. Come with us if you like, and if this aquifer is in Kunene we can look into it – you can even travel in my vehicle. But if not, don't stand in our way; I have no time for arguing with scientists.'

Cat was offended by this and it made her doubt him, just as she doubted anyone who expressed scepticism about science. She wanted to say something quickly in reply, but the Priest had already turned away from her. In that moment she had another moment of self-doubt as she remembered another of Professor O'Connor's famous nostrums – 'what science needs to be most sceptical about is science itself'. Whenever he said this in lectures, she always used to think of Uncle Tony saying, as he patted one white-faced cow or another: 'I don't know what you're thinking, but I'm thinking you need to get in the parlour.' And nearly always the beast in her beauty would walk inside.

By now the Priest was addressing the broader crowd again, halooing as loudly as her uncle did when feeling impatient and had a whole herd of white-faced kine to deal with: 'Comrades! Let us begin at once. If we're marked to die like she says, so be it.'

The Priest lifted his fist and Cat noticed on it a ring with a ruby-like jewel. Its suggestion of vanity made her doubt him even more. As it caught the sun, which was now nearly overhead, the gem seemed like an eye, one focused on the Priest but also on her: if she did go with them, what was her role going to be? If she went, maybe she could split off at some point and look for the aquifer and Mam?

More importantly right now: Nadine. Cat went over and hugged her, as she'd long been wanting to. The girl made a little intake of breath, then pulled herself out of Cat's grasp. It was almost like she didn't want to be comforted – or whatever bond they'd forged had been severed.

19

First day

The ragbag army packed the dry lakebed. The surface of the old *vlei* was now dotted with a miscellany of flags. The Priest's red cross; Spinnekop's spider web; Zowa's two crossed guns under a bowler hat, all fluttering in a slight breeze. Ma Shango's outfit didn't seem to have a flag, but she was there all right, her stolid dignity giving the impression that she was the real leader, not the Priest. What she'd said about letting me speak, well, that was one good thing, Cat thought, one good thing in all this mess.

Amid the swarm of people, engines vibrated, letting off clouds of fumes. She spotted a diesel tanker, mine lorries with flatbeds and tip-up trailers, a few large earthmovers, yellow and orange, along with flotillas of grey pickups and sundry other vehicles, including one or two battered saloon cars. In the noxious fug that billowed from the exhausts, thickened by airborne sand, horses and mules also milled about, flashing frayed hooves and tombstone teeth.

Militiamen in a bewildering variety of uniforms were rushing to secure munitions to vehicle tailgates, bouncing the weight on their thighs as they levered the large green tubes of mortars into position. The weaponry, like the humans, left no shadow, for by now the sun had reached its highest point.

With rolled-up mats strapped to their backs, along with tin buckets and babies (hardly visible under folds of coloured cloth), matronly women were trying to control older children, some of whom were running through the crowd. The kids were dodging like wasps between uniformed legs as if they were enjoying it; they certainly didn't seem scared.

The sight of children in the midst of all this weaponry turned Cat's stomach; but what was to be done, now she was in it herself? Part of her wanted to shout back across time into the ears of the Admiral, into the ears of her mother and the father she had never met, *Get me out of here* – but again, it was too late.

Yet in spite of the fear, perhaps inextricably bound up with it, was an uncertain, building excitement, spurring her on. She was well aware that it was easy, in this strange place, to make wrong assumptions. But she had decided, hadn't she, that she would go with this strange army, see what happened, with luck find her mother and the aquifer if they were indeed in Kunene, the Priest's destination?

At the very least, she needed to look after Nadine. She thought of the closeness she'd sensed playing draughts with her, and how Nadine had touched her wrist during the exchange with the Priest – as if she, too, had felt some kind of bond developing. But later she'd pulled away . . .

Processing all these uncertainties, she made her way back to the bungalow. There she paused for a few minutes, wondering tediously again if she should stay put, stick with her ordinary self rather than try to find a best version of it.

But then she began collecting items she thought useful for this expedition: a change of clothes, her maps and also her mother's (or those she presumed to be), the rest of the Admiral's money, phone and torch, the binoculars she'd found there, a sleeping bag, two bottles of water.

Fifteen minutes later, she was approaching the Priest's Kombi, having taken up his curt invitation to travel with him. Nadine, too, he'd said, should join them, and the young woman was already in the back of the vehicle, hoodie as tight over her head as any teenager back home.

Cat was about to get in the front with the Priest. On the point of doing so, she said to him: 'Actually, reckon I'll sit in the back with Nadine – more comfy.'

'Whatever you like.' His voice sounded a little sarcastic, as if he thought her use of the word 'comfy' was, in the circumstances, completely wrong. Which perhaps it was.

But that's what Cat did anyway, settling herself on one of the banquettes opposite Nadine, as the Priest bent his long legs in the front. Near where Cat sat, foam was spilling out from a rip in the pleather of the seat – clearly had been for some time, the edges having become dried, like those of a wound.

At last they got under way, a caravan of vehicles and animals and people on foot streaming out of Dekmantel behind the Priest's Kombi. He was, Cat soon thought, driving far too aggressively, spinning sand with the wheels. The pole of one of his red-cross flags – wedged between the roof rack and the front bumper – was flicking to and fro, like it was trying to achieve balance. Which is what she felt too.

Even though she'd made the decision to go with this group, it would never be the right decision, just as not going with them would also not have been right. Like she would always be wobbling as wildly as that flagpole. Feeling queasy, she had to look away from it – first opposite at Nadine, who was gazing out of the rear window, then turning round to do likewise.

There – framed in dust-smeared, gravel-scratched glass – Cat spotted João, the young man who'd lifted Nadine on his shoulders and was now riding a motorbike. His white cut-off vest displayed impressive biceps, and he was wearing a FedEx courier helmet. João seemed to have decided that Nadine was the girl for him, because he kept standing up on the footrests of the bike to make faces at her through the glass. Nadine looked down shyly whenever he did so, sometimes pulling her hoodie down even tighter.

Was he sweet or a threat? Cat couldn't decide.

Some of the pickups racing behind the Kombi, mostly Toyota Hiluxes, were filled with sacks of millet, rice or maize. Others contained sacks of yellowcake, which she presumed were being taken along for their financial value.

Most, however, were stacked high with blue-plastic barrels of water, bound down with rope. Sealed with black lids, these barrels represented the very last of Dekmantel's water supply, looted from the mines, combined with whatever the militias had in store at their bases.

Other vehicles contained the portable reverse-osmosis desalination machines, that were such a feature of this part of the country. Seeing them alongside the looted water barrels gave her a slight sense of security. But doubts about her decision to go along were still coming, seeping into her consciousness even as she tried to stop them, plugging in mental fingers like the boy in the dike. That was, of course, impossible because her mind itself felt like a pool, with more thoughts always lapping over the edge.

She began trying to calculate how long the water barrels she'd seen would last them (there were about 200 people in the convoy, she estimated), but that too was impossible. She felt frustrated in being unable to put her scientific mind to use. How much of any of this had been properly planned?

Besides those pickups carrying sacks of food or yellowcake, water barrels and desalination machines, others were mounted with what seemed like improvised combinations of weaponry: twin machine guns, rifles with very long barrels, rocket-type tubes, even what looked to her unpractised eye like turrets from light tanks and armoured cars, from which even bigger artillery protruded. Welded on with rough seams, or fixed by an intricate net of bolts and wires, these weapons had clearly been assembled by the militias over a period of years. Alongside them, ammunition boxes were piled high; where, Cat wondered, had the militias got all this stuff from?

The Priest's teenage choir sang as they walked behind, or jogged ahead of the Kombi when it got waylaid by a trough of sand. They were, it seemed to Cat, again adapting familiar hymns to martial rhythms.

João often zipped on past the Kombi to the very head of the convoy, doing wheelies as he went, just another thuggish young guy as he now seemed to Cat. He had plenty of meat on him, but mostly they were scrawny, these kids.

Scabbed faces, ragged uniforms, no uniforms, reed-like arms, bowed legs; already Cat, who kept looking back, had seen one or two who looked fit to drop in the heat. A cloud of flies hovered over those marching behind, feeding on their sweat, moving in vortices from one body to the next. Part of her was disgusted that she had aligned herself with all this. Almost on a whim, it now seemed.

And yet here she was, on her way at last to Kunene, where the aquifer might be, and her mother also. All those things that had proved so difficult in Dekmantel now seemed possible.

She looked across at Nadine, tried to get her attention, but the young woman's face was hardly visible in the hoodie. How could she keep that garment on when it was so sweltering in the Kombi?

Up front, the Priest was turning the wheel to avoid sand holes. Despite his boniness of aspect he was a strong, handsome-looking man. But when she caught his eye in the rear-view mirror, behind his black plastic spectacles, it seemed to her that there was something broken in him, something wounded.

'Why in the name of God do you keep looking at me?' he eventually shouted back to her, over the noise of the engine.

'I don't understand why you have set off without more planning,' said Cat, finally uttering something that had been worrying her.

'What do you mean? How do you know I have no planning? I've been planning something like this for years!'

'Where is everyone going to get food and water? Where is everyone going to sleep?'

'All that is covered,' he replied briskly, as the Kombi made its way up a rock-strewn gully.

'Maybe, but do you really think you can defeat the forces of a mining company?'

'Have you ever witnessed one of these militias sweep down, heavy machine guns blazing from the back of vehicles? It's terrifying, I can tell you that myself.'

Cat looked again at the rabble behind. Ma Shango's Mai-Mai, flaunting their big guns on top of the pickups, and Spinnekop's riders with their rifles, and Zowa's men, some marching in ordered infantry formation amid the turmoil, others in heavy lorries – these did seem like forces to be reckoned with; but most of the rest of the convoy really didn't. Subsistence farmers carrying hoes and machetes, women with infants, some breastfeeding. So many young people: how were they going to fare in battle?

'What about the kids, Priest?' Had to ask that question. 'You know they're going to suffer.'

Outside, many were now walking with hands covering their eyes, or with pieces of rag tied about their faces as protection against the sun and the sand and grit blowing up the gully.

'What do you foreigners know of suffering?'

She did not reply at first. Then said, with sudden emotion: 'I have suffered in my life.' And it was true.

'Oh dear, look at me!' he said sarcastically.

'What?'

The Priest gave a mocking laugh: 'So many like you come here and eventually say something like that. Like you think the desert offers some kind of therapy.'

Across from her, Nadine gave a little smile of sympathy, before beginning to take off her hoodie. At last – Cat herself was already melting.

'That's not what I meant,' she said to the Priest, emboldened by Nadine's small show of support.

'I was just saying that I've some experience of suffering, not on this scale of course but . . .'

'Not on this scale! So many of you visitors don't even see what happens here. You're too focused on yourselves. Why have you even come with us anyway?'

'I want to find my mother.' How pathetic it sounded. 'And also the aquifer, which I think is in Kunene. Both of those.'

'Yes, you told me before, and, just as I said, focused on yourself.'

If he was this dismissive, why had he allowed her to come? His attitude made her angry. 'Why did you take me then?'

'Because it may be true that there's an aquifer near there. It's in the myths of various tribes. And the fact that Scursail has set up its new shop in Kunene probably means it's true, as those miners need water too. So, in answer to your question, I brought you along because what you say might just be correct.'

'OK, but don't start accusing me of being like every foreign person who's ever set foot in Namibia.'

The Priest hit his hand on the steering wheel. 'What do you know? Have you ever been here before?'

'No.'

'Well then.'

A sudden gust of wind sprinkled sand on the windows of the Kombi. Cat turned her face away from the Priest towards Nadine, who to her surprise gave her a grin and a sudden thumbs-up.

As Nadine's coltish legs folded up under her on the banquette, the Priest continued mercilessly: 'We, us Africans, *we* are the ones who have suffered. That is why this crusade is taking place. Once we have taken our revenge, hanging by the noose those who have oppressed us, we will establish a more just society.'

'More just? Using nooses?! That sounds crazy . . .'

He again struck the steering wheel with his palm: 'No, it is the powerful countries of the world who are crazy. Crazy because they put men on the moon before curing malaria, or getting fresh water into every home. Crazy because they make guns, not things that truly help humanity. Foreigners come here to replace what they have wasted at home. Worse, when you get here you expect us all to act as if we were all, fuck, back in the 1890s. Or 1970s or eighties or nineties. It's always the same thing!'

'I'm sorry, I don't understand.'

'Of course you don't. I mean the thing called racism, the thing called colonialism, the thing called neo-colonialism.'

'Those are all different things.'

'You can quibble about the curtains, but it's still the same house.'

'I came here only as a scientist,' said Cat, knowing it wasn't fully true. She sighed inside, fearing the Priest was going to carry on raining guilt on her as if she were the token representative of every white person who'd come to Africa since whenever. Or in her case white-adjacent, something he had not seemed to have registered, which was a little blessing in the midst of troubles. Even if the blessing brought trouble of its own (there it was, the pool of her mind lapping again), in thinking this way, was she betraying the Chinese part of herself – something the Admiral had intimated during their conversations? That was, maybe, among the many reasons she'd boarded this ship in the first place.

Feeling estranged in so many ways, she looked across at Nadine again. The young woman had by now fallen asleep on the opposite banquette; she was lying on her side, head on her rolled-up hoodie.

The Priest meanwhile continued to speak with some hostility: 'So you characterise yourself as a scientist? Very well, if you like to think so. A scientist in service of the people of Namibia – nice fantasy. But it's my role to serve my people in reality rather than in theory.'

Cat shifted on the banquette, another flash of anger coming: 'Serve them? They'll perish if you make that attack on Scursail. Even before that, Cole and his people could swoop at any point, couldn't they? If you want to serve your people, save the children at least.'

He did not reply, slowing down to negotiate a rut in the sand-filled, dried-out torrent that the Kombi was going through, then stopped to allow the steering wheel, which had been shaking in his hand, to settle. But every time he revved, the whole vehicle vibrated again. Its tyres were spinning in drifts of sand.

A camel loped past with one of Spinnekop's men in the saddle, which was studded with silver tokens. Then came a truckload of Ruga-Ruga with their camouflage uniforms and carbines, their helmets caught in snatches of sunlight as they passed. All of them glanced at the vehicle, looking at the sand-grains spinning from its tyres, which Cat could hear spattering against the wheel-arches.

As the Kombi continued to tread futilely in its sand bed, the Priest shouted, 'My Lord, please!'

Others passed them, including a lone pregnant woman on a donkey. She also turned to look at the Kombi, the navel of her impressively swollen belly standing out like a press-to-open button. A member of the Himba tribe, Cat understood from the Priest when she asked him: 'Almost the last truly semi-nomadic people of my country, and they have suffered very much.'

The woman's hair was braided, and her mostly naked torso glistened red with a mixture of fat and ochre. It made Cat feel even more guilty to gawp at this incarnate example of a small tribal society that modernity had nearly swept away.

At last the wheels of the Kombi hooked into the sand. They began driving, then got stopped once more, causing the Priest to make another plea to his Lord. The pregnant woman's braids and broad face passed by again at eye level, though she did not turn to look in this time, just clutched the reins of the donkey to her bare breast and looked ahead down the riverbed, seemingly unbothered by the grit funnelling up towards her. Her little donkey trod indefatigably onward.

The sight of all this, as the Kombi got going at last, caused Cat to speak out. 'Look, that woman is pregnant. Shouldn't we let her ride in the camper?'

'She has no place in this vehicle. You expect me to let every impoverished person ride in here? Anyway, those Himba see time differently to most people. For them the future is invisible, it's the very river they are walking into, this actual old riverbed we are driving up. For them, projections into the future are senseless; so she will not expect any invitation, will immediately refuse it, even if she could understand what I say. And what would we do with the donkey, anyway?'

'You are pitiless; how do you even know what she feels?'

'I know more than you at least, and I am not pitiless. You, for example, are in here with us, and I didn't have to allow that. I showed pity in that for sure, because of all your mummy talk as much as the slight possibility of your scientific fairy tales being useful to us.' The Priest shoved his spiny shoulders back against the driver's seat, pressing on the steering wheel. 'I am *not* pitiless.'

'Coldly pragmatic, then?' She pressed on despite herself, while feeling fairly culpable about the mummy stuff.

'No, it is simply that I have learned to be strong. I do this so we can take back what was ours in older times. There was a shape to how things were then; not blessedly peaceful, I don't mean that at all, but there was a common logic, which the power of colonialism severed, detaching communities and individuals from a wider whole.'

'You can't seriously believe that golden-age crap? There's always been separation, and there's always been power of one type or another.' For it did seem to Cat that he was seeing the past too rosily, as if all those centuries behind had been a fruitful land where everyone was happy.

'Why shouldn't I believe in something?' he said contemptuously. 'We Africans can match ourselves against anyone in the world, we showed it before in what you dismissively call a golden age and, believe me, we will show it again in the future.' He flicked his long fingers back at the convoy behind them. 'And that, that's what all this is about.'

Cat's eyes were itching, streaming with sweat yet perversely gritty and dry. 'It's insanity, driving yourself on, driving all of them on, to risk death. Just for an idea of attacking a mining company!'

'Losing your nerve?' he challenged. 'You did not have to come.'

'Crazy, like I say.'

'What you call crazy, I call sanity.' He turned and looked at her derisively.

Disturbed, she dug about in her rucksack until she found the right map. She spread it out on her knees like a napkin.

'What's our route, anyhow?'

'We are heading to the coast, so we can use the desalination units, then we'll head inland to the Scursail HQ.' He raised his chin as he spoke, twisting his head back to her, as if simultaneously trying to engage with her and remain aloof.

One of the camper's wheels hit a rock and the vehicle jolted; turning backwards again, Cat watched a group of children lathered in dust, their mouths open, shouting something; glancing forward once more, she saw the Priest's face in the rear-view mirror, thin lips pursed.

And so in this stop-start manner they continued, jouncing across the riverbed.

Nadine, still curled up on the back seat, had begun to snore gently. How could she sleep, what with the roaring engine and the endless bouncing on dried-out ridges of sand?

Cat tried to sleep too, resting her head on a softish piece of upholstery on the sliding door next to her, but got nowhere.

Behind the Kombi the children and others marched on, and soon the going became harder in the rocky watercourse for both humans and vehicles. The camper van, getting stuck once more, was again overtaken by some of Spinnekop's men on their swift camels and rangy horses. Zowa's Ruga-Ruga, further behind in heavy trucks, had got bogged down too and had to be shoved out by one of the earthmovers.

The Kombi found its groove again, went on over the sandy tracts, its changing gears sounding like change itself in Cat's ears.

Through it all, Ma Shango's militia pushed on heedless, she on her quad bike like a black Boudica, passing in front of the Kombi, her Mai-Mai following in their grey pickups or at a jog trot, which seemed to Cat impossible to maintain.

But they did, sometimes shoving the exhausted, shuffling children roughly aside. Cat was bewildered by the unneeded violence in Shango's men, and when she saw these children stumble and fall she again felt angry with the Priest, who would not stop and let her out to attend to them. She said to him: 'They will collapse, those kids, if you let this go on much longer.'

She wasn't at all prepared for the Priest's reply. 'What if I cannot stop them dying? Have you thought of that? Of course I do not want them to die. But all I know is that we must keep on at as quick a pace as we can to the coast. Otherwise we will all die from thirst.'

Why had she let herself in for this, Mam or not, aquifer or not? 'What makes you think it will be better at the coast?'

'We can desalinate seawater there, like I told you.'

'I just hope you know what you're doing, that's all.'

'No, not completely.'

'What do you mean?'

'You are so wrong about many things but not about the risk of contending with Scursail. I am worried, it's true, that somewhere on our route we will be attacked.'

'So why on earth, knowing that, did you start all this?' she asked in a louder voice than she intended – which woke Nadine.

'What else were we going to do?' the Priest said as Nadine rubbed her eyes.

'You could negotiate.'

'We have tried that before. It never works.'

'When we get to Kunene, maybe you should try it again.'

'Maybe. But here in the remote desert what opponents could do is different to what they might do in your own country. I've never been there, but in Ireland I suspect enemies will pretend to behave themselves; here they will not hesitate to kill, especially if the body can be hidden in sand.'

'There have been plenty of killings in Ireland, don't have any illusions about that. Plenty of secret burials too.' Some possibly on the farm itself, if there was anything in the stories that Uncle Tony had haltingly advanced, speaking of their distant ancestor, the IRA doctor who fled to England, having had to dispose of too many bodies. Not to mention the famine, which, some seventy years earlier, had caused other bodies to be buried in the very same fields.

All of them a long way gone, decomposed in soil where roots grew and rhizomes proliferated, fed by the oozing trickle of the Well Field spring.

'What're you talking about?' yawned Nadine. 'I thought Ireland was a pretty place, that's what *Dona* Catherine always said.'

Feeling a pang, while also slightly amused that her mother had characterised Ireland in this way, Cat began telling Nadine something of the country's tortuous history, at the same time trying to keep her real identity secret.

After a while she finished – as if that story of Ireland could ever be closed like an eye, or come right with the click of numbers in Shut-the-Box. The Kombi carried on, the Priest saying nothing at all in response to Cat's tale, her counting his silence as a small win.

They carried on, passing places where the desert stretched as far as the eye could see, other places where the spikes of thorn trees punctuated the landscape. Whether flat or spiky, this relentless world was creating in Cat a melancholy feeling that she was wanting, that she had not succeeded in answering something.

Didn't you hear me calling?

Her itchy eyes filled with tears, and she was so glad when that first day of travel finally ended and the convoy made camp.

20

Second day

Soon after dawn they entered the deep inner desert, a great sea of sand. The speed of the convoy now slowed further. Tyres, hooves and feet passed in the heat over towering dunes. The only sounds were the growl of engines (oddly muted – an effect of the sand), the coughing snort of camels and the slap of carbines and machetes on thighs. The ammunition boxes, the sacks of food, even the plastic tubs of water became too hot to touch. Cat noticed that anyone lying on the backs of the trucks, where all this material was piled up, now and then needed to leap off and join the walkers.

The sweat between her thighs and trousers and the seat of the vehicle was now as slick as one of the salt licks that Uncle Tony used to hang on posts for cattle, to give them essential nutrients and encourage them to drink at water troughs. 'Thirst therapy,' he'd once called it, echoing one of the signs behind the bar at Mullarkey's. Shifting about, she kept checking her maps, making sure they were going in the right direction, but it was hard to be sure of anything.

Now and then they reached a clump of strange, primeval-looking desert trees. In the little islands of shade provided by the thin canopies above these gnarled trunks, groups of resting marchers congregated. All hope, all desire, even the thought of the next imminent action, the next merest footstep, seemed smothered by the savage power of the sun. The bonnets of the vehicles ticked with heat, the horses' hides quivered to shrug off the flies, and the camels lay their long necks on the ground, arranging their heavy heads like pieces of machinery awaiting repair.

'You must eat,' said Nadine to Cat as they sat under a tree during one of these rest stops. She held out a gunny sack, her slim fingers gripping the hessian edge, which was the same browny-black as her ringleted hair.

Cat reached into the sack and pulled out a strip of dried meat. It was like eating leather, she thought as she began to chew on it.

'How're you doing, Nadine?' she asked, as cheerily as she could manage.

'I'm OK,' Nadine replied, getting onto her haunches. João, who was sitting under another tree nearby, chose that moment to call out something to Nadine in Portuguese.

'He seems to have taken a liking to you.'

'Eeesh, that one wants sex too much. But look!'

Cat followed the direction of Nadine's pointing finger. Ma Shango: sitting astride her quad bike, yelling at some of her soldiers, her topknot shaking in a frenzy of command. Amid all the torpor, she was the exception.

'What's she shouting at them for?' Cat asked.

'Don't know.'

Ma Shango continued her angry enquiry. Back up by the Kombi, his arms folded, the Priest was also aware of this disturbance. Suddenly Ma gunned up her bike and sped towards him. Nadine rose from her haunches, a piece of the dried meat in her hand.

She and Cat watched Ma Shango say something to the Priest. He shrugged. With a swagger, she walked back to her bike.

'What did Ma Shango say to you?' Cat asked the Priest later, climbing back into the van.

'She wants to be in front,' he replied sardonically. 'She wishes to take a turn as convoy leader.'

'You did not object?'

'With her, I must be careful. She makes her own way. And anyway, others have been sometimes overtaking us as it is. So I have agreed to rotate the order in which we travel.'

The convoy got under way again, first with Ma Shango on her quad bike, then Spinnekop's men, remounting camels and horses and sweeping forward in a cavalry-like line, pressing into the burning, sand-filled wind. And then came the rest: the supply trucks, the diesel tanker and the Kombi, humbled, no longer in the vanguard, followed by Zowa the Brave and his Ruga-Ruga, orange earthmovers with scoop loaders, lumbering yellow dumper trucks and the crowd of migrating people, these trudging men, women and children, all linked by necessity to an uncertain fate.

But why am I tying myself to this group of people I don't know? Cat knew even as the thought seeped into her head that the answer was to get nearer to the aquifer and (possibly) her mother, and that any further hand-wringing was pointless.

She decided that once they got to Kunene, before any fighting began, she would give the Priest an ultimatum: either he follow her plan in finding water or she'd strike out on her own. It was time to be more like Ma Shango – making her own way.

Later that morning Cat asked the Priest, 'What's she like, Ma Shango? She seems pretty scary.'

'Yes! But people do not follow her because of that.'

'I don't understand.'

'People follow her because she solves problems so impressively. And maybe because she's actually more full of joy than at first appears, once you understand her point of view. She shares that joy, and that way of just getting on with things, with her followers.'

'I haven't seen anything like joy.'

'Yes, but you maybe will. Even though I've had many personal disagreements with her, I will honestly tell you that I wish I could be more like her myself. And have seen what she has seen. She's been all over the world, that woman. She used to be a sailor before things blew up for her. In the Nigerian Navy.'

'Really?'

'A gunner. Her real name is Mary Oduduwa; my understanding is that she was born in Fada, which is a city in central Nigeria. Not exactly oceanside.'

'When did she come here?' Cat asked, finding it weird that her false first name was the one Ma Shango had abandoned.

Nadine obviously reckoned so too, piping up to say: 'Two Marys, like in the Bible.'

The Priest huffed, as if what Nadine had said was impious, then turned the steering wheel of the Kombi to avoid a pile of burnt logs that lay in the middle of the track. 'Stupid place to light a fire! I don't know when exactly she came to these parts. Or how. I guess jumping ship in Matadi or Lobito, or in Walvis. Once, long ago, Walvis was the best-ordered, most peaceful port in Africa, not like those others. Strange how things go.'

'Strange? It's tragic.'

'Yes. It has often happened here.'

'What has?' Cat asked.

'Tragedy. Look at the Hereros, one of our tribes – almost annihilated by the Germans. Those devils, let me tell you, were rehearsing what they'd later do to Jews. And the whole time they thought they were doing good! The work of so-called civilisation. So when foreigners come here with all that in mind, we Africans have to remain sceptical.'

'You blame the colonial empires for all those tragedies?'

'Such a boring topic,' he replied. 'One, if you don't mind me saying, that Europeans often advance as a bogus excuse for historical abuses, folding it into criticism of more recent regimes here. As a matter of fact, I agree with many of those criticisms – that's why we're here, where we're at, isn't it? – but you always need to look at who's making them, and why.'

'You had your own empires,' Cat said, conscious of a sulky tone entering her voice.

'Yes, some of them massive, way back when Britain was just a shitty little island off the coast of Europe.'

She'd had enough of being lumped in with someone else's blame: 'I'm Irish, remember that.' As she spoke, the two sides of her identity erupted into conflict again. Admiral Yu, for one, had clearly thought of her as Chinese, not Irish. Once more it flowed – the thought that this was another reason 'why we're here, where we're at', as the Priest had put it.

'Same difference, in this case,' he said now.

'Not at all.'

'If you say so. But there were plenty of imperial soldiers in the past who were Irish. Like Lord Kitchener; he was Irish, wasn't he? Conquered Sudan and active in the Boer War just next door, here too actually; in fact, active in every British war till his ship got sunk in the First World War.'

'Priest, I don't want to argue with you, but I know all about Kitchener. Yes, he was born in Ireland – in fact, just a few miles from where I myself was born. But he wasn't really Irish, his family were English landlords.' She suddenly remembered something from a history class. 'About which he once said, "A man may be born in a stable, but that does not make him a horse."'

The Priest laughed at this, Nadine too. Cat suddenly felt slightly ashamed, because similar or in fact inverted types of the same argument were being used on social media, about Irish-born children of immigrants, by those of nativist sentiment. So weird, those people, emoting together online but never thinking of the whole; and what would they emote about me, if they ever found me out? Go back to where you came from, we're readied up for violence, go rank for it tomorrow. All that, as if real life were endless generations of *Assassin's Creed*. Again Cat found herself wondering about her own mixed ancestry.

Apart from Glen Cole, who perhaps had an eye for these things, no one here had commented on her slightly Asiatic looks – maybe because the whole place was something of an ethnic hotchpotch. That being so, what value did the Priest's comments about foreigners really hold?

'That's funny, I grant you,' he continued, oblivious of her thoughts. 'But you can't discount the effect of the Irish in the British Empire or what came with it, at the time and after too. What about all those Irish priests who were here? I myself was taught by one.'

They were now passing over a section of stony track in which the pebbles had weirdly lined up in different colours – grey and pink and white and brown. Almost like the beads of an abacus;

perhaps something to do with the effect of wind on pebbles of different mass.

'That's true,' Nadine said, nodding at the Priest's admission and looking at Cat as she spoke. 'Mary, Father O'Rourke was a famous man in Dekmantel. They say he was a good man.'

'Agreed, and not an imperialist,' the Priest said. 'Almost like you said, quite the contrary. But he was part of it, even if he came here long after colonialism and even if I owe him so much. The fact remains: a lot of problems here, and elsewhere on this continent, happened because colonial forces suddenly jumped at us, biting from outside, changing whole cultures in ways from which we're still recovering.'

'Maybe,' Cat replied, 'but it seems to me you're just describing what happens globally now . . . different forms of power squashing down those without it.'

'Obviously. Look, all I'm saying is, don't come here with your quick fixes, your old-fashioned do-good ideas born of the milk of human kindness. Please – not after all that history.'

Abashed at this latest ticking off, Cat tried to put into words whatever was left of her self-respect. 'OK, but it's still true that what's often happened here is now happening everywhere. We're all in a race for the last reserves, Priest.'

He turned back to her, one hand on the wheel, eyes burning. 'You are so wrong, if you don't mind me saying. Most of you people in Europe, and the US too, live in relative luxury, compared to many of us. Yes, there are now bigger middle classes in some countries on this continent, but that's still quite a small proportion of broader African populations that are growing super-fast. This whole place is bursting its sides with young people like Nadine beside you, right, Nadine?'

'Yes, Priest,' Nadine intoned obediently as the Priest's eyes returned to the track in front. But his voice kept going on, its accusatory tone grinding at Cat as if in unison with the tyres of the Kombi as they crunched over pebbles.

'Far more young people than its various nation states can manage; where you're from, Europe – it's still wealthy but old: massive elderly population! And mainly white, despite immigration.'

'You say white, but race has less and less to do with it any more – in my view, it's all become economic.'

He let out an explosion of breath. 'I'm sorry but it's just impertinent, the way you speak.'

She finally shut up then, wondering how and where she'd gone so wrong.

At the next stop, nominally for lunch on this second day of travel, there were no trees. Members of the convoy consumed their meagre provisions on a pan of glittering mica, with the sand from high dunes on either side sliding down towards them. It made a hissing noise as it rolled: the accumulated sound of each grain dragging its neighbour.

There was shouting as people jostled to get in a queue for the contents of the blue-plastic water barrels being unloaded from trucks. Cat, the Priest and Nadine went over to wait their turn, Cat getting thirstier by the second.

As the water was being dispensed, a fight broke out. It was between one of Ma Shango's men and a Ruga-Ruga, a dispute over their place in the queue. The Ma's man had stepped out of line and been slashed by a Ruga-Ruga machete. The owner of this weapon was kneeling in his khakis by the body of the man he'd just cut, watching in stupefied horror the effects of his own handiwork.

Between people's legs, on a pile of shiny mica, Cat caught a glimpse of something grey – tumbled down like a heap of shabby clothes, fallen to the floor.

Human guts, Cat realised in horror.

'This is bad,' Nadine murmured.

The Priest strode forward to confront Zowa, the Ruga-Ruga leader, who was stripped to the waist like a prizefighter but still wearing his badged bowler hat: 'You must offer him up – if you do not, the Ma will make war and we will not get to Kunene.'

'We must first investigate the facts of the case,' Zowa said solemnly before taking out a cigar and lighting it.

All this while Ma Shango looked on in silence, more or less

immobile save a ready hand on the pistol in her webbing belt and eyes that seemed to sneer at this proposal of peacemaking between factions. It was as if she was not speaking on purpose, holding back her power.

As she and Nadine reached the front of the water queue, which had otherwise continued in a fairly orderly fashion, Cat was shrivelling beneath the unforgiving sun. Scooping her own tinful of water from the barrel, she feared her legs were buckling and she'd fall onto fragments of rock.

Life-giving liquid slipped down her throat. She shut her ears to the shouting voices. It was as if she were on a wave, or, now she'd drunk at last, a wave was in her, foaming out across the dry beaches of her body, swelling her cells.

The argument between Zowa and the Priest meanwhile went on, mounting to hysteria as flies begin to settle on the guts of the dead Mai-Mai, until in the end, as people continued to wait nervously for their turn at the barrel, another of Ma Shango's men suddenly sprang forward and shot the Ruga-Ruga machete-wielder in the stomach. Ma Shango herself remained still, like a cobra waiting to strike.

Cat felt a lurch of fear and Nadine clearly did too, pulling her by the sleeve of her T-shirt and saying, 'We must move away right now.' They managed to do so a little, but it was hard to push through the hubbub and also to resist the temptation of continuing to watch the outcome of what had just happened.

Zowa, in turn, seemed to accept the killing as fate, but before he turned away from the body of his own man, who had fallen on the other corpse, he raised one finger in front of Ma Shango's face, making a circle.

'What's he mean by that?' Cat whispered to Nadine, as they looked on from the safe-seeming vantage point they'd found.

'That if it happens again there will be a feud,' Nadine replied, 'whatever the merits of her case.'

Rather than responding with violent actions or words, the Ma lifted the palms of her hands to her face, in front of her eyes. It briefly seemed to Cat that the Ma could not take in any more brutality, as if the litany of savage attacks that had maybe comprised her whole life had finally become too much to bear.

But before anyone could react, those hands were down again, and the moment of emotion that had flitted so quickly and unexpectedly into the Ma's face was replaced by the look of a warrior queen. She turned and walked back to her quad bike.

The crowd, too, moved indolently away, except for those who had not yet had their fill at the barrel. Seeing the two bodies on the sand, Cat was about to vomit but she stopped herself, knowing that the water she had just drunk was too precious for that.

Nadine was regarding her intently: 'Are you all right?'

'I'm fine,' Cat gasped as the Priest came to join them, sighing deeply.

His mood seemed to change as the three of them returned to the Kombi. Before they got in he pulled on the sleeve of Cat's T-shirt. 'So . . . I think you're beginning to see the state of things here. You must learn.'

'Learn what?' Cat asked glumly, trying to keep calm as she resumed her seat in the back of the Kombi.

'How we roll here. And how to get back on your own true path, as ordained by God.' He turned to glare at her with deep-set eyes.

'My own true path? Two men died just now while I was waiting for a drink of water. In that context, your path, all that man-of-God stuff, is just dangerous.'

'It is the world that is dangerous, not me. And if I am not mistaken, the true ordeal lies ahead of us.'

Nadine reached across from the other seat and squeezed Cat's hand.

As they continued through this second day, Cat's mood went from bad to worse, rage and anxiety mounting with every passing mile. Now and then other vehicles passed them in one direction or another, mostly trucks taking melons or goats to market, or returning from the same.

When another of these vehicles next passed, going back towards Dekmantel, she briefly thought about asking the Priest to let her get out, hitch a lift. It would be a big volte-face, in spite of her frequent wobbles, but she was tempted . . . But what could she usefully do in going back there, now that nearly everyone had left? Except perhaps help that old man with the blister on his forehead who'd given her directions when she'd first arrived. She'd not seen him among the convoy.

'It's going to get worse, isn't it?' Cat said to the Priest as they bumped along a little later. She buffed the hot plastic of the door handle with the underside of her wrist, trying to burn away the itch of an insect bite.

Looking ahead down the riverbed – up which hot, skin-peeling wind funnelled like the exhaust of a furnace – she listened to his reply, given with a sharp turn of his scrawny neck.

'Of course. But remember that these people out there are tougher than you, braver than you, prouder than you. I take my cue from them: it makes me stronger.'

'That's where you draw your resilience from, the power of others? It makes you sound like a vampire.'

'Very funny. I mean, of course, by their example. And look, if you really want to talk about this, you're going to have to come and sit up front, because it hurts my neck to keep turning back to speak with you. I need to keep my eyes on the road.'

'Hardly a road.' She wanted to ask him to drop her off, leave her to her own devices, but that would be suicide.

The Priest sighed again. 'Come up front.'

'I want to stay with Nadine.'

'It's OK,' said the young woman. 'I need to sleep anyway.'

Cat clambered through the gap to join the Priest in the front. For a while neither of them spoke.

Looking out of the window, Cat several times spotted João, following the Kombi slowly on his motorbike like a dutiful dog, now and then veering near to the windowpane on which Nadine's by-now-sleeping head was resting.

Eventually, when he had done this many times, the Priest brought the Kombi to an abrupt stop. Got out, slammed the door and shouted: 'João, rejoin the ranks!'

'I just wanted to check she's . . .'

'Rejoin the ranks!'

★

At a later stop, where there was more queueing for water from the blue-plastic barrels but thankfully no more violence, Cat was shocked by the exhaustion that so many people were showing, especially those who were younger. Waiting for water, the teenagers and kids moved very slowly now, some with bloodied feet.

She drew the Priest's attention to this and he nodded. His solution was merely to get Nadine, still fairly groggy from her sleep, to go out among all those kids with that stupid wrench and speak to them with encouraging words.

'How's that meant to help?' Cat asked.

All he did by way of reply was give her a grim, needs-must sort of smile, as if she simply didn't understand that a larger cause was in play and that there might, alas, be casualties even among this cohort of youngsters.

It was true. She didn't understand. In fact, she was horrified by how he was able so easily to sacrifice individuals to a larger cause. Yet what was she doing about any of it – either as her prospective best self or the ordinary one that still seemed to be very much with her?

That night, after yet more hours in the Kombi, they camped at a cluster of meagre palms that hardly deserved the name oasis. As food was prepared, Cat helped some of the youngest children, walking with Nadine among the fires and oil lamps, bandaging feet, dispensing scoops of gritty water from a bucket with a mess tin, putting ointment on bites and cuts.

Despite this, her feeling of not being able to do enough persisted. Watching kids claw for water and food – awful. There were just too many of them, and suddenly she found herself alone in the throng, separated from Nadine. Where was she?

The children pressed around her, grabbing at her dusty clothes with sticky hands. Her own uselessness . . . so strong a sense of it that in the end she ran away from all those pawing kids, hating the feeling of being exactly the person – a weak foreign person – that the Priest had implied she was.

The desert air dried out her lungs as she ran, beating the air with frantic arms, his words coming back to her: *tougher than you, braver than you, prouder than you* . . .

She stumbled through the galaxy of campfires back to the Kombi, and the protection of the Priest, who was sitting by a little bonfire on a collapsible stool.

Collapsed enough herself, she tried to hide her panic and confusion, but she was trembling like a pursued animal and instinctively moved closer to the small fire he had built, the logs in it set out like the points of the compass.

'All well?' he asked, looking at her with a raised eyebrow.

She nodded, holding her breath to control it. He gestured for her to sit down at one of the open doors of the Kombi.

'Have you seen Nadine?' she asked, wanting that female friendship.

He shook his head: 'Thought she was with you. Have some food.'

He gave her a bowl of greasy stew made from goat meat, along with a portion of maize porridge. It was hard to eat in near-darkness. She watched the Priest's hand moving from bowl to mouth.

Someone let off a flare and the Priest said, 'Well!'

In the explosion of light they spotted João and Nadine seated on a nearby dune. Nadine was squirming in João's lap. As the flare died she heard a squeal of girlish laughter.

'Young love,' commented the Priest, sprinkling rough salt onto his meat.

'I hope he's not making her do anything she doesn't want to. He's a bit older than her, I think.'

'Here, things that way are maybe different than in your own country. And anyway, it looks as if she likes him.'

Cat sat still, digesting the goat stew, watching dry wood burn in the fire.

'Try this,' the Priest said once they had eaten the meat. He handed her a small wooden tumbler. She took a sip of its contents, almost gagging immediately.

'What is it?'

'Camel milk. You should drink it – very healthy.'

She forced it down. Slightly warm, it tasted mouldy. A bit like newly drawn milk from cows – which she'd never liked anyway – but kind of gamier, smokier, and with a urinous tinge.

'Good?'

'No. Disgusting – sorry.'

Yawning, the Priest stretched out his long legs.

'Well, now we must sleep,' he announced.

So there they lay, the Priest and Cat, outside on blankets on either side of the Kombi. The vehicle was still radiating heat, like a ring on the hob after cooking . . .

Cold now – impossible that all that heat had dissipated – and she was shivering so much. It was not yet morning, still dark. Trying to find her torch in the middle of the night. In or at the edges of sleep, she became aware of human cries among the rumbling groans of the camels.

She sat up, flicking the torch around. But all she could see, beyond the dying glow of the fires, were the shadows of militiamen moving like hyenas between the corrugated trunks of palm trees.

Go back to sleep, she told herself. She tried to yoke the rhythm of her breathing to that of the Priest on the other side of the Kombi.

It was hard to sleep with the cold, though. Again she was tempted to call someone, go home, back to safety. *How can I do it, though?* She'd looked at her phone a few times along the way. There was very little signal in the desert. But she kept on thinking she should call the Admiral, ask for her help, or ask that pilot, Sean Morrow, to fly in and collect her. She felt almost shocked how abruptly she could keep changing her mind like this, resolution and hopelessness flowing backwards and forwards. All just happening in the head, or wherever else in the body the mind was; and sometimes that, too, seemed to change, moving through her body – now viscously, like the slime in the Well Field, now jumping like the leg of a galvanised frog on the scarred work-bench of a biology class.

On the journey to Kunene this far, the Priest had shown signs of not liking her charging her phone in the cigarette socket of the Kombi, even though he had plugged in his own. He'd told her he wanted to make sure the battery of the vehicle was always fully charged. She knew this was bullshit, as the drain from a phone was tiny if the alternator was going and they were driving.

When she'd challenged him he'd said: 'Yes, that might be so, but obviously the last thing we all need is you calling someone who might bring us trouble. You know how tech is these days, everything monitored, yes?'

True enough, but there was something lurking within her own will that had so far stopped her from texting or ringing anyone. The dual lures of adventure and that elusive best self, maybe, both still calling her on . . .

21

Third day

To begin with, the next morning, Cat couldn't compute it when – trying to find somewhere private to pee – she saw an injured girl, lying in a hollow of sand, blood near her waist. Her thigh had been cut. She immediately called out for help.

After she'd shouted a while, an older woman from the convoy appeared, one of the matronly ones she'd seen when they first set off, whose name was Helena. As they carried the girl back to the camp, Helena told Cat that other young girls were stumbling around saying they had been attacked, each cut in the same way. 'They came in the night and dragged the girls into the desert. They pulled off their clothes, then held them down, and took their turn on them. Then cut them, and left them.'

Cat started worrying about Nadine. Not one of the girls, Helena said, had so far dared point out which of the blank-faced men in forage caps had done it.

Leaving the girl in Helena's care, Cat at once went back to the Kombi, looking for Nadine, asking everywhere, but she was nowhere to be found; the Priest didn't seem to have a clue about what might have happened.

Shaking with moral horror, Cat screamed at him, pointing a finger in his face: 'Where's Nadine? Girls have been raped. Is this your plan? Is this your great war of liberation?'

Gently pushing away her finger, he replied in a voice of iron: 'We will find Nadine. You need to understand that many of the militias here rape. They do it to show their strength, and the cutting of the thigh is often left as a mark of that strength. But not my boys, they don't do it.'

'We must find Nadine. And the people who did it – punish them.'

'I think you should talk to the Ma. Her men are the most dangerous. I myself will look for Nadine.'

Cat went off at once to find Ma Shango, who resided in a large tent. Pushing past two guards, she found the Mai-Mai leader lying propped up on one elbow on an army camp bed, wearing her camouflage jacket, but no trousers, her machete at her feet. She was scooping rice pudding into her mouth from a tin.

'Your men, I believe they may have raped some girls,' Cat said as steadily as she could. 'There's one who is missing, Nadine – my friend – she was the one with the wrench.'

Ma Shango moved slightly, shaking the tangle of charms which hung round her neck. The tent flap lifted. One of her men came in, carrying a machete like the Ma's own. He gestured at Cat with it. Ma Shango hissed at him and he scuttled out.

'Rape! Your men have been raping,' Cat persisted, her voice beginning to gallop.

'Sister, no rush abeg,' Ma Shango said, hauling herself upright on the bed. 'Talk normal, we dey hear.' She put the tin on the floor, reaching down between her thighs, and slowly pulled on a rumpled pair of trousers.

'It's important, what I'm saying,' Cat replied, having taken a few seconds to interpret Ma Shango's words. But she didn't get any further response for almost another minute, standing there in stiff frustration.

Once the trousers were on, the Ma tapped her temple. 'Think well before you talk am. Calm down, make you no go bite your tongue.'

'I don't want to calm down,' Cat almost spat.

'Well remember, dis no be your domain.'

'We found a girl injured this morning, and then five others appeared who said they had been molested and marked in the same way. Those are the facts.'

'Me myself, men dem done rape me *tired!*' said Ma Shango,

breathing a little heavily. 'You no suppose tell me how men bad and rotten? I sabi so well. You speak like I never hear or see dese tings for my whole life? Eh!'

As Cat tried to get what she was saying – did *sabi* mean know? – Ma Shango let out a disdainful explosion. 'Dem type men go like make their prick our king. If I fit, I go stop am.'

Next she looked down, tapped her large bosom as if disappointed. 'But I don even get small success for myself in dat project, eh heh?'

'Whose men did it?' Cat asked, still struggling to understand, thinking of how foreign visitors to the farm sometimes had trouble with her uncle's way of speaking.

'E fit be any.'

'Yours?'

'Even. Dat possible.'

'And what will you do about it? You seem the most powerful leader around these parts and leaders should implement justice, shouldn't they?'

Ma Shango shrugged. 'Important questions you ask but not one for hia-time, not one for now-time. Wata dey important ting, or plenty plenty people fit die.'

'Wata?' queried Cat.

'War-ter,' replied the Ma, as if mocking Cat's own speech, before switching immediately back into dialect as claggy as Uncle Tony's. 'But I go shook eye into dis mata, me promise you.'

'These men have destroyed the lives of young girls. You must find those responsible.'

The Ma lay back on the little bed. 'When your mouth only talk, is rubbish-rubbish till you act. If you no get mind for doings, just fashi.'

Cat was confused again: 'What's . . . *fashi?*'

'Never mind. Words before action no be real!'

'Rape is real.'

'I tell you already, I go put my eyes into it.'

'That's all you've got to say?'

Ma Shango nodded ponderously. 'For now. I go probe, like

I say. If true men dey attack small girls, I promise catch dem, punish well-well.'

Cat stormed out of the tent and went straight to Zowa the Brave and Sol Spinnekop, but her pleas proved equally fruitless. Neither of them knew anything about Nadine, and both seemed bad-tempered, for it was now fantastically hot.

Walking back through the camp, with the gaze of so many people upon her, she told herself she'd been naive. Conscious of what sounded like shouts, maybe jeers, and sweating heavily, she passed among crowds of people, sitting, eating, smoking, standing about, sunlight glinting on weapons being greased and cooking pots cleaned . . . as if her illusions, too, were being scraped off. Enough was enough, despite all the effort she'd invested in them, those illusions. She'd ask the Priest if he'd drop her off somewhere, the nearest town. Anywhere but here.

Getting back to the Kombi, she spotted João in a group of people next to the vehicle. His head was wrapped in his muscled arms, as if he could not bear to see any of the world, and he was rocking to and fro on his haunches. The Priest was there too, bent over. Something on the sand beneath him. Moving and alive. On all fours, trying to stand up.

Cat ran over fast, as if there was nothing else that mattered: no sun, no sand, no earth. It was as if those larger systems could only be apprehended from within, from where she was, *in the hia-place, in the now-place*, as the Ma had put it.

Nothing but whatever she was trying to understand, there at the feet of the Priest as she approached, who, straightening up his own long, cane-like body, said bluntly, as if his gift for eloquence had finally been defeated by events: 'I found her in the desert, about two hundred metres from the camp.'

Nadine's hands and knees were on the sand, her head bent down over a pile of flinty stones, her legs bent too, a little blood oozing from a cut on her thigh. She was still alive but weak, on the cusp of consciousness.

Silently, Cat and the Priest carried her to the open doors of the van. Clearing a place on the floor, they laid out a blanket and put her on it, at which point Nadine lost consciousness altogether.

The Priest fetched a bowl of water and Cat cleaned and staunched the wound on Nadine's thigh.

'We need medicine,' she said eventually, so cross with herself that she'd been running about the camp, thinking of justice, when she should have been here. 'That cut could become infected.'

The Priest shook his head sadly. 'Most likely, I would say.' He went to the front of the van and rummaged in the glove compartment. 'Penicillin powder, but not much I am afraid. And bandages.'

She shook some of the powder onto the wound and bandaged it. As she was doing so, João leaped up and made a lunge for the Priest's long rifle, which was leaning against the side of the van.

'I will kill those who did this!' he shouted. 'All of them!'

The Priest reacted with great speed, seizing the barrel of the rifle and pointing it at the ground, at the same time wresting João's head under his arm and squeezing his neck until the young Angolan, spluttering for breath, went limp in his arms.

Ignoring them, Cat encouraged Nadine, who had now reawakened but was still more or less senseless, to sip a little of the precious water.

Cat kept her eyes focused on the young girl's bruised face.

'Poor love. Here.'

Beginning to come round more, Nadine started moaning gently. She kept touching her forehead with the flat of her hand.

The Priest came over to Nadine – reached across the floor of the van – held her arm.

'Do you know who did this to you?'

She shrank from his hand, calling out something in her own language.

'Leave her,' Cat said, pushing him away.

'She knows,' muttered João. 'She must know.' He had got to his feet and was leaning against the door of the van, rubbing his neck. 'But she won't say.'

'What about you?' the Priest said, looking at him. 'You were with her.'

'I was asleep,' João replied sheepishly. 'I had drunk too much spirit. Before that, we were together.' His head fell.

The Priest touched Nadine's arm again, making her jump.

'Leave her!' This time Cat shouted. 'She needs to rest now.'

Later Cat went to seek out Helena, who was tending to the other girls who had been attacked, each with a mark of shame cut into her thigh.

Don't touch me, their stunned, wordless bodies said to her as she helped Helena and other older women wash them, *I am glass*.

These other women, all from a variety of tribes and backgrounds, seemed to Cat to accept her help, even though they had no previous relationship with her, the stranger. It was as if being female, like the victims, was enough to transcend differences, despite the self-consciousness Cat felt. It gave her hope that people of various backgrounds could in fact come together and do heaven's work; even though this situation was, frankly, as grim as hell.

And as hot, for all the time she'd been washing those injured bodies, sweat had been dripping off her forehead onto them.

22

Feathers wafting backwards

The rest of that third day passed awfully: Cat sitting by Nadine on the sweaty back seats of the Kombi, mopping her feverish brow, swabbing her wound, cleaning and re-dressing it, clearing away yellow pus when it broke open, which happened frequently as the van slithered over dunes. She fed her with a spoon and – now simply barging her way through the queues during stops to get it – gave her drinks of water, sometimes heating it and mixing it with honey, which Helena and the other matrons had collected from desert trees.

The Priest, meanwhile, had begun worrying about how much time this journey to Kunene was taking. The longer they were travelling, he said, the more likely it was that one authority or another would spot them, either from the air or by report from one of the trucks that occasionally passed them.

Cat herself was worried too, but for different reasons. Her resolution to leave the convoy as soon as possible had ebbed because she perceived an even deeper duty to stay and help Nadine and the other young women who'd been abused. It now seemed as light as feathers, the way that *I want to go back home* voice had sounded so heavily in her head before. Feathers wafting backwards from the fading bird of thought.

Anyway, there was no phone signal at all now. Insofar as she was able to examine her motives and plans properly at all, she began trying to align better her own search for her mother and the aquifer with what was needed now on the convoy.

When Nadine cried out incoherently Cat jumped up and

comforted her, dabbing her face where it was running with sweat and holding her thin body as it trembled.

Mostly Nadine remained silent. But slowly, falteringly, words came. Huddled up on the banquette, hesitant as Cat herself, about to plunge into the waves at Banna or Ballybunion. But this was something so much more, different in scale and type.

Nadine eventually whispered: 'They pulled me so hard, ripped my knickers . . . put hard fingers inside me – their nails cut. And then their cocks.'

'How many times?'

'*Dona*, I don't even know, I'm so smashed up. I'm afraid of STDs, Aids.'

Cat held her hand, said, 'I know,' even though she didn't, feeling more useless than ever.

It was hard to get her to eat or even drink. It hurt to pee, she told Cat; on stops she staggered if she stood, hobbled if she walked; back in the camper van all she wanted was to sleep, and found difficulty even in that. Now and then Nadine mentioned João, but he'd disappeared, his FedEx helmet no longer rearing up by the Kombi.

As Cat nursed the young woman the convoy simply continued on, ratcheted in the mechanism of its journey, almost as if the rapes had not happened. The Priest drove, the militias bickered and fought, the children seemed more distressed with every mile. The girls who'd been raped did not appear to have been disturbed again the previous night, but on today's stops they sat with dull, half-closed eyes and drawn cheeks.

The Priest's choir band, who no longer sang, began to mutter curses during these pauses. They, too, were suffering – from coughs brought on by the previous night's fog, from insect bites that refused to heal and might be becoming infected, from stomach aches caused by pieces of camel or goat meat too green to begin with and not, in the end, sufficiently boiled. These problems were adding up for everyone; compounded by general weakness and fatigue, they were beginning to make the bodies of those involved in this popular uprising buckle.

Once or twice, Cat saw the pregnant Himba woman, slumped

over her donkey, and wanted to help her too, but what could she do? Her old life, when she had worried about academic achievement and a neglectful mother, seemed very far away. She felt helpless, exhausted, and something turbulent was happening in her tummy.

In the latter part of this third day, Cat developed diarrhoea. She pleaded with the Priest to stop, then rushed up and down the edge of the column in search of a big enough thorn bush behind which to empty her bowels. There was no real need for modesty, for no one in the long file of people was interested in her now, and plenty of others were in the same condition.

As she tried to wipe after, half tripping on her trousers, thoughts of leaving all these people and going home struck her again. Trudging back to the Kombi, she fretted about cholera but reckoned there just wasn't enough water now for it to spread rapidly: she herself had got used to the sensation of thirst, of her tongue swelling and her throat closing up.

That night a full moon appeared. And so many stars! Nadine was in the Kombi, sleeping peacefully at last, the Priest and Cat outside as before.

Cat herself finally slept, so was really annoyed to be woken by the Priest tugging at her sleeve, well after midnight.

'Come. I need your help.'

'Why – what's happened?'

'It's all right, there's no danger. The Himba woman, the one we saw earlier on the way; she's in labour.'

And so she went out into the night with that curious man, who may not have been pitiless after all but was certainly a mystery. And with him standing by, she knelt on the sand next to the squatting Himba woman, lonely creature that she was, and helped to bring a squalling infant into the world. Not something she knew how to do, but she relied on what she half remembered from helping Uncle Tony birth calves on the farm.

All around, across barren wastes of sand that glowed like paper under the fat moon, going deep into the velvety black night where the stars wheeled on through space, the cry of a baby could be heard, echoing from dune top to dune top in search of an ear to hear it.

Later, rinsing her blood-soaked arms first in sand and then using a bit of soap and precious water, the Priest standing by in silence waiting to do the same, Cat was dangerously excited, as if something had quickened inside her own body too, something that was hard to grasp.

It made her very uncomfortable, this primal excitement, and lying on her sleeping roll next to the Kombi afterwards, with the gleam of the moon still in her eyes and the snorts of camels in her ears, along with the memory of the baby's cry at its first breath (it had now gone quiet), she could not account for the mixture of feelings. There was a sense in which the experience of helping the Himba woman – helping Nadine and helping those other women – justified, or at least allayed, the whole seriously fucked-up business of her being there.

But really? I think I might still want to go home.

Hearing sand move about her in the wind, at first whistling, then booming weirdly, Cat tried to adjust her thoughts. What good had she done, how could she justify herself? She experienced another sudden wish to be back in the university rat race in Dublin, among the gloomy-minded tribe of academics, even if she suspected she'd been wasting her time there. But if buses were burning at home now, and nativist sentiment was on the rise, was that really where she wanted to be?

This mental to and fro, as she tried to edge herself into slumber, was as disturbing as the daytime swaying of the Kombi. Every time she tried to see off something bad in her head something worse said hello; but eventually all these voices gave up on her and sleep came at last.

23

Fourth day

Going the next morning to see what water could be had, Cat discovered a group of militia hammering posts into the sand, securing them with rocks at the base.

'What's going on?' she asked the Priest, who was standing outside sipping tea from a tin cup.

'You seem to have made an impression on Ma Shango. She has found out the names of the rapists and is about to give them treatment.'

He handed her the mug and she took a sip.

'What does "treatment" mean?'

'Punishment routines.'

Cat saw the soldiers affix a lateral piece of wood between two of the posts, nailing it in at each end so that it made a shape like a football goal, but narrower. There were four of these arrangements in all. Extreme unease rippled through her as she began to wonder what might be intended.

A few minutes passed, during which she continued to watch the carpenters at work. She then heard Ma Shango's quad bike, approaching not with its usual roar but with lower revs. Around the Ma moved a large group of people, filling the riverbed with tense disorder, calling, shouting, bustling about. In the midst of this crowd were four men, bare-chested, their arms tied behind their backs; or rather three men aged between thirty and fifty and, at the end of the line, one youth: João.

'Oh no,' said Cat, gasping, going nearer and staring. João lifted his head slightly but refused to meet her gaze.

'I am afraid so,' said the Priest. 'But I think we suspected this, no?'

She nodded. 'I must go to Nadine.'

The girl was on her knees in the Kombi, looking out of a window from which – somewhere in the course of the journey – the pane of glass had fallen out; the rubber seal and bare metal of the window framed Nadine's face.

She was weeping.

Cat climbed in, kneeling alongside her, hooking an arm over her shoulders. Without speaking (for what could be said?), they both looked on in stupefied horror as, one by one, each of the first three captives was raised up and hung by his arms from the posts. All of them struggled but, forced at gunpoint, they had no option but to comply.

The Ma stood by with her lieutenants, making sure the crowd, which closed in every time one of the offenders was hauled up, did not interfere with the procedure.

João was the last to be mounted on the scaffold. Beforehand, Ma Shango dragged him, half on his knees, over to the Kombi and put him in front of Cat and Nadine, still looking on.

The former Nigerian Navy gunner was wearing a white bra under her half-open jacket. 'I see you, Miss,' she said, next looking at Nadine. 'And you, little one which was hurt. This boy did it, na?'

Nadine nodded, tears still rolling down her cheeks as Ma Shango continued.

'Me, I don look on dis mata well-well. As I say I go do. As I don promise you *oyibo*, white woman there, when you take your leg come meet me dat day. We suppose behave, now show you!' She turned to her fellow militia leaders: 'No be so, Zowa?'

'It be so,' said Zowa, taking off his bowler hat and lighting a cigar.

'And when dese men dey rape, omo, from all our units dem come? Sol?'

Spinnekop nodded, making the spider's web across his face flex into a new puzzle, as if he, too, was at first trying to understand what she was saying. Then said himself: '*Ja*, we must all take responsibility.'

'Priest?'

Priest Kwambi, long fingers plucking at his lion-skin kaross, spoke thus: 'We have been living with this disease of rape for too long. I'm sorry, I – I just did not know any of my own team were involved with this, believing their hands better directed by providence than to lay them on young girls. May God forgive me.'

'Priest, abeg take your church talk other place,' declared Ma Shango. 'Dis no be the time for dat sort of yama-yama.'

Producing the blade of her machete, placing the flat of it on the rim of the empty window of the Kombi, she looked directly at Cat. 'May you for know dis, white lady: when you don hear about the raping, and come find me, know I talk am so because I get dat rape first time ever I come inside a navy ship. Officer did it, en get gold braid on shoulder!'

Cat realised then what a personal narrative this was for Ma. She turned and looked at Nadine but the young woman was keeping her head down, unable to look at the beating that Cat thought was about to ensue.

But it wasn't a beating, it was an execution.

Calling out the names of the victims, the Ma began moving along the line of posts, cutting with her machete into the screaming, thrashing men, belly by belly – until she came to João, whose pleading eyes appeared to fix on those of Nadine and Cat, still watching from the empty window of the camper. The Ma's blade seemed to hesitate for a moment before slicing into him like the others, saying Nadine's name as she did so.

Nadine shuddered under Cat's arm. Cradling her, Cat hid the face of the hoarsely sobbing girl in her bosom. Then uselessly asked: 'Are you all right?'

She certainly did not feel all right herself, not having expected this 'trial' and 'punishment' and sickened by the brutality of it. She wanted to scream, outraged not just by what the men had done but also how summarily justice was being meted out. At the same time there was a kind of flatness in her, an awful insulation of rage that was itself perhaps a numbed response to what was happening.

As the internal organs of her successive victims slid onto the sand, Ma Shango began addressing the men she was executing in a jeering tone. 'So you fit feel the pain now, big boys who forgot dey were all women's pikin. You think say you brave but no, you be cowards, nothing more.'

Cat had to look away, and noticed that the Priest was doing the same, cleaning his glasses with the sleeve of his robe. She forced her own eyes back, seeing Spinnekop spit on the sand and Zowa suck contemplatively on his cigar, his face void of expression.

The Ma turned to the crowd. 'Make una all dey take lesson-o. Make una no touch women, special no touch small-small girls. Una dey hear me so?'

Once the howls of the dying men had ceased, after many minutes, there was silence, except for the buzzing of flies. Big, green, iridescent creatures: weary jewels, looking for help from the wind to keep themselves afloat. But there was not a breath of breeze in the dry desert air. As if it were a line of grey thread unspooling down from heaven, the smoke from Zowa's cigar was soaring straight upwards.

24

Fifth day

The next morning was incredibly hot, sweat soaking Cat's clothing almost before she woke, memories of the day before twisting in her mind. Priest Kwambi and the other militia leaders were already holding a conference over breakfast as Cat joined them. Yesterday's horror was still fresh as welling water, pooling in her head, however much she tried to contain it.

'Seventy more clicks to Kunene,' announced Zowa, brandishing a map.

'You're wrong,' countered Spinnekop. 'It's only sixty.'

'Well, make we start, gentlemen, una ready?' said Ma Shango, the tendons of her throat rippling. 'Fighting dey hungry me like food!'

'Plenty of time for that, we must be slim enough now,' said Spinnekop. 'Nearer we get to Kunene, more slim even.'

'We fit start or no fit start, abi?' Ma Shango barked at them. 'My body dey do me fight-fight!'

'Of course,' said the Priest, rolling his eyes at Spinnekop and Zowa. 'But yes, we go.'

And after that the convoy went on, into the incredible heat and shining sand, over a crusted dunescape covered with indecipherable markings, beneath a sky so blue it appeared flayed of clouds.

Frequently there was no track to follow at all, and often the wheels of the vehicles sank axle-deep into the powder-soft sand. Everyone began to feel the intense strain of digging them out under the skin-blistering sun, using shovels and putting wire netting under the wheels.

And then they began again, going onward between the dunes, sending up dust clouds as they rolled along.

Mostly, during this fifth day, Cat sat in the back of the Kombi with Nadine. The wound on her thigh was slowly beginning to heal but she didn't speak much. Eventually, cradling her shoulders, Cat said, 'You can talk about it, Nadine – if you want to.'

Nadine shook her head, then said: 'I just want my mother,' and began to weep. Cat held her tighter, experiencing her own conflicting feelings, and then some guilt because their two situations were not at all commensurate.

The landscape through which they were passing became drier and drier. There was now no more thorn bush and scrub, just petrified rocks and deep-yellow sand. Some of the larger rocks had very odd shapes: chicken drumsticks, a big toe, a teapot. But there was no time for Cat to observe these formations with a scientific eye. There were more pressing things to deal with. The water in the blue barrels was beginning to run out. The Priest had ordered that the allocation be reduced and the pace increased.

At about midday – by which time thirst was making their bodies husk-like, in a process which began with the hair and eyes and lips and fingernails, then slowly crept into the rest of the physique – the buzz of a drone was heard. It flew to and fro over them, as if assessing size and military power.

The Priest stopped driving. Getting out of the Kombi, he studied the drone through binoculars, while up ahead Ma Shango braked suddenly on her quad bike.

'What is it?' asked Cat.

'Surveillance,' replied the Priest. 'Checking up on us. Most likely sent from the Scursail HQ.'

'But why?'

'Isn't it obvious? Because of what happened in Dekmantel. And maybe they have already worked out our plan.'

They heard Ma's voice: 'Suck on dis, Scursail!' She was stood up on the seat, her large body squeezed between the quad bike's roll bars as she levelled her portable Strela missile launcher at the aircraft.

'No, you crazy . . .'

The words spilled out of the Priest's mouth as he ran towards the Ma's bike – but already her missile was arcing up into the sky, making a roaring sound as the Strela's sensors sought out the drone, which quickly started making evasive moves in the sky before disappearing over the horizon.

The missile continued in vain pursuit before running out of propellant and spinning down into a dune, where a bright-orange disc of light showed, followed by a distant boom, carried to them on wind already hot as a furnace.

'Now they know we're an offensive force,' reproached the Priest, standing by Ma Shango's quad bike, eyeing the portable rocket launcher, still smoking where it rested on one of the roll bars. He seemed really angry.

'Dem sabi already, Priest,' she sighed. 'You wan comot that little church world of yours. Dem don get satellite vision too, maybe. I try just bring down dat one drone, make it no fit report.'

'If it did not report, they would send another drone.'

'Dem go send something for sure, maybe plane wey get bombs. We suppose get ready, brother.'

'There is absolutely nothing we can do against air strikes. There's no cover here.'

'Well, was you talk say make we attack Scursail base, Priest. Now make you give us anoda plan?'

'Look Ma, I didn't expect them to find out about us quite so soon. We need to move on as quickly as possible now. First stopping by the ocean to make water.'

Not long after, they hit it: a fogbound, wind-buffeted strip of sand against which Atlantic breakers crashed, each one making a creamy foam on a bleach-white beach. Nearly everyone stumbled down to wash, but Nadine held back, staying in the Priest's vehicle, laid out on one of its banquettes like an effigy, silent as stone.

The waves were very fierce, almost knocking Cat over when

she tried to put her face in them. After splashing about a bit, she went back to the Kombi and with some difficulty persuaded Nadine to come down and join them all – to clean the cut on her thigh, and also wash between her legs; she was still hobbling wretchedly. Cat watched her squatting in the waves, wincing as she cupped water with her hand to clean herself.

But it gave Cat joy to see that the Himba woman had also made it, bathing her child, who shivered with cold as she was washed.

Trying to forget for just one second all these others to whom she rightly or wrongly felt a duty, Cat bent down again to immerse her own face in the rolling, booming surf, feeling as if the earth itself was turning in her ears with each furious fall of waves. Took off her clothes eventually: who gives a shit now about how anyone looks? Splashed armpits, crotch, bum hole.

Afterwards, she saw that men from the convoy had come down to the beach. They were not watching her, though, nor any of the other naked women washing themselves, who were equally uncaring of exposure. Having rigged up a contraption involving pipes into the sea, the men were turning the handles of the portable desalination machines she'd seen earlier – pumping water into the blue barrels, refilling them.

It did not seem an easy task. Drying herself, she asked Nadine – who like her was now shivering, flicking strands of glutinous seaweed from face and hair – how the machines worked. 'Very hard: ratio of saltwater pumped to freshwater got is ten to one.'

Walking back to the Kombi afterwards with Nadine, who seemed oddly upbeat to have been asked a question that wasn't about what she'd been through, Cat suddenly thought again of the little pond in the Well Field back home in Kerry, that spring which fed the whole farm – to which she'd so often gone with her uncle to check the flow, right from when she was a little girl. He'd always talked more than usual on those forays into that field, as if his tongue loosened the nearer it got to the water source. Been better at listening, too, to her stories of school and, later, university and work.

But it all seemed very far away now, and there was a slight

sense, having been homesick before, of wanting to flush all thoughts of home away. Isn't what's going on here, she asked herself as she and Nadine, both trembling with cold, tried to dry themselves off by the Kombi, complicated enough for you? What Nadine had termed 'almost a revolution in Dekmantel', the Priest's accusations, so many difficult days of travel, the attacks on those girls, on Nadine herself, the punishments Ma Shango had meted out, and then her firing a missile at a drone: it was a lot.

How will I, Cat thought, find the words to describe all this to Uncle Tony next time we walk in the Well Field, that place where for so many years only Brosnans had walked?

25

Earlier the same day

'Well, what do you say to that?' asked de Vries, staring hard at Glen Cole, not long after Ma Shango had tried to shoot the drone. The two men were in a newly built company office in Kunene – the very place that the Priest's army was heading for – in a so-called 'decision room' festooned with monitors and other electronic equipment. Next to them stood a tall individual in pilot's uniform, for now keeping his counsel.

What de Vries was referring to was a video of the convoy in the desert that had just played on one of the monitors, transmitted just in time from the downed drone. It showed trucks and earthmovers, camels, horses and Toyota pickups, together with a large stream of people, some armed, many not.

'To be expected, I guess,' mumbled Cole.

'*Ja*, and that's what we now need to think hard about,' said de Vries. 'You too, Masuku!'

The pilot's name was Selvy Masuku. As de Vries spoke, he was shifting restlessly from foot to foot.

Wim de Vries was the boss of both Cole and Masuku, sometimes going by the codename Boomslang. A man in his late fifties who nonetheless had a thick thatch of blond hair. Formerly a colonel in the South African Army, de Vries nowadays took charge of a dark ops group on the fringes of the mining industry, offering security services.

Being in charge, he'd found, involved taking in hand one's useless employees. Masuku was a good pilot technically but was possibly a bit flaky in terms of commitment, not really enjoying his work; Cole on the other hand loved his work, but often made a mess of things technically.

Despite all that running about when the miners rioted, Cole was (de Vries observed) still just as porky as before. But reduced in bluster at least. And his boss had his number. 'You really fucked up in Dekmantel, *mompie*,' de Vries said, shaking his wedge-shaped head at him. 'Didn't see the Chinese running like you did.'

'They have a lot more troops,' Cole countered.

'No excuse. Well, from what we know they'll be into all this soon too. Driven by the same thing as us, the need for water to run uranium mines, any kind of mine. But those people we just saw on the screen, they're driven by thirst. And by some idea of social justice. More powerful forces than mines in some ways, which is why they need to be slapped down fast.'

Almost permanently cross-looking, Colonel de Vries ran Bureau 33. Or B33, as it was referred to in the southern African security community, which basically meant ex-army or air force people looking to make a buck. He had thin pink eyelids with blond lashes, and the kind of body that only a man who'd been constantly in military service since the age of nineteen could possess.

B33 was a private military company based in Johannesburg. It provided security for many companies across the continent, including Scursail Mines, Cole's own employer at the Deep, the mine he had just abandoned. On behalf of these clients, it fielded not only professional fighting men but also armour and support aircraft such as the Mi-24 Hind and Mi-8 Hip helicopters, the BMP-2 infantry vehicle and the T-72 battle tank.

The most powerful asset of the company was the Python, a multi-weapon, tilt-rotor aircraft that delivered members of de Vries's B33 unit on their missions, or brought ordnance to supply proxy forces. It flew higher and faster than most helicopters and carried more weapons and more people. Crucially, as its name suggested, its rotors had the ability to tilt. It could direct the thrust it produced towards the ground to allow it to take off and land vertically. For military aircraft buffs, who pored over its details on websites, the Python was an object of almost pornographic attention. It was nothing less than the ideal military helicopter, able to yield a total crop of fear.

Selvy Masuku, pilot of the Python, was also looking at the screen. He was wishing he was elsewhere, back at his modest cottage in Hermanus, drinking a cup of rooibos tea. Watching his wife washing up at the sink after dinner, the kids racketing around in the next-door room . . . his beloved wife, who thought he was just an ordinary helicopter pilot and knew nothing of his actual life as a mercenary. One day – the thought struck him then as it so often had before – he would have to tell her what he really did, and then she would carry that news to a pew at her church to kneel and pray, considering their mutual future.

'I always thought something like this might happen one day,' Cole said complacently, leaning on the steel table. 'These militia leaders never stay still, they're always on the lookout for the next place to attack, like vultures seeking out the whiff of a corpse. And she's one of the worst.'

The screen showed Ma Shango on the quad bike, shouldering the Strela missile launcher. And then, in the next close-up, the missile itself, succeeded by – far in the distance, a little out of focus now the drone had gone on – the Priest remonstrating with the Ma afterwards.

A couple more shots showed Sol Spinnekop and Zowa, the two other militia leaders, before the picture on the screen broke up, like someone had shaken a snow globe in front of the lens.

After all that fuzz, the camera on the drone focused on one final image, frozen on the Priest and Ma Shango, mid-argument, both almost tiny in the vast landscape that surrounded them.

'I reckon we will just have to give at least those two a *klop*,' said de Vries, looking at the image on the screen, which was now shuddering, as if the underlying software was craving release back to some more stable mode. 'And all those other folk are also in *almagtig* God's waiting room.'

He started to outline to the other pair a plan to attack the convoy before it reached them in Kunene, a plan principally involving use of the Python.

'But we can't just go in and wipe them out,' objected Masuku.

'It's been done before,' shrugged de Vries. 'I know you always squeeze your eyes shut like a little girl sucking a lemon, but you've done it yourself. These things happen, just have to happen. And anyway, we have clear cause for a military response – they fired on our drone.'

'Not the most just cause?' ventured Masuku. 'Drones are shot down every day.'

'Just enough,' de Vries said. 'Those drones are hard to get hold of, now the US has closed down Iranian supply.'

'We would need clearance from the Namibian government if we use the Python for that,' continued Masuku, hoping to find other grounds for objection. 'Otherwise it's illegal.'

'I don't answer to the government boys,' replied de Vries disparagingly. 'Only to our clients and their shareholders.'

'We should just do it, Wim,' said Cole. 'Those two and the other, the *ou* with a spider tattoo on his face, they've been thorns in my side for far too long. But we may have the Chinese to reckon with.'

'The Chinese never fight,' said de Vries. 'They're scared of pulling the trigger, just want to make cash. Any sign of that Irishwoman who was in contact with them, Glen?'

'I tried to make her leave,' Cole said. 'Stubborn.'

'Who're you talking about?' asked Masuku, puzzled.

'An Irishwoman I found tramping along the road in Dekmantel – on her way to the Chinese safe house on Spit Street, so obviously working for them.'

'You should have tried harder,' de Vries said.

Cole pulled a face. 'She's with the Priest and Ma Shango now, I expect. Dekmantel almost emptied out entirely when the water ran dry.'

De Vries's reply filled Masuku with chilly unease. 'If she is, all the more reason to do them. The very last thing we need is a group of rebels and water refugees, all driven by thirst, linking up with someone who seems like she might be a Chinese operative.'

'I don't get it,' Masuku asked guilefully, trying to hide his true feelings. 'What's an Irishwoman got to do with Chinese actions in Namibia?'

'Good question,' commented Glen Cole. 'And it's not the first time. A while back an Irishwoman called Catherine Brosnan hooked up with Captain Xin, my equivalent at the Chinese mine. Now this other one turns up, Mary McLaverty. Both Irish scientists, both looking for aquifers, both shacking up in the Chinese safehouse in Dekmantel.'

'Still don't get it,' said Masuku. 'Are you suggesting the Irish authorities are involved with the Chinese here?'

De Vries shook his head. 'The only things Ireland sends to Namibia are offal, whiskey and priests, pretty much in that order.'

'So what's it all about then?' Masuku asked.

'We've got a bug in the office of Admiral Yu,' de Vries explained. 'The woman in charge of Chinese stuff round here. *Ongelooflik!* This admiral, anyhow, had some mission for the young Irishwoman, concerned with finding that aquifer everyone's been talking about all these years, wanting to get a water permit for their own mines, no doubt. There was some odd discussion of family between the Admiral and this young woman too, but our bug went on the blink during some of those parts, so I couldn't get to the bottom of it. I was a bit mystified.'

Pausing, de Vries frowned, as if being mystified was the very last thing someone as clever and hardworking as he (*slim en hardwerkende* was how he put this compliment to himself) should experience. 'Anyway,' he continued, 'our present mission, Masuku, is to get this lot out of our hair.' He gestured again at the frozen image of the Priest and Ma Shango on the monitor.

Masuku nodded glumly, then turned his gaze towards the office window and a view which gave on to an airstrip, where a radar antenna was spinning round. The revolutions of the device cohered with his own thoughts of being caught in a spiral. He had spent too long being ordered around by this monster.

I'll have nothing to do with this is what he wanted to say of the planned attack on the convoy. But then thought of his wife and kids back over the border in Hermanus and the comfortable life they had, that little garden of riotous flowers and veggies whose leaf-nubs crowded upwards.

'OK, you go and get ready,' de Vries told him. 'We'll do it early, when they're still dozy. Six a.m. coming in from the south?'

'Will do. But how many troops?'

'Full twenty-four. There's a lot of armed folk in that convoy, even if their weaponry is mostly fairly backward compared to what we have. Off you go.'

And so Masuku went, disgusted at what he had to do tomorrow, disgusted that this whole way of life had, for so long, been concealed from his wife, disgusted mostly at himself, which was worst of all. To once again feel abjection before these white bastards, and extinguish the souls of black folk, in a place where wild waves hit ancient dunes. He thought of his grandfather, who'd been a fighter in the liberation, shot down by someone not so unlike him (another helicopter pilot but Afrikaans), and in the same kind of sandy place, an ANC base on the Mozambique coast.

'Good pilot, but worries far too much,' de Vries said to Cole when the door was closed. 'Now, about this material we have from Admiral Yu's office, it's odd because the Admiral calls the young woman Catherine at one point, which I thought was the older one's name, but gives her a ticket in the name of Mary. The recording kept fucking up, like I say, so I only heard – *weet nie*, 30 per cent of two conversations on successive days.'

'Mary was the name she used, when I spoke to her on the Dekmantel road. Looked a bit Chinese, mind, despite speaking with an Irish accent.'

'Probably undercover.'

'Nope. Well, she didn't seem so in any professional way. Completely wet behind the ears. Almost wetting herself, too, when we had our little chat.'

De Vries picked up a remote and pipped a few buttons until another image replaced the frozen one of the Priest and Ma Shango arguing. It was a satellite-derived hydrological map, showing in coloured codes current groundwater, expected underwater reservoirs and multi-decadal predicted recharge volumes.

'Complicated stuff,' said de Vries. 'And according to our backroom boys in Toronto, these maps are not to be trusted too much. This aquifer the Admiral and the Irishwoman – Catherine, Mary, whatever – were talking about is fairly near us here, in the Kunene region. Seems like the Russians knew about it too, and years ago. The main thing is there's a lot of blue there, and if we can secure that for our principals, that's more money in our pocket. *Boer maak'n plan!*'

De Vries chuckled, and Cole did so in return. *Glug-glug-glug* went their throats, both re-enacting a television commercial from their earliest childhoods, a South African ad for petrol in which a young boy filled up with fuel a toy car that suddenly came to life, roaring off through the skirting board.

26

Contact

At about 4.30 the next morning, the convoy resumed its journey, at first in darkness. As dawn began to break, they passed the weathered skeletons of shipwrecks that loomed like giant sculptures out of the ocean. They passed colonies of seals and small packs of jackals. They passed two large black crosses, presumably remembering ancient dead – but they were without legend, without name. They passed dilapidated military trucks, which reminded Cat of the tale she'd been told about the vehicle that her mother and Xin had found long ago. They passed wooden vegetable crates half buried in the beach, and so many other things – including, much more massively, the 200-foot-long, rust-red drill tower of an oil rig toppled over on its side, yellow ghost crabs scuttling over its flaking paint.

Other abandoned workings too: pieces of railway, half-dismantled crushers and washing-screens from diamond mining, even a couple of ramshackle steam tractors sunk in the sand like dying elephants.

'We'll get to the Scursail HQ quite soon,' said the Priest not much later, squatting down next to Cat at the first stop, by which time they had headed inland, away from the Atlantic and back into the deep dunes. 'Tonight we attack. I thought I should give you the opportunity to not be part of it, if you wanted.'

His words were drowned by a sudden boom. One of the dunes next to them rose like a beast on its haunches, shaking its tail wildly, scattering fragments of sand that needled Cat's face, her neck, her hands. In the sky above the sea bright glimmers showed, which at first she thought were sheets of lightning.

'Big guns!' shouted the Priest, standing up. 'Scursail attacking. Run!'

The boom came again, and this time the barrage of shells fell nearer, the force of the explosions dashing her over. Dashing over other people too, and animals, and causing those who had not yet been hit to panic and run.

Cat sat up – dazed, swaying, staring at another pillar of sand swirling up nearby. The Priest's robes got caught up in the vortex, which whipped him up and then propelled him down sharply. She heard a crack, what sounded like a neck or back breaking but could have been gunfire.

The Priest's body was obscured by a wash of exploded sand, and then another noise filled the sky: a reverberation of rotors, growing in volume.

Cat stood, fell again, rolled, stood again, staggered dizzily towards the lip of the dune above the convoy, which now seemed to be floodlit from above.

The light moved, swept over her head. Something shivered within the light, very near. Strange ordnance!

Balletic by accident, Cat found herself cartwheeling backwards, physically confused . . . what? A sudden suck of air came as something descended in front of her, again very close – half an aeroplane, half a helicopter, landing near the laagered vehicles of the convoy, which one by one were bursting into balls of flame.

Flatbed lorries, earthmoving vehicles with scoop loaders, dumper trucks, Hilux pickups, saloon cars: the windshields of each were breaking, glass loosening into starry powder. The metal structures around the glass burst in series too, each explosion triggering a chain reaction as successive fuel tanks ignited.

Among the last to go was the Priest's Kombi: Cat thought first of her rucksack, with all her precious maps and other stuff, and then – sickened by the order her own thoughts had taken – of Nadine.

Had she managed to escape? Cat started down the dune towards the Kombi but was immediately forced back by a clatter of automatic fire and further explosive blasts. Men in masks and helmets were pouring out of the doors of the aircraft. The area of the convoy's temporary camp swarmed with tangled limbs, vague forms gyrating in smoke and noise, humans cowering under the howl of gunfire, animals bolting: she spotted one of the camels shot down, legs collapsing under box-like udders.

On her knees – trying to hide – Cat saw Spinnekop's white horse rearing, next the spider-faced man himself: shot, hanging from his own reins. Then – hat on, cigar in mouth, stubby shotgun in each hand – Zowa the Brave, banging away, moving his face from side to side in a dreadful dialectic until a projectile removed it entirely, with just the right amount of force to make his bowler hat fly up.

Caught in the light of a flaming vehicle, another bulky shape materialised before Cat's eyes: a squat figure in an open camouflage tunic who ran, tumbled, knelt to fire a pistol. In a succession of shots, going the full 360 – moving her arms like they were sweeping across the face of a clock – Ma Shango took out one, two, three of the soldiers who'd emerged from the aircraft before rushing towards Zowa's headless body, finding cover behind it, lying on her back.

Cat saw it spin, Ma's empty pistol – tossed out; then a hand reaching out, first for one of Zowa's sawn-offs, then the other for his bandolier of cartridges and twin holsters, which were lying nearby on the sand.

All got occluded by vapour for a second or two. Then the indefatigable Ma appeared again, like sun through mist, cartridge belt attached, binoculars bouncing about her neck as she ran through the smoke drift towards one of the large orange scoop loaders.

Caught in the Ma's field of fire, several more of the soldiers from the aircraft fell. Others continued attacking members of the convoy, even shooting at the horses and camels. A couple of these black-uniformed soldiers ran in the direction of Cat, who then turned and ran . . . safer on the other side of a dune.

She clambered up the massive sandy incline, scorched air rattling in her lungs as she clutched and scratched at loosening grains. A shot passed her, ruffling her hair as she reached the top, before she began hurtling down . . .

Fell in a heap, sprawled and bewildered.

She was confused by the twist of the horizon and the remnant of moon, which now seemed like another spinning steel blade in an upturned, half-dawn sky. Was it that aircraft again, come to find her, shining down its lamps?

No. Here, away from the burning vehicles and the spotlights of the aircraft, it was much darker, which presumably meant safer, though she could still hear the battle continuing on the other side of the dune.

Her immediate thought was whether one of the soldiers had followed her. But she was on her own. Except that what she was hearing, what she was smelling – it was the scent of burnt protein, like when Uncle Tony was disbudding the horns of calves – felt other.

But so did the heat and roughness in her own body, and the echoing in her head. Everything seemed entirely other, as if not just the convoy as a whole but her own sense of being had been violated.

She sat at the dune's base, shaking, trying not to move but unable not to spit sand, not rub raw eyes, not pass her wrist under a streaming nose. After some time, the noise from the other side of the dune subsided a little, but she was still trembling in terror.

When it appeared that she really was unseen, Cat gathered herself. Began walking, even though she was already done in, stumbling on, scrambling on across a flat of half-lit sand that soon developed into another incline.

At first this next dune seemed to rumble back at her, as if rebuking the mumbled words coming from her sand-filled mouth. But she trudged on up until near-complete silence fell, marked out only by the abrasive sound of her feet as they moved across sand.

27

Thirst

Dawn rose above the wastes, illuminating the slight figure of a woman making her way over dunes and through granite gorges. Cat had slept a little in the night but was now well aware that she had no water, no food, no map, and that the arduous journey and recent attack had squeezed all the energy out of her. Nonetheless she was determined to keep on walking, away from the killing and the horror; but she was really flagging now, having been going for about five hours, with perhaps two hours of sleep curled up in a hollow of sand.

She looked around for signs of water, for trees or any plants, but she could only see sand, pure-white now, extending like a code of nullity in all directions. At this moment the whiteness was still cold from the night, but already the rays of morning sun were beginning to warm it, yellow it. She realised that she may have chosen death by walking away; although better that, she thought, than a death she did not choose by staying.

Thirst meant she would have to dig for water. She looked for thorn and spinifex, the best signs of subterranean H_2O, but there was only sand, billions of particles of sand. She tried to dissect the mass of it, find a way through the labyrinth, the smaller dune forms and the larger, but could see none.

She knew these dunes were all part of the big delta of the desert – an ever-changing domain, altered in its depths by the tiniest grain shift on the surface, and itself en masse affecting the whole epic sweep of the surface of the earth through a variety of scientific processes. But what did that knowledge count for when her own extinction was at stake?

The pattern of Cat's thoughts soon ceased to be rational; in fact, they were hardly thoughts at all, being entirely physical, the emanations of a walking stupor, which led her on through the loose, will-sapping drifts of sand.

She decided to go north, as far away as she could get from what now seemed to have been a massacre. She took a blinding bearing from the rising sun, which she knew was already drying and burning her skin and soon, when the skin was fully seared, would be doing the same to the flesh beneath.

It began (it had already begun) with a dry tension in her throat and a stabbing pain in her neck, accompanied by further parching of her mouth. As the sun rose higher and she stumbled onwards, the remainder of her saliva foamed, making patches on her lips and causing her tongue to cleave to the roof of her mouth. It was as if someone was holding her neck, tightening and tightening it, then moving up to pinch her face, crush her cheekbones, compress her temples, making the blood that beat within them boil.

She began to babble, half-consciously speaking of the sounds of water itself, of murmuring streams, of the sorrowful sigh of the Shannon at its widest breadth, of the ditches and ponds that formed noiselessly in Irish meadows like their own Well Field, then sluiced out suddenly with new-fallen rain. Spoke, too, of those Cork and Kerry loughs and their rippling song of wind-trembled surfaces over chilly depths, a song so pure that it seemed to come from some place before sound itself – well before the *Aaah aaah* that her tormented throat now began to emit, that her swollen tongue tried to convert from a croak into some intelligible set of syllables as she walked – no longer properly, with little awareness of either the last step or the next. And so she rambled on, tongue and feet twitching in a mockery of progress.

The plastic water bottles that Nadine had bought her in Dekmantel loomed in her mind. Little totems, raised in memory only. The foam on her lips bubbled like pork fat at the thought of the humble lusciousness of just one sip of water from them. And she now understood why the people of Dekmantel had suddenly upped and offed: because if they hadn't, they could be where she was now, almost dying of thirst.

Struggling aimlessly, Cat continued – pushed herself – dragged herself – called out at the vultures circling overhead – pissed just once – drank a bit of her own urine, cupping its scant product in her hands. *Disgusting.*

Now it was as if time and space, too, were crashing together, breaking all measure, becoming like the Atlantic. Not the Atlantic here. The Atlantic at home, where the bogs peter out and the landscape gets rockier, and Irish time and land get mixed up with what happens at the edge of the sea. *Kerry faces the Atlantic Ocean and, typically for an Atlantic coastal region, features many peninsulas and inlets, some with fascinating history* . . .

The last spit in her mouth had changed to paste, pulling at her lips, thickening the salivary crust until it became hard and crystalline, sherbet for her gibbering gums to continually champ and tear at to stop her face from stiffening.

How long has this been going on?
Uncle Tony, I just don't know.

Something was fucking up her vision – her eyelids were peeling back and it was as if she wasn't seeing the banks of the dunes but her eyes were rubbing against them, in time with the pulse of blood in her head and the crackling in her ears. Crackling that started a flame on the crown of her head, then advanced down over the rest of her body in jumping waves, causing liquid to exude from every pore, every membrane, every fissure.

After about five hours of this torture, her feet were plucking uselessly at the dune mountains, her teeth clicking, trying to produce moisture, when she suddenly saw the sea and a bank of fog. Not to her left as they should have been by her earlier calculation but directly in front of her. She had lost her bearings. She fell onto the hard, deadened surface of the dune and began pulling herself up it with sun-reddened hands, trying to get nearer to that fog, seeking immersion in it.

Her throat made the same rasping sound as before as she dragged herself up, the sand grating against the fabric of her

T-shirt, welting her chin, chapping her chest, scraping her breasts, stripping away skin until white-flecked blood started to flow, stopped when dried, then flowed again, plastered with sand, which more sand then removed.

Cat pawed at the dune, thought she was actually eating sand as the sun planted his great foot on her neck even harder. Her tongue was now a stick-like thing, cleaving her palate, cleaving her head, it felt like. But up she still went, answering the deep-buried, instinctive knowledge of water that was calling her, beckoning her to the top of the dune, where the Atlantic fog curdled on the white sand like cream on milk.

The summons of fluid seemed to her then that of mother to child, as if each kept within oneself some memory of amniotic immersion. And then she thought of her own mother, hanging out laundry on the dryer in the back kitchen, and recited the same words that she always used when Cat didn't hear her.

Didn't you hear me calling?

Her own mother, joining in the session at Mullarkey's, removed from self through drink, slaking thirst but waiting on that other thirst that would inevitably come the next morning. Her own mother, swimming in the rocking, surging, nourishing foam of Ballybunion beach, summoning her to swim as an infant, over ever-increasing distances, reaching again and again the security of enfolding arms.

Then thought of herself, her own same self, encased in a body that wasn't drying out but soaking in the bath in her Dublin digs, immersed in the costed units of water that had flowed through pipes and reservoirs and tanks down to that city; and next the other bath from which the Admiral had called her, under the slates of the farmhouse, slates she would happily now climb onto, licking the drops of rain on each one.

Water now, at any cost. *Didn't you hear me calling?*

Retching, twisting her fingers, biting her arms, she wanted to fall into her own ooze, wanted to suck her own luscious blood and the sand-scrubbed serum and curious lymph that the sun was mustering on the surface of her body . . .

When suddenly all became windy, fresh and full of the

wondrous life of which water is not the supplement but the fundamental solvent (she could almost hear Professor O'Connor's voice now, as well as her mother's), water moving between different materials and driving so much, just as she was being driven by it now.

She had reached the dune's summit, itself supplemented by a cairn and surrounded by tremulous cacti spines that lapped at the piled rocks in an effort to find shade, edging nearer to the fog drifting up from the Atlantic shore.

Cat dragged herself up and looked at the succulents through gummed eyes, thinking to grasp one of their spines and suck the marrow, when one of these spines suddenly jerked – then the mass of the cactus itself shifted, and then the next stirred, and the next, each with the same jerky movement.

Something large, animal . . . four or five big lions, some dark-maned, all with black ruffs down their bellies and gold flickering in their eyes.

Semi-conscious, her body encrusted with sand from head to toe, she realised that the felines' long pink tongues were licking at a stream of water dripping down the stones – cold, airborne droplets, sweeping up from the sea . . .

It wasn't the aquifer – she still had enough cognition to know that, just, as another fragment of scientific memory cohered. Something different . . . to do with water vapour in the air and what happens when it touches things of a different surface temperature. Yes, that was it, fog condensing to liquid as it collided with the stove-hot stones.

She watched the lions nervously as they drank. Until, unable to bear it any more, she edged forward on her sand-rasped belly . . . She pushed among their furry heads, expecting at any moment a razor-sharp claw to slice her; but she didn't care now. *Here I am already*, she thought, *where I'm meant to be*, turning over on her back, shuffling between them, cheek by jowl with that other species, with lions made familiar, almost become human – unless she had become animal, returned to that state.

The ice-cold water poured down over the stones, over her wooden throat, over her split lips, over her ravaged face, falling at last into her mouth. Alongside the muzzles of the lions, she thought she could feel their whiskers.

Above them, these two species, another laughed.

Seagulls.

28

Tiny hammers

There she was – delirious, dipping in and out of consciousness, her head under that strange fountain issuing from the rocks, lions to either side of her, seagulls above. Lions who were only harmless because they'd fed earlier, maybe, or at least were willing to put up with her as another mammal in the fellowship of water.

There she was – seeming to hear the blast of a horn. Was it Uncle Tony, waiting outside a pub in Listowel to pick her up after someone's party? Was it the horn of one of those frustrated drivers glowering over delays in the traffic queues that used to build up next to her shared house in Dublin?

It wasn't either.

There she was – when the lions scattered; even the seagulls lifted off a little. Creatures of intelligence and skill, they seemed to be, as they whirled upwards, into the freedom of the sky, even if they'd laughed at her before. She turned her boiled head to see a great orange earthmover, a gargantuan scoop loader, rolling towards her.

Then everything greyed out.

Ma Shango would tell her later that day: 'So I find you. Your eyes no wink, and your skin gone shrunk, and your heart shake like jelly for inside your ribs. Girl, you rigged out like mule wey neva see chop since dem born am. Patch and blotch fill your flesh – thanks be plenty wata from lion stone wey slushing you!'

She had woken Cat but found she could not speak, twitching when touched. With the point of her machete Ma Shango had stripped out the flesh of six or seven nara melons she had collected, and these Cat was now slopping down greedily, still lying on her back. Then, bringing the scoop of the vehicle close to the cairn, Ma Shango began to fill it with the water coming off until, after a considerable time, there was enough for Cat to lie in it as if in a bath, coughing hoarsely, now and then vomiting, shaking in spasms all the while.

Later still, the Ma hauled Cat out of the scoop and fed her, morsel by morsel, the roast flesh of a bird she had shot, but she vomited that straight back up.

The Ma cleaned her up, dressed her, got her back in the cab of the earthmover and began driving again. All this time she was like a shadow figure to Cat, just as the lions and seagulls had been.

Slowly over that day, Cat came back to life, beginning to recognise things, including her own lacerated hands and feet, which she regarded with wonderment. Also her tongue, still twice its normal size by the feel of it.

They slept in the cab of the scoop loader at nightfall, crammed together.

Some of Cat's first words on being able to speak at all, which only came on the day after her rescue, involved asking where they were cruising to, radio on, in that big orange vehicle.

'No particular way, we be wanderers now,' Ma Shango told her.

'What happened to the others in the convoy?'

'Doan fully sabi. Maybe killed. I had to take leg, like you.'

They were in fact going vaguely north-east, deeper into the Kunene interior, on a track sometimes flat, the sand spreading out evenly, and at other times going over dunes where the sand seemed on the move upwards, as if craving the sky.

No particular way.

'Did you come looking for me?' Cat mumbled as music played from the dusty radio in the cab.

'I found you by chance.' She gave a bitter chuckle. 'Or dat ting the Priest call providence.'

'But what about everyone else?'

'Stop any wahala 'bout dat. You almost die yourself.'

'What about Nadine, the Priest?'

'Look, I just doan sabi, girl.'

Cat ran fingers over her blistered forearms, feeling shock – or something; it was hard to name – about what had happened, but also horror at the awful flatness of the Ma's tone as she spoke about those who might have died.

As if sensing Cat's judgement, Ma Shango added: 'Just to comot from katakata be the main thing, then we fit begin head for Angola border, like I take do last time.'

Proper food clearly being out of the question, for a good while after her rescue Cat subsisted on melons only. There was soon more water, thank God. For they began to find wells as they drove on during that second day of travel, filling up several barrels that Ma had brought with her. She stowed them in the back of the earthmover, alongside Zowa's twin-shoulder holstered shotguns and bandolier, which she'd also carried out of that massacre from which they'd both so narrowly escaped.

Once they were back on the road, Cat again asked about their destination.

'Going Angola way,' Ma Shango repeated, sounding a little irritated now. 'Least, far side from where those *oyinbo* did dat bad thing.'

'What's . . . *oyinbo*?'

'White people, girl,' said the Ma. 'Dem who attacked us, Mary.'

It was the first time, she thought, that Ma Shango had used her name, but of course it wasn't her name, and it felt like the time to fess up.

'About that, Mary,' Cat croaked.

'What? Nobody call mi dat no more.'

After a moment of almost farcical confusion, Cat began to explain about the Admiral and the false name of Mary McLaverty she'd been given, to such little purpose as it now felt . . .

It turned out to be quite a long explanation, during which the Ma occasionally laughed, occasionally sighed, occasionally sucked her teeth and at the end said only, without any censure: 'Boy what a tangle you wey in. So if Cat you be, that fit I call you, yes?'

'Yes, and please can I have a drink of water?' For in the course of clarifying these matters her throat had become drier and drier, even if it felt so good to get it all off her chest.

Later in the day, they neared a small herd of lean cattle. Stopping the vehicle, the Ma took hold of one of Zowa's shotguns, pulling it out from among the water barrels in the back. She loaded it with cartridges and, walking over to the herd, put the muzzle of the gun right against the temple of one of the animals (who seemed to show no fear whatsoever) and shot it; then shouted over to Cat, who was watching by the scoop loader, to come over and help her drag the dead cow back to it.

To many other people all this would have been horrifying, but Cat had seen Uncle Tony dispatch cows on the farm with the so-called humane killer, which was almost like a shotgun, so it was not – certainly not after what she'd already seen here – quite so terrible as it might have been.

Almost immediately after, once they'd hauled the dead beast back to the earthmover, the Ma cut off two steaks from one of its haunches and barbecued them, having gathered branches of dry wood from a clump of spindly thorn trees.

Eating the steak (spliced on Ma Shango's machete, it had hardly taken any time at all to cook and tasted delicious), Cat asked her about the soldiers who attacked the convoy.

'Mercenaries, B33s dem called. Sent to neutralise threat to Scursail, or so I fit guess.'

The fire on the sand was dying down now, the boughs that had fuelled it keeping their shape as they reduced to ash.

'It's amazing you managed to get away from them. How on earth did you manage it?'

The reply came with a deep sigh: 'Omo, I shoot craze for dem, and then go drive dis big beast. All while my mouth pray, make no one missile blow my nyash till kingdom come. Miracle dat I escaped, but you know well girl, beta miracle I find you for dis wide desert. Like Priest go say, Baba God just choose to smile on us, sista.'

'What of him, and the others?'

'Many of dem don kpeme is my belief. Like I go tell you already.'

'What?'

'Kpeme is "dead". But maybe some of dem don get collect as prisoner.'

Zowa the Brave she'd seen killed with her own eyes, as had Cat. It did seem likely, from what the Ma was saying, that the Priest and Spinnekop were probably also dead, along with many others of the convoy.

Cat again asked about Nadine. 'You know, my friend, the girl who the Priest took the wrench from?' She caught her breath, wincing as cracked skin pulled on the corners of her mouth, where meat juice was also stinging. 'Also one of those who were raped.'

As she said this, Cat was aware that a little of the anger when she'd first spoken to the Ma on this matter – in her tent, when she didn't even know Nadine had been raped – was shifting in the undercurrent of her voice.

'I well sabi, but I no am see her. Abeg no vex at me. As for dat stupid wrench, maybe done burn am, inside the Priest's van, like so many human done burn. Powerful weapons dem sojas got. Girl, I go tell you straight, whacking my best english, I so sorry.'

'What about the Himba woman who gave birth?'

'I no see am either.'

Cat shuddered, thinking of the Himba woman and her child, looking at her own still-claw-like hands as she imagined vultures tearing their bodies. But mostly she thought of Nadine. Had she managed to get out of the Kombi at all? If she was still alive, she might be in trouble.

And if that were so, surely trying to help Nadine (and the others left behind) was more important than – whatever it was she was trying to do now?

Their journey continued until suddenly the Ma brought the

vehicle to an abrupt stop. Jumped out and began scanning the sky with her binoculars.

'What is it?' Cat asked, joining her beside the scoop loader.

The Ma stayed silent for a while, continuing to move the binoculars over quadrants of sky, doing a full 360.

'Not sure,' said Ma. 'Could be I heard another drone.'

Cat cocked an ear. But she could hear nothing save the vibrating boom of distant sand – whole dunes moving far off, setting off successive disturbances in a weird chorus, as if one dune needed the next and they were calling to each other.

What I need, she proposed to herself that evening, is some kind of revelation about what I should do next. How I should act now, rather than sleepwalking into . . . into what? I don't even know what's been lost, never mind what's coming.

As she tried to sleep that second night since her rescue, bunched up against the Ma's bulky figure, the people of the convoy seemed like ghosts already. But it was hateful to think so, and she suspected herself of too easily consigning them to oblivion only because any remedy seemed so far out of reach.

Now, as she lay by the Ma in the darkness, even though the wind had lessened a little, sand-grains were striking the panes of the vehicle like tiny hammers. *No, no, no,* they seemed to be saying to her, as if emphasising that no clear revelation about what she should do would ever come from the external world.

29

Yet another day

The shot cow lay in the scoop of the earthmover as they travelled on the next morning, the third day since Cat's rescue. Later, before the sun got too high, the Ma butchered it further, cutting more of its flesh into strips and hanging them to dry from cleats on the sides of the vehicle.

Last night's worries – anxieties about herself, and feeling so lost, anxieties about the other convoy members, whom they seemed now to have abandoned – were still piling up in her head like the dunes around them. Finally she asked Ma Shango directly: 'Don't you think we should go back and try to rescue them?'

'Dem be who?'

'Those we left behind.'

Ma Shango shook her big head. 'No be fit our purpose do dat. Myself I be a fighter, as you well sabi. But fact be, we must accept loss and waka on. Return, dat too many time in life be illusion. Romance into which we all go too willing, eh? Priest plan itself wey one such. Big error he make, we make too, stirrin up those mining folk like we did.'

'We can't just leave them back there.'

'Comot dat dream, girl. Shine your eye! Some of dem bad sojas could be following us even now, if dat was a drone I heard, come down when we no expect, and us for don perish.'

Faced with the undeniable reality of what Ma Shango was saying, as they bumped over a ridge of rising sand, Cat didn't know how to reply. The Ma seemed like the very last person to back down from a challenge – just as she didn't back down, right now, from gunning the giant vehicle up the next vast dune gradient.

As they bundled down the other side of the dune, memories of that moment in the desert came back, when she was at the end of her tether and so many lions had let her squeeze in among them, allowing her to drink. It had been, she reflected now, as if she was not an individual then, nor even a human.

She'd long had a feeling that both those categories – which had driven so many other events across human history and that of other species – were just no longer relevant now that a more holistic approach was needed. What was necessary was the modelling of the planet as a single interconnected system, such as Professor O'Connor had sometimes gestured at in his lectures, saying that we needed to treat nature as someone with whom we were having a polite conversation rather than dictating to it. The phrase he'd actually used was 'dictating to it like a copy-typist'. No one, including Cat herself at the time, had the foggiest what he meant by that.

But he was so old and vague by then, and the prospect of a solution to environmental risk just as vague. And as old. In fact, older: scientists like him had been warning, warning about the dust of wasted fields and the blind certainty of a backlash in the ecosphere for nearly a century now. It had got to the stage when earthworms themselves, the very intestines of the soil, were moving microplastics through the physics and chemistry of their own guts.

Why had the lions let her live? She remembered something else O'Connor had once said – about water carrying memory; but surely it didn't carry memory of times so far back as to reach a moment when lions and humans were biologically closer, never mind that moment when tracks collided in a common ancestor for all animals, which probably resembled something like a worm.

Humans still shared something like 90 per cent of their DNA with lions – but still, well, this was crazy thinking, she told herself. And why, on the spectrum of algae to hominid, should mammals be particular? Water, seeping from one place to another, one substance to another, like the figments of the darkest dream, went so much beyond these categories.

The only course of useful action to take now, she thought as Ma Shango hauled the vehicle up the next dune, was the one that she had intended before the attack: to attempt to find the aquifer and, if the two things could ever cohere, which she by now very much doubted, her mother as well. It was as if she had pledged herself to that double contract long ago and could not now escape from it.

'Ma, we can't just go on aimlessly, we need to find the course of the old Alfaib again, get back on track,' Cat finally said.

'What e bey again, dis Alfaib?'

'The underground river that will lead us to the aquifer, I'm sure of it.'

'But for what, why we go dere, datdat aquifer?'

'I think my mother went there.'

'Ah. I be fit see you now clear, girl. I, too, lost my mother, so I got understanding. But better we stay living, not go chase fantastical thing? Say those guys wey attack us go come after us again, like I explain? Cos everything now track with big tech, you know?'

'I know, but I have to stay faithful to why I came here in the first place,' Cat continued. 'To find my mother and for scientific reasons.'

'Which? Totally different.'

'Yes, but they've all got bound up together in me.'

'Eh?'

'Being useful feels like the most important thing. We know the people of Dekmantel cannot get water by fighting for it, but perhaps they can get water by us finding the aquifer?'

Ma laughed out loud as she turned the steering wheel: 'You don't get neva, do you? No way ever we ourself get Dekmantel people to wata some place so far away, even if dem folk still alive anyway. The best thing wey we for do now is, focus for dat Angola waka, like I say, whack any chance we can find dere.'

'I just can't,' Cat said, shaking her head as she looked at the forbidding dunescape unfolding relentlessly in the windscreen.

'I just can't do that. Everything that has happened will make no sense unless I find it; I don't mean just here, my whole life before here too.'

'I understand, for sure. When fate call, e get some certain women must arise. Even if put plenty yama-yama on our brain.'

Again Cat really struggled to understand what Ma Shango meant. It yammered her brain too, all this translation.

For a while they drove on. Cat kept wondering how Ma Shango could so quickly abandon those to whom she'd been allied. In the end she just asked her outright again: 'How can we leave them behind, Ma? Not go back.'

'It because to survive, fit be little selfish. Why not you sabi when you ask so many time and I answer same so many time?'

'I think I'm afraid to understand properly.'

'Well, you need to reswagger, girl. And more. Sometimes fit be super selfish, most so at dat article of death all must face.' She laughed again, more wildly this time. 'So don't you ever comot some spot rescue me, girl, when dat could happen my side.'

'I don't want to think about that, but I do get it.' She paused. 'But what if we really do try to find the aquifer, like I said?'

For a long time after, Ma Shango said nothing. In the silence, Cat struggled to believe there was any way forward for her at all.

'If dat be your plan, then possible make we try it,' the Ma eventually responded, speaking with great deliberation. 'Because I no got other plan for better save my skin except waka Angola and face dem crazy mugu dere. But where dis aquifer be and how we go dat side?'

To these significant, fair-enough questions Cat had no easy answer. There was a simple, low-resolution map in the glove compartment of the scoop loader, but it was of no use at all for pinpointing something like a single dry riverbed. Even with the map, they only had the vaguest idea of where they were. It seemed a more hopeless quest than ever, and Cat started resigning herself to taking her chances in Angola, whatever Ma meant by that. There was surely no chance of laughing all this off once they got to the border.

All the same, she put the map on her knees and tried to

concentrate. There were two vast river systems in the broad region, the Okavango and the Zambezi, but they were much more eastward than the dotted line of the former Alfaib River that she remembered from her mother's maps. Nearer to where she thought the aquifer might be, one river, the Kunene, flowed towards the Atlantic. Another, the Cuvelai, was hardly a main river at all, being more a drainage array of shifting small waterways consisting of hundreds of channels that dispersed water across the landscape.

It seemed likely to Cat that the place where all the water that once flowed down the old Alfaib might now be stored – in the proposed aquifer – could touch both the Kunene and the Cuvelai systems. But she also knew that once, millions of years ago, the mighty Okavango itself had fanned out, draining much more westerly than it did now, its present-day course being south and then southeastwards, ending in the vast swamp of the Okavango Delta. It was also possible that the Alfaib was connected to ancient channels that were part of the Okavango's 'paleo-megafan', as it was known in the hydrology trade.

This wasn't on her map, not at all. But when she traced what she remembered as being the supposed edge of the Okavango's earlier drainage in previous tectonic eras, and triangulated that against the present-day passage of the Kunene and the many channels of the Cuvelai, she found what seemed the most likely place the Alfaib's former flow might have halted. Where in her best guess it was presumably now charging, stopped by an ingress of sand and waiting to be released.

But there was a real puzzle, because the Russian diary mentioned a *serra*, which meant a mountain range, and there weren't any mountains in the spot she'd identified.

Alongside where the map had been, and other dusty bits and pieces, there was an old biro in the glove compartment. Fishing it out, she drew three bisecting lines, their meeting point marking the most likely location of the aquifer.

She then tried to explain it all to the Ma, whose response remained sceptical: 'E be like ghost, dis Alfaib of yours. I just hope say dat aquifer no be ghost too. But we go still try your idea, sista. What you sef think of our chances, though?'

The Ma stopped the vehicle next to another clump of thorn trees and they spread the map out on the sand, looking at it together. 'If I'm right,' Cat said – drawing her finger to the intersection of the three blue lines that she'd drawn – 'the aquifer must lie in this area, about here. About the probability of me being right, I'm sorry, I just don't know.'

'Fine nuff,' said Ma Shango, 'but plenty-plenty ground still for us to go dere. Big risk we never find am! Why you not be more exact?'

'Not enough of this land is really mountainous,' said Cat, still studying the map, which was already absorbing heat from the sand beneath it.

'So?'

'I know from a written record I have read that the aquifer lies within a rock monolith rising in a mountain range, a *serra* as they say in Portuguese.'

'What be the record?'

'That's a long story,' Cat replied, thinking of the mummified writer of the diary, found in his shroud of sand in the desert. 'The fact is, the area where the three lines I have drawn connect is here.' She pointed again to the place on the map where the contours narrowed, but only very slightly, within other lines that were wider. 'The contours mean the ground is raised a little, but it's no mountain range.'

Ma Shango leaned over, peering at the map. 'For sure, not much big lift for dat side. No *serra* dere.'

'But a monolith, just one lump of rock, would be too small to show much on a map this scale,' Cat said, sticking to her guns, even though the Ma was telling her exactly what Professor O'Connor said about the map not being the territory.

'If so you talk am, girl,' said the Ma. 'But make you show me again, as we no get fuel like that to dey waste.'

Picking up her biro, Cat made a little blue circle on the map. 'Look, our route to Angola is taking us past what I think's the source of the Alfaib anyway, so we might as well see, don't you think?'

After a pause, the Ma gave a heavy nod and said, 'OK, but dis be your decision.' Her voice, usually confident, jolly enough however dire the circumstances, did not sound like that now.

With that assent, if assent it was, they got back in the cab and changed direction slightly, bringing them nearer to the spot Cat had pinpointed on the map.

After more driving, the road passed by the dry canyon of a former river that was perhaps now flowing in fits and starts underground. Cat thought she could tell this from the topography – all her training seemed to say so; at the same time, another voice told her to be more careful and not jump to conclusions. The trail she was studying from the vehicle's window wound in and out of old, twisty trees and was bordered by steep eroded cliffs, the rock of which was cracked and time-weathered. In some places rocks seemed to be crumbling even as they drove past; in others it was as if the cliffs were still rising, climbing into the sky on their own giant steps.

But none of these cliffs were high enough to be called mountains. 'I'm so sure this is it,' Cat told Ma Shango nonetheless. 'The Alfaib.'

All she got in reply was a doubtful grunt, but her companion turned off the road and started following the river canyon more directly, causing the scoop loader to rumble as its big tyres passed over the pebbles in the deepest part of the gulch, then quieten when they reached areas of desiccated mud.

'We need to keep looking for a large, flat-topped mound of rock,' she told Ma Shango, who this time did reply, shaking her head: 'No be nothing like dat round hia.'

And yet they continued, if haltingly, along what might or might not have been the canyon of the old Alfaib River, whose dotted path Cat had traced on maps back in the bungalow in Dekmantel.

They passed over more shattered grey stone, other areas of dry mud spiked with skeletal trees, and sometimes the sour little patches of grass that were the most definite signals of the course of an underground river.

In some places dunes still obscured the old river path completely, the signs of its former passage dwindling away. In these moments, however much she checked the map on her lap, and tried to remember her mother's map, only an abstract idea of the Alfaib's trail remained in Cat's mind, if this was indeed the right river.

'You be say some big rock hia?' complained Ma Shango at one point. 'I no be see nothing like dat, girl, sure you no be wrong? If so, we need be lively up, make other plan. Go back what I say for Angola.'

Only at sunset, by which time the river canyon had deepened and widened and the driving become harder, did it seem like Cat might just be right. For there, suddenly, the object of her quest appeared. Revealed in the dying light was something that seemed to answer her doubts with the utmost certainty. A rock formation, a monolith whose silent substantiality mocked the chattering fury of sand-grains on the windscreen. An edifice about the height of an apartment building or biggish radio mast, maybe 150 metres in elevation, with a broad slope area fissured by crevices.

'Comot at last from dis!' shouted Ma Shango, grabbing Cat's neck under her arm. Her voice, so often deep-toned, was suddenly sounding as bright as the brook that fed the Well Field back home.

They got out of the vehicle, looking at the monolith through Ma Shango's binoculars.

From a distance – they were still some way away – the rock formation rose like a castle out of the desert, its rough battlements making it appear as if it were hovering in the blood-red sky.

'Well, girl,' said Ma Shango, breaking the spell, 'I for am give you maximum regard.' She raised a thumb to her topknot, which was casting a shadow on the ground below, making it seem as if some enormous plant were growing there. 'We need watch careful still, say just be lump of rock dere, no mean say wata full am?'

'Point taken,' Cat said. 'But I'm pretty sure there's water in there, Ma. I now think it's more likely to be what we call an unconfined aquifer sitting on top of one or more confined ones.'

'What fuck dat mean, girl?'

'Kind of a lake trapped inside the rock, on top of lateral layers of rock and gravel saturated with water.'

'If you dey say so. Mi no worry.'

But Cat was still worrying about a point the Ma had made earlier: there was definitely no *serra* here, no mountain range, just a single monolith in an area of more or less flat desert.

They got back into the cab and continued in the direction of the monolith, which remained frustratingly distant.

Later, as nightfall came, Ma Shango said they should turn in. Previously she'd let Cat sleep on the seats in the cab with her, but she said her back was hurting from sharing that space and Cat should sleep on the sand. Which she did, under the scoop of the vehicle, wrapped in Ma Shango's camouflage jacket.

A cold wind began to blow, stirring sand about Cat. She woke a couple of times – turned over and over, wrapping the jacket closer round her as she tried to find the right shape in the ground for her hip. Although she got a little more comfortable, she was still disturbed by the endless sprinkle of grains of sand, feeling the pock-pock-pock on the skin of her eyelids, and however much she squirmed about, her hip never married completely with the hole it was trying to make.

None of this was helped by the dolorous sound of Ma Shango's snoring, audible even through the closed doors of the vehicle. As the night went on, it was as if the chilling sand beneath her was sucking the heat out of her body, almost synching with Ma Shango's snoring, which sometimes lulled her off, sometimes woke her. And all the while an ever-stronger Atlantic wind was blowing, cinching when it funnelled through canyons, then distending when it reached the open desert.

So cold, that desert-night wind. Still scooching about in her hip-made hollow, Cat knew it would become hot, desert-day wind tomorrow – this mutable wind, which travelled according to its own system, shifting globally from somewhere to somewhere else, moved by temperature and pressure but also moving temperature and pressure by its own transition. Abstraction of all this, dealing in ideas rather than events affecting oneself – well, that was possible to a degree (still she kept trying to think as a scientist), but it was not overly helpful.

Certainly not helpful in getting to sleep. Wind also needed to be understood in human terms, or animal terms . . . each gust only usefully comprehensible as a point of contact between various consciousnesses. And when you went beyond those terms into wider frames of understanding – ecological, geological, atmospheric – you came back inevitably to the human system, and below that the individual system, each with its self-reflexive frailties.

Which was, she thought, why all the attempts to deal with climate change, the very thing (aside from her mother's example) that had driven her into science in the first place, had so far failed, just as she was still failing to sleep.

30

The others

Glen Cole, when morning came, was also subject to wind. Wind that, despite its residual Atlantic frigidity, was not evaporating rapidly enough the sweat that had gathered during his journey from a local hotel to the Scursail headquarters in Kunene, in armpits that sucked like limpets under the sleeves of his striped shirt.

That same Atlantic wind, passing over the airstrip next to the mining company's HQ, was now entering through the open windows of an office, causing metal blinds to clatter. Inside this sanctum, Cole was apprehending the possibility of finding an aquifer on a map, alongside the mercenary leader, Colonel Wim de Vries, and the Python pilot, Selvy Masuku.

Cole and de Vries were razor-cool after the killings in the desert, but Masuku felt sick to his stomach, wishing again that he was back home with his wife in Hermanus. De Vries had just finished a Teams conversation with his superiors in Toronto.

Amazingly enough, given how clean and well behaved most Canadians are (whoever met a dirty or rude Canadian?), Toronto was the location of nearly three-quarters of the world's mining companies, along with associated banks, legal firms and consultancies, all benefiting from the loose regulatory framework that had made the atrocity in Dekmantel possible.

Now another mission was being planned. 'Its purpose', de Vries said, 'is to secure what we believe to be an aquifer, having received intelligence to that effect. Now, I presume you both know what an aquifer is?'

'Of course,' said Cole. 'This is the same one that the Irishwoman and Xin were looking for a few years back, *ja*? And then the other, younger Irishwoman I met tramping along the road in Dekmantel?'

'Masuku?'

'I know what an aquifer is, Colonel. An underground layer of water-bearing rock. Or sometimes gravel.'

'*Ja ja*, but this one's a bit different. The backroom boys in Toronto have done some analysis, using satellite imagery, historical maps and past geophysical surveys. It's an elevation of rock sitting on what might be an underground lake, probably fed by a more typical aquifer as you say it.'

Getting a map up on a monitor, de Vries pointed at contours and the dotted lines of half-buried river tracks.

He said: 'Not much of a rise and very localised. It's just a lump of rock in the end, but it seems like there's water under it. From what the boffins reckon, that lump of rock is like the cork in a bottle of fizzy wine.'

'But what's Scursail's interest?' asked Masuku.

'Well, bru, it's this. The scans seem to suggest a massive expanse of water under the elevation, not just a top lake but layer on layer of water-bearing material – perhaps the biggest aquifer in the whole of southern Africa, the scientists in Toronto are saying. If so, that's very good for us; we can use it to feed new mine operations as it's in our zone of control.'

'But also good for the Chinese,' interjected Glen Cole, 'if they muscle in, or persuade the Namibians to change the zoning.'

'Too right,' de Vries said. 'And that's exactly what I think the Admiral's up to. Maybe the Irishwoman too – look at this, which we just got.'

He flipped up a drone photo on another monitor, this one showing an orange scoop loader and, standing beside it on the sand, Cat and Ma Shango, the latter looking up into the sky with binoculars.

'That's your Dekmantel girl, isn't it, Glen?'

'Yes, and next to her the Nigerian woman. What do you reckon?'

'Not sure, but they're fairly near the aquifer, so we must assume they're headed there. So may need neutralising.'

'What's the actual plan?' asked Glen Cole.

De Vries turned back to the monitor displaying the map. 'You approach by this route early tomorrow morning, Glen – by truck, with troops. It's about 225 kilometres, so to get there by sunrise you'll need to have wheels up by 2 a.m. at the latest. Me and Masuku, we'll come in the Python later as backup, along with more of our guys. Either landing or fast-roping down, depending on what we find. OK, Masuku?'

The pilot nodded, unable to speak, so torn did he feel inside.

De Vries went blithely on. 'Also, from what I'm hearing out of Toronto, the Chinese are expected to move soon, so we can't discount the possibility of their troops turning up too.'

As he spoke these words, de Vries thought: why is it I who am so blessed to bring a confluence of water and blood to the ashen desert? The answer that came to him was: *Dit is as gevolg van my ongewone intelligensie, wat my alles verdien het wat ek nog ooit gekry het. En ek sal nooit huiwer om dit te gebruik nie.* Or in English, that other language of conquerors: 'It's because of my unusual intelligence, which has earned me everything I've ever got. And I'll never hesitate in using it.'

But these *domkops* needed instruction, and so he bent again towards the map on the monitor, showing them where the monolith was and giving further details. As he spoke, the blinds on the office window continued to flutter metallically, giving cut-up glimpses of the airstrip next to the headquarters, where a windsock was filling with the wind's own voice.

31

Ray of light

The contours that de Vries had pointed out were in the same spatial sector as those previously identified by Cat. Now, on the same day as that plan was being hatched in the mining company headquarters, she was bumping along in the orange vehicle getting nearer and nearer to the monolith that the contours represented.

Ma Shango's topknot was wobbling as she sang with gusto beside her. Some Nigerian song containing the words *mami wata*, its lyrics hard to understand . . . It seemed, anyway, as if the Ma felt safe now, was briefly less haunted by her own past and the struggles they'd both been through.

Cat was still feeling guilty about Nadine, and about all those others affected by the strike on the convoy. In the part of the journey they'd done since breakfast, she had made an agreement with herself that she would at least try to find out what had happened to Nadine.

Even that seemed hard to accomplish. And about all the others, what could she do?

As Ma Shango continued singing, Cat's eye focused on a small, star-like crack in the vehicle's windscreen, near one edge of the rubber rim that housed the glass. It made her uneasy, as if the whole screen might shatter at any moment.

Underneath all this, perhaps, lay a sense that despite Ma Shango's agreement to head for the aquifer, all the other compacts Cat had made, tacitly or not, remained just as doubtful as the integrity of the glass in front of her.

Looking after Nadine, finding her mother – she had made those agreements only with herself. Part of her secretly (even if she could hardly admit it) didn't want to find her mother at all. Doing so preyed uncomfortably on a previously embedded idea of simulation: how it rankled, having to follow the model of a mother. Looking after Nadine, which she reckoned she definitely hadn't done properly so far, seemed oddly bracketed within this whole complex of feelings.

Didn't you hear me calling?

I have no choice.

Just have to be yourself in the end, that's only common sense.

All these odd voices, speaking in her head. All these odd voices, none of them her own. All these odd voices, squeaming within her. Nauseated, she looked at that fissure in the windscreen of the vehicle bumping her along, fearing that she, like it, might break.

As for the agreement she'd made with the Admiral about finding the aquifer – an agreement between two people that had committed her to innumerable risks – where the fuck was the other party in that now? Ever since leaving Dekmantel she'd been hoping that the Admiral might send that pilot Morrow, or better still a whole detachment of robust Chinese marines who'd pluck her out of this. Maybe it had not happened because of everything that had happened in the pump riot, the Admiral fearing an international incident like the one that had seemed to force her father to leave, all those years back?

They stopped at a well. Cat watched admiringly as Ma fashioned a waterskin from cowhide, filled it from the source, which was a hole a few metres deep, surrounded by stones. Who'd put them there? Cat wondered, thinking of the Himba and the other desert tribes whose home this truly was, at least in human terms.

As the earthmover got under way, her throat fresh with the new water, Cat herself started singing – teaching the Ma the words to, of all things, 'The Fields of Athenry'.

The pupil sang with particular brio the line 'Nothing matters, Mary, when you're free', as if the coincidence of it having been Cat's false name and her own real name gave them common ground.

Then she began singing the *mami wata* song again.

Now, on Cat's enquiry as they drove along, its lyrics were unpacked. They concerned a mermaid emerging from a famous beach in Lagos and how, on seeing this *mami wata* yourself, you should not run away.

'It be about no be scared, whatever happen,' Ma Shango explained. 'Good lesson datdat. All we human fit do is persist. But why you dey no stick Ireland, persist there?'

'Partly coming here was to do with my mother,' Cat replied. 'But also myself. I never really found my own level, not at university, nor at home either.'

'Home e fit important, what yours be like?'

'A farm with cows. A farmhouse. Sitting by the range with my uncle mostly, as the nights closed in . . .'

'Range, wetin be dat?'

'Kind of a stove.'

'Kay, and sound OK too.'

'Our evenings dragged, Ma. In some ways, it's better to be here with you.'

'Nice for you am say. But dis no be your place, no be mine either. Not your cause either, wata for desert people – why you risk everything for it?'

'I want to find the aquifer, and my mother too. It's as simple as that, really. Maybe also find what I'm about. But what about you?'

'Ah, now you ask big question. I always be one wanderer, maybe looking all time for that *mami wata* about dat song I you sang.'

'When you killed the men who raped, I was horrified, Ma. Why did you do it?'

'I said dat why-so back then. Because I myself got dat rape.'

'I'm sorry.'

'Not just once. E be many time.'

Cat found herself reaching out and patting the big, sweaty camouflaged thigh of the woman next to her, as if that silly gesture could in any way measure up to what she was being told.

'As per say,' the Ma continued, 'woman don wise up after

e first. I buy knife wey small pass dat matchet of mine. Next Nigeria Navy man who come for me, I make sure for en gut I cut am. Cut him body like one bonga fish! After dat, I jump e ship, take beta pistol and rifle, run for Walvis.'

'Is that how you ended up in Namibia?'

'Took so much longer, girl. From Walvis I go up to Angola, stopping in Kunene region where we be now. Burn one bloody track on and on, till I reach Congo and its eastern jungle. Dere I see men fight serious fight. Learnin' much: biig educashun! After long time and much wahala, I come start to build my own team.

'Sharp-sharp, we waka from town to town, city to city in dat Congo. Big war always go on dere. Robbing banks or taking down the richest man around: datdat one, him always be bad fella!'

Driving on, Ma Shango continued to tell how, in time and under duress (for her band was by then fleeing government troops of various countries), they'd flitted south, down through southern Congo and across Angola, eventually to become one of the Dekmantel militias, hoping to take a small pension, so she said, and rest in the desert sun.

'But not yet, alas. And so hia we be. And my band now all gone. Only you left.'

Ma Shango related this odyssey in a fairly matter-of-fact tone, but it made Cat admire her. What a lot this woman had seen, had been through. Some kind of affection was developing between them, so she thought. Weirdly enough, it was manifesting, so far as feelings ever showed themselves truly, as something more than whatever she'd ever had with her mother. Maybe, she wondered, it might have been like this if she'd had an elder sister? Someone to guide her a little in those ways that parents never could.

Not long afterwards the scoop loader passed a scrap of trees out of which – to Cat's great surprise – a pair of giraffe necks and heads suddenly popped. Under long lashes, the eyes of the animals regarded her dolefully, and she suddenly felt a more diminutive version of the same species kinship she had experienced with the lions.

But in a second the giraffes were gone – loping, cantering, lope-cantering off . . .

All this while, the lump of rock was looming on the horizon, that residual igneous lump which she'd begun to assume was maybe the collection point of both surface and sub-surface water. Cat reached for the binoculars. Were her goals at last really attainable? Maybe. Before, the monolith had still seemed far away, but now they were almost there.

The monolith must be, Cat was sure by now, the sort of unconfined aquifer of which she had told the Ma earlier. A subterranean lake of freshwater, a little like the water lenses often found on tropical islands – more or less an underground swimming pool sitting on top of a more typical aquifer, where water was distributed in porous rock, the whole thing capped by the volcanic edifice of the monolith.

It was by now about midday as they continued on towards it, this thing that had so long remained hazy, tenuous, but at last was in plain sight, and getting larger by the minute.

Ma began singing the *mami wata* song again later, slapping the steering wheel with the rhythm, making the vehicle veer. Singing the song seemed to carry Ma back into a vanished childhood, if what she said next was anything to go by, going so more deeply into pidgin that Cat could sometimes hardly understand.

'Anytime I sing dis song, e be like something special. Me, my mumsy and auntie, we always sing dat song anytime we make food. Me and dose packed-up women, with flour for our hand. Den when my fruit dem don ripe, I go enter street, alas, find trouble. Wahala with boys and guns. Ah, Lagos, dat dissolution city! Den I come begin draft plan to join navy. Biiig mistake, walai . . . errorful, dat course I take as young girl.'

She paused for a second, wiped from her cheek what might have been sweat, might have been a tear. 'Well, sista, we still waka our journey. Look at dem fingas a sand creepin up de mountain like dem be rascal hand!'

For two hours now, since Cat had looked at the crack in the

windscreen and Ma Shango had again sung fragments of the mermaid song, they had been nearing the monolith.

Some parts of the massif ascended sheer, like a wall, but mostly it was flanked by the sand canyons to which the Ma had just referred – those fingers of sand that filled chasms in the vertical rock. A few of these corridors stretched from the summit all the way down to the white dunes that flapped at the foot of the structure like the tails of giant whales, before flattening out into the surrounding plain.

She grabbed Ma Shango's binoculars.

The summit was partly a plateau or *mesa*, partly a smashed causeway that merged with some of the channels in the rock.

Squinting, the skin on her face still a bit crusted and painful from that time of thirst in the desert, Cat kept trying to look at the edifice with a scientist's eye. Some sort of igneous extrusion, but punctuated by feldspars and other silicate minerals, which sparkled like myriad jewels, turning it into a sort of mosaic.

Mosaic wasn't really a term of science, except maybe in the very deepest recesses of rock study. But approaching this thing seemed more like an event that had become more personal than scientific anyway. She corrected herself as they carried on: if there was water there in the rock, it wasn't hers alone. She remembered the tribal rumours in the anthropological literature, remembered the lions, and the giraffes they'd just seen, and extrapolated then to the many other creatures she presumed might come here if the monolith really did contain a huge pool of water. But how did animals enter it?

Eventually, the evening after they had first spotted it, they arrived at its base. They sat in the after-silence of the extinguished engine, gazing up at the rock, stunned by its visual power. It was like looking upon something summoned from the reaches of eternity, something to which human beings were of no consequence, it mattering little that we came or went, lived or died, or indeed had ever developed as a species in the first place.

Emitting a loud grunt, Ma Shango climbed out and Cat followed suit. Her limbs were stiff after the long drive . . . *Christ*, *how much more do I have to go through?* . . . and Ma Shango too suddenly seemed irritable again.

'Good we get hia, but I no see wata, girl, not one drop.' As Ma Shango spoke the evening sun was playing on her big face, highlighting the seams of her scars.

Cat approached the rock, placing the flat of her palm against it. It was warm, like the side of an animal; she was suddenly cast back in time herself, sitting on a stool with her mother on the farm in Ireland, learning how to milk a cow.

'The water's inside,' she explained to the Ma, 'with the plateau acting as a kind of lid. Or maybe too as some kind of water harvester – periodic rain falling on the monolith, running down its sides, concentrating rain in the sands beneath it, meeting a point where it added to the underground movement of water from the surrounding catchment that generated the useable aquifer. At least I think so. Look, there are some trees up there, in that cleft. That must be a sign that water is nearby.'

'E fit be true,' said Ma Shango, looking doubtful. 'Even if you blind me. But, babe, oh, how you say we fit take reach?'

'We climb . . . there's maybe a route just there, up that crevice.'

'That one go take us several hours; e go get dark soon.'

Sure enough, the sun was beginning to set again in the wide desert sky, transforming the prevailing white light that had played over the monolith into a deep red.

'Tomorrow, then,' said Cat.

'But I worry, girl, all the same,' said Ma Shango.

'About what?'

'You suppose know, as I say before, possible for Scursail people come here attack us again. They don dey track everything with koro-koro eyes, like I say! You no sabi?'

'I know, you've said already we might be being tracked, but – what's *koro-koro*?'

Ma Shango sighed. 'Like, clear vision?' Then laughed, adding: 'What you need, girl!'

They prepared some supper – more dried meat from the cow Ma Shango had shot, together with slices of nara melon, supplemented by a mouthful or two of water – and then bedded down for the night, this time the Ma settling next to Cat on the sand by the scoop loader, covering both of them with her camouflage jacket and an old, rather stinky tarpaulin she'd found in the back of the cab.

The rock's red colour shortly became purple, then dark blue, finally deep black, broken only by a sheen of moonlight and the spikes of stars, each one searching out its echo in the gleaming mica on the rock face.

'Dem ray from star,' the Ma wondered as they lay on their backs, looking up: 'What dat light go dey find?'

'Good question,' replied Cat. 'But I guess we can't say, always thinking about light in terms of its origin, or where it falls, rather than as something conscious of its own direction.'

'But everything have direction of its own. Like veggies, and human, and cow too, we all go waka for water. Water ensef, what she dey seek?'

'Water wants to go downhill. Or evaporate.'

'True. And fire, e want find air, but what light seek?'

Embarrassing, to be in the role of explainer. 'Well, it's both a wave and a particle, depending on how you describe it.'

'That not what I mean, girl. What light e *seek*, what be the target?'

'Um, that's complicated. I'd never thought of light having a point of view.'

'For sure she do,' mumbled the Ma, a few minutes later beginning to snore.

Trying to doze off likewise, Cat thought of her mother, and next of Nadine. Then found that she could not visualise either of them well. Despite the Ma's evident presence, she felt very alone.

The further she'd gone in this quest, despite having arrived at its apparent destination, it was as if she was still losing ground every second. As if she was one of those rays of light of which the Ma had just spoken, going out across the universe looking for the right object. There had been a few moments during the journey so far when she thought she didn't need anyone's assurance, wasn't vacillating as usual, but those feelings of strength now seemed to have dissipated with the coming of night.

She listened to the rhythmic rumbling produced by the vibration of soft tissue at the back of Ma Shango's nose and throat and wondered if she really was, in fact, already where she was meant to be.

32

A tumult in the clouds

Waiting in his flight suit, helmet under his arm, Selvy Masuku scanned the morning sky above the airstrip at the Scursail headquarters. It was rapidly filling with clouds, which tumbled over each other in folds of pink and red silk. Good flying weather for the Python, except for a slight sign of muddied skies on the far horizon, which could presage a storm.

The airstrip stretched out around him, amid sandy bunker tops and the tail fins of the cargo planes that had been bringing in construction supplies for the new mines Scursail was building nearby.

Behind the ranks of planes, hangars faded to a wire fence and lines of blasted trees in the distance. Despite the fine sunrise, a strong breeze was blowing from the east, making the wind-speed indicator on the top of the nearest control tower spin round rapidly.

On the edge of the runway asphalt a small knot of paramilitaries, members of B33, were checking their gear as they waited for Masuku's Python, along with a fire truck and a bunch of airport operatives in overalls, one of whom had a pair of paddles for directing aircraft, which he was tossing up into the air and catching as he waited.

It was as if the whole world spun with those paddles. Masuku was plunged back into memory, recalling playing table tennis for the first time – someone having had the bright idea of making an outdoors table out of concrete at the centre of the South African village in which he'd grown up.

Masuku was brought back to himself by the sound of a zip. At the feet of each soldier were long black canvas bags containing an assortment of automatic weapons, two cans of ammunition, a hunting knife, four blocks of plastic explosive, a first-aid kit including a morphine needle, a canteen of water, three days' supply of rations, two fragmentation grenades, a raincoat, helmet, boots, gloves, a powerful UHF radio and an extra change of socks and underwear.

Soon these men would be winging their way north in an aircraft flown by him – the fabled Python, the special bird. Masuku sucked air into his lungs, trying to contain his fury that he was still mired in all this, as if the freedoms Mandela had won from these *umlungu* so long ago counted for fuck all. Yet, given what he was doing, he was perhaps the very last person to say so.

In his flight-suit pocket Masuku had a printed location target for the aquifer. It was strange, given that everything was also electronically lodged, that the system still produced these flimsy dockets. He watched one of the B33s sharpening his trench knife, rhythmically moving the blade against a stone, before the sound of a vehicle caught his attention.

Masuku next observed a staff car making its way onto the runway. Out of one of its doors stepped Wim de Vries.

As their commander approached, the troops stood to attention as elegantly as they could manage in their battle gear. An NCO started forward to speak to de Vries, but paused when he held out a restraining hand. 'Give me a minute, Neuman. I need to check something with Cole.'

He acknowledged Masuku with a cursory flick of his blond head. 'You're up for this *jol*, right?'

Masuku nodded, trying to contain his feelings.

'Better go get the Python then.'

De Vries touched the miniature mic integrated into his battle tunic and spoke a few words into a high-powered UHF radio. 'Boomslang and friends confirmed at Kunene. Ready for off.'

As de Vries continued speaking into the little plastic comma on his collar, Masuku was driven away to the hangar in the same staff car that had brought de Vries, that creature of violence who fancied himself as Boomslang.

The genesis of de Vries's codename was a large, venomous snake native to Sub-Saharan Africa. Its name meant 'tree snake' in Afrikaans (*boom*: 'tree'; *slang*: 'snake').

'Briefing, men!' announced the bearer of this forbidding sobriquet after his radio conversation with Glen Cole, who was already nearly at the supposed aquifer, having set off the night before in a truck full of troops.

The NCO who had approached de Vries brought out items of equipment from one of the kitbags and passing them to his commander, who began attaching them to a utility belt as he spoke: grenades, knife, camel bag . . .

The B33s gathered round their colonel as he explained how they would land the Python on an expanse of sand and make what he described as 'a neat capture' of a lump of rock, his Afrikaner accent giving a harsh inflection to the vowels. 'Should be a simple job,' he added at the end.

'Any defenders?' asked one of the soldiers.

De Vries was now threading a webbing belt through the loop of his battledress trousers. 'Unlikely will be much. We just slot any dog who's there, anyways. Got it?'

The soldiers nodded in assent.

He was distracted by the approach of the plane. The Python ERICA Quad Tilt-Rotor, to give the special bird its full name, was now rolling from the hangar onto the airstrip with Masuku at the controls. ERICA stood for 'Enhanced Rotorcraft Innovative Concept Achievement' but de Vries preferred Python. Good brand name for what the thing was.

De Vries looked at the four large-bladed rotors that would control the aircraft's descent, now motionless, twisted down for land operation, and the front rotor, which was driving its motion towards them.

As it was moving the Python bounced a little, going over a pothole on the runway. De Vries spat on the ground, then muttered, '*Hy het op sy gat geval.*' 'He fell on his arse': a reference to Selvy Masuku, because the pilot had not avoided the pothole.

Within the cockpit, the subject of this comment switched off the engine. The noise of the rotor began to subside, but it still kept turning for a while, sending gusts of air and sound over the airfield. De Vries felt the subsiding *lub-lub-lub* of it wash over him. Technicians began moving around the black flanks of the fuselage, attaching fuel hoses, adjusting settings on the tail unit.

His lips pressed together, de Vries put on his helmet, fastening the strap beneath the chin with a hard tug, cocking his head in the opposite direction as he did so. Then, without a word more to his troops, he turned and headed towards the door of the Python, where an automated set of stairs was appearing.

The other troops, black-clad and bulky, followed de Vries to the stairway that, one by one, delivered all the B33 men into Masuku's aircraft, where they began strapping themselves into their seats.

Sitting in front of the instrument panel in the cockpit, Masuku had already reached underneath his own seat to assure himself of the parachute pack – always the first check. He next plugged in his helmet and begun going through his other checks. The routine of gyros, radio, fuel pumps. Air pressure. Starter motors.

Now, as he pressed a button and the rotors began functioning again, the noise in the cabin increased with every rotation.

Masuku made more checks and adjustments, fixing the location of their destination in the onboard computer against the one on the flimsy target docket.

He opened the throttle. The Python's engines roared towards full capacity and the rotors began to speed up further. Compressing the air between the wings and the ground, they lifted the craft into the shaken sky. There was a feeling of buoyancy as the sunrise seemed to wrap itself round the cockpit.

At 800 feet a shudder passed through the hull as Masuku altered the Python's main rotors to the horizontal. There was a sudden surge, a forward thrust. Masuku kept his eyes on the instrument panel, checking speed counts, radar blips, fuel gauges.

Finally, the weapons systems. In this technical world he felt safe, secure from other complications.

On a monitor – one he had switched off on a previous journey, during which de Vries had thrown two prisoners out of the open door – he could see what was happening in the cabin. As the sky grew into light outside, the low-level lighting back there went off, causing the strange gleams that had shone on the matte-black composite material of the troopers' body armour to disappear.

Most of the men were lying back in the uncomfortable seats trying to catch up on sleep. A few munched on chocolate or sipped coffee from canteens. Others adjusted their weapons, digging about in their kitbags for squirt cans and stained rags, which they applied to their armaments with loving care.

Drops of moisture began to slide across the Plexiglass that separated Masuku's eyes from the onrushing clouds. Soon, certainly enough, the Python would arrive at its destination, but the pilot himself was feeling very uncertain. He did not want to be part of this, any more than he had wanted to be part of the attack on the convoy a few days earlier. He again thought of his wife back in Hermanus. To be by her side was what he wished for, and he was nowhere near achieving it.

What impulse had first driven him to it, this tumult in the clouds?

33

Common sense

Half an hour before dawn, Cat sat bolt upright. A frenzy of images, voices, memories immediately began contesting in her head; she felt estranged, in limbo, hyphenated. The horror of thirst returned: the lidless sun, the bands round the throbbing throat, the unfurling skin. She reached in panic for the waterskin the Ma had made, unlaced it with one hand, leaned over, brought her cracked lips to the nozzle.

Slowly, in semi-darkness, she began to piece together her surroundings: vehicle shape, rock shape, very big, in a space of sand, billowing dunes at the rock face, all foreshortened by a bulky shoulder beside her – rising, falling and making a noise.

The sound was only Ma Shango, of course, still snoring. Cat rubbed crusted eyes, looking across at the Ma's face. It had taken on a grey pallor in the early light – for some reason making her think of Nadine.

I should have gone back for her.

She tried to re-dress her mind in rationality. The grey on Ma Shango's face was that of coming dawn, not the grey of death. There was no point in being miserable about Nadine till she was able to find out exactly what had happened. Job to do here, finish it at last. Find out once and for all whether this is the aquifer or not. But then what? And Mam, what about her too?

She stood, walked a little away from the sleeping woman, looking at the encirclement of light on the dunes, parts of which were still in black shadow from the rock.

Other areas of sand were growing reddish over the dunes, the shade of the fuchsia in the Well Field hedge, on the house side of which Uncle Tony kept a small kitchen garden, growing potatoes, beans, radishes ... Sometimes he swapped produce with the neighbours, the Finucanes, despite historical argy-bargy about boundaries between the two families. In those moments of exchange, what they held in common seemed more important than the arguments about who owned what, one side or other of a crumbling stone wall.

Despite the beauty of what she was looking at – the reddening sunrise casting its glow over the lee of a dune – Cat felt so homesick at this moment. She wanted to be out of danger, but the world had not signed her release. Had she'd been stupid in not agreeing to Ma Shango's Angola plan, even though the Ma had implied it was a shithole? She didn't know, looking again at the light spreading across the dunes, as if she might find an answer there.

A rumble came, sounding through her feet, and she was sure this time it wasn't Ma Shango's snoring. Something more subterranean, but what?

Through all this process that humans call dawn, the rock itself had seemed unchanged save for the glances of light that were now falling on it. Despite these, the monolith appeared powerfully resistant to any influence, truly awful in its immobility.

Basic rock, though she was convinced that she had just heard it speak, like the Well Field used to speak its language of puddles, mouldering stones and tussocks of marsh grass. Cat thought again of the lions letting her drink beside them, as if there were common sense between two species; but even if that was what had happened, and she wasn't sure it was, that affinity would surely never apply to basic rock? The monolith was inert, at least it was so in most human timescales, broadly unable to connect with us or to gain the kind of awareness that we have. But what was 'us' now, what was 'we', when the planet was transmitting so powerfully the effects of human action upon it?

She almost kicked herself, wanting to refute her own thoughts, to counter this vain attempt to *connect* with everything, which had happened so often on this journey. It was as if she had been infected with some sort of mind-virus.

The rumble from the rock came again, almost at once, as if answering her questions direct. But if this was really some movement of the subterra, why hadn't she heard it last night? Cat was so consumed by the strangeness of all this that she did not hear the tread of Ma Shango behind her – jumped when the Ma said, 'Reckon you look in wrong direcshun.'

She turned to see what her companion meant. The Ma was standing stock-still, staring into the desert. With a hand raised above her eyes, she was following something on the clearing horizon.

'What is it?' asked Cat.

Ma Shango did not reply, instead running over to the earthmover, half climbing inside as she rummaged in the glove compartment for her binoculars; returned to the same spot with these fixed to her eyes and was once again silent.

'Well?' said Cat.

The Ma shook her head. 'They waka come here quicker than I for think.'

'Who?'

'I bin say you before. Eyes dey see us for sky!'

'Whose eyes?'

'B33 eyes. Scursail Mines sojas. Dem us dey follow who attack before.'

She handed Cat the binoculars and, raising them to her own eyes, Cat discovered what was concerning Ma Shango. In the distance a military truck could be seen.

'Omo, dey reach hia so soon-soon,' said Ma Shango. 'We must climb dat rock right now. We go drive round the back, see if fit hide dis dumper.'

Cat was seized by panic. 'Wait, why don't we drive away?'

'No time, girl, sabi? Make we shift!'

Even though there was urgency in Ma Shango's voice, it wasn't like she seemed as scared as Cat was feeling. Why had the Ma really taken the decision to come here and not flee to Angola like she planned? The only reason Cat could think of was that the Ma actively embraced the idea of risk and mission, even if in this case the risk was incalculable and the mission unclear.

It took them about twenty minutes to drive round to the other side of the rock and roughly the same amount of time, once on the other side, to find a suitable crevasse in which to hide it.

'We need suppose slippy,' Ma Shango said as she manoeuvred the scoop loader into a slice in the rock. Not an easy task. 'They go waka here soon.'

The Ma clambered out of the vehicle and immediately began looping the leather ties of the waterskin onto her back. 'Jump down now, eh?'

Cat was rooted to the passenger chair in the cab. Fear was holding her back again.

'You just gonna sit there, sista?' exclaimed Ma Shango, now hooking the double holster of Zowa's sawn-off shotguns onto her back, next to the waterskin. 'Abeg, carry your little bum-bum comot for dat seat!!'

Cat did get down at last, her mind running in every direction as the slam of the vehicle door behind her seemed to close off all other possibilities than that of finally facing the reality of climbing the monolith. After all the innumerable risks and decisions she'd so far half-thinkingly taken, hoping they'd lead her to some kind of intimacy with her mother and the aquifer, here she was, getting into something much deeper.

They stood next to the vehicle in its new hiding place in a large crevice of that vast rock. The Ma explained again that their best option was to climb high into it and find a hiding place of their own.

Cat hesitated once more: if the Scursail people really were so near, surely they'd be better driving on, in spite of her own mission. Again, she told Ma Shango so.

But the Ma was indefatigable, gathering her weapons and the waterskin about her and beginning to haul her body up a steep, broken sort of path that ran along the side of the massif. Ma Shango's movements seemed so definite, so *real* compared to her own uncertainty, that Cat thought she had no choice but to follow her up the path. She'd spent far too much time in contemplation rather than action, and overthinking had often (far too often, in fact) turned awry the current of her life . . .

So up the rock she went, struggling to keep pace with the Ma, who despite her greater bulk was much more nimble, Zowa's holstered shotguns jiggling on her back.

After sitting in the earthmover for so long, Cat felt a perverse pleasure in the pain in her limbs as she scrambled up the rock, coping with the underfoot rush of scree, feeling gradations of height from the cliffs and convolutions in her brain. Ma Shango all the while pressed on, going up at a pace, seeming then a better model for herself than her own mother.

She was doing it again, wasn't she? Stopping to think (gasp, actually!) for a second about her propensity to copy not just her mother but any powerful woman who came into her orbit. When all that was needed now was her own breath, her own sweat, her own handholds and footholds.

Ma Shango turned and said: 'Girl, just get a move on, will you? You need to spring from where you are to the next place.'

It was only common sense, what the Ma was saying, but it seemed so hard to keep going. Now and then the path almost disappeared, leaking into the scree-strewn landscape either side of it as they reached the flattened-out tops of cliffs – before going deeper again, cutting between more cliffs as they rose.

34

The path we follow is always our own

The plan at first was just to hide. To that end, Cat and Ma Shango continued scratching and scrabbling up the hardness of the monolith, welcoming now and then slight stirs of breeze as they climbed, kicking out stones, avoiding the hazards of crevasses and gullies where safe-looking stones turned into sliding gravel.

Sometimes, when she looked down into chasms on the side of the monolith, Cat was more scared of a submerged urge to throw herself off than of the need to keep on climbing, but above her always was Ma Shango, going assuredly upwards.

It was exhausting, under the strobe-like pumping of the sun: not yet anywhere near its highest, and Cat was again having flashbacks to her ordeal in the desert. But now Ma Shango was sharing that sun. She was such a good example in taking on fear as a measure of self-respect, and showing how contradictions can't be always solved by analysis, only by action, with all the grunting and sweating that entails; and by now Cat was doing a lot more grunting and sweating than the Ma.

More than an hour of ascent in a hurried frenzy, more than an hour of jamming toes and fingers into tiny cracks and fissures, brought them to a slab of sunbaked rock where they were able to catch their breath and take a gulp of water from the waterskin.

'We must comot of dis, go on,' said Ma Shango, panting. She reached out and grabbed Cat's wrist. 'Ah, girl, your looks don dull finish-o, but tire or no, we must waka on.'

Cat looked at her bleeding fingertips. 'I'm OK,' she said, uncertainly.

'You be mystery, woman-o. Sometimes you soft, cry-cry like pikin wey no get mama, other times you dey show plenty-plenty strength.' With these words the squat, piratical figure of the Ma bent down and helped Cat to her feet.

They continued up the devious path, climbing and resting, climbing and resting, until a moment came when Ma Shango stopped, turned with a sudden anxious look. 'Listen!'

Cat stopped moving and from far below heard the unmistakable grind of a truck engine. 'So they're here; what do we do now?'

'Make we sharp or we go die. If dey come roun' dis rock side, e go easy for dem to spy us.'

Ma resumed the climb, faster than ever now, moving upwards at astonishing speed for someone so large, sometimes reaching up for the high holds or stretching out a foot, at other times seeming to scramble along the indefinite, stone-encumbered path like a crab.

Following, Cat could feel her breath whistling in her chest and pain building up in her muscles and joints. She passed the next half-hour in a kind of trance, swaying and sweating in the Ma's wake, the barrels of the holstered shotguns making a V that swung from side to side on her back.

They were still not at the top of the monolith – in fact, there were hundreds of little rocky eminences to be surmounted, chasms to be jumped over, troughs, cracks, places to twist your ankle in, projections to crack your knees against, but eventually, after much expense of effort and the occasional outburst of cursing by Ma Shango, they approached the summit, coming at last to the final sun-blasted crag.

They worked their way through a narrow indentation until it suddenly opened onto a vast, anvil-like plateau. Out of this numerous black-basalt outcrops protruded like teeth.

Between the largest of these were large pools of yellow sand (all the redness of the sand they'd seen earlier was gone by now, the sun being higher). This sand had evidently been whirled up by wind and then settled on the plateau. Some of it yesterday maybe, Cat thought, some of it years ago, if the different compaction levels she noted were anything to go by. Walking on it, she could actually feel this difference as it sometimes slushed, almost like half-melted ice, at other times broke like a pie crust.

The whole aspect of the summit plateau was extraordinary, like a different planet with its saucers of sand interspersed with jagged outcrops of rock. Cat was about to remark on this when the Ma, still panting from the climb, said: 'Right, girl, make we go find better shelter, nice place where we go fit hide. We no go want make they come here catch us, else they go flog us well-well.'

They began searching for a suitable place to make a camp among the basalt outcrops, ideally somewhere with an overhang to protect them from the sun and with cover in case they were attacked. As Cat wandered off a short way through this blasted moonscape her eye fell upon a fault in the rock.

The fault widened as it drew away from her line of sight – rising, developing into a large gorge with ramparts of boulders on either side. There was a little fig tree halfway down, scrabbling for life in a patch of sand and, next to it, the remains of a gate and then some kind of collapsing structure made of wood and corrugated iron.

Surprised by this sight, Cat approached the fig tree across the litter of rock, which seemed almost to be trembling under her feet. After a short while the boulders cleared. She came to a patch of golden sand, in the middle of which was a small pond, evidently keeping the fig tree alive. A surge of excitement came on realising that there really was water here after all.

Between the pond and the dilapidated structure was a narrow path, fringed by scanty stalks of grass on either side. Alongside the path ran a rusty pipe, the end of which dipped below the surface of the dark-green water. Intrigued, she knelt down beside it; the pipe appeared to be made of small metal sections fitted together.

Some of the sections were rusty, flaking, some glinting brightly; she could hear the patter of water between the joints.

Tins, for goodness' sake! They were food tins pushed one into another and the water was running through them. One or two of the tins, she saw, had deteriorated labels in Cyrillic, the Russian script overwriting images of crab and tuna. But most of the tins were bare, their labels worn off.

Cat followed the pipe of tins past what might have once been a gate bisecting a ragged fence of staves. Beyond this perimeter, so far as it still existed, she discovered an upturned plastic chair minus two of its legs – and a human skeleton, minus its skull. On the sand round about lay small pieces of shredded, sun-cured army uniform, looking like overcooked bits of bacon.

It was shocking to see human remains. She flinched on seeing them, those headless bones, would have yelped aloud if she had not been so stunned. Slowly, remembering the details of the diary, she knew it must be the body of the KGB officer, whose death that document recorded.

Horror aside (if it ever could be), this did at least mean the path she'd taken here was her own: no more imitation zone. For this surely was, she knew it now, the place she had read about in the Russian diary; somewhere that had a connection to the body that her mother had found with Xin. But were these really the remains of the KGB man mentioned in the Russian diary? They could be someone else's. She'd learned to doubt that words represented reality, at least not directly.

Yet the proofs (she was again thinking scientifically) were pretty evident, even though so many years had passed since the diary was written. Here was a clay-brown Tokarev pistol lying on the ground; here were broken pieces of china; here was the ragged, corrugated-iron roof of the hut mentioned in the diary. The roof was half collapsed, a radio aerial wire coming out of the top, splitting into a dipole strung between adjacent crags. Another cable led out of the hut to a generator, half engulfed with sand . . .

All from so long ago. What was it, fifty years? Half a century. Should almost be approaching this like an archaeologist rather than a hydrologist, she said to herself as she crunched nearer to the ancient objects, over what felt like even more ancient sand.

And now again, beneath that self-same sand, it seemed as if the monolith was rumbling, trembling under her feet like a warning.

'Who be the stiff, den?'

Cat whirled round.

'Ah, sorry, girl. I no mean to make you jump like antelope. That's some very old body dere.'

'A Russian soldier. There were Russians here in the 1980s, and Cubans. They fought the apartheid regime.'

'Fightin' the fight. Dis their base?'

'Something like that. This is the place, Ma. This is the aquifer.' She spoke almost with joy.

'Well, if so you say,' replied the Ma, looking at her somewhat askance.

'It's true. I read about it. It's partly why I came here. This is what I was trying to tell the Priest and you, back in Dekmantel. It was some sort of gun emplacement.'

As Cat spoke, a mechanical sound echoed up from below the plateau. 'Stay for hia,' said the Ma, her brows knitting. 'Make I go for scout back down the gulch.'

35

About that likewise too

On the scraggy top of the monolith, sat on her haunches outside the abandoned Russian hut, Cat waited for the Ma to return from her look-see back down the path. With a prickle of anxiety released by the sudden silence, she found herself hit again by the realisation that she really was in the shit here. The idea that she was on some simple-sounding quest for her mother and an aquifer now seemed very far away indeed.

Following the excitement of realising that what they'd found up here was connected to the Russian soldier who had written the diary, she was now experiencing successive jolts of fear-soaked doubt again: what was the point of climbing the monolith at all if the Scursail people were only to pursue them up here, leaving her and Ma Shango totally trapped?

Did Ma Shango really have any plan at all? *Have I put too much trust in this woman, who seems so practical and persistent, so full of fire and so free of doubt herself?* Cat was beginning to worry about that too.

Now, here, at what seemed almost certain to be the source of the mysterious Alfaib, that half-active river, most of it running (when it ran) underground, she paradoxically remained as uncertain as that dream of water itself. How she longed to be more fixed on course like the piped water back home, which came reliably from a tap and with determinate physics.

But they were where they were, and something inside her told her she just had to trust the Ma's instincts. What choice did she now have anyway?

As these thoughts slid across the threshold of her mind, which seemed to be in an almost liquid state, she reckoned that she might as well have a look in the abandoned Russian hut, the opening of which lay just before her, a space that at least might afford her a small understanding of where she was.

Smelling musty, the hut contained: bedrolls; lamps; a rickety table; more plastic chairs; a cabinet upon which sat a very large radio with Cyrillic markings on the dials and knobs, its grey metal case connected by wires to a large battery on the wooden floor. Everything was covered in a thick layer of dust. She turned on the radio, but of course no sound came out.

Cat was still looking at the dials and knobs, thinking about the Russian diary and what it had told her about this place, when Ma Shango returned, puffing after having run up the gorge, binoculars banging against her chest.

'We shift now o. Dem sojas from the mine dey come for sure. I see dem start climb the cliff. About ten, twelve, proper military. Do sharp-sharp, my girl, we suppose run quick-quick!'

'Run *where*?' asked Cat quietly, and without any interpretative delay, for she had by now got the gist of the Ma's language.

It seemed to her that they were out of options, up there on that lunar time warp of the monolith. It was as if all her worries about Ma's plan had come home to roost.

'Make you no worry about dat!' Ma Shango unholstered one of the shotguns from her back. 'If you wan survive for dis world, no just look back – continue move!'

Cat was about to follow the Ma when she spotted something. 'Look,' she called, pointing, 'at the back! What do you think's in there?'

Ma Shango turned, her eyes following Cat's finger to the back of the hut, where a piece of frayed green canvas formed a kind of curtain across a tall aperture in the rock. This was, in fact, also the terminus of the gorge up which they'd climbed.

'OK,' said the Ma. 'We go see, but very little time, girl.' Even though time was short, as the Ma had said, Cat experienced a glitch of irritation about being continually called girl.

Through holes in the tin roof of the hut the sun burned Cat's neck as she pushed aside the canvas to reveal the opening to a large cave. They both walked forward a little, whereupon the intense sensation of heat on the skin was immediately replaced by cool. A strong, dank smell filled Cat's nostrils.

'What be disone now?' murmured Ma Shango.

She took a flashlight from her pocket and played it over the cave, the smooth floor of which sloped down sharply into a large chamber. As she shone the light, they both became aware that along the top of the cave ran a long metal object, cylindrical in shape, which rose at an angle to a point high on the ceiling above where they stood: the Pion, Cat knew at once, the Russian supergun mentioned in the diary.

'By the saints!' said Ma Shango in wonderment. 'Dat one big barrel, Cat. Very big. But why no dey open the top of the rock for it shoot? E no make any sense.'

Cat looked up at the roof of the cave and saw that the end of the barrel almost touched it. Examining this enormous piece of artillery, Cat heard the subterranean rumble again. It was a stirring from deep below, down in the belly of the monolith – she was certain of that now – the guttural sound of underland, but now louder than before.

'Did you hear that, feel that?'

'Yep, girl, and for some time. Dat be voice of deep rock, churning like she always churn. Why you be so surprise, with yo science an' all? But dis big gun no less surprise, my what ting it be!'

It was true, about the science. Geologists used acoustic patterns from rocks to identify unstable regions below the surface where there was potential for earthquakes or eruptions. These signs of subterranean dislocation tended to increase in pitch and frequency the nearer one got to a cataclysmic event. But it was all quite far (even in the broad church of earth science, never mind science as a whole) from her own area of study.

The Ma was meanwhile shining the torch downwards. They both saw that the barrel stretched so deeply back into the cave, after which it was absorbed into a gun carriage supported by two large wheels at the front and two smaller ones at the back.

Either side of the gun carriage large shells were lined up, along with wooden crates tool-stamped with Russian writing, and many sacks of what looked like pasta or rice, one or two trailing white lines in the ghostly light, evidently having been gnawed open by rodents or burrowed into by insects.

Grey-green in colour, its lines softened by the poor light in the cave, the giant artillery piece looked like some great prehistoric dinosaur.

'Biggest cannon me ever see,' said the Ma. 'Though I no fit get how e come enter here. Unless they done construct it inside?' She clambered down to inspect the gun carriage.

'Do you think we can use it against the soldiers?' asked Cat, staring at what was clearly a very powerful weapon.

'Shell still dey for the breech!' shouted the Ma, sitting on the firing seat. 'Dis remind me of those times when I still in Nigeria Navy.'

But the expression on her face was puzzled. 'But no fit shoot, with dis kain barrel so near roof. How it get hia, I just doan get.'

'Craned in?' suggested Cat. 'But how?' She stamped with her foot. 'The floor's wooden. Maybe there's . . .'

But the Ma wasn't listening, looking instead at the ceiling. 'Blow-wow!' she cried, clambering back up to the opening. 'Dat roof – explosive charges wire up dere!' She pointed at a line of ancient, plastic-looking slugs along the roof of the cave, each one connected to its neighbour by a black wire.

'Ah, now I dey get,' Ma Shango said. 'Is false roof of rock and earth. Fi wan use gun, dem blow 'am. Not sure will help our crisis, sista, but we try, girl, always must try.' She patted the long shaft of the gun. 'Plenty bang in dis one. But make we dey waka rapid before those sojas reach here.'

'So what are we going to do?'

'Make you no worry, I don buck up with some notions of own sef. And reckon more weapons fit for hia, if dese boxes look like I am see.'

Holding the flashlight in her mouth, the Ma took a knife from her belt and began opening the dusty cases, the splintering sound echoing loudly in the cave. The first three crates contained bottles of vodka and cartons of cigarettes, tins of food, some kerosene lamps, matches and fuel.

The Ma gave her torch to Cat to free up her hands and then, on opening a fourth box, gave a cry of triumph, turning open six AK-47 rifles, still in grease. Another box contained rounds of 7.6 mm ammunition, and another fragmentation grenades, closely packed, like fruit ready for market.

'Ah, we don get more firepower now, though old and maybe no fit work,' said the Ma grimly, lighting a kerosene lamp so she could see better. 'You know how fi use one of dese banana guns?'

'I've done a little shooting,' Cat said, as she almost tripped over a coil of rope. 'We shot pigeons on the farm at home.' As she spoke, she was very aware that killing people was very different from killing pigeons.

'Any pikin can use an AK.' The Ma paused, lowering her voice, sounding serious. 'Dem be on us soon, girl.'

Sitting on a piece of rock that stuck out from the cave wall, the Ma began de-greasing the rifles, wiping them with a piece of old sacking. She fitted a magazine to one, then to another. Stacked the readied weapons like sheaves.

Again they heard the mysterious rumbling, but quieter now. Muffled by rock, Cat thought. Soon after, a sharper sound came from high above: metallic, repetitive, causing the air in the cave to thump.

'You clock am?' said the Ma. 'Helicopter too now, maybe same fancy one as attacked us with Priest.'

But, down on her knees in a corner of the cave, Cat was not concentrating fully on what Ma Shango was saying. She was following a small pipe that ran along the wooden floor to a diesel-powered pump covered in dust. The suction end of the pump went through a hole in the floor. Despite the flashlight and lamp it was still quite dark, so she had to peer to see more closely to see what she was looking at: a rectangular metal shape cut into the run of wooden planks. The object was a small handle.

36

Inside datdat aquifer

As Cat stood over the trapdoor and pulled up its handle, she again heard the subterranean sound – before guttural, later like a whine, now it was more like a repeated screech. The higher pitch and frequency suggested that if dislocations really were underway beneath, they were now happening at a faster rate. All this worried her, but there was too much else to think about.

'Hey,' she cried out, her breath catching. 'Ma, it's here!' Under the planks of the floor, now shimmering under the play of the torch, was an underground lake. Water. This must mean that the monolith *was* the home of the aquifer. It was real, the thing she had been trying to envisage for so long.

The Ma didn't reply; was she up at the entrance of the cave? Still worrying about what was coming, she must be . . .

Cat let her eyes slide over the surface of the lake as she considered the vastness of the water that must be beneath, lodged in pores of rock. Time slowed; she was like a child seeing something for the very first time, something strange, going beyond what could be attested. As she moved her torch it dropped spangles of light into the browny-black, depthless-seeming lake.

She suddenly thought of her mother, as if each of those little dips of illumination were, in fact, soft-melting murmurs of grief, lapping to and fro rhythmically. If Mam had seen this place, she must have been excited, as Cat was excited now. What a thing to be able to tell other researchers about later.

As her eyes adjusted, the water below now seemed completely clear. An odd change. Cat's torch created a beam of light through it that seemed as if it might go on forever. But before she had time to fully comprehend the sublime beauty of the lake, which already seemed much larger than she had at first thought, there was a shout from the mouth of the cave followed by a burst of automatic gunfire.

'Cat, they don waka come here-o!' shouted the Ma. 'I seen dat Cole guy.'

Cat couldn't see at first, only hearing shots, then got back nearer to the opening, where Ma Shango was firing from the hip as soldiers tumbled through the opening between the cave and the hut.

As quickly as Cole's men came in, she downed them. Five to ten men. The noise and smell of automatic fire filled the cave. No less automatically, a pile of limbs and weapons developed by the opening to the cave, the sides of which were now wreathed in tendrils of smoke.

Creeping nearer, Cat took cover behind an outcrop of rock.

'Stay for down, blocking your ear,' shouted the Ma. 'And take dis.' She slid one of the AK-47s across the wooden floor. 'When I don dey move, make you fire at the opening.'

With that, the Ma scrambled up and made a run for the box of fragmentation grenades. She seemed to roll, slipping from side to side as fire poured down on her from the opening, where more soldiers were now using the bodies of their comrades as cover.

Cat aimed, pulled the trigger; the rifle kicked in her hands, sending a fusillade towards the pile of bodies, the bullets thumping into dead flesh with sickening efficiency. She turned away, disgusted at herself, letting the rifle slide out of her hands to dangle by her side on its shoulder strap.

She saw the Ma pick out one of the grenades and, removing the pin, throw it towards the entrance, just as another incoming soldier began to top the grisly barrier made by the tangled bodies of his comrades. Cat covered her ears – the movement of her arms sending the strap of the AK-47 sliding off her shoulder, and the rifle to the ground – but still the sound of the explosion entered her eardrums like driven nails as the force of the blast washed over her.

The cave filled with smoke, and small pieces of rock began to drop from the ceiling.

And then, suddenly, it was quiet. Cat crouched behind her boulder at first, feeling as immobile as a statue, then summoned up the courage to return to the trapdoor above the lake, which seemed like it might be a place of greater safety.

'Ma?' she shouted in panic over her shoulder on the way there.

'Level, I dey hia, sista.' She appeared from behind a rock and let off a backward shot at one of the twitching bodies by the entrance. 'But me I fear disdis party don finish; you sabi what I mean?'

'I found the water. Through this trapdoor. I think it's the top of the aquifer.'

'You don find am? Good girl! Make I come over.'

She came to join Cat, who again lifted the trapdoor. There was barely a glimmer on the water until she shone the torch down, whereupon it lit up again like crystal. The Ma leaned over to look, wincing, but with a delighted smile on her face all the same.

Blood was seeping through the side of her jacket, Cat saw. 'You're hurt.'

'Pain mean nothing to me, sista. I sabi that dirty fella too well.'

For a second it was quiet, and then they heard the sound of rotors above, echoing in the cave. Cat was unable to move, tears pricking at her eyes.

Ma Shango sighed. 'Weird copter coming, sista. And we seen dat one before. E fit come down soon. And plenty more troops fit follow am, na I reckon so. Make you be hush now. E for beta make you waka enter dat wata hole.'

'What about you?'

The Ma looked up at the charges in the roof, at the little white lozenges with black wire strung between them. 'I get small something arrange for dem. Girl, waka enter for inside dat wata right now. Carry flashlight.'

Again Cat was immobile, paralysed.

'Get in the wata! Move!'

No more words passed between them. Cat sat on the edge of

the trapdoor, then, as she shuffled her bum forward to let her feet and ankles slip down into the water, saw Ma Shango roll under the gun carriage, finding a place where a metal plate covered her. Ma drew one of Zowa's sawn-off shotguns from its holster, and then the other. Rolling onto her back, she lifted both guns in her hands and aimed at two of the white charges on the ceiling.

The water was icy-cold. Sat with her ankles immersed, Cat put the end of the torch in her mouth. Next, sliding down, using one hand to reach up and pull down the door on top of her, she hung with the fingers of both hands hooked over the edge of the opening, caught uncomfortably between the trap and its door. Instantly registering something like an electric shock, she suddenly saw a white blaze through the crack above her, then felt a thump of explosive force.

The edges of the cave seemed to curl up. Large pieces of stone rained down, amid them dead soldiers, their limbs grossly distorted as they fell like puppets. Above the big Russian gun, the rock ceiling was collapsing, opening to reveal the sky.

37

Guillotine

Having let go of the edge of the trapdoor at the moment of the explosion, Cat splashed into the water. Cold immediately crept into her bones as she kicked to keep her head up. As the door above fell shut, she gripped the metal end of the torch harder, hurting her teeth, terrified of the complete dark that would otherwise come. The flashlight got doused once but she jerked her chin back in panic. She managed to keep it up out of the water and it continued to shine. The interior walls of the cave seemed to spin around her, their gleaming stone slick with runnels of condensation and the slime of algae.

Treading water, she was very afraid. *What am I going to do?*

She kicked harder so that she could take the torch out of her mouth for a second or two. Above the smell of the water, her nose was becoming alive to rotting things, ancient carcasses.

Taking it out of her mouth, Cat played the torch through 180 degrees until she saw a little ledge across the water. She put the torch back into her mouth, and it was then that she first thought she heard a noise, a scratching. She swam quickly to the ledge.

In the cave above, Ma Shango leaped onto the metal gunner's seat of the cannon and pulled back the firing pin. Setting off the charges in the roof had been the 'small something' she had arranged for the attacking troops, but now she had something bigger in hand; in fact, a whole fistful of intentions. She'd found some ear-muffs so that was a start.

★

Above Ma in turn, the Python hovered, its rotors wobbling in the air directly in front of the big gun. De Vries was in the pilot seat now, feeling inadequate to the immense power within his hands as well as a residual rage that his pilot, Masuku, that *fokken skapie*, had bailed on him, putting the craft on autopilot and suddenly jumping. *Ja*, the pilot had leaped out, throwing himself on the mercy of the desert, hoping his parachute would open. Well, good luck to him, out here on the Skeleton Coast. *Mompie* was cutting his own throat.

Cat's fingers touched the ledge at the edge of the cave, which was as slippery as soap. With some difficulty, she pulled herself onto the narrow shelf of rock and sat there shivering, listening to the echo of her own breath and the faint noises of fighting above. She turned off the torch, thinking she should save the battery. She turned it on again a few seconds later, having heard a splash; she was sure now that there was something else in the pool.

But she couldn't see anything, just the surface of the water and, on the ceiling, long milky veins of fungus. The underground lake was, she estimated, about the size of a hurling pitch. The planks of the wooden roof above her – or, more properly, the floor of the Russian gun chamber – only covered part of it; the rest was rock, into which the ends of the wooden planks had been chiselled.

Somewhat in confusion, as he struggled with the unfamiliar controls of the Python, that ideal military helicopter, de Vries perceived down on the ground some way in front – leisurely enough, as his mind went through the reflexive process of making out the meaning of what he was seeing – a large woman wearing ear defenders. It irked him after the fact, this feeling of aboriginal sensation upon which he'd taken too long to bring rational categories to bear.

A woman whom he recognised from a screen in Scursail's Kunene headquarters – he was copying it again in his head, but slowly enough – as that same Ma Shango who'd been on the surveillance camera of the drone back at HQ.

Now she appeared to be sitting at the base of an enormous artillery piece just in front of him as he hovered above the broken-open top of the cave, the ground in all directions now littered with fragments of the Russian hut and pieces of rock.

The woman was smiling in satisfaction, and de Vries suddenly began to understand what she was going to do. He wished that Masuku was still in control after all, as the handling of this Python was way *te moeilik* for him to understand.

Ma Shango was indeed satisfied, highly so. The action she was about to take seemed to her like something redeemed from long ago. As if each and every one of her ancestors was speaking through her lips as she said again: 'Disdis party don finish!' This utterance came only a few seconds before the shell from the cannon she'd just fired took out the Python's main rotor. She'd been aiming for de Vries himself, but still, it was pretty amazing that the old gun had fired at all.

All this happened just after Cat smelled a tang of feline urine, much more pungent than the ammoniac smell that had hung over Dekmantel. Then she saw the eyes. At first it seemed impossible, but there they were, on another ledge on the opposite side of the cave: three black-maned, yellow-furred lions, all lying on their bellies, motionless apart from pink tongues continually flickering in and out, taking salt from the rocks.

A deafening boom came from above, and then a crashing noise. A few pieces of stone were falling through gaps in the timber ceiling, making splashes in the water. Along their own narrow ledge, one of the lions stirred in response, seeming to shoulder forward on its squat legs, moving like a robot.

There was now nothing human in its malevolent muzzle. In fact, it seemed to Cat the stuff of nightmares, as far as could possibly be imagined from the companionship-in-water she'd previously experienced, out there in the desert. The beast that had moved . . . just the sight of its teeth made her shudder.

Cat suddenly realised that Serra dos Leões, in the phrase of whatever Portuguese adventurer had first named this place, didn't mean 'mountain range of lions' at all – *serra* referring to the way mountains on the horizon could seem like the teeth of a saw. No, it meant something more like 'place where lions cut' or 'place where lions saw' – with their teeth, upon humans. Something had been lost in translation.

She swept the torch across the water only to realise, with an even deeper shudder, that there were other ledges, other lions. A whole pride, perhaps. They lazed as dogs do, some younger, some older. There must have been about ten of them, she thought, the pink ends of their darting tongues catching gleams of her torchlight.

On one ledge were what seemed like eggs; no, they weren't eggs, they were . . . skulls. Three human skulls, their dead eyes looking back at her across the water. Next to one of these, which still had some skin with a tuft of dark hair attached, was a Russian Army cap.

She knew it at once. The same absurdly large cap with metal grommets, airholes, internal leather headband, Soviet red star above the brim, and plastic chin-strap that used to hang from a hook on the door of her mother's bedroom.

The lions were gazing at her now, slowly blinking their eyelids. It was as if they were trying to tell her something, maybe like the ginger tom had seemed to do back in that north Kerry barn.

Lying there in terror, like a dank mermaid on the edge of a beached world, she realised that several things might be being messaged across the water: first, that she had spent far too long in her own head, not looking about her; second, that her prejudices and obsessions really got in the way; third, that one of those skulls must be that of her mother.

Of these, the last was the most shocking (almost too shocking to be dwelled upon), not least because it really did feel as if the lions were telling her that her mother was dead.

She wanted to vomit, but couldn't, as she imagined one of their forebears masticating her mother, for who else's could one of those skulls be? Eating her from the hands up, crunching her finger bones, consuming the hands that had sometime slapped a daughter, crunching radius and ulna and clavicle and all the interconnecting fascia and flesh and muscle and tissue and everything else with equal relish, all this digested by stomach juices. And that was before even starting on the main torso and the delicacies that lay inside, making a right turn at the neck and beginning the long feast downwards – which is what Cat was now projecting for herself too, panting at the horror of it.

One of the other skulls must have been Xin's, her father's, Dad's . . . though she had never thought of him like that.

The third skull – a pair of gold-rimmed glasses lay nearby it – did it belong to the lion researcher Max Cloete? Hadn't the pilot, Sean Morrow, mentioned gold-rimmed specs when he told her the story of her mother dancing with the lion scientist in the fire-light? Cat could well believe that Mam had dumped Xin for someone more like her, a scientist rather than a sailor.

What had gone on? Why were their skulls all here, laid out in some kind of love triangle? Had the two men, as men do, competed to get her mother to the aquifer, this lake of death? But it was far too late for detective work.

A lion slid into the water and began swimming towards her; she could see the tips of its mane moving across the surface.

As the creature advanced, the wood above the water began to splinter, crack. The structure of the Russian gun emplacement was shaking, collapsing, the planks pulling away from the ancient sections of rock into which they had been wedged. Cat hardly had time to realise that the roof of the cave was disintegrating even further when an enormous black shape – something mechanical, burning – fell through into the lake, its fire-seared parts hissing as they were doused in the abyssal water.

The lions – including the one in the water – at once disappeared, going deeper into what now seemed like a cave system. Suddenly aware that this might be her only chance to escape, Cat dived into the water, the surface of which was now filthy with rock dust and ash. She began swimming back to the trapdoor, skirting timber shafts, flaming plastic, feeling all the while that the manes of lions might be brushing against her belly.

She scrabbled through the water until she came to splintered planks, seven, eight inches wide, still just about nailed together.

She pulled herself up, water streaming down her face, her breasts, her stomach – water and blood, because somehow she had injured her face, the skin above her eye having snagged on something.

Hauling herself onto the small shelf of ceiling that was still left, digging her fingernails into the wet wood, she clawed to get purchase . . . then the weight of the planks changed – it was like being on a see-saw. And she was sliding down the other side.

As she fell from the planks onto which she'd just climbed, did she again see the lions gliding towards her, presaging claws and blood? But it was not animal movement: it was water itself that was moving, water being sucked away, going down through the rocks, deep into the underground pores of the aquifer.

It was lighter above her now, real sunlight was coming down, as most of the roof had gone. Only a hole there now, with ragged edges of rock and wood. What remained of the floor of the gun chamber had tipped up and was unsteady.

There was now a vast hole in the middle of that remaining part of the floor. Fallen within the enormous gap was, Cat was slowly beginning to realise, the fancy helicopter of which Ma Shango had spoken, the same one which had attacked them in the desert.

Piles of rock lay everywhere, rock and ripped sacks of provisions, pools of water between the rocks and the sacks – and no sign whatsoever of Ma Shango. The giant cannon had slipped over so that it was at an odd angle, swaying precariously on one wheel of its carriage.

Finished, gone, sobbing, Cat lay back on a rock, unheedful at first of those auditory signals of subterranean activity that had dogged her since she arrived. Where was she, the Ma? Then the higher-pitched noises, those warnings of cataclysm, screeched unignorably.

But Cat didn't have time to think more about the science of all this because at that point something mechanical rather than auditory happened: a movement so large that it began to unbalance the Russian cannon.

Suddenly the barrel of that great steel beast from so long ago fell down like a guillotine.

38

The nature of crisis

Faint and unsteady, Cat felt detached from her own body. Slowly she came to her senses, rebuilt her actual world, experienced the rock as rock beneath her, her heels in a crevice.

The barrel of the cannon had missed her, just. But where was Ma Shango?

And then she saw a figure, moving up the gorge, portly and carrying a handgun.

Not Ma Shango. Glen Cole.

Suddenly she was angry, full of righteous justice, all dreaminess gone. She wanted to destroy them all, the destroying men. She picked up one of the rifles that Ma Shango had called banana guns.

Cat clambered out of the crevice, blinking because of the sunlight. The AK was heavy in her hands. She shot off a volley of fire, the gun jumping between her fingers like a live animal. A shout came from further down the gorge. She wondered if she had wounded him, but it sounded more like a curse than the voice of a man who had been shot.

He was there, below, behind a rock, aiming a pistol at her over the top of it.

'Your friends have caused me a great deal of trouble!' Cole shouted. 'That is going to stop, and stop right now. De Vries might have got himself *bliksemmed*, but well, here's Glenny!'

Frightened as she already was, frightened now by the pistol in his hand, Cat still almost laughed on hearing these remarks, which seemed like those of a man possessed by deranged self-assertion, as if he wanted to out-act all the other devils who'd plagued the region's history.

'Fuck you!' she replied. 'This water is not going be used for mines and factories. It's too valuable for that.'

Cole's laughter echoed off the boulders.

'Value? Value is determined by exchange, baby. For instance, what would you give me for . . . this?'

He pulled up, with great difficulty, by a bunch of hair with an unmistakable likeness to the leaves of a pineapple, the slumped figure of Ma Shango, clearly wounded.

'Drop the rifle,' he shouted. 'And then come down, with your hands above your head.'

Shocked, but still training the rifle on him as best she could, Cat called back, 'Let her come up first!'

She felt faint again, unsteady. It was now with the sunlight coming through extremely hot, and the ground seemed to tremble, as if the age-old team of temperature and pressure had got more firmly in harness.

Cat heard Cole's voice echoing up the gorge. 'Do you take me for a fool? Then you will both just climb back down into the depths of that lump of stone! If you come here, I will let her live.'

'Why should I believe you?'

In answer – he shot off his pistol. The bullet winged the rifle, making it spring out of her hand and clatter on the rock. She reached down for it and immediately another bullet zapped past, very near, spraying her face with chips of stone.

'Now, you come!' commanded Cole, his voice echoing up the gorge. 'She's nearly had it anyway, it will not take much to finish her.'

As Cole spoke, another sound emanated from the ground, rising to her ears at the same time as his words.

Trying to ignore the noise, Cat watched Cole shove Ma Shango onto a patch of rock, then grab her topknot again, holding his pistol against her temple.

'Don't!' Cat shouted. 'I'm coming down!'

As she spoke, the earth shook. An even huger thunder sounded from the core of the aquifer. The gun platform was promptly flung upwards by a great column of foaming white water; simultaneously, another body of water seemed to come in from outside, as if it was galloping fast across the sand towards what was left of the monolith. At the same time, more sunlight shone in, almost as if God himself had turned his torch on the scene, just as Cat had earlier.

There was another crash as the cannon fell further, tipping and joining the Python in the remains of the lake. Cat jumped to one side, flailing in the rising water. Then in an instant, but one during which time seemed both to stop and restart, Cat saw Ma Shango and Cole knocked over in a single blow, as if being squashed between the two walls of water.

And then she herself was being tumbled over and over by foaming surf, which caused an abrupt block to the sunlight that had been falling into the cave. In the midst of this, Cat spotted Ma Shango's body, a great jumble of camouflage, whipping past her – whereupon she herself lost consciousness, her last sense being water drumming against her feet . . .

Human actions (the firing of the supergun, the downing of the Python) and other non-human ones, some coincident tectonic shift probably, had combined to push the water that had just drained into the pores of the aquifer back out again, along with more water, so much more from other channels beyond – discharging with all the hydraulic power of which a quake-driven flood is capable.

The firing of the supergun and the impact of the falling helicopter might have been the catalysts. Now the supplement to something more elemental, they were nonetheless human impacts that seemed to have changed 'the biophysical facts of the environment', as Professor O'Connor – and even Cat herself at another moment – might have said.

But, being half drowned, Cat saw none of this anyhow, so wasn't able to judge. And maybe nobody would have been able to say or assay for sure what had happened. It had all taken place remarkably quickly, after all, that explosion of water back into the cave and the weird onrush of further water which seemed to have come from elsewhere, all occurring in not much longer than it takes for an ordinary domestic loo to refill after being flushed. Was it that there were so many tunnels underneath, and that the firing of the gun had somehow blocked previous drainage channels, and this was the angry result? She didn't know, but whatever was happening had enormous kinetic energy.

When Cat came round – to a dead, heart-sunk silence – she was draped over the rear axle of the gun carriage, which was now sticking up vertically from a bed of jumbled rocks.

The AK rifle that Cole's shot had sprung out of her hands was beside her; she picked it up and hugged it to her, even though it would be of absolutely no help against the natural forces she now was facing.

There was no identifiable underground lake any more, no identifiable roof or cave, just what appeared to be a smallish island of rock surrounded by a huge expanse of grey mist, on which the remains of the supergun, and Cat herself, now rested. Whatever had happened in the subterranean depths of the aquifer, the whole region in fact, had forced up this pall of mist that engulfed everything through 360 degrees, making it hard to see. Condensation again, but on a much bigger scale.

Now, on that rock island, the half-destroyed gun carriage on which Cat was perched poked into the enshrouding mist like a strange sculpture, mocking with its mass the rifle that Cat was clutching.

Trying to peer through the mist, Cat's first thought was: so much water, stretching so far; impossible that all this had come up from a single aquifer. Something had happened which connected to much wider water systems.

Second, she thought about the precariousness of her position on that supergun carriage, which had toppled onto what appeared to be an island that had suddenly formed in the middle (was it really the middle?) of an inland sea. It felt like the last island ever.

But where was Ma Shango?

No sign.

The hour had arrived, Cat thought, but hadn't it arrived several times already? The real crisis was upon her – but she had felt it had come so many times before that this was no longer a novel crisis, however little sense that made.

She felt angry that all this was happening, angry that finding her mother had turned out to be nothing more than glimpsing a skull that might or might not have been hers, angry above all that her efforts had not produced any of the social good she had vaguely (very vaguely) hoped might come of this journey.

She looked out into the mist but could see nothing, so, putting down the rifle, she climbed down from the supergun carriage into the water next to the island, which came up to her waist.

As if this whole event had not been weird enough, the water was now clogged with something – blurry, lumpy, whitish in colour . . .

Wading through this particulate stuff (it was a bit like soap suds), feeling dizzy, yet hoping to spot Ma Shango amid the murk that was greying her vision – going nowhere really, splashing about, cursing when she stubbed her toes on rock and wiping her forehead because the murk seemed a bit acidic – she slowly realised that this water, this half-solid water round her, was filled with pasta from the soaked Russian sacks she'd seen in the hut.

Expanding and spreading, the pasta was forming a frothy surface coating amid which crates and boxes floated, along with pieces of the old hut and fragments of the burnt-out helicopter.

She stood bewildered for a second or two, looking at it – at this macaroni, pasta, whatever name the Russian had used in his diary. There was a lot of it.

And then from amid this whitish gloop there appeared, like a vision to Cat's eyes – Cat's crisis-ridden, explosion-struck, water-soaked eyes – a camouflage jacket.

Someone was hauling herself out of that pasta soup, sitting up, spitting out bits of it as if they were Tom-and-Jerry teeth.

'Never liked that stuff,' grumbled Ma Shango, splashing across towards Cat, stirring the white mess away from herself with her machete, using the point to flick it.

It was like the whole world had been redeemed on hearing Ma Shango's voice.

Approaching Cat, Ma Shango leaned heavily on her with one hand. The Ma was holding another hand to her own side, which was bleeding more heavily, staining the pasta-sea red.

Together they went back to that little island of rock, which seemed the ultimate island in a drowned world, the broken part of the gun sticking pathetically out of it.

Even as she helped Ma Shango get there, Cat was puzzling about how a drought world had suddenly become so wet, wetter even than those north Kerry fields she knew from childhood. Professor O'Connor had always said that such changes were to be expected in what he called the new normal, or new non-equilibrium, but it was so different to experience in reality what you had previously been told in theory. Possibly it would not much longer be possible to think of floods or droughts at all, in their categories, only of an endless series of uncertainties.

But there were, right now, far more urgent things to deal with. 'Thank God you are alive – but you need a bandage on that at once,' Cat said, looking at Ma Shango's copiously bleeding ribcage.

'Small sleep my body need now. I don tire bad-bad, sista.'

Cat made Ma Shango, who did not say anything more for a while, as comfortable as one could make anyone on a rock, then looked about to see if there was, in the floating crates and cartons, anything with which she might ease the Ma's condition.

And as she did so, she suddenly remembered that Glen Cole had been here too. He might, like the floating crates and cartons, still be about.

But, looking around, there was no sign of him.

Could she, after all this, after all these crises that had mounted one upon the other like the steps of someone climbing a mountain, afford to relax at last?

Possibly so, but first she had to find some way of helping Ma Shango, who was still bleeding out beside her on that island of rock, surrounded now by expanses of shallowish water, in which wooden boxes and broken bits of timber were floating, along with the pasta and random items of equipment. It seemed such a wrong end to the hopes of that great alleviation of thirst of which she and her mother had dreamed.

39

A major event

Searching for something with which she could staunch Ma Shango's bleeding, Cat found that she was able to wander through the detritus, albeit stumbling over submerged rocky protrusions and falling into sudden plunges. The level mostly came up to her waist – till the water got precipitously deep, before shallowing again.

She flopped around like this until by sweetness of providence she found, in fact, exactly what she needed: a first-aid kit, floating in a sealed tin with a red cross and more indecipherable Russian writing on it.

Returning to the island, she took out a dressing and bandage from the box – both were very stiff and friable, the brittle material almost seeming to come apart in her hands – and helped the Ma remove her blood-soaked camouflage jacket. There was a very deep gash in her ribcage where a piece of bullet-splintered rock had gouged out flesh.

Having tried to clean it, taking out pieces of rock with tweezers, Cat shook on some ancient, caked antiseptic powder and applied the bandage, making Ma sit up as she wound it on.

'Not sure how much help this is going to be,' she said in a worried voice. 'You've lost a lot of blood.'

'No worry, I go dey all right. I don experience the wey worse before, sista. Much worse!'

'It does look bad, Ma.'

'I all right . . . you very good to me,' was all the Ma said in reply, wincing. 'Well, we no go dey sunbathing, dat one na sure thing. What even cause dis havoc?'

'I don't fully know,' said Cat, looking around. While there were probably scientific reasons why the massive insuck and outpush of water that they had experienced had happened, testing those, understanding those, well, that was another thing altogether.

She rubbed the sweat from her eyes, half aware of Ma Shango lying back down on the rock with a groan. Cat looked around again. The idea that part of this desert, the world's oldest and driest, had become engulfed by water was messing with her mind, just as the water about them was messed by ancient Russian pasta. Remains of the *makaroni po-flotsky* mentioned in the Russian diary were still dispersing in the to and fro of the water.

The Ma gave another groan.

'Ma, you are not all right.'

'For sho, I am. But I no wan hear about wata, ever again. I don tell you, good sleep I need.' She was wheezing with pain now. 'You yourself must comot, waka go check dis strange land, else we go straight hell. Make sure say no other soja out dere, being sneaky. You dey hear me so?'

'I don't want to leave you.'

'Take leg, checkit. I no fear nothing. And take dat rifle too!'

As the Ma closed her eyes on that flat boulder in the middle of the rock island, her machete beside her, glinting in the dull light, Cat picked up the rifle.

She waded through the accumulated muck to the edge of what must once have been the massif – a distance of about 200 metres – where she stood half immersed, looking at the expanse of misty water, trying to work out what had happened; at the same time trying to stay aware of threats, as Ma Shango had advised.

And then a revelation came.

For Cat had suddenly realised that the whole expanse between the aquifer and the two great river basins of the Okavango and the Zambezi must have been subjected to an underground earthquake so large as to bring to light all sorts of previously unapprehended comprehensions. Many scientists believed the hydrological equilibrium of the Okavango, so far as it existed, to be entirely unconnected to that of the Zambezi – but science had not always thought so, and perhaps reality had now overtaken the recent science, producing new paradigms that were themselves non-equilibrium; again, she didn't know.

The missiles of the falling helicopter or the shells of the gun might have caused the aquifer to open, but at the same time the land along the course of the old Alfaib must have fallen, plunging large areas of former desert into the tumultuously rising water table below.

The more she thought about it, the more she knew it could be true. This was a major event, maybe something to be examined in future analysis of African hydrogeology as a moment when human actions had coincided with natural ones (but how can one make it, she thought, that separation?) to produce something cataclysmic, perhaps proving at last the advent of that still-unofficial scientific concept, the Anthropocene, when human activity started to have a significant impact on the planet's climate and ecosystems.

But how far away Professor O'Connor's voice, speaking in her ear alongside all the others, sounded now. She held the rifle to her, as if that, too, evidenced his theories, pressed the butt into her belly. Not just his theories. Mam's too. Her lost river, the river they'd both searched for, was suddenly alive. And becoming part of a great new inland sea.

Triumphant thoughts, glorious thoughts, and ones soon corrected in her mind as she rubbed off from the belt of her trousers a thumb-slick of grease from the rifle.

Corrected because: if this massive flooding had really happened, there would be a human cost – villages, maybe whole towns, that had become submerged. The scientific opportunity, the social opportunity, might also be a human tragedy; and that was before one even began thinking about the effects on plant life, animal life, across species that for so long had got used to being amid conditions of water scarcity.

Cat was reflecting on this astonishing turn of events, looking across the miracle of a water-invaded desert, when she suddenly saw Glen Cole's bloated body floating past. Staring at it – the slob was decorated with pennants of pasta – she heard Ma Shango's voice again, this time shouting almost as loudly as Big Business.

She turned to where the sound came from. For the second time that day, the injured woman was being carted along by her topknot. A tall man in black military gear was hauling her through the water.

The face of the man dragging the Ma was pitted, almost bubbling, a mixture of burnt flesh and melted Plexiglass from the stoved-in, burnt-out windshield of the Python helicopter – from which he must have somehow escaped, Cat dully realised.

'Howzit?' the man said as he got nearer, grinning crazily. There was something very wrong with one of his eyes.

The Ma was struggling in his demonic grasp, her own machete held at her throat. 'Cat!' she twice screamed, loudly at first and then more huskily.

'I'm here,' Cat said softly, shakily levelling the AK at the man in front of her. 'Who the hell are you?' she asked, speaking more loudly.

'He be dey top boy of B33,' Ma Shango groaned, holding her side, 'de Vries, dat be his name. He must fit be on dat helicopter but how he not kpeme, I just don't know.'

Still holding Ma Shango by her hair, de Vries side-slapped her with the machete, exactly on her wound, which caused a yelp, and then said: 'That's right, and this be the *antie* who has been such a *pyn in die gat*. You too, Irishwoman. So put down that rifle or else she gets it.'

It was his left eye that was wrong, standing out of his burnt face like a coin that had worked its way to the surface of a Christmas pudding.

De Vries progressed towards her, dragging Ma Shango, the latter dripping water like the mermaid in her song, the former (maybe appearing this way to Cat because of his charred face) seeming like a sweating labourer in a foundry.

'You're an animal.' Cat slipped off her rock and retreated into the water, taking care to keep the rifle trained on de Vries.

'That's just a word.'

There was a moment when she should have shot, but it all happened too quickly.

De Vries put the machete blade between his teeth, in order to be able to peel a strip of conjoined plastic and flesh off his cheek. Another remnant of the Python.

He made to cast off this piece of shedded skin in the water, but it stuck to his fingers like Sellotape. Giving a little phut of frustration, he rubbed it off on the front of his battle tunic before regrasping the handle of the machete.

Observing all this in stupefaction, Cat missed a second chance to shoot him. Mainly she'd been afraid she would hit Ma Shango, who seemed to have lapsed back into unconsciousness.

Holding up the rifle, Cat waded backwards, fearful she'd trip on one of the rocks strewn about, beneath the surface or sticking out of it.

'What do you think gives you the right to kill?' she said, looking at him with bitter revulsion, wanting again to shoot off the rifle.

'Lady was dossing, so I woke her up, hey? Probably would have croaked anyway, from the look of her.'

'Just a killer, nothing more.' Cat was determined to overcome this man.

'You talk too much.' He fingered the blade of the machete, approaching her unsteadily. 'Cheeky. Know what I'm gonna do?'

'Haven't a clue.'

His enraged face seemed to bubble even more. 'I'm gonna give you a *snotklap* with this.' He held up the machete. 'Then chuck you in this big pond you've made and make you swim for it!'

Cat shook her head, in which hammered an idea of revenge for what he was doing to Ma Shango. She didn't care what happened to herself now. 'That doesn't make sense,' she told him. 'I'm already in it.'

'You think?'

He came for her faster now, moving through the water, but hampered by Ma Shango's weight. She really didn't seem to be at all conscious now . . .

Cat raised the rifle higher but again was too indecisive, too full of self-doubt, to pull the trigger.

The protuberant gaze of de Vries's damaged eye – silvered with metal or chemicals – appeared to travel before him. It was as if the eye were pulling the man along.

As de Vries moved forward, he seemed to pause, his good eye looking down at his leg. Puzzled, he let go of Ma Shango.

His leg twitched.

What at first appeared to be the snout of a terrier snapped out of the water, rising and sinking in pulses as it bit repeatedly into de Vries's thigh.

It was just a cub, but a lion's a lion.

He gaped at it. Then cried out, 'What the *fok?*' in a kind of extended squeak.

He recovered, he resolved, held the machete tighter – hacked down with it.

This action seemed to call forth a quivering in the water, its currents going awry. Suddenly it was filling with other lions, their manes and tails cleaving the surface as they bore down upon de Vries.

His body started to tremble uncontrollably, his good eye now fixing no less a spectral stare than his bad one had on Cat, who was rapidly retreating from the water, fleeing the thrashing tails and raking claws to clamber back onto that bigger island of rock. There the remains of the supergun drooped pathetically, its self-slaughtered cannon covered in droplets of water . . .

She didn't quite understand what was happening except that de Vries was being attacked by the lions and she hadn't been, at least not yet.

Perhaps she had just been outrageously fortunate. She hoped that Ma Shango had been lucky too, but of her there was again no sign at all; she must be under the water, Cat thought in panic, wanting to do something but not knowing what.

Cat felt useless, finding hope only in those attributes of Ma Shango that she knew enabled survival – endurance, courage, a will to live . . . even as she judged her own lack of those qualities.

De Vries flipped up. The last she saw of him was his agitating legs kicking in the air. The water quieted suddenly, as if covered with a glassy calm. A few minutes later she heard a dragging sound, but couldn't see where it was coming from.

Sat there on the apocalyptic solidity of her rock, Cat waited for the lions to climb it, come for her in turn, to grind her flesh and bones into edible paste, which is what she imagined was happening to de Vries now – his mauled body carried in jaws somewhere safe, somewhere the lions had already found within the expanded landscape of this aquifer that she and her mother had envisaged for so long, that had been the source of so much trouble and claimed so many lives.

Shuddering, Cat wondered what she had done, or not done, to deserve this fate. All she'd basically been doing was trying to get power over herself, somehow. And do it graciously, with kindness to others.

She thought of all the promises she had made to herself – about Nadine, especially, but also Ma Shango – and felt unworthy. Far from being a saviour, she had done almost nothing, acting throughout this episode of her life, perhaps the whole of her life, under the influence of others. Even the predominant issue of thirst, which had seemed so important, to both her and Mam, seemed now to have been subsumed under the particular effect of another flow in her body. That of adrenaline. Its passage in her heart and airways, the blood vessels within her skin and her adrenal gland again (everything came like karma round again) was ebbing now but still a sense of danger remained.

Sat on that rock of the damned, she continued trying to come to terms with all that had happened, reflecting that at least she had finally discovered what had befallen her mother. Even if her head still hummed with questions about that in its detail. Even if, once again and so annoyingly, the process of simulation of her mother seemed about to recommence, as it was so likely that the lions would come for her too.

Crouched on the rock still, by now (despite the earlier heat) feeling as cold as an earthworm, she stared down at one of the rock's features, just there by her left-foot Puma trainer. Crystalline, the formation had almost the shape of a polygon; or several polygons. Because as she looked closer, it was as if there were a smaller copy of the exterior polygon in the interior one.

She got down on one knee – the rock hurt her, pressing in as if it, too, were alive. Looked closer . . . the formation really was like a copy with another copy within it, and possibly others too, all in the centre of their parent larger shapes, in a process of recursion.

There was, obviously enough, no self-awareness among these geological objects depicted within themselves, but it still seemed like their successive forms were talking to each other somehow, just like it had seemed that the lions were communicating with her when they'd let her drink with them. Did that, too, mean recursion, some sense of mutually going back to a previous state?

It was impossible to think so, after seeing de Vries get torn to pieces in the water like that. Worrying again that lions might still be about, she got back up from inspecting that little fragment of rock, rubbing her sore knee, rubbing all her limbs in an attempt to keep warm.

How odd the thoughts that come when we are at the end of our tether . . . how often they seem to involve some sense of non-compliance with a higher authority, one telling you, *I told you so*; all this was going through Cat's head as she continued rubbing her arms and legs.

She lay down, tired, so tired of fighting. Sprawled on her particular rock – shivering, frightened, torn to pieces herself – Cat then began to hear the voice of her mother, that mother with whom she shared not only a name, but also a tendency towards impetuousness and occasional stupidity.

Didn't you hear me calling?

This voice seemed to Cat – so far as she was competent to hear anything, having been tossed, dashed, harried, hunted, and before that strangled by sun – the answer to her search for clarity. But it remained confused in itself, upsetting essential categories as its sequences sounded in her head:

I am Catherine Brosnan; she is Catherine Brosnan; Catherine Brosnan is the woman lying on this rock. They are who we are, two selves conversing in a void, both strangely familiar.

Didn't you hear me calling?

To anyone else, these words she was mumbling – sprawled there – would have seemed gibberish that they could not understand, noise for nothing . . . general symptoms, all the same, of a virus of replication, or contagion of copying. There was no sticking plaster to put on the fact of the matter: she'd copied her mother and was now suffering the consequences, as were others.

This double voice multiplied further in her mind, becoming ever more plastic, ever more pliant, in its provision of alternative modes of itself. Squirming inside, Cat sat up on her button of extruded rock, thinking that, of all the people she'd met, Ma Shango was the one most authentically herself, expressing her own inner being rather than acting like anyone else.

Someone who acted, just did it – and at that moment acted again, rearing out of the lake, half covered in blood, then swimming in Cat's direction. How on earth had she survived?

At the same moment the lions, too, appeared again, rushing open-mouthed towards Ma.

I myself need to act now, Cat thought, hoping to draw them away from this woman who'd given her so much strength. She took a deep breath and slid into the sacrificial water.

40

Sunday by the lake

It had been a very long journey for Uncle Tony, his first time out of Munster, never mind Ireland. As the story of Cat's death became national news, the Irish authorities had quickly expedited the passport that he'd never before possessed. But still, bureaucratic time passed in its glacial way, and it was almost two months before he arrived.

A long journey, and a big shock facing the strength of the sun here in 'Africa', as he insisted on calling the country in which he'd pitched up, unshaven and disoriented and soon very red in the face. Quite hard to find calamine lotion, but he'd found some other goo with which to plaster his burnt skin.

Uncle Tony was disgusted that the casket in which Cat was to be buried could contain pieces of other human bodies . . . *and the saliva of lions, for feck's sake!* . . . plus, possibly, rejected parts of other creatures that they may have tried to eat before consuming Cat. Very little had remained of her anyway, as recovered by divers of the Namibian Navy at the instigation of the Irish government; and that was why he'd decided it wasn't worth repatriating the casket for burial at home.

What there was of her, in that little box, was interred at a funeral lead by the Priest, who had survived the attack on the convoy. He superintended a modest enough ceremony at his old mission school church in Dekmantel – of which he now had custody. Took it by right, as he thought, shooing out the official Ecuadorean priest at gunpoint.

The pilot Sean Morrow and Ma Shango were also in

attendance, along with a small band of other survivors. The Ma had more or less recovered from her injuries after that close escape from the lions, but her face was now even more scarred than before. Her heart too: listening to the obsequies, she felt both anger and sorrow about Cat's act of self-sacrifice. So often in the past she'd successfully beaten down empathetic feelings, but now she was finding it harder to do so. For Cat was a seeker like she was.

As the committal got under way, Morrow meanwhile was processing – more self-forgivingly than Ma – a measure of guilt that he had not replied to Cat's attempts to contact him by phone from the desert.

Nadine was absent from these proceedings, being in a sorry state, having become mute after the terror of the attack on the convoy: a state of trauma about which the Priest was much exercised, not knowing how to help her. He, Nadine and only a few others had survived by doing just what Cat had – rushing under a torrent of gunfire to the next dune and escaping the onslaught. The Priest and his companions had slogged through the desert to the nearest town, then reached Dekmantel by bus.

It was in the course of this journey that Nadine's present condition of silence had developed. During the final stretch of that awful travail, she had stopped moving as well as speaking. The Priest had to carry her off the bus. The motionlessness, at least, had since ceased, but he remained very worried about her.

Now, as Cat's ceremony took place, Nadine was lying in a bed in the Dekmantel clinic under fluorescent tubes – whimpering inside because, hungering for mental calm, what she wanted to say was: *This light's too bright, too white, can't you turn it off?* But her lips were sealed as tight as the edges of an oyster-shell – even as her internal thoughts tried to feather between them.

Admiral Yu was also among the attendees at the funeral. Watching it, she was feeling sad about the death of her nephew and guilty about the death of his daughter, in whose fate she recognised she'd had a hand. The whole thing had not been managed well, and she acknowledged that she was partly at fault.

As the casket was lowered, the Admiral's gaze landed on Sean

Morrow, the pilot she'd commissioned to bring Cat into the desert. His eyes were the colour of blue chrysanthemums. *Ju hua*, the October flower, apt for funerals, with which it was often associated. Also, at least in the Chinese Navy, a euphemism for the arsehole, because its skin folds are comparable to the flower's small, thin petals.

As she thought about that linguistic quirk, Admiral Yu considered her own past behaviour, remembering how she'd set Cat on her way, genuinely hoping it would be good for both of them . . . anticipating that Cat would find her parents and maybe achieve some scientific success, and that she herself would fulfil Party orders to secure new water supplies for mining activities.

She began walking slowly away from the graveside, sifting through the hundred-pocketed times of her life – remembering chiefly the cheerless, long-ago days when her marriage had broken down, mainly because she had started ascending so rapidly the fragile emerald tower of a career in the navy. That progression in which every step could be a wrong one, shattering the jewel of the hoped-for prize.

Something very hard for a woman in particular to do. She remained the only female admiral in the whole organisation, an achievement that had brought her to this remote place, with so little joy on the way. Her own husband had been an arsehole himself, as were many of the predominantly male colleagues and superiors she had to deal with.

But maybe I, too, have erred, she considered as she walked back towards her staff car, in how I've dealt with this whole business. If only the Americans didn't flex so much in how they deal with us, all this mess could have been avoided . . . The truth (she wished she could tell her counterpart this, the Admiral at the new US Navy base being built in Ghana, to counter their own in Walvis) is that Chinese people are not fighty people, not in the first instance, but if pushed fight like dragons.

The hostility between the two countries was not something to be easily eradicated, however much people of both nations hoped that one day it could be. And, personally speaking, it was far too late to think of such things anyway. The older she got – and she was by now far too old to be doing the job she was doing (she'd lost a tooth last month, and sometimes staring at the computer screen was like looking into an unpolished mirror) – the more preposterous the path that she had chosen seemed.

Smelling the fragrant shoots of bamboo that had suddenly grown up by the shores of the new lake, she wished that she'd somehow been of more use to the world, well aware of the irony that this was what the Party had been enjoining ever since she was a young woman like Cat.

Be useful. It was not the worst nostrum. And the sad thing was that she knew Cat had been hoping to be useful too.

In the car her driver was waiting, a fellow of subaltern rank, currently scrolling through his phone, she could see as she approached. She hoped he'd keep it silent on the way back to Walvis, not offering to play crappy music like he had on the way here. Today was a Sunday, but there was still so much work to do.

By now the lake of the expanded aquifer had spread as far south as Dekmantel itself, submerging its old dried-out *vlei*, in the environs of which both mining companies had resumed operations.

Already Scursail and Karunga were using the new water source for mining operations, even though neither the local community nor the Namibian government water bureau had given their permission. It was as if the communal voice and even the idea of democracy itself were nothing more than outmoded twentieth-century shibboleths, things that could be turned away like the flick of a page. The idea of any inquiry into the massacre had also been turned away, edited out of history like a rogue apostrophe.

The flood from the aquifer had caused enormous damage, but also opportunities. Small informal settlements – collections of huts constructed from a mixture of natural and man-made materials, lengths of overlapped wood, mud bricks, scraps of plastic sheeting, panels of corrugated iron – had developed on the edges of the lake. Some of the inhabitants of these dwellings were subsisting on the aquatic species that – in the mysterious ways fish and crabs and prawns, or things similar to prawns, suddenly appear in such places – were now flourishing in the wide, shallow lake fed by the water supply that had slipped southwards. It kept growing larger, drawing on the seeping aquifer in Serra dos Leões, far up in the north.

Others in these little lakeside villages had begun harvesting the new shoots of bamboo that were growing on its edges, shredding them for animal or human food or fermenting them to make alcohol.

All this agricultural activity existed on the old horizontal model – so different from the vertical farms that were by now springing up everywhere in more northern climes as it became clear that food might, if things were not better managed, run out globally. These and other matters were fermenting change across the world, and nobody really knew where it was all going.

Except perhaps the Priest, who'd always taken a long view of the sociopolitical and ecological whole. Usually – even in recent weeks, after his crusade had gone so bloodily wrong – he was as secure as a saint in his ideas about how things would turn out over time, absorbing like a sponge every action and reaction, every tension and paradox that threatened to undermine his onward-to-Jerusalem way of thinking.

But right now, his funeral duties over, there was a need to temper such grand visions and focus on one individual rather than reach for unattainable unities. He felt he could not escape that responsibility.

So once the ceremony was over, he rushed over to Ma Shango and Uncle Tony in order to make known to them his concerns about Nadine – saying that the young woman needed looking after and he didn't have the resources to do it properly.

Later, Ma Shango and Uncle Tony walked by the edge of the lake, near those informal settlements, the one's claggy dialect half understanding the other's, but mostly understanding that they'd jointly loved Cat, about whom they had both shed bitter tears, wishing so much that she had survived. They talked a little, too, about the future of Nadine, wondering if they could assist the Priest in his hope of help for her.

Uncle Tony haltingly advanced to the Ma a vague plan involving Nadine coming to Ireland to get more of an education, maybe living on the farm . . . 'In honour of Cat, like? And to loosen the poor girl's tongue.'

'Or e fit spoil things – do dat, we could go make dem worse,' the Ma replied.

Tony sniffed, not sure what 'we' meant in circumstances that seemed to him, so far from his Kerry townland, so strange as to be imaginary.

What would Cat have wanted? He didn't know, except that it was likely more than where they'd got to, but said all the same to Ma Shango: 'You could be right altogether about doing harm, but we don't need to slabber on too long about all this. Only act.'

'Dat be my own philosophy always,' she replied.

He was surprised to hear that long word from her, a word he'd certainly never used himself. More like Cat talk, or Catherine talk.

Looking askance at the Ma, as she moved beside him on the shoreline, both under the too-hot sun and her under a new camouflage jacket nonetheless (*body dey need fresh cloth*, she'd told him earlier), he next shyly added: 'Yourself could come too, you know?'

He'd felt so lonely in Ireland, which without his sister and niece didn't much feel like home any more, all of which emotion surfaced now like a plea: 'Mind, it's pretty grey back there, far shout from these golden sands. And the immigration service could mither us.'

Ma Shango laughed, giving neither assent nor dissent. They carried on walking by the lapping water, talking of this and that, till Tony felt it was time to up his game. As warmly as he could manage, he told her: 'Where I live, and I really mean that invitation by the way, there are lots of myths about water. Some meaning bad luck, some meaning good. I feel I've failed my niece, perhaps my sister too, and I thought by helping that young woman I could make amends. Sort of like the good-luck water was flowing back to her?'

'If you fit say,' replied Ma Shango. Ever ready for what was contingent and provisional, she was not one to fall under any illusion about lucky futures, watery or not, but what he was saying was better than any other plan she had. Yet it was always necessary to keep up the appearance of the unwitting outlaw.

They rested on a conveniently low rock. There continued talking of many things as the sun warmed their backs and water kept sculpting the sand at the edges of the lake.

In the far distance, much further away than either of them could hear, a lion roared at last, all earth and sky loud with its terminal voice. Scenting out the next meal, any prey whatsoever, its muzzle was snouting along another shore of the same lake by which those two humans were sitting – the lake which was once a starveling underground river, fitfully fed by the aquifer at Serra dos Leões.

The lion knew, just as those humans knew, that soon dusk would come. Sunlight would fail, darkness would fall, the air would become colder and, being less warm, the sand grains through which it was snuffling would no longer lead it to what it sought.

Yet it kept on in hope, pressing its nostrils to the shore, swishing its nose to and fro. Doing what was in nature, according to its instinct.

Acknowledgements

I'd like to thank the following for their invaluable help and support, of many different types, during the writing of this book: Aidan Buckley; Ally Ireson; Bruce Lankford; Christina Franco; Corinne Hua; Darran McCann; Daniel Hickey; David Barton; Eromo Egbejule; Gill Ballard; Ian Pindar; Jekwu Anyaegbuna; Jem Bailey; Lisa Shakespeare; Miranda Collinge; Nkiacha Atemnkeng; Otosireze Obi-Young; Philip Lee Harvey; Rémy Ngamije; Robert Atwater; Rowan Whiteside; Tim MacGabhann; and Yan Ge. Thanks also to my agents, Jim Gill and Amber Garvey at United, and to Lettice Franklin, Sarah Fortune, Alice Graham, Ellie Freedman, Kate Moreton, Linden Lawson, Holly Kyte, Virginia Woolstencroft and all the wonderful team at Weidenfeld & Nicolson. Particularly I must thank Emma Bamford, without whom . . .

GILES FODEN grew up in the English Midlands, the West of Ireland, and numerous countries in Africa. At Cambridge University, he won the Harper-Wood prize in poetry and literature. He has since held academic positions at Royal Holloway, University of London, the University of Limerick, the University of Maryland and the University of East Anglia. For ten years he was an editor and writer on the *Times Literary Supplement* and the *Guardian*, and his writing has been published in *Granta*, *Vogue*, *Esquire*, the *New York Times* and *Condé Nast Traveller*. His fiction includes *The Last King of Scotland*, *Ladysmith*, *Zanzibar*, *Turbulence* and *Freight Dogs*. *The Last King of Scotland* was made into an Oscar-winning feature film in 2006.